Year One

A Quincy Harker, Demon Hunter
Collection

Year One

A Quincy Harker, Demon Hunter
Collection

John G. Hartness

Falstaff Media
Charlotte, NC

ISBN-13: 978-1523800780
ISBN-10: 152380078X

Published by Falstaff Media
Charlotte, North Carolina

Printed in U.S.A

ALSO BY JOHN G. HARTNESS

Bubba the Monster Hunter Short Stories
Voodoo Children
Ballet of Blood
Ho-Ho-Homicide
Tassels of Terror
Monsters Beware - Bubba the Monster Hunter Vol. 1
Cat Scratch Fever
Love Stinks
Hall & Goats
Footloose
Monsters Mashed - Bubba the Monster Hunter Vol. 2
Sixteen Tons
Family Tradition - A Bubba the Monster Hunter Prequel
Final Countdown
Monsters Everywhere - Bubba the Monster Hunter Vol. 3
Scattered, Smothered and Chunked - The Complete Bubba
the Monster Hunter Season 1
UnHoly Night - A Skeeter the Monster Hunter Short Story
Love Hurts
Dead Man's Hand
She's Got Legs
Dead Man's Party - Bubba the Monster Hunter Vol. 4
Fire on the Mountain - A Beauregard the Monster Hunter
Story
Howl
Double Trouble

Co-Edited with Emily Lavin Leverett
The Big Bad: An Anthology of Evil

The Black Knight Chronicles

Volume 1 - Hard Day's Knight
Volume 2 - Back in Black
Volume 3 - Knight Moves

The Black Knight Chronicles (cont'd)

The Black Knight Chronicles Omnibus Edition
Volume 4 - Paint it Black
Movie Knight - A Black Knight Short Story
Black Magic Woman - A Black Knight Short Story
Gone Daddy Gone - A Black Knight Short Story
Knight UnLife - Collected Black Knight Shorts

Other Work

Headshot
Balance - Tales of Alternate Reality
Genesis - Return to Eden Book 1
The Chosen
Returning the Favor and other slices of life
Red Dirt Boy

The Christmas Lights

Acknowledgements

A very heartfelt thanks to Melissa Gilbert of Clicking Keys
for her all her help.

Thanks to Adrijus at Rockingbookcovers.com for the
awesome cover.

Special thanks to my patrons!
Sheelagh
Melinda Hamby
Patrick Dugan
Charlotte Babb
Ray Spitz
Lisa Kochurina
Jim Ryan
Bill Schlichting
Scott Furman
Steven R. Yanacsek
Theresa Glover
Leonard Rosenthol
Salem Macknee
Trey Alexander
Joe & Theresa Hood

Want to add your name to the list?
Go to www.patreon.com/johnhartness and make a pledge!

Raising Hell

*A Quincy Harker, Demon Hunter
Novella*

CHAPTER 1

I fuckin' hate demons. That's what ran through my head as I got out of the car and walked up the sidewalk to the Garda home. It was a nice place, for the suburbs. There was a two-car garage off to one side, a neatly manicured lawn leading up to flowerbeds in front of a nice little porch, and an SUV in the driveway because I'm sure the garage was full of bicycles, tools, lawnmowers and other shit that I only see when I get a call out here in the 'burbs. I live in a condo in the middle of downtown Charlotte, so the only time I see lawn equipment is when I get lost in a home improvement store looking for a new mallet or maybe a new wheel for my grinder.

I walked up to the pale yellow siding nightmare of a home and stepped up on the front porch. The welcome mat was a little askew, the only imperfect thing in an otherwise totally *Good Housekeeping* image. I took a deep breath and closed my eyes, opening my Second Sight and taking a look around. My third eye saw nothing out of the ordinary on the porch, no roiling black evil miasma ready to consume my soul and suck me down into the depths of Hell. It looked just as Martha Stewart in the supernatural spectrum as it did in the visible one. *Good, I thought, maybe the little darlin's just on the rag and I can get the fuck out of here and back uptown before the game lets out and traffic gets stupid.*

I opened my eyes and snapped back to the mundane world. After a second to adjust back to seeing the world with my eyes instead of my soul, I rang the bell. A dog immediately went apeshit on the other side of the door, as if the real trouble wasn't already in the house. A couple of shouted "shut up"s later, the door opened and a flushed forty-something man opened the door. The top of his balding head stopped at about my nose, but I'm tall, so I was used to that. His polo shirt had sweat stains under his man boobs, and it stretched tight across his spectacular belly. He looked up at me, close-set brown eyes set deep in a florid face, capped off with a red nose that only happens when you've hit the bottle pretty hard for a pretty long time.

"You Harker?" he asked, glaring up at me.

"Yep," I said.

"You got ID?" he asked.

No. I just randomly wander up to houses in suburbia and pretend to be an exorcist, hoping to arrive at the exact time their appointment was set for. I bit my tongue before that one could escape and just handed him my card.

"You got any photo ID?" He had that belligerent tone of a middle manager, the kind of guy that shits on all his employees' good ideas until somebody smarter than him hears them, then takes credit for the good one.

I didn't bother to hold back this time. "You want my badge number, too? This shit doesn't exactly come with a union card, pal. You called me, remember? I'm here, the right time, the right address, now let's see if I'm in the right place. I'm Quincy Harker. You got something needs banishing, or should I just go back to my sofa and NFL network?"

"Sorry, sorry. No need to be a—" he cut himself off, but I didn't.

"Dick? Yeah, I'm a dick. You're the stupid bastard who lets a demon into his teenage daughter, yanking me off the couch in the middle of the first Panthers playoff run in living memory, but of course I'm a dick because I didn't immediately take off my hat and wipe my shoes before entering your fucking Ikea palace here. Now point me towards your daughter's room and get out of my way before I do something really dickish, like turn you into a toad."

I pushed past the stammering jackoff and stomped towards the stairs, registering him mumbling something about the bedroom at the end of the hall. I didn't need his instructions; as soon as I stepped onto the second floor, I could feel what I was there for. This time the sense of evil, of just *wrongness* was so strong I didn't need my Sight to find it. It almost knocked me over the second I turned toward the door.

The hallway was just like a normal two-story house, scene for slaughter in so many slasher flicks. There was a small bathroom to the right of the stairs, and three bedrooms arranged around the left-hand hallway. One of these would be the master bedroom, with its own bath, and the other two would be the kids' rooms. The one on the left had pictures of motorcycles and rock bands with more makeup than KISS, but the one at the end of the hall was unadorned. Just a simple brass nameplate announcing it as Kayleigh's room.

I could tell from thirty feet away that Kayleigh's room had some seriously evil shit in it. I rolled my head and cracked my knuckles, then opened up my Second Sight to get a good look at the evil in the magical spectrum.

I slammed my Sight shut almost as quickly as it came into focus, shaking my head to clear the images from my mind. But there is no Visine for the mind's eye, and I was stuck with that shit forever. Whatever was on the other side of that door wasn't human, was powerful as shit, and was really hungry. It was also in a really good mood, which disturbed the fuck out of me. There's nothing worse than a happy demon, at least as far as the humans around it are concerned.

"Mr. Garda?" I yelled down the stairs.

"Yes?" his voice came back. I might have heard ice cubes jingle in a glass. Good—if this was as bad as I thought it was, he was going to need to get seriously drunk.

"Who else is home?"

"What do you mean?"

"I mean, who else is in the building? Is your wife here? Your son?" I left off the "jackass," but it was pretty well implied.

"No, they're gone. My wife is out of town on business for two weeks, and my son has been staying at a friend's house since Kayleigh got sick. It's just you, me and Kayleigh." *And whatever has got its claws wrapped around Kayleigh's soul.*

"That's good. You might want to make yourself scarce for a little while." *Please don't ask a lot of fucking questions.*

"Why?"

Shit. "Because what I'm dealing with up here is pretty dangerous, and I don't want you to get hurt." *And I don't want this fucker to have another vessel to jump to if your daughter suddenly becomes uninhabitable.*

"I don't think I can—"

"Would you please just get the fuck out so I can quit worrying about your fat ass and save your daughter?" I yelled. Maybe a little direct, but I really didn't want to have to fight this thing more than once. I heard a clatter of footsteps and then the front door slammed shut. Nice. I didn't believe he'd actually leave. Maybe that panicked edge in my voice was useful after all.

I turned back to the door. "Just you and me, now, buddy. So why don't you come out of the girl and let's handle this like men?"

The voice that answered rang through my head like a dentist's drill, piercing and ululating. "I can't come out. Not yet. But when

I do you'll see that I'm nothing like a man."

Then it laughed, and in that laugh were the screams of millennia of tormented souls, all shrieking together to make one terrible sound.

"Then I guess I have to come in," I said, and strode to the door. I lifted a size 11 Doc Marten and kicked the door just beside the lock. The jamb splintered, the door flew in, and my worst nightmares were realized.

"Oh fuck me," were the only words that came to mind as I looked at the picture before me. Geiger couldn't have imagined a sense of greater torment. Hieronymus Bosch had nothing on the cruel artist that created the image before me. I didn't throw up, but only because I learned years ago never to have breakfast before an exorcism. You puke on a couple of nuns and that gets drilled into you pretty fast.

The thing in the bed used to be a pretty little girl. I knew this because I'd seen enough pictures of her around the living room and on the walls going up the stairs to figure it out. There wasn't anything pretty about what was in front of me. It still kinda looked like a little girl, if that little girl's face was stretched into new positions from screaming for the last two days, if that little girl's pajamas were covered in piss, shit, sweat, blood and pus, if that little girl's matted hair was stringy with vomit and other bodily fluids. If that little girl, who probably stood around five-two and weighed maybe a hundred ten pounds last week looked like she was about to give birth to a goddamn baby elephant.

The demon hadn't possessed Kayleigh Garda. It had *impregnated* her. And it was about to deliver Hell on earth.

I staggered back from the shock and the stench and raised my Bible in front of my face. The thing laughed. I realized that I wasn't talking to Kayleigh, or the demon that possessed her—I'd been talking to her soon-to-be-born half-demon child this whole time. Kayleigh was gone, dead from the inside as the demon consumed her body and soul. And in a couple of hours, it was going to burst free of Mommy and move on to eating anything and anyone it could find. I backed slowly out of the room, then turned and ran down the stairs, almost tripping over an Xbox controller in my mad dash to the front door. I took several deep breaths, then stepped out onto the porch where Kayleigh's dad stood chain-smoking Camels. I guess he hadn't really left after all.

I walked over to him and leaned on the porch rail.

"Well?" he said after a moment's silence.

"It's worse than I thought."

"How bad is that?" His voice went up a little on the end, like he was fighting off panic. I didn't blame him. I was a little, too, and it wasn't my little girl up there. Of course, I did have to live in this dimension, so demons running loose sounded like a terrible idea to me.

"Your daughter is dead. I'm very sorry."

"But I heard her, she was talking just a minute ago!" He spun around to rush back inside, but I grabbed his arm right above the elbow.

"That wasn't her. That was the demon. It was using her vocal chords." *Please don't make me explain.*

"What? That's stupid. It was Kayleigh. She's up there, and she's in trouble, and you're too chickenshit to help." He pulled against my grip, but got nowhere. I'm a lot stronger than I should be for my size.

"Demons don't have voices like you and I do. If they're possessing someone, they can control their body completely, use their voice perfectly. You'd never know it wasn't Kayleigh if it didn't want you to. But this thing, it won't have to use Kayleigh's voice for long."

"You mean it's going to let her go?" I hate it when they hope for the best.

"I mean it's almost through with her. It's killed her and has devoured almost everything it can. When it's finished, it will leave Kayleigh and come out here looking for another meal. If that happens, it will be almost unstoppable, because it will have one foot in our world and one foot in Hell. Usually demons can't stay in this world past sunrise, but not this one. It won't be bound by normal demonic rules, and it will be very, very hungry. I need to destroy it while it's still in your daughter."

I watched him process as much of that as he could, and thought he got pretty far for a mundane, but I could almost see the moment when hope made him go stupid again. "But you can save her, right?"

Yep, every friggin' time. Sometimes I think we should have left Hope locked in Pandora's box. It causes as much trouble as it fixes. "No. She's dead. Her heart is still beating, but Kayleigh is dead. The demon inside her has eaten her soul. All that's left up there is a meat suit that a demon is wearing with a face that kind of looks like Kayleigh's, but not really very much. And if I don't get up there, and send this thing back to Hell before it delivers, we're going to all be in a lot of deep shit."

I saw the realization cross his face a second or two after I said the word "deliver." "Deliver? You mean my Kayleigh is pregnant with a demon? But, she's only fifteen! She wears a promise ring! This can't happen! We had the talk, we agreed that she should wait... She doesn't even date." He collapsed into a chair on the porch and I just stood there, staring at him. The man wasn't the least bit surprised that his daughter was possessed by a soul-eating demon from Hell, but the mere thought of his precious little girl bumping uglies with some senior in the back of daddy's Lexus reduced him to tears. People and their fucking priorities.

I went back inside, but not before popping out to the trunk of my Honda for a few extra goodies. I sealed the door behind me both mystically and physically. Mystically with a spell of warding designed to provide a non-lethal shock to humans trying to get in, but a lethal shot of balefire to anything from any of the lower realms. Angels could come and go with no problem, although I wasn't expecting anyone from the upper reaches to come join my party. Physically I wedged a chair under the door.

A few strides and a lot more deep breaths found me outside the bedroom again. I so did not want to do this. But it's my job. This was why they paid me the little bucks.

I raised my foot to kick the door in again when a soft voice called from within. "Come in, John Abraham Quincy Holmwood Harker. We've been waiting for you."

CHAPTER 2

I fucking hate demons. I hate them even more when they know who I am. There's power in names. That's one of the things you learn early in my family, and I understood it before I could read. Names identify things, and people, and if you can find out the true name of someone or something, you have a great deal of power over it. Fortunately, the names our parents give us only very rarely match up with our true names, so knowing my full name only gave the demon the tiniest hold on me. But it did give the monster a pretty good idea of what I could do, which was information I was trying to keep quiet until it became important.

I opened the door. The Atrocity Formerly Known As Kayleigh sat up in bed and grinned at me.

"Hello, Mr. Harker. Are you here to celebrate my birthday? Are you my cake? Because childbirth always leaves me hungry." Kayleigh's once-lustrous hair was dark with sweat and matted all around her face. I knew what it meant. Demons aren't born the normal way, the anatomy doesn't work. They consume their host from the inside out, starting with the soul and moving on to the mind and then the flesh. They feed on pain and fear, and once they've taken all a host has to give, they burst out of the body and go looking for more places to cause pain and fear. It leaves the host body looking a little like the soldiers from *Alien*, only tenfold. From the look of things, this demon was going to burst out of Kayleigh any minute and go cause trouble all over Charlotte, and all over the world if left unchecked.

That's where I came in—the checking. I began the Catholic rites for exorcism, speaking slowly and under my breath, more to distract the demon than to actually try to pull it out of the girl.

"And what are you trying to do, Harker? Exorcise me? You know that takes faith, and a direct line to something higher than yourself. Do you even believe there's a higher power, Harker? What do you pray to when you get down on your knees every night? Tell you what. I'll be outside this little womby-womb in a few minutes and then you can get down on your knees in front of me." The demon's voice was shrill, piercing, a dentist's drill to my brain.

I closed my eyes to focus on my ritual. I mumbled my way through the litany, the part that's supposed to be performed with an audience chanting along either in unison with me or call-and-response style, depending on the line. I've never been one for the litany. I'd rather keep the innocent bystanders out of the room, bystanding where they can't get their souls munched on like canapés.

"I command you, unclean spirit, whoever you are, along with all your minions now attacking this servant of God, by the mysteries of the incarnation, passion, resurrection, and ascension of our Lord Jesus Christ, by the descent of the Holy Spirit, by the coming of our Lord for judgment, that you tell me by some sign your name, and the day and hour of your departure. I command you, moreover, to obey me to the letter, I who am a minister of God despite my unworthiness; nor shall you be emboldened to harm in any way this creature of God, or the bystanders, or any of their possessions."

The body on the bed writhed and screamed at me, shouting profanity in about seven human languages and three demon variants that I recognized, then it flopped to the bed and lay still. I watched it for a few seconds then shook my head. It's always the same thing. I walked over to the bed, well within arm's reach, and leaned down, far too close to a monster who had a thing for biting.

All demons have a thing for biting. And fucking, and killing, and desecrating holy places, and raping, and pillaging, and burning. Burning is one of their favorites. But this one liked to bite, I could tell from the way it had morphed Kayleigh's teeth to sharp points as it had taken over her body. So I did what any reasonable human being would do—I put my face right next to its ear and whispered, "I know you're faking, you son of a bitch."

It reacted about like I expected. It was fast, the body of a coltish preteen with years of community league soccer behind her meshed with the unholy might of a hellspawn enabled her to lunge from the bed faster than any human could react. A normal priest would have been lying on the floor with his throat ripped out.

I'm not a priest, and I'm sure as hell not normal. I'm Quincy motherfuckin' Harker, and the blood of Dracula himself runs through my veins. I dodged the demon's bite, yanked the silver cross from my belt and brought it around and down through the back of What Used to Be Kayleigh's skull. I put the tip of the cross right on the little ball in the back of her head where the skull meets the spine, the soft spot that just barely protects the medulla. It didn't protect it enough. The three-pound crucifix, blessed in holy waters from the font of St. Peter's Church, crunched through the thin bone walls and severed the brain stem, shutting down all neurological activity instantly. She died so fast her body didn't know it was dead until a couple of seconds later, when it stopped getting signals from the brain. She collapsed face-first on the hardwood floor, limp, dead.

I knelt beside her. I turned her over and pulled her the rest of the way out of the bed so she was lying on the floor looking up at the ceiling. I sat down, cross-legged, and pulled her head into my lap as the last light of Kayleigh fled her eyes, and then I closed them. I closed my own eyes and felt a tear slide down my nose. I took a deep breath, looked up at the ceiling and said, "If you're up there, you son of a bitch, and if for once in your worthless existence you're paying attention—take care of her."

God and I have an interesting relationship, to say the very least.

I closed my eyes again, took another deep breath, and then opened them to look down at the dead girl in my lap. "You can open the eyes now, asshole. I know you're still in there."

The demon opened his eyes and smiled at me. "Why Harker, I must thank you for this gift. This body is young, strong…" The demon trailed off as it realized there was something wrong.

"Paralyzed?" I offered.

"What did you do? How did you do that? Why can't I get out? Why can't I make it work? What's going on?" The demon's eyes were darting side to side, looking for a clue, but it had no mobility from the neck down.

"Oh, sorry about that. You see, I knew you'd just about finished eating Kayleigh's soul, so I only had a few seconds to get her out of there before you were done with her, and then her soul would be gone, with no chance of Heaven. That didn't seem very nice to me, so I decided to fuck with your plan. And while I was fucking with your plan, I decided to just fuck with you at the same time. You see, when I crushed Kayleigh's brain stem, I didn't just kill her body and free her soul. I left her body a quadriplegic, and that gives you a whole lot of fuck-all to work with." My mom always told me I swear too much. I told her she was provincial and old-fashioned. She told me that both statements were true. She was right. I swear too much. But almost always only at demons. Except when I swear at people. And angels. And minor elder Gods. And traffic lights. And a lot at elevators. Fuck it, I swear too much.

"But why—"

"Why can't you just jump out, like you always do? Yeah, that's the necklace I slipped on little Kayleigh while I was praying. It's got these twelve little charms on it, all around the cross. One for each apostle."

"You put me in a Saints' Chain? You son of a—"

I punched him in the face. It wasn't terribly effective, since his body was dead and he didn't feel pain, but he was surprised, and it did shut him up before he said anything bad about my mother. I don't abide anyone saying anything bad about my mother.

I leaned in so my face was uncomfortably close to the demon's. "Here's the deal. You can stay trapped inside that dead body by the Saints' Chain and hope that in a few hundred years the body will decay enough for the chain to fall off the neck and let you loose, or you can tell me what I want to know and I'll banish you right here and now. So what's it going to be, a couple centuries in a lead-lined box, or scurry on home like a good insect?"

He glared at me for a long moment, which would have been unbearable for most people. I've had what some people would call an interesting life, and what sane people would call an absolute fucking nightmare existence, so being glared at by a demon didn't even register.

"Fine, what do you want to know?" it asked.

"Who summoned you?"

"Like I have any idea. I don't know, and I don't care. All I cared about was getting out of Hell and up here on furlough for a couple weeks until some self-righteous prick like you found me and sent me home. You know, it's not too late—we could still party." I felt the demon's essence pressing on my mind, trying to worm into the cracks in my consciousness and take hold. I blinked twice, then focused my eyes on the demon's and pushed with my own being, flooding the demon's mind with the essence of me. And the essence of me isn't very pretty. You know you're an asshole when a glimpse inside your head makes a demon draw back, and that's exactly what happened.

"Wanna play some more?" I asked.

"Hell no! I'll tell you the whole thing, just let me go after that. It was a frat party, Saturday night, Omega Sigma Iota. Some horny fucktards called me up to persuade the girls at the party to be just as horny as they were. It didn't work out quite like they had planned. They all got laid, just like they instructed. But maybe they didn't all get laid by who—"

"Or what?" I interrupted. I'd had a few conversations about human sexuality with demons in my past, and they had pretty flexible views on inter-special relations.

The thing inside Kayleigh grinned at me, and my stomach did a couple of flip-flops and a barrel roll or two. Thinking about what the demon made those boys have sex with made me really happy I'd skipped breakfast.

"Or what," it confirmed. "They expected a fucking. They got one. I held up my end of the deal, and I got this barely-used meat suit all to myself. Until you came along and fucked it all up. So send me home, shitheel. I'm going to have a world of trouble with the boss when I get home."

"You mean Lucifer?" I asked.

"No, fuckwit. I mean my wife. The last time I got a chance to run off after some young live bait, she did macramé with my intestines for a millennia. And that was her idea of a warning." Good to know even demons had women troubles. Not that I had enough time to chase women to give me troubles.

"I'm going to have to have your name to banish you." True Names have power, and someone who holds a demon's True Name can call or banish it from anywhere. I could see his reluctance in giving me his real Name. I didn't blame him. I wouldn't trust me with it, either. But he didn't have a choice. He whispered his Name to me, and I repeated it until I got all the syllables right. Demon language is kinda like all the nastiest-sounding parts of Latin and German thrown in a blender with a bunch of apostrophes and just a little bit of Klingon sprinkled in for garnish. I finally got it right, and was ready to proceed.

I reached into a pocket of my leather jacket, pulled out a vial of holy water, and sprinkled it on Kayleigh's forehead. "Begone from this vessel, Krag'tharisman'teak, in the name of the Father, and of the Son, and of the Holy Ghost, I banish thee." I opened myself up to the Source, closed my eyes, and *pushed*. I felt the demon leave Kayleigh's body and opened my Sight.

Before me stood a humanoid figure, shimmering from within with a reddish light. The demon's spirit manifested as a nearly seven-foot tall winged human with goat hooves and clawed hands. It looked at me, eyes wide in, I don't know what, surprise that a human could actually banish it? Shock that someone without any real faith could perform the ritual? I couldn't tell, and the demon's soul didn't stick around long enough for me to ask. I watched closely as a small hole opened up in the aether behind the demon, and the soul was sucked back to Hell where it belonged.

I stood up, Kayleigh's limp body in my arms, my knees protesting from sitting on the floor too long. I put her in the bed, pulling the covers up tight around her neck and taking the Saints' Chain off her body. If you ignored the blood seeping from her neck wound, it looked almost like she was sleeping. I knelt beside the bed and put one hand on her forehead.

"All right, God. I know you're up there, probably watching something stupid like soccer or *The Dick Van Dyke Show* reruns, but this one needs a little help. She didn't deserve what happened to her, so she doesn't deserve to deal with your usual Purgatory bullshit, or some stupid line at the Pearly Gates, or whatever crap you've cooked up this year to keep the humans cooling their heels outside of heaven while you and your band of merry fuckwits sit on clouds and play harps or whatever it is you bastards do. So let her in, and take care of her like you didn't do while she was alive."

"You know, Q, one day he's going to actually listen to one of your 'prayers,' and I'm pretty sure he's gonna be pissed." The voice from behind me was cultivated and slightly British. It was also female, which made it all the worse.

"Hello, Glory." I stood and turned to the angel in the corner. "Was she one of yours?"

"No. She wasn't mine to watch. Sorry, you'll have to blame someone else this time." Glory leaned against the wall, casually gorgeous like a woman who is beautiful the minute she rolls out of bed, all Heidi Klum class and Sandra Bullock girl-next-door sexy rolled into one stunning package that stood about five and a half feet tall and had blonde curls falling down her back like a waterfall of gold. She was dressed for work, not business, which meant jeans, boots and a silky-looking tank top that made me want to run my hands all over her torso. I thought better of it quickly. Copping a feel on a celestial body is a good way to get disintegrated.

"Who was her angel?" I asked. Yes, guardian angels are real. Yes, everybody has one. No, they're not really worth a shit, as was evidenced by the dead girl in the bed I was standing beside.

"I'm not going to tell you, Q. It's not your day to die." Glory was my angel. As such, it was her job to keep me from dying before my appointed time. I didn't make it easy on her. Picking fights with angels is a good way to get dead, and I've done it more than once.

"So it's Michael? Gabriel? One of the big boys?" I pushed, trying to see if I could get some*thing* out of her. I needed to punish someone, something for this girl's death, and sending the demon back to Hell just didn't feel like enough. I have a thing about supernatural beings fucking around in the heads of innocent young women. Call it a family issue.

"I'm not telling you. I will tell you that it was her time. She was dead by tomorrow no matter what. If she didn't go to that party and get possessed, then she would have wrapped her car around a tree on her way to school in the morning. Or maybe she would have had a massive aneurism. Or just tripped going down the stairs and broken her neck. I don't know the how, I just know the when, and this was all part of The Plan."

"Fuck the Plan."

"You seem to do everything in your power to do just that every single day. But not today. Now what are you going to do about her?"

"I'm going to find the frat boys who thought it was a good idea to summon a demon just to get a little underage pussy on a Saturday night, and I'm going to emasculate them with a blender and a bottle of Tabasco sauce."

"That's not what I meant. You have a dead teenage girl in her bedroom and the murder weapon with your fingerprints all over it. How are you going to deal with the whole not going to jail thing?" I hate it when she talks like a Joss Whedon character.

It's bad enough my guardian angel ripped off her name from a *Buffy* character, I really can't deal with it when she starts talking like the show, too.

"I've got a plan."

"Is it better than your last plan?"

"I don't remember my last plan." I totally remembered my last plan. This one wasn't all that much better.

CHAPTER 3

It took a little mojo, three fairly complicated spells, a minor summoning that wasn't exactly on the white side of magic and a whole lot of arguing with Glory, but by the time I left the Garda residence, Kayleigh's body was exorcised and sanctified, Mr. Garda was on his way to the drugstore to buy some Nyquil for his sick daughter, and the toaster was rigged to blow the gas oven sky-high about ninety seconds after I got into my car. I hated to do that to the poor guy, he'd really lost enough for one day, but most people's minds aren't built to deal with the kind of shit I spend my life dealing with. So a little suggestion mixed with some fairy dust I keep in my toolbox for situations best forgotten, and Mr. Garda would never remember that his daughter died in her bed a couple of hours before delivering literal Hell on earth.

He'd feel guilt, of course. He was a parent who'd lost a child, and I could only imagine what that felt like. Fortunately, given my line of work, it looked pretty unlikely that I'd ever have to find out. Which meant I also wouldn't spawn any demon-summoning, high-school-girl-raping, overprivileged doucherockets like the ones I was about to visit some seriously unholy vengeance upon. Although, thinking about it, my plans for the fucktards that got Kayleigh knocked up with a demon baby pretty closely mirrored some of the smiting the Almighty did back in the Old Testament days, back when he actually paid attention to what happened down here, before we got to too much begetting for him to keep track of.

I pulled up in front of the frat house at about two in the morning, but you'd never know it was late from the music blaring and the drunk kids hanging out of the windows and lounging on the porch and front yard. I walked up the sidewalk, my boots making a solid *thunk-thunk* rhythm that sounded a lot like the beat of fists on flesh. That thought almost cheered me up a little as I bounded up the steps and flung open the door.

"If you're not a member of this frat, get the fuck out." I didn't say it very loudly. I didn't have to. I *pushed* my voice to make sure everyone in the building heard it, and put just enough suggestion behind it laced with imagery of fire and bloodshed that a veritable flood of bimbos and hangers-on cascaded down the stairs and out of the house like rats following the Pied Piper.

"What the fuck, dude? Who the fuck are you? Where the fuck is everybody going? We still got a party goin' on here!" A shirtless, blonde college-age Justin Bieber lookalike with a square jaw and more abs than an Olympic sit-up team walked up to me and bumped chests with me.

I stared at him. He actually *bumped his chest into mine*, like we were fucking gorillas in a mating ritual or something. I backhanded the little fuck to the ground and stepped on his balls. "I'm the motherfucker that just ended your party, shitbird. Now get the rest of your brothers into the living room. I've got questions. You've got answers." He scurried backward until he could reach the stairs, then scrambled to his feet and started rounding up members.

Another one came up to me, all full of bluster and righteous indignation. "What is this about? I'll have you know, my father is Jacob Marlack; he's a very important attorney in this city and I know my rights—"

I cut him off by grabbing his throat in my left hand and marching him backward into the living room where most of his fraternity had gathered. I steered him to the couch and shoved, forcing him to sit. "I'm going to say this once, and I get irritable when I have to repeat myself, so pay attention. I don't give a fuck who your daddies are, how much money they have, or what they do for a living. I don't give a flying shit if you can buy Rhode Island. I'm here for information and the faster I get it, the fewer of you bleed. Are we clear?"

I looked around the room. A couple of the boys looked like they wanted to say something, but the ones next to them either smacked them or just shut them up. And they were boys, for fuck's sake. Most of them had three chest hairs between them and they'd already summoned a demon. They were so fucked and they had no idea. I felt bad for them for about a second and a half, then I remembered what Kayleigh looked like, lying in her bed, dead at my hand because these assholes wanted to bang an underage girl. These stupid fucks that could have had their choice of college tail but wanted something different. And I had to clean up the goddamn mess.

"Last Saturday night you boys had a little party."

I started, only to be immediately interrupted by the drunkest of the Overindulged Ones. "We have a fuckin' party every fuckin' night, asshole. You're going to have to be more spefi . . . scepifi . . . specific." He grinned and high-fived the brother sitting on the couch next to him.

I gathered my will and murmured, "*Sobrietate.*" Then I pushed my will at him. He went from happy drunk to a little green, then pale, then sweating, then miserable and holding his head as he went from tanked to stone-cold sober in about three seconds. I was impressed that he didn't puke.

"May I continue?" I asked. There were nods all around. The boys were looking from me to their now-sober friend with what I thought were appropriately frightened glances, so I thought I might make some headway this time. "Now, at this party was a cute girl named Kayleigh. She looked a lot like the girl in this picture." I produced a snapshot I'd pulled down off the wall in Kayleigh's house. You know, before I burned it to the ground with her demon-violated corpse inside.

"Anybody recognize Kayleigh?" Lots of shaking heads. "Really? You guys are absolutely certain you've never seen her before?" A lot more shaking of heads, but several sideways glances, too. Most of them landing on Mr. My Daddy's a Lawyer. Big surprise.

I walked over to young Mr. Entitled. "What's your name, kid?" He was exactly the kind of kid I would have hated in college, if I'd gone to college. Tall, thin but with a layer of muscle that said he'd spent his time on the lacrosse field or cross-country team. The kind of confidence and good looks that come from decades of breeding and successful parents. He had perfect teeth, brown hair that curled artfully down just over his eyes in a tousle that looked like it took at least an hour to perfect. I wanted to punch him in his perfectly straight Roman nose.

"I don't have to answer any of your questions, fucktard. I know my rights." He seemed determined to tempt me to violence.

I took a deep breath, let the mental roulette wheel land on "fuck it," and gave in to temptation. I punched him in the nose. "You have the right to tell me what I want to know, or you have the right to bleed. Your call." I leaned in close, where his buddies couldn't hear what I was saying, and whispered "I'm not a cop, you little shitball. I'm your worst fucking nightmare. I'm somebody who actually gives a shit about that little girl, and really wants to do bad things to the people that hurt her. And your name is on top of my list. So tell me what went down, and I might decide that you're not worth the time and effort to destroy." I pulled in a little of my will and lit up my eyes with soulfire. It's a cheap parlor trick, but it scares the shit out of the mundanes. It did the job this time, too.

"Fine, fine, I'll talk, but not here. Let's go to the library." He stood up, and I backed off enough to give him a little room. He turned to the rest of his brothers and said "This is nothing, just a protective big brother who needs to look at some security tapes to make sure we didn't take advantage of his precious little darling. Eric, can you come help run the computer for me?" He walked off, obviously expecting everyone to just go back to normal now that he'd made his proclamation. Must be nice to have minions. A big kid with close-cropped red hair and sprinkling of freckles that would keep him getting carded well into his forties got up and walked close behind. I shrugged and followed them.

My idea of a fraternity house library was a room with a couple of ratty desks and a huge stack of *Penthouse*. These guys had different ideas. They led me through the house, every room looking pretty much like I expected, decorated in video games, beer signs and posters of half-naked women. Until they led me through a pair of heavy wooden double doors that opened into the kind of library that would make a dedicated bibliophile fall to their knees weeping. The room was lined with ceiling-height bookcases, and leather spines stared out at me from every angle. No paperback bestsellers here—I spied a complete set of legal manuals from three different countries, about fifteen different Bibles and holy books, and one entire corner shelf unit glowed in my Sight so brightly that the magical aura bled over into the real world, casting pale purple light on everything within four feet of it.

The lead kid noticed my squint and chuckled. "Impressive, isn't it? We have one of the largest occult libraries in the South, and no one suspects it. After all, what kind of idiot would trust a bunch of drunken frat boys with some of the most powerful magical texts in history?"

"An amoral idiot that doesn't care what happens to anyone who wanders by the front door would be my guess." I sat on the arm of an overstuffed leather chair, making myself the apex of a triangle that let me keep one eye on the door and the other on the shelf of spell books.

"Careful, Mr. Harker, that's my father you're talking about."

I opened my mouth to speak, but he held up a hand. "Yes, I know who you are. You don't dabble in the occult circles in this town without learning who the other players are, so to speak. I knew you the second you walked in, all billowing duster and self-righteousness. How is little Kayleigh? Has she delivered yet? Is it a boy?" The smile on his face made me want to punch him again, and keep punching until my hand got tired, but I thought better of it. This kid was way more than he seemed, and I needed to know where he learned his tricks before I killed him, so I could go and kill his teacher, too.

Just for the record, I don't kill every bad guy I come across. I don't believe that killing is the best solution to every problem. I'm not one of those "every problem is a nail" guys. I just kill the monsters that are so far removed from human that they'll never feel or show a shred of remorse no matter what they do or who they do it to. And frat boys. Apparently, I kill frat boys, too, because this little bastard was in dire need of defenestration.

I took a deep breath and shoved all my murderous thoughts way down deep inside. "You seem to have me at a disadvantage, Mr...." I let the name trail off as I made my way over to the shelf of magical goodies. The texts there were pretty typical, if incongruous by their setting. There was a *Necronomicon*, a *Satanic*

Bible, the collected writings of Aleister Crowley, a treatise on the Marquise de Sade, an entire shelf of introductory spell books, and several volumes of Martston's *Creatures of the Otherworlde,* an encyclopedia of things that go bump in the night. I had about four volumes myself, but had never seen a complete set. The shelf before me was missing only *Volume Seven - Sasquatch to Vampire.*

"Alexander Marlack," the kid said, extending a hand. "And this is Eric Brown, our chapter President." I shook his hand, managing to keep from wiping it on my jacket when he let go. Marlack gestured to a pair of sofas that faced each other across a coffee table. I sat in the center of the one facing the door. I watched *Deadwood;* I know what happens when you sit with your back to a door.

"So you knew you were putting a demon inside that little girl," I said as I sat down. I tried to keep my voice even, but it was pretty hard since most of my concentration was focused on not burning the two little bastards to ash where they sat.

"We did." Marlack's face was expressionless, like we were talking about the weather.

"Why the hell would you do something like that?" I asked. I suppose I hoped somewhere deep down that there was a piece of these little shits worth saving.

"I wanted to see if we could actually summon a demon. And when we did, we needed somewhere to put it. Kayleigh wasn't someone we'd miss, so I stashed the demon there." The smug prick could have been talking about a tech stock split, the level of emotion he was showing.

"And you knew that it would eat her from the inside out and then go on to wreak indescribable havoc until it was banished, right?"

"That fit with what I'd read, but as I had never summoned a

demon, I had no proof." He leaned back and crossed one ankle over the other knee. "But what is that to you? Why are you here?"

"Why am I—you soulless piece of trash—I'm here because less than four hours ago I put a cross through the back of that girl's head to keep her from destroying the entire neighborhood."

"Oh, so you murdered a little girl and you're here to make yourself feel better because we're the monsters that put a demon in her?" His friend hadn't spoken, but at least had the good grace to look ashamed at what he'd done. Marlack just grinned, stood up and started pacing the room like he was making a closing argument. "You killed that girl, Mr. Harker, not us. And don't tell us that there was nothing you could have done—there are dozens of exorcism rituals available if you're willing to look for them. You just didn't look. You did what you do—you rushed in there, guns blazing, coat swirling in the mist at your feet and killed that child. Admit it, you're worse than the demons you claim to hunt!" He timed himself perfectly, finishing his little spiel right in front of me, bent over with his finger in my face.

The only problem for him was that I was a few years past being intimidated by rich college kids in expensive libraries. I stood up, grabbing his extended finger in my fist and bending it back sharply. As I stood, he dropped to one knee and started pawing at my hand, trying to get me to cut loose. Wasn't happening.

"Listen to me, you entitled little fuckbag. I came here hoping there was a better answer for what happened that night than statutory rape and demon summoning, but now I find out that it was worse. You weren't just an ignorant pawn; you knew exactly what the fuck you were doing. And instead of trying to find some way to make it right, or even show a scintilla of remorse about the little girl that died because of you, you rabid fuckmonkeys sit there and try to turn this around on me! Well, Mr. Marlack, I guarantee you one fucking thing. You've hurt your last little girl." With that, I reached out into the world around me and drew in my will. I focused my eyes full of soulfire on little Alex Marlack and shut out everything but the screams.

CHAPTER 4

I walked out of the room about ten minutes later feeling pretty good about myself. That feeling lasted all the way to the front door, where I first caught sight of the flashing blue lights and the three cop cars surrounding my beat up Honda. There was a woman in a dark pantsuit leaning on the front fender of my car, and my heart sank through my kneecaps when I saw her.

Detective Rebecca Gail Flynn, rising star of the Charlotte Mecklenburg Police Department, fervent non-believer in anything supernatural and spectacular pain in my ass. She'd decided a couple of years ago that I was a fraud, and that it was her sworn duty to bring me in. Since then I'd had a ridiculous number of jaywalking tickets, broken taillights, random license checks a block from my house and a couple of anonymous tips called in about my arsenal of automatic weapons. None of her best efforts had ever turned up anything incriminating, but they certainly made it harder to do business with a certain level of my clientele who are uncomfortable with their business dealings being observed by a mortal, much less a mortal police detective.

Of course, I'd never killed a teenage girl in her bed and burned down her house three hours before running into her, either. Detective Flynn looked positively radiant illuminated in flashing blue LEDs as she walked toward me flanked by two gigantic officers with biceps the size of my thighs and no necks. *Good thing I didn't inflict any* physical *damage on the assholes here,* I thought.

"Mr. Harker, how are you this fine evening?" she asked.

"Well, Detective Flynn, I'll have to admit that I was having a glorious night until you showed up. Blue isn't exactly my favorite color, you know," I replied. I stood on the sidewalk in front of the frat house, arms folded. Flynn and her gorillas had me blocked from my car, and they knew where I lived anyway, so there was no point trying to get away from them. I decided to hang tight and see what her game plan was.

"Let's see if you prefer orange. I hear it's the new black, you know." She smiled at her pop culture reference. I didn't. If she was talking orange jumpsuits, she must have thought she actually had something on me for a change. "Would you like to come down to the station and answer a few questions for me, Mr. Harker?" It was phrased like a question, but it had all the earmarks of an order. Too bad I've never been the obedient type.

"Nah, I think I'll just go home and catch up on *Downton Abbey* if it's all the same to you." I stepped forward, reaching out as though I'd open the door to my car, but one of the no-necks moved into my path.

"It's not. All the same to me, that is. Come with us, Mr. Harker." She gestured to one of the waiting cruisers.

"I'll follow you in my car." I reached again, and the no-neck put his hand on my chest. I looked up at him, judging whether or not I could take him. I could, but he'd slow me down enough for his friend to Taser me.

"You'll ride with me," Flynn said, and walked past me to the most obvious unmarked car in the world. The dark blue Chevy sat a few yards in front of my car, engine running. I shrugged and followed her, since I wasn't going to get to go home until I dealt with her questions. I slid into the passenger seat and pulled out my cell phone.

"Who are you calling?" Flynn asked.

"I thought I'd give my lawyer a call. Since I'm being held by the police and all."

"You're not being held, Mr. Harker. You're just being casually questioned about an assault that was reported by one of the fraternity brothers here."

"I've never seen you do anything casually, Detective Flynn. I might like to watch that sometime."

"Don't hold your breath. And give me your phone. You don't need to call anyone."

"I don't think you get to make that determination," I said, but handed my phone over. It didn't matter; I'd already sent the text to Uncle Luke telling him that I was getting arrested again. It happened so often since Flynn put me in her sights that I had a shortcut programmed into the phone.

We rode without speaking to the police station, Flynn tapping the steering wheel in time with the radio. It was never good for me when cops were in a good mood. I followed her into the station and down the hall to Interview Room #3. This wasn't my favorite of the interview rooms, but I didn't complain. They were all pretty much the same. Room #1 was a little bigger, but was often disgusting from previous interrogations. Room #2 was the same size as #3, but the chairs wobbled, and Room #4 was small, almost as though it were for juvenile offenders only.

I took a seat on one side of the table and Detective Flynn sat across from me. There was a tape recorder in the center of the table, with a small microphone next to it. A pair of security cameras monitored the room from the corners of the wall near the ceiling, and the obligatory two-way mirror covered one wall. I murmured a quick disruption spell under my breath as Flynn closed the door, gathered my will and pushed out at the cameras and the recorder. I smiled a little as the red lights on the cameras winked out. I was pretty sure there didn't need to be a record of anything we said tonight.

Flynn sat down and pressed the button on the tape recorder. "Just to make sure we don't have any misunderstandings, right, Mr. Harker?" Flynn said with a fake smile.

I returned her smile with one of my own, equally fake. "Absolutely, Detective. I certainly want to cooperate to the fullest with the lawful authorities."

Her smile flickered momentarily when she noticed the tape recorder wasn't working. She turned to the mirror and said, "The recorder in this room is out; can someone bring me a spare?"

A few seconds later one of her no-necks came in carrying a fresh tape recorder. She set it on the table beside the one I'd already cooked and reached down to the floor to plug it in. As soon as her eyes were off me, I murmured, *"Adflicto Affligo,"* under my breath and pushed my will at the new device.

Detective Flynn successfully plugged the recorder in and smiled as the red light winked on when she pressed the Record button. I smiled just as widely as it flickered out a couple of seconds later. She turned back to the mirror, but before she could speak, I said, "I'll just break the next one, too, Detective." I pitched my voice low, so the people on the other side of the glass couldn't hear me, but there was no mistaking my words.

Flynn whirled around and glared at me. "You did this?" She gestured at the recorders. "How?"

"Magic. I've explained before that there are stranger things on heaven and earth than are dreamt of in your philosophy, Detective. But I'd suggest you keep your voice down or your compatriots on the other side of the mirror will think you've lost your mind. Again." My last little barb was a reference to some department-mandated therapy the good Detective had undergone after being first on the scene to a school shooting several years back.

Her eyes narrowed, and I could almost see her calculating the best place to start cutting to keep me alive the longest and still inflict the most pain, but all she did was turn back to the mirror. "This recorder's on the fritz, too. I'm going to take my notes manually."

She turned back to me. "What do you know about a fire in Midwood this evening? The Garda residence, to be specific."

"I know nothing."

"Bullshit. You were seen leaving the house moments before the first 911 call was made. A girl died in that fire, Harker, and I know you had something to do with it."

"Let me guess. An anonymous tip placed me at the scene, right?"

"And then we pulled the Garda's phone records and saw that someone in that house called your cell phone this afternoon and spoke to you for four minutes. That's a lot longer than leaving a message, but not a casual chat. That was you, booking an appointment at the Garda's for tonight, wasn't it?"

I tried my best to look chagrined, but I'm very bad at it, so I'm sure I failed. "Yes, Detective, I did have an appointment at the Garda's house tonight, to discuss the possible possession of their daughter. But she was fine when I left her, and the house was intact." Technically true, since in comparison to having a demon in her womb, dead was certainly further along the scale to "fine."

"And then what were you doing at the Omega Sigma Iota house?" Flynn asked.

"I was working on a case."

"The same case?"

"I'm not at liberty to discuss it."

"Get liberated." Detective Flynn probably had a finely tuned sense of humor, with a rapier sharp wit and an appreciation for

Jerry Lewis movies. It just never showed its face when I was around.

"Yes, it was the same case. It seems a couple of frat brothers summoned the demon which possessed Kayleigh Garda." I was never terribly cautious discussing the details of my cases with Detective Flynn, since she didn't believe in what I did anyway. I've found that bland honesty goes a long way into making people ignore the truth, particularly when the truth is hard to believe.

"What was Kayleigh Garda doing in a frat house?" Flynn asked.

I felt my neck start to get a little red. "Well, Detective, I bet she was being stupid, which is the inalienable birthright of the high school student, which is why there are things like laws and police departments to protect them. But good job, Flynn. I bet you passed 'Blaming the Victim 101' with flying colors."

"Don't give me that shit, Harker. I'm just wondering how anyone that young even finds out about a party at a frat house."

"Good lord, woman, did you even go *near* a college? You don't have to know about a party at a frat house, there's *always* a party at a frat house. All Kayleigh Garda had to do was walk past the house on the sidewalk wearing a little bit of makeup and her slutty best friend's shoes and they would have thrown open every door and poured her first drink for her!" I've found my tolerance for police stupidity has decreased as I've grown older, and I'm older than almost everyone I know, dashing good looks aside.

"Can the attitude, Harker. I don't need it. I've got a suspicious fire with your fingerprints all over it, a prominent citizen's kid getting harassed, again with you neck-deep in it, and a dead teenager in her house with injuries that don't look like they came from a fire, and once again the evidence points straight at you, so maybe, just maybe, you want to cooperate with me for once instead of giving me a bunch of bullshit about demons and witches and things that only exist in fairy tales. What do you think of that?"

"I think I want my lawyer." I leaned back in the chair and crossed my arms. There was obviously no way I was getting her to see sense, so I may as well move along to the "spend the night in jail" portion of my evening.

"Fuck your lawyer. You tell me what I want to hear or I'll put you under the fucking jail." Flynn leaned over the table and got right in my face.

I leaned in, getting uncomfortably close to her, but she couldn't back down or she'd lose face in front of everybody watching through the glass. Then I whispered, so low that she had to get even closer to hear me, "You want to know what happened tonight? Well here's the real fucking deal, Detective. I've shit all over your cameras and recorders so nobody can hear this but you, so here you go. Those overindulged fucktards at the frat house summoned a demon and let it play with Kayleigh Garda. It fucked her fifteen-year-old body and destroyed her mind. Then it impregnated her, with a demon. Not a baby, not a human, but a fucking demon that ate her from the inside out, starting with her soul.

"By the time I got there tonight, Kayleigh's soul wouldn't fill a thimble, much less her body. I stopped the demon from completely destroying her soul, and sent it back to Hell where it belonged, but it killed Kayleigh in the process. Then I went to the frat house and found a couple of junior sociopaths who don't give a fuck who they destroy so long as they don't miss their tee time. I had just finished bringing down a fuckton of fiery vengeance on the little bastard who called up a demon to rape and destroy Kayleigh Garda when you showed up. I know the drill from here, so why not just call one of your pet apes to take me down to holding for the night until my Uncle Luke shows up to pay my inflated bail in the morning?"

She leaned back, shook her head briefly, then leaned in and slapped the shit out of me. "Fuck you, Harker. And fuck your bullshit stories. One of these days you're going to fuck up and leave some evidence we can use, and then you're done. Game fucking over." She reached into a pocket and pulled out a handcuff key. She dropped it on the table and said, "You know your way out by now. Don't make me waste the time walking you out."

"Keep your key, Detective," I said, shaking my wrists and letting the loosened handcuffs drop to the table. "I was out of those things before you ever stepped into the room." I stood up, brushed some imaginary dust off the front of my jacket, and headed for the door.

I bumped shoulders with the no-neck partially blocking the door in the hallway, and forgot to check my strength until I'd almost knocked him flat. I flicked out a hand and caught the front of his uniform shirt before he hit the ground and pulled him back to his feet. No point in completely pissing off every cop in the building.

CHAPTER 5

Uncle Luke was waiting for me outside the station, his Mercedes convertible purring in a No Parking zone and roundly ignored by all the dozens of cops walking past. Uncle Luke looked the same as ever — short, high cheekbones, wavy dark hair, skin the white of a fresh notebook paper and piercing eyes that took in everything around him. Uncle Luke didn't miss anything, and didn't mind people knowing it. I walked around the car and slid into the passenger seat, flipping the radio to a classic 90s station. Luke immediately flipped it back to show tunes and we battled over that for a while before Luke finally snapped the radio to OFF and reached over and cuffed me on the back of the head.

"What the hell were you thinking, setting fire to the house?" he asked me, his sibilants getting that extra little hiss that told me his fangs were out and he was really pissed at me.

"Seemed like a good idea at the time," I muttered, rubbing the back of my head. Uncle Luke, as he had decided to be called this generation, packed quite a punch for an old dude.

"Much to my chagrin, your mother said the same thing about conceiving you."

"And look how awesome that turned out, Unc. Her and pops both rotted away to dust, but you and I are still kicking! Ain't immortality grand!"

"Oh, fuck off." He drove in silence for a couple of minutes, but it didn't take long for his curiosity to get the better of him. "What was it?"

"Demonic possession. A bad one. It had a little girl. I had to take pretty drastic measures."

"You couldn't exorcise her?"

"Possession isn't the right word, I guess. It was more like demon impregnation. And she was about to give birth to it."

"Fuck me."

"Fuck us all. If that thing had gotten out..."

"You couldn't banish it." For a converted bad guy, Uncle Luke had a pretty good handle on right and wrong.

"Nope. It would be native to this plane. An immortal, amoral, incredibly powerful monster that could never be sent home. Just what I want hanging around the suburbs."

"Yeah, that would send property values straight into the shitter." When you live as long as Luke, real estate speculation is a long-tail game.

His cell phone rang as we were turning into his driveway. He pressed a button on the steering wheel and spoke into the air. "Card here."

A reedy voice came over the car's speakers. "Master, sunrise approaches. Will you be home in time?"

"I'm almost home now, Renny."

"Very good, Master. I will prepare your rooms."

"Renny? I've told you not to call me Master. It's a new century. We need to change with the times."

"Yes, Master, I'll try to remember." Renfield clicked off and Uncle Luke just shook his head.

He looked over at me. "They never change, do they?"

"At least as often as you do, Mr. Luke Card. Or Mr. Alucard. Isn't that the name you used when you hired Dad? Why not just own it? Be fucking Dracula. I bet nobody would believe you."

"I'm sure they wouldn't, but I don't want to take the chance. Besides, if I have to invent new identities every few decades, what of it? It just gives me opportunity to see the world."

"At night," I reminded him.

"Yes, at night." Luke let out a little sigh as we pulled into his four-car, light-tight garage. His entire house, all eight thousand square feet of it, was outfitted with lightproof shades and light locks for all the doors. Luke slept most days, but if he needed to be up, he could go anywhere in his home safely. And since those shades were all bulletproof and the walls reinforced with plate steel, pretty much anyone inside was safe, too.

We walked through the garage into the kitchen where Renfield waited for us. He'd been a college student in the sixties, studying hotel management. Uncle Luke was looking for a replacement for his last Renfield and offered this one a live-in position as housekeeper, butler, personal assistant and chef. He didn't mention the blood-drinking thing until the contract was signed. But Renfield VI took it all in stride and deposited the paychecks. He was getting close to retirement age now, and had begun looking over recent Johnson & Wales hospitality majors for a replacement. I wasn't sure what Luke had planned for Renfield when he retired, but I'm pretty sure it involved memory wiping and white sand beaches. I'd been with Uncle for four Renfields counting this one, and he always provided for their well-being after they left his employ.

"Master, you didn't tell me you were bringing Mr. Quincy," Renfield chided. Only the Renfields got to scold my uncle; it was a perk of the job. I guess if you're going to be Dracula's manservant, you're going to grow nuts of steel pretty quick.

"My apologies, Renny. My… nephew wasn't planning on visiting today, but he ran into some difficulties last night that required my services."

"Oh dear. Mr. Quincy, are you injured? Should I fetch my sewing kit?"

"No, Ren. I'm good. I just got arrested for burning down a house, that's all."

"Oh. Well, if that's all, then. I shall fix you some breakfast. Eggs and bacon?"

"Kippers?" I asked. Some things you never outgrow, and I'm a turn of the century boy at heart. Turn of the twentieth, that is.

"No, sir. I'm sorry, but North Carolina seems to be lacking in good kippers."

"You can only expect so much from the Colonials, Ren. No matter how far they've come, they still drink shit beer and don't understand proper football. I'll take the bacon and eggs, though. Poached, please."

Renfield laughed at my soccer joke and went off to the kitchen, happy to have someone to cook for. I knew that Uncle sometimes sat with him and smelled the food just to make Ren feel better, but it wasn't the same. I made my way into the den, where Luke sat waiting for me. I took a chair across from him and waited for it.

He didn't make me wait long. "So you burned down the house to hide the evidence of demon infestation?"

"Yep."

"How did you get caught?"

"I went after the assholes who started the whole mess. They summoned the demon, raped the girl, then let the demon play with her. I think I convinced them that was a bad idea. One of them had a rich daddy. He made up some bullshit about seeing me leave the house right before the fire broke out and called the cops. There's no evidence. I can't be convicted."

"It may be inconvenient enough for you to merely be charged. Your identity cannot become known."

"I have good documents."

"I know. I had them forged for you."

"So what's the worry?"

"Who was this rich daddy you speak of?"

"Some asshole lawyer."

"Good god, child, talking with you is like pulling teeth. Does the asshole lawyer have a name?"

"Have you ever thought, *Uncle*, that maybe the reason I don't always give you much information is because it's something I want to handle on my own, without you drinking the bad guys. Maybe every once in a while I don't want you to get involved."

"I am involved, Quincy. I just got you out of jail."

"Fair enough. His name is Jacob Marlack, and he's got a serious collection of black magic texts that he lets his idiot son play with."

Uncle Luke didn't respond for a long time. I hate it when he does that; he gets all super-still and just sits there, like a statue covered in clown white makeup. After a couple of interminable moments, he looked at me and said, "Fuck."

Uncle Luke doesn't swear much. And when he does, it's usually pretty old-school stuff. For him to drop an F-bomb was a big deal. "What's the deal with Jacob Marlack?"

"I know him. He's a powerful witch. I met him many years ago when he was just beginning his study of the dark arts. I thought I had persuaded him to stop. Apparently I was wrong."

"Why don't I know this guy?" I've worked with Uncle Luke almost since we moved to the States, right after my parents died.

"I met him before I met your father. He tried to kill me in Romania."

"Wait, what? You knew him before—"

"Yes, before all that. Before your mother, before your father, before that fat shite Van Helsing, before any of them."

Yeah, all that happened, apparently. All I know outside what's in the book (which Uncle Luke wrote, by the way) is that as far you'd know from Luke, Van Helsing's first name was "fat shite."

Uncle Luke went on. "Marlack was a young wizard then. This must have been shortly after your President Lincoln was shot by that actor."

"John Wilkes Booth," I added.

"Yes, him. Well, a few years after that, I was in my home in Romania when I heard a pounding at the door. It was rather uncommon for me to receive visitors at my home during those years—"

"On account of the whole 'eating the villagers' thing, and the fact that everyone for fifty miles was terrified of you."

"I could do with a little healthy fear on your behalf, young man." He smiled when he said it, so I was pretty sure he didn't want to rip my throat out, but it was good to keep in mind that Uncle Luke was really Dracula every once in a while. This was shaping up to be one of those nights that I didn't want to lose track of the fact that one of history's greatest monsters was sitting ten feet from me.

He continued. "I answered the door, hoping it was just a lost traveler. It was late, and I felt the need for a snack. But when I opened the door, I faced a man holding a massive silver crucifix and brandishing it in my face. I instinctively flinched, but there was no power in the talisman other than the native pain I feel in the presence of silver. I felt nothing of the repulsion I had often felt when in the presence of holy symbols and holy men. That's when I realized two things: that holy objects only held sway over me when wielded by true believers, and that this man had no more faith in God than I do."

"I'm pretty sure he believes God exists, but I don't think

they're friends on Facebook," I quipped. Renny brought my eggs with a large glass of orange juice and a Coke. He set the whole meal up on a little folding tray complete with silverware and tiny solid gold salt and pepper shakers. It was just like room service, but I didn't have to tip. I started to eat as Uncle Luke went on.

"I smacked the fool's hand away and pulled him inside. I looked into his eyes, wondering what kind of fool comes to a supposedly haunted castle in the middle of the night, and saw no fear there. That gave me pause, and as I hesitated, the fool pulled a clove of garlic out of a coat pocket and shoved it in my face."

I snorted back a laugh and orange juice almost came out my nose. Luke continued. "Exactly. I pushed the garlic away; not because it harms me in some way, but because the smell was so strong it made me gag. My senses are very heightened, so strong smells are unpleasant, and I never liked garlic even when I was alive. The Gypsies cooked with garlic. It makes me think of them. And I hate Gypsies. So I looked at the man and asked him if he had anything else he wanted to try. He pulled out a vial of holy water, but I stopped him before he could throw it on me. I think I broke his arm at that point. I dragged him into my den and put him in a chair, then demanded an explanation as to why he had sought me out."

"He told me his name, Jacob Marlack, that he was from the United States, and that he was looking for books of magic. I told him I had none, and that for humans to meddle with forces beyond their reckoning was folly. I then offered to feed him to my wives so that he could gain a greater understanding of the powers of which I spoke. He declined my offer, and demanded to be given my magical texts. I repeated that I had no such things, and he grew angry with me. I have long since lost any fear of a mortal's anger, but this was something more. This Marlack was no longer just a man, and as his rage grew, his scent changed. He no longer smelled human, but began to reek of sulfur. I wanted him out of my home, so I called upon my servant to dispatch him."

"Was this the first Renfield?" I'll own it—he had me wrapped up in the story. Luke doesn't often talk about the old days, so any time I get a chance to see behind the curtain into his past, I'm all over it.

"No, this was Curtis. He was my valet and my guard. Curtis had spent time with the English Army in India or some other sweltering place, and he was a man of some size and great strength. But when he laid hands upon Marlack, the American flung him aside as though he were a child. Curtis' skull smashed against the stone walls and he died instantly. I was quite annoyed at this point, for good servants are difficult to find, and discreet ones even more so. I rose and advanced upon Marlack, determined to drink from the fool and perhaps bespell him into a few decades of servitude for his insolence, but when he spoke, the voice was not his own, or anything belonging to this world.

"It spoke of power, and hunger, and ageless times before men walked the earth. It spoke of destruction like I had never witnessed, even I, who had walked the earth for half a millennium, and I was afraid."

Luke looked at me, and I'd never seen that expression on his face before. "I was afraid of that creature then, and I am afraid of it now. I forbid you to pursue this investigation further. I will speak no more of this."

"The hell you say," I said. "You don't forbid me shit, Uncle, because I'm not your kid, I'm not your blood, and I'm not your goddamn servant. I'm going after this motherfucker, and I'm going to bring him down. Now you can either finish the story, and maybe I can get some good info out of it on how to bring him down, or not. But either way, there will be justice for Kayleigh Garda, and I'm going to bring that justice down around Jacob Marlack's old demon-possessed ears. I've fought demons before. They don't scare me."

"A fact I understand all too well. But this is more than just a demon, and it's more than a sorcerer. It is some evil blend of the two, and you should be scared."

"I'm not."

"Then you're a fool."

"Not the first time that charge has been levied, Unc. Now what happened with you and Marlack?"

He took a deep breath and looked to the sky as if for help. Both were oddly human gestures for a vampire as old as Uncle Luke, and they made him seem more vulnerable somehow.

"He spoke to me for a long time, Marlack did. He tried to persuade me to work alongside him, using my natural abilities and his magic to enslave entire countries. I was not interested. I was still a feudal lord at heart; I had my keep, I had my villagers paying tribute, I had my servants—I had no need for globalization. I was perfectly happy with a virgin to eat once a month and plenty of donors for the between times. Once Marlack understood this, he ransacked my library looking for magical texts that simply weren't there, then left, muttering about 'provincial fools' and 'bumpkins' under his breath the entire time. I stood atop my battlements and watched him go, hoping that my path would never cross his again. I know that humans consider me to be a monster, and perhaps I am a creature of my appetites, but that man is more than a monster—he is pure evil."

CHAPTER 6

I leaned back and digested both my eggs and Uncle Luke's story. After a while, I spoke. "So he didn't do anything but change his voice and that made you think he was carrying a demon around in his head?"

"The fact that his eyes glowed purple may have had something to do with it as well," Luke replied.

"Okay, that's something to go on. Purple fire may be his demonic signature," I said.

"Like always saying the wrong thing at the wrong time is yours."

"Kiss my ass, Unc. I'm going to go upstairs and get some sleep."

"Then what?"

"Then tonight I'm going to pay Mr. Marlack a visit, and we're going to discuss the etiquette of statutory rape, demon impregnation and having me arrested. I expect the conversation to turn violent. It may even start there. Thank Renny for breakfast for me. And Uncle," I said, standing up and heading for the door.

"Yes?"

"Thanks for bailing me out. I really didn't want to have to deal with this bullshit while I was awaiting trial for murder."

"You're welcome. After all, what is family for?" He laughed, one of those old-school super villain laughs, then flashed into smoke and disappeared.

I looked around the study. "I hate when you do that!" I yelled to the empty air, then headed upstairs to my room to catch a few hours' shuteye.

I live in an apartment near Uptown, but I've kept a room at Uncle Luke's for as long as I can remember. We all did—my brother, my sister and me. I walked into my room and looked at their picture on the dresser. It's the only thing I've got from the old days. I'm not Luke, I don't drape my walls in velvet tapestries and bitch and moan about days gone by and gripe about all the "horseless carriages" and the general decline of civility. I just keep one photo, taken when we were all in our twenties, of me, James and Orly. That was before we realized how different I was, how much of mother's blood was changed and passed down to her firstborn. That was back when we thought vampires were just stories that mother told us at night to make us keep our windows locked from the inside.

I looked at the picture, yellowed and brittle and framed for its own protection, and thought about how much I felt like that paper some days. Old past my time, frayed around the edges and getting brittle with age. Then I shook my head, tried to derail my self-pity train, and poured myself a stiff drink. None of that OJ and Coke shit, either. A proper drink, Scotch with no ice and one lone drop of water to release the flavor. I knocked back the first one, and used the second to chase a couple of Vicodin down the old windpipe. It promised to be one of those days—the kind where my dreams are way more real than I want to deal with—so anything I could do to hold them at bay would be welcome. I checked email and surfed the web for a little while looking for information on Jacob Marlack, then when my eyes got heavy and the whiskey and painkillers started to take effect, I kicked off my shoes and sprawled, face-down and fully clothed, on the duvet and nearly drowned myself in goose down and opulence.

I awoke some five hours later, undrowned in feathers and with a taste in my mouth like the sewers of Riyadh City. I looked around the room and saw a fresh can of Coke sweating on the night stand where by all rights my Scotch should have been, but Renfield is an industrious and slightly morally superior fellow, so I chose discretion over drugs and whiskey and chugged the soda. I stripped down and walked into my bathroom, finding the customary towels and washcloth laid out for me.

I don't know if Renny just comes in and does these things when I'm here, or if there's some little magical spell he casts each day to freshen up the linens in the room, but everything is always sparkling and dust-free, no matter what ridiculous hour of the day or night I happen to wander in. Sometimes I wonder exactly who is thrall for whom in my uncle's relationship with this Renfield, then I decided I don't really give a shit, as long as he doesn't get in the way. And he never gets in the way.

A quick shower later, and I dressed in a change of clothes from my armoire. In any other place I'd call it a closet, or if I were feeling particularly genteel, a wardrobe. But in Uncle Luke's place, it was an armoire. And I offered up another silent prayer of thanks to Saint Renfield for the clothing in there, because it all fit and had been mended since the last time I dressed there. That had involved a werewolf and a misunderstanding about a gambling debt. Actually, he'd understood the amount of my debt perfectly, just not my complete and utter disinterest in paying. That led to an unpleasant discussion and little bits of fur and brain matter becoming rather embedded in the fabric of my jeans. Renfield had either replaced those jeans, or done an amazing job of getting wolf brain out of the knees, because they felt like brand new. I only knew they were my old pants when I found a spare fang in the right front pocket.

I got dressed and headed downstairs, groaning a little when I remembered that my car was still at the frat house. Gods only knew what those little fuckwits had done to it by now. Renfield met me at the bottom of the stairs, a little smile on his lips.

"Mr. Quincy, good evening. I trust you feel better after your nap?"

"I do, thank you for the Coke. I would join you for dinner, but I have to get going. There's some pressing business I need to attend to with a man who calls demons for fun. Could you call me a cab?"

"Of course, Mr. Quincy. You are a cab."

"You know, just because a joke never gets old, doesn't mean it was ever funny in the first place. Now how about arranging some transportation for me?"

"Certainly, sir. Your keys are in your duster, on the hook by the front door. Right front pocket." Of course. Renfield was a manservant, an old-school, get-shit-done kind of manservant who didn't need to be told to go get his boss's nephew's car from out front of the house where he'd been arrested the night before, he just did it. And we won't talk about how he got those keys from the pocket of the pants I was sleeping in, but it explained the dream I had about Salma Hayek in the movie theatre watching *E.T.* Well, it explained part of the dream, anyway.

"Thanks as always, Ren. You're the best."

"I know."

I chuckled a little as I walked past him and out the front door. The sun had set, but that didn't give me a good gauge on time. It was fall, so that could be anywhere from six to eight in the evening. Either way, it was about the right time to go pay Mr. Marlack a visit. A visit I sincerely hoped he was not going to enjoy.

CHAPTER 7

I wasn't surprised when I found out that Marlack's office was on the top floor of one of the massive monuments to small penises and corporate dickheads downtown. I also wasn't surprised to find that he was still at work at 8:15 PM on a Thursday. I was surprised to find magical wards poured into the concrete on the building's cornerstone and etched into the windows in the lobby. The wards on the windows flared briefly as I pulled the heavy glass door open and stepped into the atrium. My boots thunked across the marble floor, and I watched as the wage-slave security guard struggled awake behind his huge circular desk.

"Don't worry, Frank, it's just me." I waved my library card at him as I walked past the desk to the bank of half a dozen elevators.

"Huh? My name's Dennis. Who's Frank? And who are you?" The guard was almost fully coherent by the time the express elevator dinged open and I stepped inside. I gave him a little wave as the doors slid closed, then pressed the button for the sixty-fourth floor.

Nothing happened. The button lit up for a second, then went dark. I looked around, then noticed the card reader set above the bank of buttons. Obviously Mr. Marlack didn't want any unexpected or unauthorized visitors.

Since the next time I willingly walk up sixty-plus flights of stairs will be the first, I pressed my fingertips lightly to the card reader, focused my will on the device, and whispered, "*Laborious pro merda*," which loosely translated into, "Work you piece of shit." I pressed the button for the top floor again, and this time the elevator jerked into motion. I leaned against the back wall of the elevator car, arms crossed, feeling pretty darn satisfied in myself. After all, I'd saved the girl's soul from Hell, figured out who was responsible, and was about to go do some serious smiting. That was a pretty good couple of days for me, even with an arrest thrown in for good measure. All I had to do was bludgeon Marlack into losing interest in the occult, and then finish showing his son the error of his ways. No problem.

Until the doors opened on the sixty-fourth floor and I stepped out into the biggest damn casting circle I'd ever seen. The elevators sat in the center of the floor, and the second I stepped out, I felt myself cross a magical barrier that had every hair on my body standing at end. And you have no idea how uncomfortable that is while wearing pants. I turned in a slow circle, trying to take in all the unnatural details I could before I opened up my Sight. As bad as this place looked in normal light, I really didn't want to know what it looked like in the magical spectrum, but I was pretty sure I wasn't going to have that choice.

The floor was black marble with gold inlays. To a normal observer, the gold was in random patterns, but if you turned your head just a little and squinted just right you could see the runes set into the floor. That kind of precise gold work must have taken months, and cost millions, but given the kind of critters Marlack's kid played with, Daddy obviously knew enough to set his defenses. I was standing inside one edge of a ten-foot circle, and I couldn't break it if I tried. The second I stepped into it, the circle invoked, bringing up a mystical barrier between me and the rest of the known universe. Nothing was getting into that circle unless I, or someone else, summoned it. That wasn't the part that worried me. I was much more concerned with the fact that I couldn't get *out*.

The rest of the floor, as much as I could see through the

shimmer of the magical wall, was decorated in early twenty-first century office dickhead. Lots of exposed chrome and uncomfortable seating, a lot of track lighting and no plants or magazines anywhere. The whole place was designed to make you think the man in the office was very important, and that you aren't. As soon as my eyes lit on the doors to the office, some dark wood double doors that were probably brought back personally from an expedition down the darkest reaches of the Amazon, the golden knob turned and the doors flung outward. Following in their wake was a tall man, thin but not gaunt, wearing a very sober pin-striped suit and a classy red striped tie. He looked every inch the captain of industry, and appeared to have no more magic than poor old Dennis down in the lobby.

Until I closed my eyes and *looked* at him. That's when I saw the power swirling around him like a heavy green fog. That's when I could read the sigils carved onto his soul from twenty feet away and knew I was in the presence of a man who lusted for power like I lusted for Angelina Jolie, and would do absolutely anything to get it. He walked across the floor, his perfectly polished loafers making a thin *click-click*, the brisk click of his steps counting down the remainder of my time on earth, I'm sure.

"Mr. Harker, I presume?" He stopped just in front of me and held out a hand.

I looked at the hand like it was something disgusting, which it was. After a few seconds, he pulled it back. Marlack looked up at me with a rueful grin. "I suppose civility was too much to ask for. So be it. What do you want?"

"I'm here to tell you to stop."

"Stop what?"

"Playing around with things you don't understand. You're messing with stuff humans have no business getting involved in,

Marlack."

"I've been involved with those things, things like your Uncle Luke, since long before you were born, Mr. Harker. I don't think I'm going to stop now just because you don't approve of my son's recreational activities."

"Recreational?" I spluttered. I couldn't even get the word out right. "You call summoning a demon and letting it rape a little girl recreational?"

"No." Marlack's smile disappeared and his eyes went cold. "No, I call it stupid. And I appreciate you dealing with the situation before it got out of hand. But it has been dealt with, and now your services are no longer needed. So, thank you for sending the demon back to Hell. Now, please leave my office."

"I don't think so, pal. You've got a lot to answer for, not the least of which is giving that douchecanoe you call a son the books to raise demons with in the first place. What the hell were you thinking?"

"I was thinking that he needed to start learning to use his gifts, the gifts I worked very hard to bestow upon him. And if he decided to use those gifts on some whore at a party, then the world loses one whore, and nobody notices. Even you only care because he happened to pick an underage whore. If she'd been eighteen and white you wouldn't give a damn. But Laws a'mercy, we gots to help the little brown girl! We gots to take our liberal guilt and uncle's money and help the poor little wetback!"

"Fuck you, pal. Your kid raised a demon, and you taught him how. There's a price for that, and now it's time to pay up."

"And who appointed you the Morality Police, Mr. Harker? Who gave you the badge and the gun and told you to clean up Dodge City?" He was right in front of me now, less than five feet away, inches from the edge of the circle, which he could obviously pass through without any trouble.

"I did. When I promised that little girl's father I'd try to save his daughter." An image popped into my mind, one I'd worked very hard to keep buried for the past several days. It was a little girl looking at me through the back window of a car as it drove away. I blinked a few times to shove the image back down inside and focus on the asshole at hand.

"Well, Sheriff, I suppose we are at an impasse," Marlack said.

"I don't think so," I said, and stepped back, crossing into another circle as I did so. The barrier that had surrounded the two of us flicked out of existence as the new circle invoked. His power flickered to life in the material plane, and a solid barrier of will sprang into existence along the edges of the circle he stood in, freeing me but separating the two of us. I reached out and touched the surface of the circle, watching the vibrant green magic swirl and pool around my fingertips. I pushed against the magic, and it turned hot to the touch. I snatched my fingers back.

Marlack laughed. "You can't think my circle is so weak, can you, Harker?"

"I don't know," I replied honestly. "I haven't tested it yet." With that I drew a silver dagger from the small of my back and jabbed it into the barrier. The blade penetrated about an inch into the circle, then stopped, slowed as if I had stabbed some almost solid mass. The green magic swirled faster, focusing on the blade, and the silver dagger turned red, then white-hot, and melted, falling into two puddles separated by the circle's scribing.

"You're going to have to do better than that," Marlack said with a smile.

"I can." I didn't boast. I didn't yell. I just pulled out a 9mm Glock pistol and fired fifteen rounds into the magical barrier. I angled the shots off to the side, away from Marlack's face and more importantly angled the ricochets away from my own. Green lights flared up with each impact, and I saw Marlack's brow furrow, but his circle held.

"Now are you beginning to understand what you're dealing with, boy?" Marlack asked after the ringing in my ears subsided a little.

"I'm getting a pretty good picture," I said. I stepped into the office and began pulling thick law books off the shelves. I took my time building a nice little two-foot wall around the outer edge of the circle, all the time ignoring Marlack's queries. Once I had the circle completely ringed in bound paper, I pulled out my Zippo, drizzled a little lighter fluid across the tops of the books, and lit them on fire. The books with lighter fluid on them blazed to life, and the fire quickly spread to the entire ring of books. Marlack was perfectly safe from the flames within his circle, but unfortunately for him there was still plenty of air traveling through his magical barrier.

I walked across the office and looked for a way to open his floor-to-ceiling windows, but apparently they don't allow that sort of thing in high-rises. So I put my fist through the glass, shattering it and letting some fresh air in. At least for me. The added oxygen just made the book fire blaze up even higher, and Marlack began to cough. I pulled a chair over from Marlack's desk and sat by the window, keeping the worst of the smoke from my eyes.

A fire alarm blared to life, but a whispered, "*Silencio*," shut the fire alarm system down before the sprinklers kicked in. Marlack coughed inside his precious circle for a couple more moments, then with a wave of his arms and flash of green light, he dispelled his protective barrier. Another wave of his hands and my circle of burning books broke apart and flew into all corners of the room. Some of them even hurtled through the air and out the open window I was sitting next to. I would have been concerned, but there was too much smoke for Marlack to see me, much less throw a book at me.

I got up and walked over to the coughing wizard. Tears streamed down his face, and soot stained his forehead. I grabbed him by the throat and pulled him upright. "Now we're going to talk about your book collection, and then we're going to talk about what kind of punishment your son gets to face."

Marlack glared at me, then coughed up a mouthful of sooty air in my face. I blinked and wiped my face to clear my vision, and when I could see straight again, Marlack was standing several feet away, perfectly composed. There was nothing in my hand but his necktie. I hate illusionists.

"That was a good trick, Mr. Harker, but not quite good enough."

"I think it did alright. It got my hands around your throat." I stepped forward, shoving myself forward with my enhanced strength and speed, but Marlack vanished as my hands went right through his neck. I really, really hate illusionists.

I spun around, looking for the annoying magician. Marlack stood in the center of the room, in a circle surrounded by more circles and sigils than my eye could trace. I looked down, making sure that I wasn't trapped in any of the room's many inlaid circles myself, and started toward him.

"*Debilitatio.*" Marlack pointed at me, and a bolt of green energy flew from his fingers. I leapt into the air, but the spell was cast on me, not just hurled in my general direction, so the magical arrow bent like a guided missile and followed my every move. It struck me square in the chest as I came down from my leap, and all my limbs turned to jelly. I landed on the inscribed marble in a heap, unable to move or feel any of my extremities.

I listened to those goddamn dress shoes *click* across the floor again, thinking about what kind of pansy wears hard-soled shoes to a fight as Marlack stepped over me. He reached down and rolled me onto my back before kneeling beside me. "Now I think it's time for this charade to end, Mr. Harker. Let's stop pretending that you are any threat to me, and I'll stop pretending that you're going to live through the night. *Vis vires.*"

With the murmured Latin, his hands glowed a deep purple, almost black against his pale skin. He reached out with his long fingers and wrapped one hand in the collar of my shirt and the other around my belt. Marlack stood, and hefted me over his head as he did so, like a professional wrestler hoisting a child. My two hundred and forty pounds bounced in his grip like it was nothing, and Marlack strode to a window, hefted me once more, then chucked me through like so much battered garbage.

I felt my skin tear as the glass shattered across my face, then the cold wind rush by as I made my rapid descent. I had just enough time to think that maybe Marlack was more than I had expected when I spun over in midair and saw what was rushing up to meet me.

I had just enough muscle control to mutter, "Oh fuck," before I landed face-first on the roof of a parked Suburban.

CHAPTER 8

I lay there, face full of broken glass and Chevrolet factory paint, thinking about the poor choices I'd made in life.

That's total bullshit. I lay there thinking, *Fuck that hurt*, until the first flashing red and blue lights showed. Then I shifted my internal monologue to just, *Fuck*. I still couldn't move, although I wasn't sure if it was due to Marlack's spell or the grievous injuries I'd just sustained, and I could tell by the sirens that there were ambulances and police arriving on the scene. The last thing I wanted to do was explain to some overzealous public servant exactly how I was still alive after a sixty-plus story fall onto several tons of Detroit steel.

That's more bullshit. The last thing I wanted to do was fight Marlack again, but the next to last thing I wanted to do was deal with the cops or the EMTs. So I made myself move. I peeled my broken body off the roof of the broken car like the coyote in a Road Runner cartoon, leaving a fair amount of blood, skin and a couple of teeth behind. I knew from experience that the blood and skin would replace itself in a few hours, but the missing teeth were going to be a problem for the next couple of days.

I had just rolled to the ground and pulled myself up to my knees when I heard one of the last voices I wanted to hear right in that moment, the usually welcome tones of Detective Rebecca Gail Flynn.

"Mr. Harker. This is where I would typically say something witty like 'fancy meeting you here,' except that I am totally and completely unsurprised at seeing you here. After hearing reports of strange flashing lights, explosions and a man falling to his doom from the upper offices of the Pantheon Building, it brings me no surprise at all to see you here in the middle of an explosion of blood, broken glass and property damage. I'm not even surprised to see you alive, no matter how bizarre that may be." She reached down, helped me to my feet, then continued helping me right into a spin that ended with me face-down on the hood of the destroyed Suburban with handcuffs clicking shut around my wrists.

Flynn hustled me into a nearby squad car and gave the uniform behind the wheel strict instructions to take me to jail, directly to jail, and not to allow me to pass "Go" or collect my two hundred dollars. After a quick thump on the roof of the car, Flynn receded in the back mirror and I turned to face the driver.

"I don't suppose you'd consider a detour through the emergency room, would you? I think my everything might be broken," I said through the Plexiglas divider.

"Detective Flynn said straight to the station. So you go straight to the station." He never turned, not even flicking his eyes up to the mirror.

"But do you want to be the one that 'just follows orders' or do you want to be the guy that takes compassion on a fellow human being that's suffering?" I tried to make myself look suffering. It didn't take much, since I was still bleeding from a dozen cuts and my left eye was swollen almost completely shut, but my escort still wasn't looking.

"I want to be the one that's not playing crossing guard outside all through the winter. So you're the one that's going straight to the station." He kept his eyes firmly focused on the road, leaving me to bleed and throb at my own pace.

The drive to the station took a solid twenty minutes, during which the worst of the bleeding stopped and a couple of small shards of glass expelled themselves from my face as the cuts there started to heal. I decided that I had lost three teeth in the fall, and hoped I hadn't swallowed them. That always made for an unpleasant morning after. Officer Silence held a hand on the back of my head to keep me from further injury as I got out of the car, a nice touch I thought. He perp-walked me in through the back door and up to Central Booking, where I was fingerprinted (again), had my mug shot taken (again), and was escorted to the drunk tank for holding (again). I settled in on my bench and rubbed my chafed wrists while taking stock of my situation.

I'd failed horribly in my attempt to beat Marlack into submission, or even understanding of his wrongdoings. He wasn't just unapologetic; he was gleeful about his depravity. I'd ended up in jail, where I was somewhat less than effective in both avenging Kayleigh Garda and protecting any other girls from Marlack's brat and his fraternity brothers. All in all, I had to admit it was a pretty godawful night. I was sitting there, minding my own business and listening to my blood clot, when a voice jarred me from my moping.

"That's my seat." I looked up at a lump of a head atop a mountain of flesh sitting somewhere near seven feet off the ground.

I stared at him, not moving. My mind flashed back to everything I'd ever learned about predators, both human and not. Then I thought *fuck it*, and stood up. "If this seat means enough to you to die for, then have it. I'll go sit over there. But if you start some bullshit about that being your seat too right after I get comfortable, then we're going to have a problem. The kind of problem that involves somebody washing a lot of your blood down the drain in the center of the floor and me quite possibly causing serious injury to my hand while beating your fucking face in. Got it?"

The mountain held up both hands and backed up a couple of quick steps. "Hey man, I don't want no trouble. You can sit wherever you like. I was just gonna say that I'd been sitting there before I had to go pee, and could you scoot over a little. Okay? But I'll go sit somewhere else. Just don't beat me up, please?" His voice was a lot higher when he was scared shitless, and on second look he was just a fat lush spending his weekend in the drunk tank, not some hardened criminal trying to establish jailyard supremacy.

I stood up. "Never mind, buddy. Total misunderstanding. I'll go sit over here. You have a nice sleep." I crossed the room to the other bunk, all of eight feet away, and sat down facing the now-terrified drunk.

A dreadlocked head popped over the bunk, looking down at me. "You are not a nice man." The head said, then broke into a grin. "I'm Jake."

"I'm not interested."

"I'm not trying to pick up a date, bro, just making conversation. What happened to you? You look like you got run over by a steamroller."

"I fell down."

"Shit, man, how far?"

"About sixty stories."

"Bullshit!"

"Fuck off then." I lay down on the bunk and put my hands behind my head. Jake's head disappeared for a minute, then the rest of him spun into view as he dropped down off the top bunk and sat at my feet. He was a skinny black dude with long dreads, a pierced nose, the bloodshot eyes of the cosmically stoned, and a Bob Marley *Legend* t-shirt. I shook my head. I tend to immediately discount the musical opinions of people wearing shirts with records that were released before they were born. Of course, before I was born they were making music on wax cylinders, so I suppose I'm only a poseur if I wear a Mozart shirt. Which I never will.

"Hey man, I'm just trying to be friendly. How did you fall that far and live? Did you go, like, super-limp or something? Are you like a superhero? Or are you just really, really fucked up? I mean, I read once that if you're fucked up enough, you don't get tense at the moment of impact, and you can like live through almost any fucking thing. Like getting hit by a bus or whatever. Is that what happened to you?"

It took me a minute to parse the sentence, but when I did I just shook my head. "Go away, kid. I've had a really shitty night and I just want to sleep this off, get up in the morning, post my bail, and go home. I don't want to deal with fighting for turf, I don't want to deal with making friends, and I don't want to talk about my night. You got all that? Good. Now get your ass off my bunk and leave me alone."

"Nah, I don't think so." He leaned back and grinned at me.

I sat up, looking around for a weapon. That's when I noticed that no one else in the cell was moving. At all. Not like they were asleep, like they were frozen in time. Or like I was suddenly *outside* of time. I jumped out of the bunk and stomped across the cell, trying to find something to kick that wouldn't hurt too much in the jail slippers I was wearing.

After a minute of fruitlessly looking for something to use as a weapon, I turned back to my bunk, where "Jake" was now sitting cross-legged in the center of the bed, smiling at me like a cat with a bellyful of canary. Then I realized what was happening.

"Goddammit, Glory, what the fuck are you doing here?"

"Guardian stuff. You know, making sure you don't become somebody's prison bitch while you sleep, that sort of thing." My angel's voice sounded strange coming through Jake's weed-scarred vocal chords, but it was probably doing all sorts of good things for him being inhabited by one of the Host.

"Yeah, like that was going to happen." I looked around the cell and waved at the others in my little twelve by twenty room. There was Tubbo, the innocuous fatty that I'd given up the first bunk to. He was probably three hundred fifty pounds of Jell-O and milquetoast, not exactly the stuff my nightmares were made of. Then there was skinny Jake, too high to tie his own shoes, much less subdue me. That only left one little guy stretched out on the top bunk across the room, a banker-looking dude about five-eight with wire-rimmed glasses and a receding hairline. He looked too timid to take eleven items through the express lane at the grocery store, much less attack anyone.

"It was. The guy whose body I'm inhabiting? He killed three people last night in a psychotic break. In the movie in his mind, you're his high school girlfriend and this whole conversation has been taking place after prom. You two had been waiting months for this perfect moment, and he was about to seal the deal with you."

"Not while I'm still breathing," I said, looking back over at Jake. He looked harmless, if high. "Are you sure he's delusional?"

"He thinks Fox News really is fair and balanced," Glory replied.

"Yup, batshit crazy," I agreed. "What about these two dweebs? Weren't they going to help?" I pointed at Tiny and Tubbo on the other bunk.

"They aren't the 'get involved' type. The fat one is so scared he pees a little every time anybody speaks to him, and the other one is a complete blank to me." Her brow furrowed as she said that.

"What do you mean?" I asked.

Glory stood up, in Jake's body, and walked over to the side of the bunk where the little guy was frozen. She stared at him for a few seconds, then turned back to me. "Run."

"What? Where?" I asked. Glory/Jake had this look of pure terror on his/her face, like nothing I'd seen before. What the hell could scare an angel? I found out as the little nebbishy guy, who looked like a less butch Les Nessman off the old TV show *WKRP in Cincinatti*, sat bolt upright in bed, bounded across the room, and wrapped his legs around Jake/Glory's neck. The second he touched the angel, time started moving at its normal pace again, which is to say way too fast for my comfort.

Nebbish had his legs locked around Jake's neck, and I could tell from the look on Jake's face that he had no idea how he'd gotten there. Apparently whatever was in the other prisoner bounced Glory out of Jake on contact. Then Nebbish straightened his legs out and twisted at the hips, crossing his ankles and pushing himself upwards on his hands in a sitting position. The twist he put on Jake's neck resulted in a very unhealthy-sounding *POP*, and the dreadlocked head lolled to one side, eyes going blank in death.

Tubbo saw the body drop to the floor in front of his bunk and curled up the fetal position. I could smell the urine flowing from across the cell. *No help coming there.* Nebbish dropped from the top bunk, straightening his shirt as he stepped up to me.

"Mr. Harker, what a pleasure to meet you. I was instructed to tell you that Jacob Marlack sends his warmest regards. And by 'warmest,' he is referring to the Hell he has hired me to send you to. Have a nice trip." Nebbish threw a punch at my midsection that probably would have sent his fist out through my spleen if it connected. I decided that it shouldn't connect, so I sidestepped the punch and grabbed Nebbish's wrist. I pulled, and he flew past me to crash face-first into the bars of our cell.

He turned around, and the look on his face made me take an involuntary step back. The little bastard was *smiling*. Blood was streaming down his forehead from where his head impacted the bars, and he was grinning at me through the red drops. He came at me again, keeping his hands low and outside to prevent me from going around him this time. I saw what he was doing, so I didn't go around him. I went straight at him instead, diving headfirst across the floor, rolling over onto my back as I slid between his spread legs, and kicking upward with a front snap kick from the floor. My slipper caught him square in the nuts, and he toppled forward. He recovered fast enough to turn his tumble into a forward roll, and was back on his feet facing me by the time I scrambled to my feet.

"What the fuck are you?" I asked.

"What am I?" Nebbish repeated. "You ask the wrong question, mortal. I am not a what, but a who. I am the Grand Marquis Fornas, leader of twenty-nine of Hell's legions, corrupter of the sciences, defiler of the experiments, and despoiler of the philosophies. I am a warrior, a poet, a scholar, and your doom." He lunged at me again, but I'd used his monologue to maneuver us around so that Tubbo was right behind me, and when Fornas leapt, I dropped flat, leaving the Grand Marquis to fly face-first into a great big pile of terrified, gibbering drunken pee. He shrieked with rage and turned to fling himself at me again, but with enough time to think for once, I caught him in midair and pressed my right hand to his forehead.

"*Exorcizo te, omnis spiritus immunde, in nomine Dei Patris omnipotentis, et in noimine Jesu Christi Filii ejus, Domini et Judicis nostri, et in virtute Spiritus Sancti, ut descedas ab hoc plasmate Dei, quod Dominus noster ad templum sanctum suum vocare dignatus est, ut fiat templum Dei vivi, et Spiritus Sanctus habitet in eo. Per eumdem Christum Dominum nostrum, qui venturus est judicare vivos et mortuos, et saeculum per ignem."*

I wasn't sure if it would work with me not knowing Nebbish's True Name to cast out the demon, but I poured my will into my right hand and felt the tattoos flare to life along my arm and my palm. They burned as the power of The Word coursed through me, and Nebbish dropped to his knees screaming. I screamed right along with him, because having holy magic run through your arm feels an awful lot like sticking your middle finger in a light socket while being struck by lightning and peeing on an electric fence all at the same time.

The air around us went dark as noxious purple-grey smoke billowed from Nebbish's mouth, nose, ears and eyes, and all I heard over the sound of screaming was more screaming and a faint fire alarm in the distance. Finally, after what felt like a year but was probably all of thirty seconds, Nebbish's eyes went back to normal human hazel eyes, all the smoke in the room cleared in an instant, and I fell to the floor with a diminutive accountant on top of me.

I lay there trying to catch my breath and wondering exactly how I was going to explain this to the nice man lying on top of me when suddenly Nebbish's weight was lifted off me and I was hauled roughly to my feet. My eyes were still trying to focus, but I got a good look at Detective Flynn as the two uniforms dragged me out of the cell and down the hall.

"I warned you, Detective, I'm the reason we can't have nice things," I said, giving her my best saucy smile. Then I passed out.

CHAPTER 9

I came to in Interview #1, appreciating the upgrade to the bigger room this time. I wasn't handcuffed to anything, and there was a bottle of water in front of me, so I drank it to try and get the taste of demon smoke out of my mouth. Even three-day-old grocery store sushi can't hold a candle to the nasty that is demon funk.

I downed the water in a long pull, squeezing the sides flat as I went. I held it up and shook it at the camera in the corner of the room, then turned it upside down in the universal sign for "more?" No dice. I set the empty bottle on the table, turned to the big two-way mirror in one wall that served as an observation window and waved, then pointed at the empty bottle again.

"Service in this restaurant sucks. I'll have you know that my review will reflect as much," I said, pushing my chair away from the table. I'd just put my feet up and leaned back when the door opened and Detective Flynn stomped in. She strode across the room, knocked my feet off the table, and sat down across from me. I sat up and scooted my chair forward, putting my elbows on the table and situating myself directly in front of the microphone. I fully intended to blow it up, but I wanted to make it look good for the observers.

"What the fuck happened in there, Harker?" Flynn asked.

I raised an eyebrow. "Why Detective, such language is unbecoming a professional like yourself. I don't know that I will ever be able to repair my image of you."

"Go fuck yourself. Now what happened in that cell?"

"Why should I bother telling you? You won't believe me."

"Try me."

"I've been trying you for three years now. Every time you haul me in, I start off with the truth and have to go further and further afield of it to find something you'll believe. Why don't you just tell me what you want to think happened in there and I'll agree to it?"

"I don't know how you did it, but somehow you managed to goad a man in custody for shoplifting into fighting with you in a holding cell, and then you set off some kind of smoke bomb, filling the jail with smoke and obscuring exactly what was going on in there, while for some reason the shoplifter and a low-level pot and Adderall dealer got into an altercation, leaving the dealer dead, and the shoplifter attacking you, of all ridiculous people. Those are things that I know happened. Now I want to know *why*."

"I told you, I can't explain it in any way that you will believe."

"And I told you to try me."

"I'm tired of wasting my breath, Detective. And I'm tired of being here. So why don't you either put me back in holding, or show me to the door?"

"Why don't I just fast-track an arraignment on murder charges, hold you here until that happens, and then throw away the key? I'm tired of this, Harker. I'm tired of all the weird shit happening when you're around, I'm tired of not being able to explain anything to anyone, and I'm tired of the goddamn mess you leave behind!" Flynn was standing with her hands on the table, sweat staining the neck of her dark purple blouse, and her hair falling from the usually neat ponytail. Her jaw was clenching and unclenching rapidly, and a vein had popped out a little on her forehead. My expert analysis revealed that she was *pissed*.

Unfortunately for Detective Flynn, any electronics in the

room, and my own chances of getting out of jail that night, I was in pretty shite mood myself. I stood up slowly, doing that twitchy thing I know I do with my fingers when I'm about to lose my shit, where I tap each finger in succession off my thumbs, faster and faster until I just make a fist and really get the shitshow started. It goes back to when I was younger and tried to keep my temper by counting to ten. Usually I lost interest in counting along about the fifth language, and just hit whatever was pissing me off. I was really hoping I could keep my shit together enough not to punch Detective Flynn. I kinda liked her, and really didn't need the drama that punching cops brings in America.

"Detective Flynn," I began slowly. "If you think it's tough being around me, having to occasionally clean up some of the mess when I leave, being thrust into the middle of pieces of my strange and cursedly interesting life, please take a second and think how it must feel to *fucking live it*. I don't get to go home after filling out paperwork about the man who died in the cell tonight, I get to go home and see his face in my dreams. I don't get to put a neat little label on the fire and smoke that billowed through your precinct tonight, I have to live with the fucking scars." I rolled up my sleeves and showed my tattoos.

Usually they aren't visible, being applied with a magically enhanced UV ink. But when I call upon the power stored there, they burn out the ink, the hard way, by setting the ink on fire while it's still in my skin. That leaves a nasty set of burns that takes weeks to heal. Then I have to go back in to a mystical tattoo artist and have the work redone. In UV ink again. With spells entwined into the design. Spells that take a piece of my soul to fuse to my body and my being. It takes about three weeks to be healed enough to get the tattoos done, then about another four weeks to heal from the tattooing. So I don't burn those up lightly.

Also, having second-degree burns running the length of both arms and down each finger hurts like a son of a bitch.

I went on. "Now I'm going to tell you what happened in that cell. And I'm going to make sure that everyone behind that glass can hear it this time. But there will be no recording. Are we clear?"

"What do you intend to do about that, Mr. Harker?" A voice came through the grill under the window.

"This." I replied. I held my arms out toward the ceiling, spread out from my shoulders in a "Y." "*Futue te ipsum!*" I said at the top of my lungs and pushed my power out through my fingertips. The camera on the wall exploded in a shower of sparks, the table recorder in the center of the table flew six inches into the air and landed on its back, smoking. The two-way mirror shattered, and three very surprised men in suits stood staring at me from the other side. One man sitting at a computer suddenly jerked a set of headphones off his head and threw them to the ground, cursing as sparks flew from his laptop. A high-pitched squeal came from Detective Flynn's pocket, and she jumped up, reached into her pants, and threw her smoldering cell phone onto the ground. I smirked as all the men in the observation room did the same.

"Now that we can chat undisturbed by all these electronic toys, let me give you all the lowdown on what happened here tonight. If there's anyone in that room that you don't think is high enough in the food chain to hear what I'm about to tell you, now's your chance to send them home." The suits looked at each other, then at the technician, who was still rubbing his scorched ear. After a couple of seconds of silent consultation, one of the suits with a square jaw and air of authority tapped the tech on the shoulder and pointed at the door. The skinny tech pouted for a second, but then looked at me and apparently decided that he wasn't that interested in finding out the truth if I had anything to do with it.

"Good," I said. "Now let's be clear about this—there are things in this world that men and women aren't meant to understand. We aren't supposed to know these things exist, much less how to fight them. The things that go bump in the night, the monsters in the closet, the shadow out of the corner of your eye—that's where I live. These are the things I deal with every fucking day, and neither your gun, nor your badge, nor that little medal of St. Jude you wear on a silver chain around your neck will protect you from the shit that is going down in our fair city these days. Nice choice, by the way, St. Jude. I've always tossed an extra coin his way when I make an offering. I figure if anybody's gonna look after me, it'll be him."

"Why don't you tell us exactly what it is that's got you so scared, Harker?" Flynn asked. She was back in her chair, burning pants forgotten as she pretended to be having just another normal day at the office. Her left hand trailed up to trace the medal under her shirt, but she caught herself and with a visible effort pulled it back to the table.

"Jacob Marlack," I said.

"Yeah, he's the one who filed the most recent complaint against you," Flynn replied.

"Like I give a fuck about his complaint. I'm much more concerned about the fact that he's summoning demons. Actually, it's worse than that. He's letting his fratboy son summon demons and use them to seduce and rape underage girls."

Flynn looked at me for a long moment and then sat back down, leaning on the table. "Why is it never just drugs? Other detectives get meth heads flipping out and shooting their wives and children over a fucked up batch of bastardized cold medicine. I get an overgrown Harry fucking Potter and his evil wizards."

"I guess you're just lucky, Detective," I said.

"That's not exactly what I'd call it." She turned to where the mirror used to be and spoke to the three men standing there. "I assume since you haven't called for the men in white suits with the jacket that buckles in the back that you're taking this seriously?"

The men looked at each other, then the one with the square jaw walked out of the room. A few seconds later the door to the interview room opened and he stepped in. He walked like twenty years of military, and had a "don't fuck with me" set to his jaw. He pulled a chair from the wall over to the table and sat down, sliding a badge holder over to me. I opened it, and staring back at me was a picture of Crew Cut with the name "John A. Smith" under it in blue block letters. Written over the picture were the words "US Department of Homeland Security" and on a line right below that, in much smaller print, "Paranormal Division." A gold badge on the facing side displayed the Homeland Security logo with an assortment of the world's major religions' holy symbols arranged in a circle on the shield the eagle was holding.

"Pleased to meet you, Mr. Smith," I said, sliding the badge back over to him. "Looks like we're in the same line of work."

"And what do you call your line of work, Mr. Harker?" Smith asked. He didn't return my smile. I decided not to feel hurt.

"I call myself a security specialist."

"You lying sack of shit, you call yourself a demon hunter." Flynn leaned back in her chair, arms crossed across her chest.

"Same thing, Detective. Same thing."

"What can you tell us about Marlack?" Smith asked.

"What else do you want to know? He summons demons, lets them screw little girls, and then casts them aside like so much garbage," I said. "Now are you going to help me kill this motherfucker, or what?"

CHAPTER 10

I gave Crew Cut my most charming smile, which I've been told reminds people of Anthony Hopkins from *Silence of the Lambs*, but he didn't even blink. In fact, he stared at me so long without blinking I started to wonder if he had eyelids. Finally, he nodded a little and waved to the other two men.

One came into the room and Smith said, "Bring us some more water. I think we're going to be able to work with Mr. Harker here."

"Are you fucking insane?" Flynn asked. "Because he is. You heard what he was babbling about, right? Demons, monsters, things that go bump in the night? What the fuck, Smith? You can't possibly believe in this shit." Flynn stood up and started pacing around the interview room muttering to herself.

"Detective, you're still in this room as a courtesy," Smith said. Flynn froze in her pacing and turned slowly to stare at the back of the agent's head. "Now if you'd like to sit down and contribute to the discussion, that's fine. If you'd like to sit down and keep your goddamn mouth shut, that's also fine. But you will sit the fuck down, right the fuck now, or you will leave this room. Do you understand me?"

Smith never raised his voice. He never changed the cadence of his speech one bit, and didn't even turn to look at the stunned detective. But there was no question in my mind that he was not a man to fuck with. And I am not widely regarded as someone who knows many boundaries. Flynn stood there gaping for several seconds until the door opened and the other suit came back with three bottles of water. He set the water on the table and stood there, awaiting further instruction. Smith waved a hand,

and the suit in the room with us and the suit still in the room behind what used to be the two-way mirror both left and made themselves scarce.

"They'll take up positions outside the doors to make sure we aren't disturbed. Now, Detective, we have a problem to deal with. Are you part of the solution?" He motioned toward Flynn's chair, and she sat.

I unscrewed the cap on a bottle of water and sucked it down, still trying to get the taste of exorcism out of my mouth. "So what can I do for you, Agent Smith?" I asked.

"Just exactly what you intended to do before meeting me — kill Jacob Marlack."

Flynn's head whipped back and forth between Smith and me. "What? Are you serious? We can't just — " Smith held up a hand, and Flynn cut her words off like a spigot.

"He kicked my ass the last time I tried. You got something to help even the odds?" I asked.

"Information," Smith replied.

"You want to elaborate on that, pal, or are we going to play cat and mouse all night?" I downed the last of my water and reached out for another. Smith gave me a little "go ahead" with his hand, and I took another drink. Rate I was going, I supposed I could drown Marlack in piss if nothing else came to mind.

"We think Marlack has been at this game for quite a while, and may have some enemies that could come in handy." He pushed a piece of paper across the table at me. I took it, and looked at the names written there. My eyes widened at the third name on the list.

"These are some of Hell's heaviest hitters. You're telling me that Marlack double-crossed these guys and lived to tell the tale?" I asked.

"Somehow that's exactly what he's done. And along the way he's done a lot worse than just giving a few teenaged girls over to be demon meat. He's engineered mass killings all over the world, with his fingers in pies from Cambodia to Haiti. For about the last century and a half, if there's been incredible bloodshed and suffering, he's been involved.

"But never the front-page stuff, only the stuff where the 'civilized' world won't pay attention," Smith continued.

"You mean he only kills brown and yellow people," I translated.

"Pretty much. That keeps him off the radar of the people with the resources to root him out and take care of him once and for all."

"Until now. What's different now?" I leaned back and put my feet up on the table and sipped my water while studying Smith. He was a white guy, late forties but still looked like he could kick a normal human's ass pretty well. He probably ran, did calisthenics, took target practice three or four times a week, that kind of thing. He wasn't a golf course and gym kind of lean, he was the walk into the woods for a week with a bandana and pocketknife kind of whipcord muscle. But there was something in his eyes that held me. This was a man that had seen some serious shit, and walked away from it, but not without leaving some pieces of himself behind.

"I'm different now. We have a very small department, but we have the full force and authority of the Department of Homeland Security at our disposal."

"Like the boys in those *Mission: Impossible* movies. All the toys, but none of the backup. If we fuck up, we're on our own. Right, Agent 'Smith?'" I put a little extra emphasis on the name to let him know that I knew it was fake. He smiled a little half-smile that was as close as I'd seen him come to a grin.

"That pretty much sums it up. Now I've given you some valuable information about our friend Jacob Marlack. Do you know what to do with it?"

Then it clicked. "You can't do it yourself. That's why you want me. You don't have enough magic to light a fucking candle, do you?"

"Not even the tiniest bit," Smith confirmed.

"So I get to be the sword."

"And I'm the arm. Exactly."

"Well loosen your grip on my johnson. I've got this."

"And where do I fit into this little magical Justice League?" Flynn asked.

"Do you want in, Detective?" Smith asked her, and something in his tone told me he was asking a lot bigger question that his words would indicate.

Flynn must have heard the same thing, because she didn't answer right away. She looked at Smith, then at me, then at the shards of glass on the floor. "This is one of those moments that no matter what I say, I'm probably going to look back on it in twenty years and regret my decision, isn't it? If I say yes, I go down the rabbit hole with you lunatics and my career stalls at Detective. I'm done with any kind of real career advancement, and any good things that happen to me in my job, I don't get to tell anyone about. If I say no, I spend the rest of my life working cases and saying, 'What if?'"

"If it makes you feel any better, the odds of you living twenty years in this line of work are pretty slim," I said. That's my idea of being helpful. I kinda liked Flynn. She was a pain in my ass, but she was a constant, something steady that I could count on. I wasn't sure I wanted her involved in my world, not really.

"I'm in." I was afraid of that. No detective worth a damn

could turn down something like this, and Flynn was one of the best I'd ever met.

"Fine, then. Let's get Mr. Harker out of here and see what can be done about our friend Marlack. Mr. Harker—"

"Call me Q. Looks like I'm stuck with you for a little while, no need to stand on formalities. Right, Smitty?"

"Sure," the agent replied. I'm sure he gave not a single shit what I called him, as long as I killed what he wanted killed and didn't rack up too big a civilian body count in the process.

"And what would you like me to call you, darlin'?" I looked at Detective Flynn. "Becky? Gail?"

"Flynn will do just fine. And if you don't mind horribly, I'll keep calling you fucknuts. At least in my head." She stepped to the door and opened it. "Let's go. I'll have to do some fast talking to get your release paperwork processed, but—"

"I've got it covered, Detective," Smith said. "I might not be able to light a candle magically, but when it comes to paperwork, I'm the greatest wizard you've ever seen."

I stood up and followed Flynn out the door. "Why Agent Smitty, did you just make a joke? Was that an honest-to-Jebus federal agent sense of humor? I thought they removed those when you stepped in the front door of Langley."

"They reissue them when you're assigned to smartass wizards with vampire DNA." Smith shouldered past me through the door as I stood there gaping. *Shit. He knows about Luke. I'm so fucked.*

CHAPTER 11

The ride from the police station to Marlack's office building was a circular exercise in me trying to get information out of Smith and him deflecting my questions into questions about what we knew about Marlack. Which resulted in a whole lot of him not learning fuck-all new, and me not learning fuck-all, period. We pulled up in front of Marlack's high-rise and I was impressed to see that the ruined Suburban was gone and the glass in the front of the building had already been replaced.

"It's an illusion," Smith said as we got out of the car. "No way he could have spun glass out of the air that fast."

"It's not an illusion, Smitty. It's called a fuckton of money. He didn't have to spin glass out of the air. He just called an emergency glass repair place and paid them triple their daytime rate," I said. "There's not a hint of magic anywhere on the outside of the building."

"I assume that changes as we move inside?" Flynn asked.

"Yeah, if you had a magical Geiger counter that thing would blow your eardrums the second we stepped off the elevator. Speaking of which, is there a plan? Because I can speak personally to the fact that just going in and punching him in the face isn't very effective. And there are no SUVs out front to break our fall this time," I said.

"Marlack's not here. We're just searching the place," Smith said.

"With what warrant?" Flynn asked.

"With this one." Smith drew his pistol and rapped on the front door with the butt of it. When the guard came to the door,

Smith pointed the gun at his forehead, and the door opened.

"Key card," Smith said to the wide-eyed guard. It was Dennis, the same guard I'd bespelled earlier in the evening.

I reached out, touched his forehead with one finger and whispered, "*Somnus.*" His eyes rolled back in his head and he collapsed in a heap on the floor. "Take a nap, Dennis," I said.

Flynn knelt down and felt around for a pulse. "What did you do to him?" She asked.

"Would you believe a sleep spell?" I asked.

"Why not?" she asked. "How long will he be out?"

"A couple hours. He'll wake up feeling refreshed," I lied. He'd wake up feeling like the worst hangover in the free world, but I was pressed for time.

We rode the elevator up in silence, by the thirtieth floor everyone was humming along to "The Girl from Ipanema." The doors dinged open on Marlack's penthouse office, and again I marveled at how quickly things could get cleaned up if you had more money than God.

"What are we looking for, Smith?" Flynn asked. I wandered the office studying the characters scribed in the protective circles on the floor. If I could get a sense of the origin of Marlack's magic, maybe I could get a hint on how to stop him. I found a few symbols I recognized, then came across a set that looked familiar, but I couldn't quite place them. I pulled out my cell phone and dialed a number.

"Hey, why didn't your cell phone blow up?" Flynn asked.

"Because mine was confiscated, remember? We had to stop by and get my personal effects out of hock before we left the station?" There was no way I was going to fight a badass wizard in the jail slippers they'd put me in after they confiscated my Doc Martens. I listened to the phone ring several times, then a familiar voice came on the line.

"What do you want, Quincy, I am getting ready for bed," Uncle Luke said. He sounded grumpy. I must have interrupted his bedtime snack. I just hoped whoever he was munching on didn't bleed out.

"I was calling for Renny, Uncle Luke. That's why I called his phone."

"You call my Renfield, I decide if he can answer." I knew I should have waited another ten minutes for sunrise, but I decided time was of the essence. Put another check mark on Quincy's List of Bad Decisions.

"Sorry about that, Uncle. But I need to talk to Renny. I need him to research some symbols for me."

"Get your own Renfield. Mine's busy."

"No he's not. He's probably just standing there waiting for you to hang up the phone and go to sleep so he can take your nightcap away and give her a cookie and glass of orange juice." I could almost hear Luke look around the room, realize I was right, and hand the phone to Renny.

"Mr. Quincy, what can I do for you?" Renny's voice was crisp, not at all like someone who was a thrall to a vampire and got kept up to all hours of the night dealing with my uncle and then run ragged all day cleaning up my messes and managing Luke's business interests. I decided to continue to ignore the exhaustion he must be dealing with and just keep being the inconsiderate ass my uncle raised me to be.

"I need some help, Ren. I've got some symbols here that I know are mystical, but I don't know where they're from. If I could find their origin, I might be able to inflict serious carnage upon a very bad man. Do you have time to help a brother out?"

"Does this have anything to do with the unpleasant situation the other night that left a young girl dead and her family's home burned to the ground?"

"If I had anything to do with anything like that, which I'm not saying I did, then this would directly lead to me beating the ever-loving shit out of the man responsible," I said, keeping an eye on both Detective Flynn and Agent Smith as I fenced with Renny. Normally I would have dispensed with all the bullshit, but I still saw a greater than zero chance of one or both of them trying to put me in jail for a very long time.

"Send me the images. I'll commence to research the moment I have dispensed with my duties here," Renny promised.

"Thanks, Ren." I hung up the phone and texted the pictures to Renny, then walked over to where Smith and Flynn were poking around a large desk and bookcase at one end of the room. I walked over to join them and sat on the edge of the desk.

"What did your uncle's man have to say?" Smith asked.

"That's a little annoying, you know?" I shot back.

"What, the whole bit where I know who you're talking to and everything about you and you know nothing about me?"

"Yeah, that."

"Too bad. Now what did Renfield know?"

"Nothing yet. He'll do some research and let us know. You find anything in his files?"

"Nothing," Flynn said. "It's way too clean for any legit businessman. There's not even a receipt for a strip club or any record of his pulling even a minor tax dodge. It's perfect. That's how you know he's dirty."

"So where do we go from here?" I looked at Smith.

"Until we hear back from your guy, we're done. We knew this wasn't a case we'd make in the material plane. It's on you to find something on Marlack."

"Why do I need anything on him? He admitted to me that he summons demons. He admitted that he lets the demons have their way with innocent girls. What more do I need?" I might have raised my voice. I might also have stood up and waved my arms a little. There might have been a little glow around my fingers that made Smith pull back a little.

"What else do you need? You need a way to beat him. Or did you forget the bit about being thrown out a window the last time you tried to go toe-to-toe with this guy? I don't give a shit about evidence. I haven't been looking for proof, because this motherfucker's never going to trial. I've been looking for a way to kill him, or at least send him to Hell where he belongs."

"What the actual fuck are you saying, Smith? We're not arresting Marlack?" Flynn put herself right between me and Smith, and she was tall enough to get right up in his face. Not so much me, I'm pretty tall.

"Arrest him? Where have you been, Detective? Do you think that your jail could hold Harker here for a second longer than he wanted to let you? Then what good do you think it's going to do against the guy that kicked his ass?" Smith didn't back down an inch. I'm not sure he knew how.

"Could we just stop going on about him kicking my ass? Just for a minute. Because, you know, I'm going to have to go do it again. And I'd like to have one tiny shred of confidence left, if it's quite all right with you two," I said.

"So due process is out the window?" Flynn asked, still nose to nose with Smith.

"Due process isn't even in the same zip code, sweetheart."

That's when it happened. I'd been waiting for the tragic slip for a couple hours. It's the same mistake men over fifty with crew cuts always make with really smart women in their early thirties. They can hold it in for a while, but eventually there's a misplaced "sweetheart" or "darling" or, when it gets really good, a "cupcake."

Flynn decked him. Smith was a solid-looking man, a good two hundred pounds and a hair under six feet tall, and it looked from the bulges in his cheap government suit that had some muscles under that jacket. It didn't help. Flynn uncorked a right hook that came from her knees, and she's a tall chick. At five-ten or so and probably one-eighty, she was no wilting lily. Flynn looked like she worked out, and from the way Smith's head rocked back, she had a hell of a punch. She caught him on the point of the jaw and he dropped to one knee, reaching out for the edge of the desk to keep from going all the way down.

"Let's be crystal fucking clear about one thing, Smith. This might be your show, and we might play by your rules, but I'm nobody's fucking sweetheart. I am a gold-shield detective, a veteran of the US Marine Corps, a marathon runner, a sharpshooter, a certified pilot and a black belt in three different martial arts. If you need backup, I'm your girl. If you need somebody to patronize, look elsewhere."

"Sorry about that, sunshine." Smith shot her a sideways grin from his knee. "Sometimes my prejudices slip out. I'll try to keep my chauvinism in check if you promise not to hit me every time I mess up." He reached up, and Flynn grabbed his hand and pulled him to his feet.

I cleared my throat. "If you two have decided who has the bigger dick, and my money's on Rebecca Gail, I've got news from Renfield." I waggled my phone at them.

"What have you got?" Smith asked.

"Renfield says that the symbols on the floor indicate an alliance with Gressil, a prince of Thrones, sort of a colonel in the army of Hell," I said.

"Does that help us?" Flynn asked.

"Yeah, it tells us who Marlack is working with, and I know how to use that. But it's not going to be pretty, and it's going to be really dangerous. You two might not want to be around for the next part."

"I'm not letting you out of my sight, Harker, so you can get that idea out of your head." Flynn turned the same look on me she'd just used on Smith. The biggest difference was, I didn't care.

"Fine. Suit yourself. But I'm not going to have time to look out for you two, so I'd suggest when we get there I draw you a circle and you stay in it, no matter what."

Flynn opened her mouth to argue, but Smith touched her on the arm. He gave her a little shoulder shrug, and she let it go.

"Great," I said. "Now let's go. We've got to get to Marlack's house before sunrise, and I still have a stop to make."

"What's the stop?" Smith asked as we walked toward the elevator.

"24-hour grocery. I need a late-night butcher who has plenty of pig's blood around."

"Why does he even bother asking?" Flynn muttered under her breath as she stomped off toward the elevator. I don't think she'd gotten the memo on the enhanced vampirish senses yet.

CHAPTER 12

We pulled up in front of Marlack's house in Smith's Government Issue black sedan with blackwall tires. He wouldn't let me get out at paint "FED" on the hood in Day-Glo yellow, no matter how obvious he was being with his choice of vehicle. I know, I asked several times. Smith rolled down his window at the squawk box by the gate, but I leaned forward between the front seats, pointed at the closed wrought iron gate and said, "*Lane patescit.*"

A few sparks sputtered out from the control box to the left of the squawk box, but I wasn't planning on Marlack being around long enough to care. We drove through and up the long circular drive to the front steps. I got out of the car and walked around to the trunk. Smith popped the latch and I dug out two pints of pig's blood, four wax pillar candles, a stack of porno mags big enough to keep a varsity football team occupied for a month, and a small box of sidewalk chalk.

"Keep the dogs from fucking up my circle, will you?" I asked Detective Flynn as she got out of the car.

"What dogs—" She started, then drew her sidearm as four SWAT team rejects with MP-5s and Dobermans came out of the house and leveled their weapons at the three of us. I ignored them and went about my business drawing a circle on the driveway and reinforcing it with pig's blood. Smith had his badge in one hand and a Smith & Wesson pistol in the other, so I decided the security goons were pretty unlikely to interfere.

At the cardinal points of the circle I took out my pocketknife and blended a little of my blood with the pig's and placed a candle to lock the circle in this dimension. I lit the candles walking widdershins while murmuring an incantation I learned from a voodoo priestess in Charleston. She taught me a lot of things about magic, and the different ways to use bodily fluids in conjuring, and my left hamstring still twinges a little when I think of her. But I always smile.

Once I had the candles lit and the circle invoked, I stepped out and placed the porno mags in the center of the circle. Then I raised both hands to the sky and said, "Glory, if you've still got any juice with the Big Guy, I'm gonna need a fuckton of forgiveness after this one." Then I focused my will and shouted, "*Asmodeus, conjure te!*"

Nothing happened.

I did it again, this time adding a few drops of my blood splattered into the circle as I summoned Asmodeus.

Still nothing.

The third time I shouted the invocation I didn't stop with Latin. I moved into French, German, Italian, Spanish and finally finished by slicing another gash across my palm, flinging a good tablespoon of my blood into the circle and shouting "Asmodeus, you horny motherfucker, get your three-peckered ass up here and take my goddamned offering, you putrid bucket of herpes!"

"That's my boy." A sibilant voice issued from a cloud of crimson smoke that billowed into existence in the center of the circle. "Hello, Quincy."

"Hello, Asmodeus."

"It's always so good to see you. You're looking well."

"You look like someone lit a bloody fart."

He laughed. That was a good sign. I tried to keep the demonkind amused, or at least off-kilter. If you let them get their feet under themselves, you're fucked. "Quincy Harker, you know I love the women of your plane, but why are these only photographs? What kind of weak-assed shit is this?"

"This isn't a social call, Az. You've got a problem."

"I'm a Prince of the Seraphim condemned to Hell for all eternity, never to see the face of my Lord again and to spend the rest of my days licking the ass of that fuckup Lucifer. I've got more problems than you've got blood cells, vampling. What is it this time?"

"Gressil," I said simply.

"That idiot? He could fuck up a wet dream, I'll give you that, but he's more of an annoyance than anything."

"He's building an army. He wants your spot." I watched the smoke carefully. If it stayed red, Az was interested. If it turned black, he was pissed. Any other color, and he already knew about Gressil's treachery and I'd wasted two pints of pig blood and four perfectly good candles.

The red darkened slightly. "Talk," Asmodeus said.

"He's been working with a human sorcerer, Jacob Marlack, to send little demons through and breed here on earth. Only one reason he'd be making more demons where you couldn't see them. He's coming after you." There was another reason, but Asmodeus was too proud to realize it. You see, most demons are pretty stupid. They like to eat, fuck and kill, not necessarily in that order. Marlack was giving these baby demons a chance to do all three, and they got to stick around our plane for a little while afterwards and kill a lot of brown people. A bonus for any demon that didn't think too far down the "What's in it for this guy?" path.

"That fucking asshole. I knew he'd been spending a lot of time with his pet human the past hundred years or so, but I didn't think there was anything more to it than some death and debauchery. I should have known he was working another angle. Motherfucker!" The smoke was black now, so I made my play.

"Well, Az, tonight's your lucky night. Guess whose front stoop I summoned you onto?" I waved my hand at the mansion in front of me.

"What's your piece of this, Harker? You don't do shit out of the goodness of your heart, especially not for my kind."

"He hurt a little girl. I don't like that. I want to see him suffer, and he kicked my ass when I tried to take him out."

"So you want me to be your enforcer?"

"I want you to put your lieutenant in his place. Best way to do that is to take out his pet wizard. Solve my problem, solve yours."

"What do I get out of the deal?" Az asked. The smoke was back to red now, but there were enough flashes of black throughout his form that I knew I still had him. Asmodeus didn't get to be a Prince of Hell by being forgiving of treachery.

"You get to kill the wizard and anybody left inside the building two minutes from now." I sent a raised eyebrow at the security guards, who had frozen in place as soon as the demon summoning started. Smart guys, they didn't need to end up dead. One turned around and ran inside while the other three bolted around the right side of the house, taking the Dobermans with him. They were less concerned with their guns than the dogs, because their rifles clattered to the porch in their wake.

"And what's to keep me from just breaking your little circle and eating your soul right now?" Az asked.

"This," I said. I opened my shirt and showed him the medallion hanging around my neck. He saw it, and a flash of blue shot through the red smoke.

"Where the fuck did you get one of those?" the demon asked.

"Not on the list of shit I feel like sharing with you, Az. Now do we have a deal?"

"I will enter the house and kill Jacob Marlack. I will also kill anyone still inside the house after I enter."

"Then?" I prodded.

"Then I will return to Hell." He would be pulled back to Hell at sunrise anyway, because the transition between day and night broke all summonings, but I wanted to make sure he didn't linger a second longer than it took him to finish his mayhem inside the house.

"And you will harm no one that is not within the walls of the main house."

"And I will harm no one not inside the main house."

"Then you are free to hunt, demon." I reached out with a toe and scrubbed a break in the circle, setting the Prince of Hell loose on the earth. Asmodeus took on what I've always thought of as his fighting form when he stepped out of the circle. He had long legs that ended in hooves, red skin, arms that hung almost to his knees and ended in wicked claws, and a narrow mouth full of long pointed teeth. He turned his black, pupilless eyes on me and smiled.

"One day we're going to dance like this and I'm going to decide that it will be worth the punishment of Lucifer to break our covenant, Harker. That will be the day I wear your intestines for a necklace as I face my judgment."

"That will be the day I give you an enema with holy water and fuck you in the ass with a dildo made from the true cross, you nasty bastard. Now go kill that motherfucker."

Asmodeus gave me a grin that made my blood freeze and said, "We'll see, Harker. One day we'll see." Then he turned and strode into the house, kicking the double doors in with one huge hoof.

As soon as he was out of sight, I slumped against the car and reached in my pocket for a bottle of Wild Turkey from one of my other stops. I knocked off about a third of it in one slug, then held it out to Smith, who took a long pull and passed it over to Flynn. She shook her head and handed it back to me. I screwed the cap back on and put it away, still leaning against the car.

"Was that a real demon?" Flynn asked. She was staring at me, but hadn't come any closer.

"As real as your…" I let it go. I know I'm tired and terrified when I can't even make a smartass remark about a cop's boobs.

"Yeah, it was real," I said.

"That's fucked up," she said, staring into the house. We kept hearing random crashing from the house, but I could tell that Az hadn't found Marlack yet. Then the light show started, and I knew it was just a matter of time.

"Fucked up is my life, sweetheart." I took another pull off my bottle and offered it to her again. This time she took a slash.

"Like I told him, I'm nobody's goddamn sweetheart." She held the bottle out to me, then the first scream rang out from inside the house. It was a high-pitched thing, like an animal being tortured, and it went on far too long. Flynn took another drink of whiskey and handed the bottle back to me. I finished it off, then tossed the empty into the bushes by the porch.

"Aren't you worried about fingerprints?" Flynn asked.

"Mine aren't on record anywhere," I said.

"Bullshit. As many times as I've booked you, your prints are—"

"Mysteriously missing from your system, Detective," Smith said.

"I think I hate you both," Flynn replied.

"That's the safer sentiment," I said. Smith nodded. The screams from inside the house stopped, and a couple of minutes later Asmodeus walked out, picking his teeth with a claw.

"My work here is done, Harker. Are you sure you don't have anyone else you want me to kill?" the demon asked.

"That's a long list, Az. And I don't think all the Unholy Host could get to my whole list by sunrise. Good night, and good luck with Gressil."

"That fuckwit needs the luck. He's going to be spinning coals in the lowest level of the pit for the next five thousand years." Az stepped into the circle, shifted back to smoke, then billowed out of existence. I blew out the candle and scuffed another few bits of the circle out of existence, just for good measure.

"You got this?" I asked Smith. "I'm fucking beat."

"What, you're just going to leave? I thought you wanted justice for that little girl," Flynn asked.

"I got it. Marlack's dead. And just like I expected, it didn't bring Kayleigh back. At best it erased a little of the dark from my soul, but I probably put as much black on it by consorting with Asmodeus as I took off by bringing that cocksucker to justice."

"And what about his kid? I thought that was important to you?" Flynn kept poking.

"Tomorrow morning your cyber division is going to get an anonymous link in their email pointing them to a backdoor onto the Omega Sig server. That server will have video files on it of several high-ranking fraternity members, including young Master Marlack, forcing themselves on young women. Some will be students at the university, some will still be in high school. That should take care of his ass."

"When did you set that up?" Flynn asked.

"When I talked to Renny on the phone tonight."

"Your uncle's butler is a hacker?" Smith asked. It had taken me all night, but I'd finally managed to surprise the fed.

"A Renfield is a lot more than a butler. He's my uncle's daytime eyes and ears and business partner. And yeah, this one's a CIA-level hacker. Now can I do like the book says and go the fuck to sleep?"

"Get in, I'll drive you home," Smith said.

I was snoring in the back seat before we pulled out of the driveway, dreams of little girls walking through the gates of Heaven dancing in my head.

STRAIGHT TO HELL

A Quincy Harker, Demon Hunter
Novella

CHAPTER 1

"I don't get why I'm stuck with the babysitting detail. I'm a fucking gold shield, for God's sake, I don't do babysitting!" The gold shield in question was Detective Rebecca Gail Flynn, currently sitting on my couch bitching about a new assignment from her boss, Agent John Smith of the Department of Homeland Security. Flynn had shown up on my doorstep unannounced about half an hour before bearing a twelve-pack of OMB Copper and a bad attitude. Since then she'd been sitting on my couch consuming one of those things and sharing the other pretty much nonstop.

"You understand that we're not friends, right, Detective?" I asked from my chair. It's not that I had anything going on, I just wanted to make sure any change in our relationship was approved by all the appropriate higher powers and that I was notified beforehand. Rebecca Flynn spent most of the last three years trying to throw me under the Mecklenburg County jail, and I hadn't quite gotten to the "forget" part of "forgive and forget." Frankly, I wasn't laying too heavy odds on forgiveness, either.

Flynn stopped mid-tirade and looked over at me. "Wait, what?"

"You come in here like we're middle-school girlfriends and start pouring your heart out to me. I'm not interested in decorating our Trapper Keepers, I'm not letting you paint my toenails, and I'm sure as fuck not going to braid your hair. You've tried to throw me in jail at least a dozen times in the past dozen months, and now we're supposed to be BFFs just because we work for the same anonymous dickhead? I don't think so, Detective. But thanks for the beer. You can bring that by anytime."

She stood up and stomped to the door. "Well, excuse the ever-loving fuck out of me, Harker. I just wanted to vent for a minute to one of the few people who I can talk to about this shit. I mean, I can't even tell my boyfriend what I'm doing because it's so goddamn classified."

"Why not just tell him?" I asked.

"What?" Flynn looked confused by the question.

"Why not tell him anyway? Who gives a fuck about their security clearances? Jesus, Flynn, don't you ever do anything you're not supposed to do? You want to tell the guy you're banging about our work, tell him about it. Especially if it means you don't interrupt *Monday Night RAW* to bitch to me."

She stomped back to loom over my chair. "You'd like that, wouldn't you? I tell him some classified shit and get him and me both fucking disappeared to Gitmo or Area 51 or some other place that doesn't even officially exist. Then you wouldn't have to deal with me anymore."

"I don't mind dealing with you."

"You just said..."

"I said we aren't friends. We're not. Friends hang out. Friends check up on each other. Friends give a little more of a fuck than I'm really capable of giving, and certainly more than you give about me. But that doesn't mean I don't like you. I just want you to know where we stand. You know, so when you eventually succumb to the inevitable sexual tension and decide to jump me." I took a long pull off my beer and waited for the explosion.

I didn't have to wait long. "What the actual fuck are you talking about? The inevitable sexual tension? Are you that fucking high on yourself?"

"I'm a pretty good-looking guy. You're a very attractive

woman. We face intense situations full of adrenaline and endorphins and emotion. That's the kind of shit that gets all fraught and stuff. So, you know, if you ever just want to tear your clothes off and throw yourself at me, I want you to know that I'm here for you." I finished off my beer and pulled another from the box on the coffee table.

Flynn stood there for a minute, just staring down at me. Her mouth opened, then closed, then opened, then closed. I was just about to make a remark about fish when she finally looked me straight in the eyes and fell onto the couch laughing. "Holy shit, Harker, I thought you were serious there for a minute."

"I meant every word," I said, deadpan.

Flynn froze in mid-guffaw, stared at me, then collapsed into laughter again. "You asshole," she said when she finally got her breath back. She sat up on the couch wiping tears from her eyes and took another beer. We clinked bottles together and she sat back. "Oh fuck, I needed a good laugh."

"And I needed you to quit bitching, so let's call this a win-win. Now about that boyfriend?"

"What about him?" Flynn asked.

"Tell me about him. You never mentioned a boyfriend before."

"I never mentioned anything before, Harker. I was always arresting you," she reminded me.

"And doing a terrible job of it, by the way. What was your record, twenty arrests and nothing ever even made it to trial?" It helps when all the crimes you commit are against monsters that usually turn to ash or slime when they're killed. And all those breaking and entering charges were really hard to prove when the perpetrator always wears gloves. Good thing for me they were in fashion when I was coming up.

"Fuck you." But she grinned when she said it this time. Used to be she would draw a weapon when she told me to fuck off. I considered this an improvement.

"So?" I asked.

"So what?"

"So what about your boyfriend?"

"Why do you want to know?" Flynn grinned at me and I knew we'd moved from hanging out to flirting. I was okay with that. Flynn was a good-looking woman, and as long as she had someone to go home to, I could probably keep my baser instincts at bay.

"I want to know what kind of competition I'm facing." I gave her my best rakish grin. Since I learned about rakish grins when rakes were still a thing, my rakish grin is pretty good.

"He's an EMT. His name is Roger. He's tall, dark and handsome, and he's absolutely crazy about me."

"So he's a good person, good-looking, and probably has a solid, working-class, pull himself up by his bootstraps attitude. I think I hate him already. Show me a picture."

"Why? If you hate him, why should I show you a picture?"

"So I can see if he really is better looking than me, then I'll know I hate him."

She pulled out her phone and pressed a couple of places on the screen, then swiped at a couple of other things and handed it to me. He was a very good-looking man, milk chocolate skin, short cropped hair, big smile full of perfect teeth, lots of muscles and his arm around Flynn in that relaxed manner that only the exceptionally handsome have, when they know they have nothing to fear from mere mortals.

"You're right, he's better looking than me. I definitely hate him."

"Are we friends now, Harker? You hate my boyfriend, I

brought you beer, and you listened to me bitch about work. I think that makes us friends." Her dark eyes told me she was enjoying the game, but I knew better than to push my luck. That way lay madness.

"Nope, still just adversaries thrown together by the heat of battle. That makes the sexual tension better. That way, when we eventually succumb to the inevitable and screw each other's brains out in a night of torrid passion, probably right after surviving some completely implausible terrorist attack or serial killer kidnapping, we can wake up not only to our personal recriminations but to millions of angry emails to our producers about how everyone in the universe feels cheated by our rushing through the bumping of uglies instead of falling slowly like that cheesy movie *Once*."

"I liked that movie!" Flynn protested.

"Proving, without any physical exploration whatsoever, that you do indeed, have a vagina."

"You're fucking incorrigible."

"And you're fucking Chocolate Superman."

"I'm telling him you called him that. He'll probably kick your ass."

"He'll probably love it and want to give me a half-assed bro hug when we finally meet. Then we can talk about the Panthers draft and how they always need another receiver or a better o-line, and I'll pretend that I don't hate him."

"You don't hate him." She turned suddenly serious in that way women have when you know you're tap-dancing drunk through a minefield. Fortunately for me, I ran out of fucks to give long before Detective Flynn was born. But I let her off easy this time.

"I don't hate him, Becks. I don't even fucking know the guy."

"What did you call me?" She'd gone from casually flirting, to defending her man, to strangely concerned in a span of seconds.

"I called you Becks. I figured since we're just one step away from sharing mani/pedis, I could come off the formality a little and maybe not always refer to you as Detective Flynn." I looked at her, and she just stared back for a long minute before she replied.

"No, it's fine, it's just…my father used to call me Becks. Nobody's called me that since he died. It just…took me by surprise, I guess."

Fuck. I knew that. Well, I guess my subconscious knew that. I knew Flynn's father. Sergeant Paul Flynn, CMPD, the reason little Rebecca Gail put away her dolls at the age of eight and instead picked up a set of toy guns and a plastic nightstick and proceeded to beat the shit out of every boy in the neighborhood that dared play Cops & Robbers with her. Flynn the elder was shot and killed while pursuing a mugger. At least that was the official story.

In reality, Paul Flynn stumbled on a young vampire having a snack in one of the few alleys downtown Charlotte had to offer, and when he stepped into the alley to confront what he thought was a sexual assault in progress, the newborn turned on him. Baby vamps are dangerous — they haven't yet developed much in the way of impulse control, and this one had been a crack addict before she was turned, so it wasn't exactly of sound mind in the first place. She never should have been turned, and I'd been splitting my time between hunting down *les enfant terrible* and its maker, and I stumbled into the alley just a few seconds too late for Officer Flynn.

Killing the newborn vamp was child's play for me. I took its head with a katana I carried everywhere at the time, due to a ridiculous fascination with the *Highlander* TV show and a desire to have hair like Adrian Paul. But Flynn was down, his chest torn open by the vamp. I didn't have to worry about him coming back turned — there's more to it than just being ripped apart by a vampire, but I felt responsible for his death. If I had focused on the fledgling first, then the maker, I probably could have saved him.

I sat by him in the alley as the life fled his eyes and listened to him talk about his little girl, his pride and joy. He told me to tell his daughter he loved her, to tell "Becks" that he was proud of her, then he asked me to watch out for her. If I'd know what a pain in the ass she was going to grow up to be, I never would have agreed to it. But I did, and as her father bled out in my arms in an alley, Rebecca Gail Flynn and I were tied together for the rest of her life. And all that led in a convoluted way to her sitting on my couch talking about her boyfriend and me pretending I had no interest in seducing a woman a century or more my junior.

I shook my head and tried to focus on the present. *Her dad — go with that.* "Oh yeah, and he died, right? Sorry, I won't call you that again."

"It's fine, Harker. You can call me anything you want —"

"Don't worry, doll face, over the course of our relationship, I have called you pretty much everything I've ever dreamed of." It's true, too. Detective Flynn had been a thorn in my side for several years until we were both recruited to work for Homeland Security, which reminded me. "So what's this babysitting detail Smith's got you on?"

"Oh, that bullshit," she replied, but with a lot less fire than before.

I supposed I was a good little girlfriend and let her get all her bad feelings out or some such shit. There weren't a lot of sleepovers in my adolescence. When your parents were two of the people responsible for "killing" Dracula, your life starts off weird and goes downhill from there.

"I'm watching some Ethiopian prince or baby duke or something. He's studying architecture and there have been some threats," Flynn continued.

"What's so special about this kid?" I asked.

"Apparently somebody is convinced that he's a true descendant of David and the Lion of Judah personified, so they want me to keep an eye on him."

"The Lion of Judah that opens the seven seals in Revelation?"

"Yeah, that's the one?"

"And he's here in Charlotte, with a security detail of one human detective?"

"I'd like to think I'm a pretty damned exceptional human detective, thank you very much!" Flynn sat up straighter, her dark eyes flashing under a careless lock of brown hair. I resisted the temptation to brush her hair back out of her face, which took a *lot* of restraint on my part.

"You are, Becks, you're fucking spectacular, but you're still not fuck-all against the kinds of things that will want to break those seals. We gotta go." I stood up, going to the closet to get my jacket and my gun. And maybe a couple of amulets. This had the very high probability of getting extremely fucked up.

"Where are you going?" Flynn asked, still on my sofa.

"*I'm* not going anywhere. *We're* going to architecture school."

CHAPTER 2

The drive to the college took about twenty minutes, and then almost that long looking for someplace to park where Flynn's cop car wouldn't stand out like a neon sign screaming "PO-PO HERE." We finally just stuck the blackwalled cockblock on wheels in a garage and took up a position on a bench outside the kid's apartment.

"You know us sitting out here means that at some point you're going to have to make out with me," I said, leaning back and lacing my fingers behind my head.

"You remember what the world was like before my grandfather was born. I don't think so," Flynn shot back, pulling out her phone. She pressed a few buttons and I heard Smith answer. "We're here," Flynn said.

"How did you get him to come with you?" I heard Smith ask.

"I mentioned coeds and he jumped at the chance."

"Good one. All right, I'm leaving now. You two have this 'til dawn?"

"No problem." Flynn slipped her phone into her pocket and leaned back on the bench, mimicking my posture and letting out a contented sigh.

"Nobody likes a smartass, Detective," I said.

"But you're a smartass, Harker."

"And nobody likes me, do they?"

"Oh don't be such a baby. So I played you a little, what's the big deal? At least we got a couple beers before we had to go on stakeout."

"Yeah, about that. I gotta piss. I'll be back in a minute." I walked around behind a tree and relieved myself, opening up my Sight in the process. Through my third eye, the whole area surrounding the apartment complex lit up like a magical Christmas tree. I stepped back, almost splashing my shoes, and quickly closed down my Sight.

I walked back to the bench and sat down. "Somebody has laid some serious wards around this place. Whoever is looking out for this kid has some heavy juice at their disposal."

"Anything look out of place?" Flynn asked.

"No, everything looks hunky-dory. Wake me up if that changes." I turned sideways on the bench and laid my head down in her lap, preparing to go to sleep. She gave my shoulder a shove and dumped me onto the grass.

"Get up, dipshit. We're on duty."

"Correction, *you're* on duty. I'm helping out a friend. I'm not getting paid for this shit, and while there are plenty of things I'm happy to do in the company of a beautiful woman at this hour of night that don't include sleeping, watching some over-privileged African prince sleep is not on the list. Besides, I'll hear anything out of the ordinary and wake up faster than you can say 'what the fuck is that?'"

"I don't know. I can…what the fuck is that?"

"That wasn't very fast," I replied.

"No, really. What the fuck *is* that?" She pointed to the roof of the complex. I followed her arm with my gaze and saw what looked like a man running the roof beam of the apartment complex. I opened my Sight and saw nothing out of the ordinary. Whatever his intentions, he was human.

"That's a dude. He's nimble as fuck, but he's human. That makes him your department." I try not to fight humans any more than is absolutely necessary. I tend to break them. Permanently.

Flynn was already on her feet and headed to the central stairwell in the apartment building. It was one of those twisting jobs with a pair of apartments separated by the staircase on each floor, so she had a bunch of little flights of stairs to get to the kid's third-floor doorway. She made it just about the same time as the ninja-garbed attacker swung down off the roof and onto the landing. I sat on the bench watching.

"You gonna help her?" came a voice from beside me.

"If she needs it. You bring popcorn?" I turned to see Glory, my guardian angel, sitting beside me.

"You're terrible. I thank the Father every day that you're not my partner."

"I'm worse, sweetcheeks. I'm your responsibility."

"That's the truth," the angel muttered. I could tell that I had an effect on the angel's spiritual well-being because I'm pretty sure I have the only guardian angel in history that mutters, grumbles and bitches this much.

"What's up, Glory? You didn't just come down here to admire the form of Detective Flynn's posterior as she kicks that ninja dude's ass. Or did you? I've always wondered about the sexual preferences of angels."

"We're neuter, Q, we don't have sexual preferences."

"No wonder you're so fucking boring."

"Thanks, Q. Love you, too. Now are you going to help her, or what?" Glory pointed up at the landing, where Flynn had the first ninja down and handcuffed but didn't see the second one sneaking up behind her with a drawn knife.

"Hey, Flynn!" I yelled. "Watch your six!" She didn't look, just lashed out with a mule kick that caught the second ninja in the gut and dropped him like a sack of potatoes. I was pretty sure I heard the *thunk* of his head hitting concrete even from fifty yards away.

"That wasn't exactly what I had in mind, Q," Glory said.

"Yeah, but you're a better person than me."

"I'm not even a person."

"But I set the bar pretty goddamn low. So what brings you down here slumming? It's not just to bust my balls about not helping Flynn win a fight she can win on her own, so spill it."

I looked at Glory, and she looked away from me. A lot of people won't meet my eyes, either because I make them uncomfortable or because they've heard stories about Uncle Luke bespelling people and are afraid I'll put the whammy on them. Glory never looks me in the eye because she says they really are windows to the soul, and she's a little scared of what she sees there.

"Spill it, Glory," I prodded.

"This kid? The one you've been assigned to protect?"

"Yeah? What about him?"

"He's the real thing."

"What real thing?" I asked. Glory just sat there. "Wait, you mean he's really the Lion of Judah? Like, descended directly from David and everything? Like, can open the seals that bring about the end of the world?"

"Yeah, like all that. He's the real deal, Q, so you might want to pay attention to your partner." I looked over to Flynn, who was now tangling with a third ninja, and this one looked like he might have the edge on her in one-on-one combat. I turned back to Glory, but the angel was gone.

"Fuck," I muttered under my breath and started to the apartment at a dead run. The first ninja was up again and had gotten loose from Flynn's handcuffs somehow. I figured I had about six seconds before she was overwhelmed. Good for her I'm a little faster than most people. I made it to the front of the building in three, turning the last dozen yards into big bounding leaps, sending me higher each time. I landed right in front of the building and sprang straight up, easily clearing the railing on the third-floor landing and scaring the shit out of the new ninja, who was about to close with Flynn.

He had a black-bladed tango knife in one hand and wicked curved thing in the other. I didn't waste time sparring with him, just grabbed both wrists and jerked him forward, simultaneously planting my right foot on the ground and sticking my left into his sternum. He came to crashing halt, both shoulders dislocated with an audible *pop*, and I let go of his wrists and kicked him backward to fall on top of the second ninja, who was just starting to rise.

I turned to the first ninja, who was advancing barehanded on Flynn, flicking out kicks and punches as he eased in toward her. I drew my Sig from under my arm and put three in his chest over Flynn's shoulder, dropping him instantly. I turned back to the broken ninja and put two in his forehead, then pointed my pistol at the third ninja's face.

"You want to die?" I asked.

He shook his head.

"You gonna talk?" I asked.

He shook his head again.

"That's not the right answer," I said, then shot him in the left thigh. He writhed around on the porch but didn't scream. I had to give him a little credit, he was a dedicated son of a bitch.

"Now you gonna talk?" I asked.

He shook his head again.

"I think you see how this is going to go, don't you?" I asked. He nodded, but I shot him in the left thigh this time. More writhing and flopping, but still no screaming.

This time I pointed the gun at his crotch. "Would you like to reconsider?" I asked.

"Harker, stop!" Flynn said from behind me.

"We need to know who sent these fuckers, Flynn, and I don't know if we have time to ask nicely."

"That's fine, but he's not going to tell you anything."

"I'm pretty sure if I start shooting inches off Mr. Winky here, he's going to get persuaded pretty fucking quick."

"As much as I appreciate the save, Captain Fuckwit, their vocal chords have been severed." She held up the head of the first ninja so I could see the jagged scar across his throat.

"Oh, shit." I remembered hearing something about assassins that would have their tongues or voice boxes removed so they couldn't reveal details about who hired them. "Well, that sucks," I said and shot the third ninja in the forehead.

"What the fuck, Harker?" Flynn asked. "You can't just go around shooting people."

"I didn't. I shot the bad guys. All of them. Now we don't have to shoot anybody else."

"But you can't just kill everyone we run across," Flynn protested.

"Yeah, I kinda can. As a matter of fact, I'm pretty sure that's exactly my job. You see, these guys weren't just bad Jackie Chan movie rejects. They were real ninjas. Assassins. Hired killers. You get the picture? They weren't here to dance, they weren't here to chat, and they sure as fuck weren't here to be reformed. They were here to kill us and take the kid. By the way, have you maybe checked on him since the whole attempted kidnapping thing?"

"I was going to do that as soon as I called for backup," she said. "I thought it might be good to get the dead bodies off his doorstep before we knocked."

"Good call. But call Smith, not the cops. This needs to

disappear, not turn into an all-day lovefest downtown." I leaned down and picked up one of the bodies, then tossed it over the rail onto the ground. The dead ninja flopped over onto his face and lay there, looking not much different than me on more than one Friday night. I deposited his friends beside him and motioned to the door.

"You want to do the talking? I ended up with all this new blood on my clothes, so I thought I should disappear for a second." As she stepped to the door, I summoned my will and murmured "*cameleon.*" The air swirled around me, and my vision went a little blurry at the edges as the spell bent light around me and caused me to blend in perfectly with my surroundings. No point scaring the kid, and a blood-covered goon with a pistol on his doorstep at three in the morning is usually cause for alarm.

Flynn rang the bell, then tried the knocker, then the bell again, then the knocker. After a solid couple of minutes, a trembling voice came from inside the apartment. "Fuck off! I've got a gun and a dog! And I've called the cops!"

"Charlotte-Mecklenburg Police, is everything all right in there?" Flynn held her badge up to the peephole. Peepholes are the worst inventions in the modern world for security. It's way too easy just to shoot somebody through one. But Flynn wouldn't do that. Hell, she didn't want me to kill the ninjas, which is kinda like not wanting to step on a cockroach.

"Yeah, we're fine. What happened out there?" The voice seemed a little less shit-scared now, and more curious. And maybe a little stoned.

"Firecrackers," Flynn said. "Can I come in? I have a few questions for you."

"Umm…sure," the voice came, then the sound of several locks being undone. The door opened, and I followed Flynn in right on her heels. My spell kept bending the light around me, but the brightness of the apartment made it a lot harder to stay unnoticed. I took up a position by the door and hoped nobody else came in.

"Are you Wallace Gubegna?" Flynn asked, looking around the apartment. It was your basic college place, decorated in early Spencer's Gifts and stoner chic. A poster of Bob Marley dominated one wall, and the other was taken up by a huge television with an expensive game console and surround sound system. A Salvation Army couch lined one wall, with a montage of landscape photos above the sofa. They were the usual kind of things, sunsets, beach scenes, all blown up and taken from interesting perspectives. I looked at the art, then chuckled as I caught sight of a three-foot high bong sitting on the floor next to the couch. Some things are universal for young men — experimenting with wine, women and drugs was definitely on the menu here. My college experience had been a little different, focusing more on the absinthe and necromancy than the marijuana and cheap sex.

"Yeah, I'm Wally. You a cop?" Wally Gubegna was a good-looking kid of about twenty with dark brown skin, long dreads and an easy smile. He stood about five-ten and weighed maybe a buck sixty soaking wet, so he was a skinny little dude. He never would have stood a chance against those ninjas, not that very many humans would have. He flopped down on the couch and put his feet up on a milk crate that served as a coffee table.

"I am. I'm Detective Flynn with the Charlotte-Mecklenburg Police Department on assignment to Homeland Security. We believe that some people are trying to abduct you. Do you have any idea why?"

"Because I'm the Lion of Judah and can open the seven seals that bring about the apocalypse?" He said it so matter-of-fact, like "it's cold outside" or "I smoke a ridiculous amount of weed," that I almost didn't catch it, but when I did, it was all I could do to hold onto my concealment spell.

"Well...that's certainly one theory," Flynn said. She was rattled but trying to hold it together.

"Oh come on, Agent. Or Detective, or whatever. You take out three assassins on my porch and come in here with a wizard under a masking spell and I'm supposed to think this has something to do with the fact that my second cousin is the President? I'm not in any kind of line of succession, have nothing to do with politics, and frankly have only the slightest interest in ever returning to Ethiopia. So you must be here to either start or stop the end of the world."

CHAPTER 3

I dropped my spell, since the kid already knew I was there. "Good call, Junior. We're here to make sure you don't go around breaking any seals. Been to the circus lately?" I asked as I stepped into the apartment's kitchen. Silence came from the living room for several seconds, then Wally laughed as he got my "seals" pun. I opened the refrigerator and took out a beer. I popped the top open on the edge of the scarred countertop, the scratches in the Formica evidence that I wasn't the first person to forget a bottle opener in that kitchen. As kitchens go, it was definitely one, and one that belonged to multiple college-aged boys. There was beer in the fridge, along with mustard, a jar of pickles and two pizza boxes of indeterminate age. The dishes in the sink weren't yet sentient, but I'd have to consult Glory on the souls of fungus before I could wash anything with a clear conscience.

I walked back into the den and sat down in what must have been the primo gaming chair. I knew that because I immediately felt a sharp pain in my ass and pulled a PlayStation controller out of the seat. "So yeah, we're here to save the world. Got any idea who wants to wreck it this week?"

"Man, I have no idea, but that shit is getting tired, you know? I thought when I got here, all this Revelation shit would be over, and I could just be me, be Wally for a while. I guess that was too much to ask, huh?"

"It was when you went around throwing out the Lion of Judah line to get laid, you dumb fuck." I turned the chair to face him and got the satisfaction of seeing him blush through his dark complexion when I called him on it.

"Who told you that, man?"

"I was twenty years old once, Wally. I know what it's like."

"Yeah, in 1895," Flynn muttered so low that Wally couldn't hear her. I gave her a look that very clearly told her I could.

"It was just this one chick, man. She seemed cool. We were hanging out over at Boardwalks," he said, naming a local oyster bar that turned into a meat market on the weekends. "We were hanging out and talking philosophy, and that turned into talking religion, and I'm like an agnostic, you know, but I might have mentioned...well, you know."

"I know that your dick might have brought about the end of the world, you little jackass," Flynn grumbled.

"Oh come off it, Flynn. Most of the worst ideas in the world were because of a guy trying to impress a girl. I mean come on, look at the Cuban Missile Crisis. That was all to get Marilyn in the sack again. And let's not even talk about Pearl Harbor. Wally just wanted to get laid. Everybody wants to get laid. It's the fact that he's such a fucking stoner that he can't keep his mouth shut that pisses me off."

Wally stood up and puffed himself up with the righteous indignation that can only be mustered by those under thirty. He stuck one arm out towards the door and said, "I think the two of you should leave. I appreciate your assistance tonight, but I can handle anything that comes to visit by myself. I have a handgun by the bed and a shotgun in the closet."

"That's good, Wally. That's excellent defense against human attackers. *Debilitato*." I reached out and touched him lightly on the forehead and pushed my will at him. He instantly fell to the floor, writhing in pain. "What good is your gun now, jackass? The people coming after you are bad fucking news, and since we took out their Plan A, they're going to have to improvise. That never goes well for the target. *Libertado.*" With a word, the spell released and Wally sat up, staying on the floor and putting his back to the sofa.

"Okay, okay, I get it. What do we do?" he asked, once he could speak again.

"We split up and cover the apartment the best we can, hoping that the reinforcements for the bad guys don't arrive before the reinforcements we called in. Agent Flynn stays in here with you and tries to keep you from doing something else stupid, while I wait outside and hope that I don't have to clean up any more of your messes."

"Why are you going out there? Aren't you better off facing them in here?" the kid asked.

"That depends. You got sprinklers in your apartment?"

"I don't think so."

"Then I'd better wait outside. We took out the ninjas without blowing anything up, but I don't have a whole lot of faith in my ability to do that twice in one night."

I stepped close to Flynn and whispered, "Don't let him out of your sight, not even to piss. He's scared enough to go full-on stupid." Then I moved past her and opened the door. "Try not to get anybody killed while I'm out there," I said, then stepped out onto the landing. Smith hadn't shown up with his cleaners yet, so I pulled out my phone to send him a text message. Nothing like trying to get your boss killed texting while driving to liven up a night.

I didn't get a response, so I walked back to the car, wrapped myself in a concealment spell again, and sat down on the hood. It was cold, but not too bad, and I don't suffer from hot or cold nearly as much as normal humans. Nothing stirred in the still night, so I waited patiently for about twenty minutes until Smith drove up in another car that screamed "cop" at the top of its lungs. The only thing more government agent than his car was the man's suit—navy with pinstripes, cheap dress shoes that looked like shit to run in, and a red tie with little blue diamonds on it. With his stick-up-my-ass posture and high and tight haircut, Smith screamed "ex-military government hired thug" louder than Wally's dreadlocks and tie-dye screamed "college stoner." Part of me just wanted to lock the two of them in a padded room for three days with a plate of hash brownies and a bottle of Jose Cuervo, but the rest of me figured that probably would bring about the apocalypse.

Just to make sure I had my quota of stereotypes for the evening, a black SUV pulled up behind Smith's car and a pair of neckless giants got out wearing tactical pants, combat boots and turtlenecks. I slid down the hood of the car and intercepted Smith at the bottom of the stairs.

"Harker," he said as I got close.

"*Aperio*," I said as I fell into step behind Smith. "How did you do that?"

"I heard you."

"Bullshit. Nobody hears me unless I want them to."

"Then I smelled you."

"Also bullshit. I don't wear cologne, I don't use hair products with scent, and even my deodorant is fragrance-free. I'm a stealthy motherfucker, but you just called me out without even trying. What are you, Smith?"

He turned and looked me in the eye from one step up. Smith was a solid man, six foot and slightly north of two hundred pounds, but I'm tall, so he didn't gain much height advantage being a step up on me. "I knew you were there because it is my job to know where you are. It is my job to never be surprised, and to never, ever let anyone or thing get the drop on me. And I am very goddamn good at my job. You want to know what I am, Harker? I'm a grumpy fucking civil servant that got called out of bed to clean up the mess left by a pair of very junior agents who had one job—"

"Watch the junior shit, Smith. Let's not forget that I'm old enough to be your grandfather. And as far as our one job, we did it. Wally's alive. That was the job, right? Not let the kid get killed or kidnapped? Well, we covered that one. There might have been a few more bodies than you like, but at least I piled 'em up nice and neat for your zombies to get rid of. Yeah, recognized them. Gonna take a little more than a turtleneck to hide the death-funk from me.

"So what's the problem, Smith? We kept the kid alive, killed the bad guys, and didn't even get the local constabulary involved. What more did you want out of us?"

Smith actually took a second before he answered, and when he did, it was like talking to a human being instead of a federal agent. "I'm sorry. You're right, you did exactly what I asked you to do, and the Lion is still safe. What does he think is going on?"

"He thinks somebody wants to use him to open the seven seals and bring about the end of the world." I couldn't help myself. I needed the chuckle I got when Smith's jaw dropped open. "Yeah, he knows. He's known since before he came here. And in the 'big fucking surprise' category, he told a girl about his destiny to get laid."

"Fuck me. You're joking." Smith actually face palmed himself right there on the steps.

"I wish. Not the fucking you part, but the joking part. Have you actually met this kid?" I asked. Smith turned and started back up the stairs. I followed. I had more questions, and while stubborn, Smith was still a better option for info than the zombies.

"No. I've read his file, but that's it."

I reached out and grabbed Smith's elbow before he reached for the door. "Does his file say he's a big stoner?"

"No, but who really cares? Everybody in college smokes a little weed."

"I'm not talking a little weed, I'm talking a bong the size of a bazooka. This kid is a major pothead."

"Well, that wasn't in the file, but I don't see how it's going to affect our protection detail."

"Then you've never spent any time with serious stoners. Getting him to take this shit seriously might be an issue."

"He can't be that bad," Smith said, then turned to knock on the door.

"Famous last words," I muttered as the door opened and a cloud of marijuana smoke billowed out.

CHAPTER 4

"Nice," I said, walking into the apartment. "You're a cop, Flynn. You couldn't keep this little shithead from blazing up for ten minutes?"

"It's been like half an hour, bro," Wally said from the couch where he sat cross-legged with his bong between his legs and a lighter in his hand. He had the relaxed grin of somebody who's smoking some really good shit. I took a deep breath. It was some really good shit.

I sat down next to Wally and said, "Let me hit that shit." I held out my hand and he put the bong in it. I took the lighter and lit the weed, sucking in a good lungful of smoke. I leaned back, holding the marijuana smoke in my lungs for most of a minute before I let it out in a long breath. Then I reached over and smacked Wally in the back of the head.

"Now stop being a fucking idiot," I said. I stood up and walked to the small kitchen, dumping the last of the weed in the sink and giving the bong a quick rinse.

"What the fuck, man!" Wally was on his feet after me like a deranged spider monkey, and when I turned around to put the bong in the dish strainer, he bumped chests with me.

"What the fuck? You wanna know what the fuck, you fucking little douche?" I slapped him across the face, not hard enough to break the skin, but hard enough to get his attention. "What the fuck is a yard full of dead guys who were trying to kidnap your dumb ass and you're in here burning one like it's a goddamn Dave Matthews concert. What the fuck is a team of highly trained fucking professionals working to save your worthless ass and you not having any more respect than to tell some cheap coed slut that you're the motherfucking Lion of goddamn Judah just to tear off a piece of college tail!"

"But you smoked my weed," he whined.

"I'm the fucking adult in the room, I get to smoke all the fucking weed I want. When you're as old as I am, you can smoke all the weed you want." I didn't mention that he'd have to get to a century and a quarter to be as old as me or that I metabolized marijuana quicker than humans, just like I did all drugs.

"But it was my weed."

"Shut the fuck up."

"Are you children finished?" Smith asked from the door. "Because I have a few questions for Mr. Gubegna, and I'd like to get them answered before we leave."

"Leave?" Wally asked. "I'm not going anywhere. I live here. You assholes can leave anytime."

"Mr. Gubegna, I'm Agent John Smith with the Department of Homeland Security, Paranormal Division. I don't officially exist, nor does the division I'm a part of. Do you understand what that means for you?" Wally shook his head.

"That means that as soon as I stepped out of my car, you ceased to exist. With one phone call from me, you're gone. Erased from this world. All records of your birth, education, immunization, junior soccer league, high school prom—all gone. Everyone who ever knew you will forget about you, or they'll disappear too. Now do you understand me?"

Wally nodded, then walked back to the couch and sat down. I felt so bad for him I almost gave him back his bong. I looked at Smith, who had no more expression on his face than ever. That was a seriously scary dude, even to me.

"Now what do you know about being the Lion of Judah?"

Smith said.

"It's all bullshit, man. It's some religious shit that my grandma believes in. Something about Cousin Morrie being President, and my uncle David being a true descendant of *that* David, I'm the crossroads for a whole bunch of hereditary lines and stuff. According to Grandma, that makes me the Lion of Judah, and I have the power to bring about the end of the world by opening the seven seals. I can't do any of that shit man, I'm just trying to study architecture and get a job in like New York or San Francisco, yeah, San Francisco, where I can get my medical marijuana card and draw awesome buildings and shit, man."

"That might not be in the cards, Mr. Gubegna. There are some very bad men who very much believe that you really can bring about the end of the world, and they plan on using you to do just that," Smith said. "So you need to come with us until we can make sure there is no threat."

"How you gonna do that, man? You gonna kill me? Because from what I see, that's all your boy here knows how to do." He pointed at me.

"Not true," I protested. "I also bake. I make a molten chocolate soufflé that is out of this world. But I do kill a lot things," I admitted.

"We aren't going to kill you, Mr. Gubegna, but we need to make sure no one can use your abilities, either," Smith said.

I stood up. "This is bullshit, Smith. Are we taking him with us or not?"

"We are. I would like it to be voluntary if possible."

"But you only kinda give a fuck, right?" I asked.

"Pretty much," Smith agreed.

I turned to Wally. "You have sixty seconds. Pack a bag. Don't forget underwear and deodorant. Leave the weed. If you're not back out here in one minute, I'm going to come into your bedroom, knock you unconscious and carry you to Agent Smith's car. If you try to climb out the window, the agent on the ground out back will knock you unconscious and carry you to Agent Smith's car. So within the next three minutes, you will be in that car and you will be leaving this apartment. Your decision is whether or not you're awake to see it, and if you remember clean underwear. Do I make myself absolutely clear?"

"I'm not going." He got right up in my face and glared at me with a faceful of twenty-something bravado.

I raised one eyebrow and said, "Forty-five seconds."

"I said I'm not fucking going, you fucking pig!" A little drop of spit flew from his lips and landed on my cheek just below my right eye.

I reached up, wiped the spittle from my face and said, "Thirty seconds."

Wally stood there for about another ten seconds, then he turned and stomped into his room. I heard a closet door open and close, then listened to drawers open and close for a minute or so. After a little over a minute, Wally came back out, tennis shoes on and a windbreaker on over his Grateful Dead t-shirt.

"Did you remember deodorant?" I asked.

"Yes, asshole."

"Underpants?"

"Fuck you."

I slapped him again. Still not hard by my standards, but my patience was wearing thin, so it probably came across a little harder than I expected. Either way, it spun Wally around and dropped him to the floor.

"The fuck, man!" He bounced back up, fists clenched at his sides.

"Bad idea, son. I'm the one that kills things, remember? Now get your fucking bag and get in the car. And if you decide to open your goddamn mouth to me again, try not say anything that's going to make me want to knock your punk ass out, okay?"

"Whatever," Wally grumbled as he pushed his way past me to the door.

I turned to follow, but Flynn put a hand on my arm. I held back and let Smith leave first. "What was all that about?" she asked.

"I was getting bored. This is where we were going to end up anyway, with the little shit going with us and being all pissed off about it. I just moved up our timetable by about half an hour."

"What aren't you telling me?"

"Lots of things, Detective, some of which I'll never divulge except under torture. Feel free to tie me up sometime and find out." I grinned at her, and Flynn rolled her eyes.

"I mean what aren't you telling me right now?"

"That whoever sent those ninjas has had plenty of time to realize they aren't coming back and move on to Plan B. And I'd like to have the kid secured long before Plan B gets here."

That's when the first explosion came from the apartment's parking lot. I pushed past Flynn to the door, where I saw the SUV that carried Smith's zombie goons burning merrily away in the parking lot.

"Fuck. Plan B's here," I said.

CHAPTER 5

I vaulted the balcony railing, landing in a crouch just past a puddle of blood left behind from the zombie cleanup crew. That's a problem with certain flavors of undead—their vision goes to shit quick, so they don't always pick up on all the little details that make the difference between a place really being cleaned up and just having all the corpses and major organs swept under the rug.

I didn't have much time to worry about the mess the zombies left behind because Smith's car slid to a stop right behind the burning mass of metal and glass that used to be a Suburban. Both back doors flew open and Smith and Wally scrambled out. Wally stood stock-still beside the car, making a prime target of himself in the firelight, but Smith hit the ground running, sprinting around the car and grabbing the stunned stoner around the waist. Smith's driver got out of the car and moved to the trunk, which opened at the push of a button. Never wasting a movement, the agent reached into the trunk and slipped on a bulletproof vest, then slapped a Velcro holster with a pistol onto his chest and came back up with an AR-15 in hand. He walked backward toward the apartment, sweeping the rifle right to left in a classic cover pattern.

I sprinted past him, using my enhanced strength to up my speed way past human levels, and shouted, "More guns in the trunk?" as I passed him.

"Yeah, another AR and a shotgun," he yelled back, then squeezed off a short burst of automatic fire down the driveway.

I got to the car and hung the rifle over one shoulder on its sling, then grabbed the shotgun. I grabbed a black case that looked to be full of spare AR mags and turned to make my way back to the apartment before whatever blew up the SUV made its debut.

I wasn't fast enough. Not by half. I got about two steps from the car when a red dragon the size of a city bus dropped out of the sky and wreathed the driver in a stream of fire. He was engulfed in seconds and dead on the ground heartbeats later. I ran past the dragon, scooped Wally up over a shoulder, and jumped from the ground to the balcony.

"Take cover!" I shouted back to Smith, then I flung the door open to Wally's apartment and shoved him inside. "If you come out before I come get you, you fucking deserve every bad thing that happens to you." I slammed the door in his face and hopped back to the ground.

I found Smith taking cover under the lowest stairwell, rifle poking through the space between steps, and plinking at the dragon. "That's not going to do anything," I said.

"I can see that, smartass. Any suggestions?" Smith growled.

"Yeah, I just need you to get his attention so I can find the little bastard," I replied.

"What little bastard? That thing is huge!"

"That's an illusion. There's no such thing as dragons," I said.

"And you know this how, exactly? If there's anything I've learned, it's that there's some weird shit in this world."

"Oh there's plenty of weird shit, Smitty, but if there were dragons, I'd know."

"Oh?"

"For fuck's sake, do we have to do this now? Uncle Luke wanted one for a pet, so we spent forty fucking years combing Europe and Asia for a goddamn dragon, okay? There's no such thing as a motherfucking dragon! But there are fucking illusionists, and I hate fucking illusionists."

I cast a camouflage glamour on myself and stepped out from under the steps. Smith ran out, firing at the dragon with every step. The beast turned its attention toward him, and it belched out a huge fireball that Smith managed to avoid but took out all the bushes in front of the apartment building. Just before the fireball, I saw a little shimmer of light off to one side of the driveway and opened my Sight.

"Gotcha, fuckwad," I murmured as the streams of magic forming the fireball and illusory dragon jumped into view, all streaming back to a point about four feet off the ground and about a hundred yards in front of me. I unslung the AR from my shoulder and knelt down, putting my eye to the scope. There was still nothing visible to my naked eye, so I started with a short burst, sweeping side-to-side and hoping to hit something I didn't like.

There's something to be said for shooting things—even if you don't hit what you're aiming at, usually just getting close will annoy or distract somebody enough that they can't cast delicate magic, like, say, maintaining the illusion of giant red dragon floating through North Carolina. I spun off the last of my magazine in the general direction of the spellcaster, and the dragon flickered out of existence. So did the fireball, and suddenly I was looking through the scope at my illusionist.

"I fucking hate illusionists," I muttered, and squeezed the trigger. Nothing happened. I pressed the button to eject the magazine, then saw that I had dropped the ammo bag halfway across the front lawn. "Fuck me sideways," I said as I stood up. I pointed at him and yelled "*Sagitta*," conjuring a bolt of mystical energy and sending it across the distance between us.

"Eat my Magic Missile, motherfucker." I watched the wizard fall and grinned as he hit the ground clutching his shoulder. He wouldn't die from that shot, but a blast of magic to the shoulder would keep him down until we got Wally someplace safe.

Which the gunfire from behind me told me would not be his apartment. I turned and saw Smith drop a pair of black-clad military types, obviously mercenaries, with two quick three-shot bursts from his AR.

"You okay up there?" I yelled. Smith gave me a thumbs-up over the balcony rail, and I started off in a quick jog to his car, hoping that his driver left the keys in the ignition and I wasn't going to have to dig through his Kentucky Fried Bodyguard for them. I was lucky for once — the keys were there. I slid into the driver's seat and drove the sedan right up under the balcony in front of Wally's apartment, ignoring the grass and curbs in the way.

I got out and shouted up to Smith, "Get Wally!" He stood up, kicked in the door, and disappeared into the apartment. He appeared back in the doorway seconds later, motioning for me. I hopped onto the roof of the car, then up onto the landing.

"Where's Wally?" I asked.

"Gone. Flynn's hurt. I need you to help her."

"What can I do?"

Smith just looked at me.

"Oh no. I don't do that. Ever. That's totally not my thing." I held up both hands and stepped back.

Smith grabbed one arm and pulled me into the apartment. Flynn was lying on the floor of the living room, three dead mercs around her. She'd given as good as she got, but the numbers game eventually got to her. She was bleeding from bullet wounds in her thigh and shoulder where her vest didn't cover, and there was a cut over her left eye that looked pretty nasty.

"You've done it before. I've seen the records," Smith said.

"Yeah, then you know how well that fucking ended," I spat.

"She'll die before an ambulance can get here and you know it."

"She's a cop. She knew the risks when she put on the badge."

"She's your friend, dammit."

"I don't have friends, Smith. I have people that I kill, and people I watch die. Guess which fucking category Flynn falls into."

"We need her, Harker. She may be the only person that knows where they took Wally. And without him, it's all over. Everything."

"Do it, Q." The new voice came from behind me, and it could only belong to one person. Well, not even a person, really. I looked around and time had stopped. Smith was frozen in mid-berate, the dust and debris raining from the ceiling was hanging in mid-air, even the noise of the burning bushes below was silent. I turned and faced my guardian angel, who was leaning in the doorway holding a bottle of wine.

"Glory," I said, trying not to fall too much in love with the angel. She was five-six or so and the kind of beautiful that you think might melt your eyeballs if you stare at her too long. She wasn't rocking the wings tonight, just a leather jacket, tattered Guns n' Roses tour shirt and ripped jeans. Her blonde hair was tied back in a ponytail, and she had a pair of sunglasses perched on her head.

"Did I tear you away from a hot date at a Scorpion concert?" I asked.

"I was watching over a nineties metal guitarist. He has more trouble staying alive than you do. Now would you save the girl so we can move on?"

"You know I can't do that, Glory. And you know why."

"No, I don't." Her voice lost the usual lilt and turned to steel. "I know that you're being a fucking child while the fate of the world hangs in the balance."

"I don't think I've ever heard you swear before, Glory."

"You're a bad influence. Now do it."

"No."

"You know you're eventually going to do what I want, so why fight me?"

"I'm not fucking healing her, Glory, I can't take it. It almost killed me last time."

"The last time you didn't know what would happen. Now you do, and you'll be able to control it better."

"There's no guarantee of that."

"I can help." That was new. Usually Glory wouldn't interfere personally on our plane, so she was taking this Wally shit seriously.

"How? You know what this takes from me."

"I know, Q. I know the bond is deep, and I know it's hard for you to deal with, but I think I can help make it easier on you this time. And Q?'

"Yeah?"

"We need her. *You* need her. She's important to the work we have to do."

"So you're telling me to suck it up and heal the cop?"

"Suck it up and heal the cop, Q."

"Fine." I turned back to the apartment and the world blurred into motion again. I turned sideways past Smith and knelt beside Flynn in the middle of the floor.

"Hey, Flynn, nice pincushion impersonation. Are there any

bullets you didn't decide to stop with your body?" I asked, taking her wrist in my hand.

"Yeah, the ones I put in those three motherfuckers." Her voice was thready, but her attitude was intact. That was good because this was about to be a wild ride.

"Flynn, you're bleeding out. The bullet in your leg nicked your femoral artery and you'll be dead in minutes if I don't take some pretty drastic measures. I can save you, but it's not going to be easy on either of us."

"Do it. I've been shot twice and caught four in the vest tonight, I think I can handle anything you can dish out."

That's what you think, I thought. I looked down at her and said, "All right, do exactly as I say."

I pulled my pocketknife out and made a slash across her wrist, then made one just like it across my own. "Drink," I said, pressing my wrist to her lips. She struggled, but she was too weak to resist much, and as my blood flowed across her lips, the magic in my body kicked in and she started to drink. I pulled her arm to my mouth and drank from her as she sucked on my wrist. We locked eyes and I pushed my will out, diving into her consciousness with my own.

I felt my hold on my own body grow faint as I dove past Flynn's mental defenses, opening my mind and soul to her completely. I watched her first steps, her first bike ride, her first kiss, the first sloppy fumblings in the back of her tenth-grade boyfriend's Prelude, her first real love, her first real heartbreak. I lived every moment of her life in the seconds our souls entwined, and I felt her footsteps through my memories as she relived all the decades of my life—my loves, my triumphs, my many, many failures, the people I'd lost, the loved ones I'd watched grow old and fade away to time, the monsters I'd fought, the monsters I'd called friend, and all the pain of the last woman I'd shared myself with this completely.

"Come back, Q." The voice was faint, and I tried to ignore it. It would be easier to just stay here, hide inside Flynn's life for a while and then fade away quietly. But that's not how I'm going out, I know. I'll never go quietly into that good night, so I turned and reached back to myself, finding Glory's hand reaching back for me. She clasped hands with me, then wrapped her arms around my soul and drew me back into myself. I felt her leave my body, leaving behind just enough of herself to dull the pain of the memories the healing dredged up, and came back to myself staring into Flynn's eyes.

Flynn stared into my eyes, her eyes locked on mine by my will. I blinked, and the spell was broken, the world snapped back into motion. Glory was gone, Smith was yelling, and I felt fear like I hadn't felt in decades. Flynn pulled her wrist from my lips and jerked her whole body away from me, curling up into a retching ball on the carpet. I fell back onto my ass, feet splayed out in front of me and my head swimming with memories, sensations and the taste of fresh blood, a taste I hadn't had cross my lips in more than fifty years. Flynn shook and retched again, convulsed once in sharp pain as her body expelled the bullets forcefully from her healing wounds, then pulled herself up onto Wally's blood-spattered sofa and covered herself with a throw blanket.

She took a corner of the blanket and wiped my blood from her mouth, looked over at me and said in a shaky voice, "What the bleeding fuck was that?"

I opened my mouth a couple of times, but nothing came out. I wiped my face with the back of my hand and rolled over onto my knees. I pulled myself to my feet using a chair and staggered into the kitchen. I pulled three beers out of the fridge and popped them all open on the edge of the counter. I drained one, then went back into the fridge for another. I walked back into the den a little steadier, collapsed into a chair and held out a beer for Smith, who was sitting on the arm of the couch alternating concerned looks at Flynn and me.

I handed the other beer to Flynn and said, "That was a blood bond. It's a way that I can heal someone who is mortally wounded, but the cost is high."

"Define high," Flynn said, trying to calm her shaking hands enough to get the beer to her lips.

We're bonded now. I thought, and saw her eyes widen at my presence in her head.

"What the fuck was that?" Flynn asked.

"Exactly," I said. "We're linked together now, you and I. Closer than you'll ever be with anyone in the world."

"For how long?" The words came out almost in a whisper.

"You already know the answer to that," I said.

I watched her eyes as she searched through my memories, then saw the color drain from her face as the realization hit her. "Fuck me."

"Yup," I said. "Forever."

CHAPTER 6

"Am I a vampire now?" Flynn asked, looking around. "Everything looks different, sharper somehow. And I can hear— fuck, I can hear everything! Is this what the world is always like to you? So loud, with so much...everything going on?"

"Yeah, kinda, but I've had a century or so to get used to it. It'll fade into background noise eventually."

"But what about..." *This?* she asked inside my head. *Is this forever?*

"Yeah, but it's affected by a lot of things. Like distance, for one, and how tired one of us is. It takes more out of you than you think, touching somebody's mind like that. So I try not to do it often."

Flynn was only half-listening, standing up under new legs and moving through the apartment slowly, looking at everything. She was like a giant newborn, or a college kid on a really good shroom trip, exploring everything, wanting to touch everything. I decided to step in when it looked like she was going to lick the wall.

"Flynn," I said. She ignored me. "Flynn." I called her louder. "Goddammit," I muttered, then focused my will on her. *FLYNN!* I mentally shouted, and she whirled around, clutching her temples.

"What the fucking fuck, Harker! That hurt!" She sat back on the couch and sucked down the last of her beer.

"We still have a stoned Lion of Judah to save and an apocalypse to avert, remember?"

"Yeah, okay, I remember. What's the play?"

Smith came out of his shocked silence at the same time Flynn did, so he took over. Good thing, too. I only had so much "leader" bullshit in me, and I was about to run out. "What did they look like? The men that came in here?"

"They looked like the first guys, like low-rent ninjas, but these were more like a tactical squad than the cliché black outfits. They had guns and flash-bangs and came in fast-roping off the roof. They were definitely pros. They sacrificed the first guy, but once he was in and had me engaged, they threw in two flash-bangs to disorient me, then swung in with smoke grenades going. They were in and out in seconds. I saw them go back out the way they came in, but I was too busy dying to see where they went from there. What was going on outside?" Flynn asked.

"An illusionist made a fake dragon and threw some fireballs at us. Once I convinced him to drop the smoke screen, we took him out pretty easy. But he was enough of a distraction to make it easy on these guys up here," I said.

"How did you know the dragon was an illusion?" Flynn asked.

"Holy shit, did you two go to the same cop school for dumbass questions, or what?" I threw up my hands. "There was a while in the thirties when the Nazis were looking for objects of power. My uncle wanted to make sure as much powerful magic as he could lay his hands on stayed the fuck out of Hitler's grubby little paws. So we spent a lot of time traipsing through Europe looking for magical shit. One of the things we were looking for was dragons. Not only did we never find one, we never found any indication there had ever been any. Ergo, there are no dragons."

"That logic sucks," Flynn said. "How do you know there aren't dragons in South America?"

"I don't care if there are dragons in South America. I've only ever cared if there were dragons in Europe and if there was a dragon on the front lawn fifteen minutes ago. Fortunately for me, there were no dragons in either place. Because there are no fucking dragons! Now can we get back to Wally, the dope-smoking, tail-chasing end of the goddamn world?"

"Good idea," Smith said. "We need to find him. That's probably going to be your job," he said, pointing at me.

"Motherfucker," I sighed. "Can't you people do *anything* without me? How did you ever make the goddamn dryads go extinct with this kind of work ethic?" I knelt by a blood spatter at the shattered sliding glass door, dabbed my fingers in it, and brought it to my nose. Different type than Flynn or any of the corpses she generated, so it must belong to one of our escaped baddies, or Wally. Either one would be just fine.

I walked to the dinette and sat down at the table, sweeping aside a pile of homework or D&D character sheets, I couldn't really tell which. "I need a bowl of water, a needle, a tongue depressor and a stick of chewing gum," I said to Flynn.

"And I want a pony," she shot right back. "Come the fuck on, Harker, where do you think I'm going to get that shit in a dope fiend's apartment at two in the morning?"

"Get me stuff that looks close. But start with the bowl of water." She brought me a cereal bowl that was mostly clean and filled with water, then went off in search of supplies.

"Is she going to be okay?" Smith asked.

"You know she can hear you, right?" I asked.

"Yeah, but I want to pretend like things are normal, for a little while longer, anyway."

"You got a weird definition of normal, Smitty. But yeah. She'll be fine. She's already healed physically, and the more we work together, the easier it'll be for her to learn to shut me out."

"What about you?" he asked.

"I have a lot more trouble shutting me out, but I'm a persistent bastard with myself." I dipped my bloody finger in the water and swirled it around widdershins, or counterclockwise. The blood diffused off my hand and turned the water a very pale pink, and I took my finger out.

"I mean, will you be okay?"

"First off, you don't really give a shit, so let's not pretend that you do. Secondly, I've got a pretty fucked up definition of okay myself, so yeah, I'll be fine."

Smith opened his mouth to press, but Flynn walked back in just then. I heard enough to know she'd been waiting for a break in the conversation to come back in, and she knew I knew. *Thanks.*

No problem. Are you okay?

As okay as I get. Now get outta my head. I mentally closed the door between us and said, "Let's see what you found."

She handed me a wooden pencil, a sewing needle and a pack of Juicy Fruit. I opened the gum and took a piece, starting to chew as they both watched me. "What? Magic is thirsty work, my mouth gets dry," I protested.

I dipped the needle in the pink water, pushed it through the eraser on the pencil, and then dipped the whole end of the pencil, needle and all, back into the mixture of water and blood. I focused on bindings, on the forces that hold things together, the connections that make us who we are, and pushed my will into the needle. "*Corpus ad corpus, sanguinem sanguini. Corpus ad corpus, sanguinem sanguini. Corpus ad corpus, sanguinem sanguini.*" I repeated the incantation three times stirring the needle through the blood/water mix counterclockwise the entire time. After the third repetition, I held the pencil aloft and twirled it slowly between my fingers. When the needle pointed to the broken sliding glass door, the tip began to glow a bright white.

"They went out that way," I said.

"We knew they went out that way, jackass. We were out the other way," Smith said.

Flynn stared at the glowing tip of the needle. "What did you do?" she asked in a whisper.

"It's called sympathetic magic. I mixed the blood with something unlike itself, but it remembers what it was like to be whole, with the rest of itself. So it'll point the way to the rest of it."

"So it'll lead us to more of whoever's blood that was." She pointed to the floor.

"Yeah, so we're hoping that guy didn't bleed out in the woods a hundred yards away. Then we're screwed."

"But for now we can follow the needle?"

"Just like a compass," I said, doing just that. I walked to the sliding glass door, stepped through onto the balcony, and when the shine of the needle didn't waver, I jumped down and started toward the woods behind the apartments.

"Hey, wait for us!" Flynn yelled, then jumped over the balcony rail to land right behind me. "Whoa," she said. "I didn't know I could do that."

"You won't be able to for long. Once your body metabolizes my blood, the strength and speed will fade. The senses, too, but not as much."

And this?

This you're stuck with. There was more magic to the bonding than physical, and this is part of it. I jammed part of my life force into you so you wouldn't die, so now you and I are magically linked until we die. Sorry about that.

So far it's not so bad.

I haven't made my weekly pilgrimage to the Uptown Cabaret yet. I flooded my mind with images of nubile girls writhing on top of me and felt Flynn withdraw from my head with the sensation of a slamming door.

"Slow down, you inhuman bastards," Smith panted as he caught up to us. We were walking at a good clip, but Smith was only human, and he was jogging to keep up.

"Humans say the sweetest things," I said, but slowed down to a comfortable human pace.

"Do you have any plans for what we're going to do when we catch up to them?" I asked Smith.

"I have a couple of ideas," Flynn growled. I looked over at her and she shrugged. "The fuckers shot me. That's not on the list of stuff I forgive easily. Cut a girl some slack, will ya?"

Not to mention that she just got a blood transfusion from a pseudo-vampire, I thought, working to keep my thoughts my own. We picked our way through a couple hundred yards of woods, led by my enhanced vision and a glowing sewing needle. After one particularly dense patch of kudzu, we broke through into a little tuft of grass bordering the parking lot of a local strip mall.

"Well, shit," I said, turning and trying to get my spell to pick back up.

"What's wrong?" Smith asked, leaning over with his hands on his knees.

"They're out of range."

"How were you able to follow them this far?"

"They must have had a car waiting here. If the guy was still bleeding, then that—yup, there it is!" I pointed to a couple of drops on the pavement. "He was still bleeding, so the magic was able to find more blood from the same guy, but this is as far as we go."

"Fuck. Now what?" Flynn asked.

"You're the detective, sweetcheeks. I just make magic and cast out demons."

"You'll need magic just to walk if you ever call me sweetcheeks again, asshat."

"Fair enough," I said. "But seriously, without something closely tied to Wally, I'm not going to be able to track him with magic. And I mean something that meant a lot to him, not hairbrush samples and the shit you dredge up out of the bottom of the shower."

"So let's get to detecting," Smith had caught his breath and took back control of the situation. "Let's take this party back to police headquarters and start looking up internet chatter and poking through airport security camera footage."

"Not me," I said. "I'm heading to Luke's to get some rest, some decent food, and some research. I hate to admit it, but Christian mythology is one of my weaker spots, so I'm gonna need to study up on Revelation if I'm to have any shot at getting us through this. Plus, Renfield's there."

"What's that got to do with anything?"

"The man is a hacker with backdoors into every system in the country. If our kidnappers came in by air or rail, and they have any record anywhere in the world, Ren will find them. Besides, he makes the best Western omelet in North Carolina, and I'm starving."

CHAPTER 7

I called Luke while Flynn and Smith were waiting on their ride back to the apartment complex, and he pulled up in his newest ride, a jet black Mercedes S-class with leather everything. Smith raised and eyebrow at me when he saw it, and I could feel Flynn's motor rev higher just looking at it.

"Not my ride, kids, but Uncle Luke has always had a taste for the finer things in life," I said, walking around to the passenger door.

"That I have," Luke said as he stepped out of the car. "Quincy, my boy, aren't you going to introduce me to your—" the "friends" or whatever froze on his lips as he locked eyes with Flynn. I saw the subtle signs of challenge, watched his pupils dilate, his nostrils flare and his back arch, almost like he was a cat ready to defend his territory. For her part, I saw Flynn instinctively clench her fists and shift her body weight to her back foot, ready to react if Luke pounced.

"Ahem." I cleared my throat and they both gave themselves a little shake and looked away from the other quickly, neither wanting to meet the other's eyes, but neither wanting to give ground either. "Thanks for picking me up, Uncle Luke, but hadn't we better get going before the sun comes up?" We were half an hour from his house with less than an hour before sunrise, a lot closer than he usually liked to cut things.

"Yes, of course. A pleasure to finally meet you, Detective." He slid back into the car, smooth as butter even though the introductions had certainly *not* gone as planned. I got into the car and Luke pulled out into traffic, weaving the performance sedan through the light traffic on our way to his place.

"You did it again," Luke said almost before we were out of the parking lot. He shifted gears and sped through a yellow light, then cut left across several lanes of traffic taking a winding back road at a good bit more than the posted speed limit. I wasn't worried about Luke's driving, but I was a little worried about deer running across the road suddenly.

"She was dying," I said. I looked over at Luke. He gripped the steering wheel so tight he was making indentations in the plastic, and you could carve granite with the line of his jaw. "I had no choice, Uncle."

"There is always a choice. You should have let her die." The words were hard, flat, emotionless, and probably right. Luke sighed, and I watched the set of his jaw relax a little. "You didn't have to watch what it did to you last time, Quincy."

"I had to live through it," I reminded him.

"But you couldn't see the full effect it had on you. When she died, it almost took you with her. I don't want to, I mean, I don't want *you* to have to go through that again."

"This is different, Luke." I reached out and patted him awkwardly on his shoulder. We weren't a touchy family, so those kinds of things never came easy to me. "I had to do it. Glory told me so."

The car actually wobbled as Luke turned to stare at me. "The angel told you to meld with this human to save her?"

"Umm, Luke, could you maybe — Look out!"

His attention snapped back to the road long enough to whip the car around a stopped city bus and thread the needle between two semis passing through a traffic light in opposite directions. We blew through the red light leaving screaming tires, blaring horns and heart palpitations in our wake.

Luke pulled over into an abandoned parking lot and turned to me. "Tell me everything. Leave nothing out." He didn't compel me to tell him, his mental powers don't work on me, but he used a tone I'd only heard a few times in my very long life. I told him the whole story, from finding Flynn on the floor bleeding out, to sharing blood with her, to bonding souls with her, to the connection I felt to her even now, half a city away.

"And this is different, Uncle. When I bonded with Anna, that was one thing. That was love, she was the woman I wanted to share my life with. This…partnership with Flynn isn't like that. The bonding is different, like we can go deeper in some ways, but it's also easier to lock her out of my thoughts than it ever was with Anna. It's strange, but…I think it's going to be okay."

"I don't know about okay, but I agree that it sounds different. But I worry, Quincy. What happened with Anna was devastating for you, and I'd hate for you to suffer that way again."

Join the club. I remembered little about the aftermath of Anna's death, just images and flashes more than a coherent thread. I remembered holding her body, a Nazi officer's bullet lodged in her brain. I remembered holding that officer's heart in my bare hand, his body lying in the snow at my feet with a fist-shaped hole in his chest. I had a flash of me attacking a squad of German infantry, and then an image seared into my brain of dozens of dead soldiers around me. There was nothing after that, just a period of blackness where my grief and loss totally overwhelmed me. The next thing I remember is being in France with Luke and his Renfield of the time and killing a lot of Nazis with the French Resistance. I remembered a lot of wine in France, a lot of Scotch across the British Isles, and not much else for a few years. My memory kicks back in somewhere around 1946 in the Arizona desert, with no Luke or Renfield anywhere around. I reconnected with them in New Jersey after a few years wandering the desert and annoying the various shamans I found there. We never spoke of Anna again, until tonight.

"I need to borrow Ren when we get back to your place," I said, desperate to change the subject.

"Of course," Luke said, his shoulders relaxing as we got on safer ground. I'm pretty sure Luke's never been scared of me, what with the whole being Count Dracula thing, but I do think that I sometimes make him nervous, and I know he likes me enough to miss me if he had to kill me, so it was better to stick to the shallow end of our conversation for a few days, at least until he was more comfortable with the idea of me bonding to Flynn. Hell, until I was more comfortable with the idea, not to mention Flynn. I could still feel her, just behind my eyes, no matter how far she and Smith drove. I could feel her right now, the uncomfortable way the seat belt dug in between her boobs... *whoa, definitely don't need to be thinking about Flynn's boobs. Not now, and sure as fuck not when she's around. She hears that...*images of what a Sig .40 could do to even my superhuman healing ability flashed through my head.

"Naturally, Renfield will be at your disposal once he finishes his morning duties," Luke's voice snapped me back into the car and safely away from Flynn's chest.

"Unc, this is a little more important than him making sure you've had your warm milk and cookies before beddie-bye," I said.

Luke glared at me. "Making the house light-tight and securing all entrances is more than 'warm milk,' you insolent whelp. It is the peace of mind that allows me to garner any rest at all. Not that I shall find an easy time of it today, with the news you sprang on me weighing so heavily on my mind."

Oh. My. God. Luke was laying it on thick today. He knew as well as I did that the second the sun was above the horizon, he would sleep the sleep of the dead, only waking in situations of extreme danger or pain. I'd spent a decent part of my adolescence testing the limits of Luke's sleep, often with hilarious results. My favorite was the time I put makeup on him to look like my mother. I took a photo with an old flash camera, which was enough to wake Luke and send him into a double fury—one for waking him up, and the other for making him up to look like a very ugly woman.

"Fine, I'll be in your study reading the Bible. Send me Renfield when you're done with him."

"The Bible? You? We must truly be at the end times if you're reading the Bible."

"Uncle, that is exactly what I am trying to prevent." On that brilliant note, Luke pulled the car back out onto the road and headed toward his house, double-time.

CHAPTER 8

"What can I do for you, Master Quincy?" Renfield asked as he stepped into the library. I really was reading the Bible, brushing up on my Book of Revelation in preparation for dealing with the upcoming Apocalypse.

"I need to stop the end of the world, Ren. Got any ideas?" I closed the New International Version Bible I was reading and put it on the stack beside me. I'd already worked my way through a couple of King James versions, the English Standard, The New Jubilee edition, the American Standard Version, the Concordant Literal Version and two different Illustrated Bibles trying to cull as much information about the end of the world, the seven seals, and The Lion of Judah as I could. It all started to blur together after about three versions. I never claimed to be much of a scholar. That was Uncle Luke's deal. And Orly's, but he was long gone.

Orly was my youngest brother, the only one of us born long enough after "the book" came out to reap the benefits of our family's fame. By the time he came along, my parents had become the darlings of the university lecture circuit, so Orly tagged along and got the chance to spend his childhood in great libraries and reading rooms all around New England. His favorite smell was bookbinder's glue, and his favorite pastime was looking up obscure facts. James and I were more robust, not to mention older, so our bookish little brother traveled with Mother and Father while we bounced around boarding schools playing cricket and rugby.

"Well, Master Quincy, I suppose if we're to stop the end of the world, we should first make sure we can keep the seven seals intact, shouldn't we?"

"That makes sense. All of the versions I've seen say if all the seals are broken, then we're fucked. Is that about it?"

"Indelicately phrased, but accurate," Renfield agreed.

"So if I'm reading these stories right," I waved my hand at the stack of Bibles, "the first four seals release the Four Horsemen of the Apocalypse."

"They are commonly considered to be metaphorical, and many scholars consider those seals to have been broken long ago, with each Horseman being symbolic of a period of great tribulation experienced by the Jewish people, the Chosen Ones."

"Yeah, I'm pretty sure Jerry Falwell has something to say about that Chosen people thing. But what if they're more literal? What if these seals unleash some kind of physical threat into the world that has to be taken care of or the world ends?"

"You mean like actual men on horses?" Renfield asked. "That's a bit literal for most religions, isn't it?"

"Yeah, but if the Four Horsemen aren't Ric, Tully, Arn and Barry, then we have a problem." Of course, that's when my phone rang. I looked down and saw "Flynn" on the display. I opened myself to our link and felt her worry. "Looks like we have a problem, Renny old pal."

I slid my finger across the screen to answer the phone. "Yeah, what is it?"

Flynn's voice came on the line, and I would have heard the fear in her voice even if I didn't feel it in my heart. *This is going to be a pain in the ass,* I thought. *What happens when she gets laid?* I shoved those thoughts aside, figuring if we didn't stop the Apocalypse, that wouldn't be an issue. "What's up, buttercup?" I asked.

"We're so fucked," she said.

"You want to be a little more specific, Detective?"

"There's been a break-in at the CDC in Atlanta. White male, late twenties, six foot, one-eighty busted in the front door shouting about the end times and shot up a bunch of doctors and security guys on his way to the Hot Labs. He shot his way in there and took aerosolized botulin toxin, anthrax and smallpox samples."

"Well, that sucks for Atlanta, and probably the world in general, but I think we're going for more of a 'think global, act local' approach right now, Becky."

"Don't call me Becky, asshole. The break-in was five hours ago. The car was last spotted getting off I-85 north at Brookshire."

"Heading right for downtown," I said.

"Local enough for you?" Flynn asked.

"What's the play? The sun's up, so Luke's out of commission. I'm pretty well exhausted, so anything we do is going to have to be fast and mostly non-magical."

"I'm at headquarters. Come pick me up and we'll move out from here."

"Smith with you?"

"Yeah, I'm here. What do you need?" Smith's voice came on the line. She must have had me on speakerphone.

"Intel. We need to know where he's going."

"We need to know what he wants first."

"I got that covered, Smitty. He's the first Horseman, and he's on a pale horse. He's Pestilence, and he wants to infect as many people as possible. So you figure out where the biggest impact of a biological attack downtown would be, and Becky and I will try to stop him without getting dead."

"I told you not to call me—" I hung up on her.

"Ren, I'm gonna need a fast car."

"Gear up, Master Quincy. I'll be out front with our ride in two minutes." The stocky middle-aged manservant sprang out of his chair and hightailed it to the door, his short little legs almost a blur. I chuckled a little to myself.

I went upstairs and threw on a black leather jacket and my Doc Martens. I slipped a Sig 9mm into a shoulder holster under my left arm and tucked a Ruger LC9 into my right jacket pocket. A couple of knives got tucked into my belt and a wrist sheath, and I was ready to go. I hustled down the stairs and out the door, to find Renfield parked in front of the house with Uncle Luke's H3 Hummer rumbling by the curb.

"Didn't want to draw attention to yourself, Ren?" I asked as I opened the door and climbed in. The Hummer was high enough that even I needed the running boards, and I strapped my seatbelt on tight as Ren pulled away from the house.

"If the end of the world is nigh, Master Quincy, I do not intend to be a spectator." He reached down beside his leg and patted the stock of a shotgun.

"Damn, Renfield," I said. "I didn't know you even knew how to shoot one of those things."

"When your uncle found me, I was little more than gator bait down in the Louisiana swamps. I learned how to shoot before I learned how to read."

"I never knew that." This Renfield had been with Luke for the last twenty years, and I'd been in the American Southwest studying Coyote magic when the last one retired. When I reconnected with Luke, he was established in North Carolina with a new Renny.

"Yup, that's why my gumbo be so good, donchaknowboy?" he said in a bayou patois the likes of which I hadn't heard in decades. We both laughed until he pulled up to the curb in front of Police Headquarters.

I pulled out my phone to text Flynn but put it away when I saw her walk out of the station. She looked up and down the street, shielding her eyes from the morning sun, then hustled toward the idling behemoth when I rolled down the window. "You could have tooted the horn," I said to Renfield.

"Your uncle replaced it with an air horn. I really don't think you wanted me to 'toot' that, did you?"

"Point taken," I said. "What's the story, morning glory?" I asked as Flynn slid into the back seat.

"Morning glory, buttercup, fuck a duck Harker, you'd think I was a goddamn florist or something. Take a left on Davidson," she said. "Renfield, I presume?" she asked.

"Indeed, Detective. The pleasure is all mine."

"I'd be a lot more pleasurable if there wasn't a psycho with a shit-ton of aerosolized death heading to the convention center," Flynn replied. She fiddled with the straps on her bulletproof vest and checked the magazine in her sidearm.

"Are we sure that's where he's going?" I asked.

"You're sure he thinks he's one of the Four Horsemen of the Apocalypse?"

"I'm pretty sure he *is* one of the Four Horsemen. Pestilence, to be more specific."

"Then I'd bet all our lives on him going to the convention center. The Southern Baptist Convention National Meeting kicked off with a prayer meeting twenty minutes ago, and delegates from all across the country will be there for the next four days," Flynn explained.

"That would be pretty much perfect, then. He crop-dusts the place this morning, they have the sniffles when they go to the airport Friday, and the disease is spread throughout the country by the time they change planes, go out to dinner Saturday night and go to church feeling like crap Sunday."

"But they can't miss church because they were the delegate..." Flynn chimed in.

"And probably have some kind of show and tell or report or some such shit," I agreed.

"So Monday morning our pandemic begins."

"And the first seal is broken all to fuck," I finished.

Renfield pulled the Hummer up onto the sidewalk in front of the Convention Center and got out, grabbing his shotgun. "Then we'd better make sure none of that happens. Shall we?" he said, then slammed the door.

A startled security guard came out the front doors at us, but Flynn badged him into silence. "Have you seen this man?" She held up a grainy surveillance photo that could have been any white guy with a baseball cap.

The cop stared at the photo, then shook his head. "He's not going to know anything," I said. "I'm going to have to do this my way."

"What's your way?" Flynn asked. "Magic?"

"No," I replied. "Noise and firepower." I stepped through the main doors of the convention center and fired one shot into the ceiling. All the men and women within a hundred feet ducked, screamed, and started running in the opposite direction. I looked up, actually aimed this time, and fired again. This time I hit something instead of just randomly firing, and when I shot the top off the sprinkler, it triggered the failsafe in the system that douses everything in that wing if the system is damaged. So the fire alarm started blaring, the sprinklers showered the hallways in water, and people started to stream out of meeting rooms, heading for the exits in droves.

"Follow me!" I shouted and ran down the length of the hall. I stopped at the top of a set of escalators and pointed down. "Our guy is in one of two places—the main ballroom or the exhibit hall. You two go clear the exhibit hall. If you make enough ruckus by the front doors, everybody will haul ass for the loading dock doors. That's what you want. Get everybody clear, and the guy who doesn't want to leave, that's your bad guy."

"What are you going to do?" Flynn asked.

"I'm going to the only other place where he has a ton of targets at eight in the morning, which also happens to be the only other place where they shut off the smoke detectors because of the fog machines used in the performance. I'm going to church."

CHAPTER 9

I got to the main ballroom only to find my path blocked by a smiling young volunteer with perfect teeth, perfect hair and sparkling blue eyes. He had creases in his dress shirt, creases in his blue jeans, and I wouldn't have been surprised to find creases in his underpants. He held up one hand as if that was going to slow me down, then got in front of me when I didn't look like I was stopping.

"I'm sorry, brother, but we can't interrupt Pastor Steve's message." He pointed to a monitor, which showed a twenty something kid with a lot of hair product and skinny jeans exhorting the crowd to do something.

"Junior, I'm going in that room, and I'm going in there right now. Your only decision is how much of your blood ends up on the floor," I said, giving him my best *Don't Fuck with Me* look.

He smiled right back up at me and said, "I'm sorry brother, but I can't let you —" His words cut off as my fist smashed his perfect lips into his perfect teeth and sent his perfect head careening into the perfectly solid door behind him. He slumped to the floor and I yanked the door open.

I immediately felt like I'd walked into a rock concert, or maybe a political rally. Hell, maybe it was both. The stage was a good fifty feet wide with more lights and sound gear than I saw on the Grammys. There were three or four guys stationed around the room on camera platforms, plus a huge boom and a couple more dudes wandering the stage with cameras on their shoulders. The room was packed with believers, at least five thousand strong. Finding my nutbar in the middle of this crowd of nutbars was going to be worse than finding one specific stripper in Las Vegas.

I looked around, trying to decide where I'd be if I wanted to disperse a lot of germs into the crowd all at once. The guitar player hit a power chord, the crowd leapt to their feet, and the lights started flashing and moving around in time with the music. It all looked a lot more like a KISS concert than a prayer breakfast, but I'd spent a lot of time with Buddhists in my life, so I was used to a quieter style of praying, with less kick drum. All the concert trappings made something in my head click, and I started for the backstage area at a run.

"Backstage" was really behind some portable curtains set up across the hotel ballroom, but they still had security guys with lanyards guarding the area, just like at a concert. I didn't waste any time explaining myself, I just laid out the security guy with a punch to the jaw and kept running. I scouted backstage quickly — sound guy, no; wardrobe lady, no; guy messing with the foggers, no — then I froze and backed up. Kneeling with a silver canister in front of a huge fogger was a white guy, about six foot, and a bit under two hundred pounds, wearing a baseball cap and a black jacket. It was the jacket that gave him away. All the other crew guys wore khakis and black polos, but this guy had on a jacket and ball cap. Sitting on the floor next to him was a small aluminum canister, like the kind they used for chemicals in all those disaster movies.

I moved up behind him, my Docs not making a sound on the carpet, and pressed the barrel of my Ruger to the back of his head. "You twitch and I'll aerosolize your brain."

"You can't stop what's coming, heathen. The signs are clear. The end times are upon us, when the earth shall open up and disgorge the faithful and we shall ascend!" He stood up, his arms spread wide. I looked down at the canister, but it still looked intact. I couldn't read the writing on it from the distance, but the markings on it were unmistakable — Bad Shit Inside, Do Not Fuck With.

"What the hell is wrong with you, man?" I asked. "Why would you want to destroy the world?"

"I'm not destroying it, my child," said the idiot in front of me who was at least seventy years my junior. "I am helping to cleanse it! And we are beginning right here, with these false prophets!" He turned to face me and I saw vials strapped all over his chest, wired together with what looked like det cord.

"Fuck me," I whispered as I stepped back from the psycho wired to blow disease all over the room. He held a trigger in his left hand and another length of det cord in his right. I'd interrupted him before he could wire the canister to blow, but there was still enough biological agent on him to kill everyone in the room three times over. Not to mention what all that det cord would do to my complexion.

He raised a hand, and I mimicked his movement, focusing my will on the trigger. "*Cataracta,*" I said just before he squeezed the trigger, and suddenly all the water vapor in the immediate vicinity coalesced into a waterfall pouring over his hand and through the trigger, preventing the det cord from doing any det-ing. He looked at his hand, brows knit, then turned to me.

"No matter, I can—" I didn't care what he thought he could do, all I wanted him to do was die. I raised the Ruger to his face and squeezed the trigger twice, putting two 9mm rounds into his forehead. I stepped forward and caught his sagging body, lowering him to the ground with the greatest of care. I rolled him over onto his back and cut away his explosive germ-dispensing vest, carrying it and the canister several feet away.

A stagehand walked over to see what the noise was, but

I pulled the badge out of my back pocket and whispered, "Homeland Security. We're investigating some irregularities with gun permits at the church headquarters." I figured it was probably true for at least one church there, and this guy didn't look like he cared one way or the other. He just held up his hands and backed slowly away from the man with the gun and the corpse.

I pulled out my phone and pressed the speed dial for Flynn. "Did you find him?" she asked. "It's a nuthouse down here, but no sign of our guy."

"Yeah, I got him. I'm backstage in the main ballroom. We're going to need a way out of here that doesn't involve carrying several samples of the world's most infectious disease out the front door through thousands of Bible-thumpers, though."

"Don't worry about that, Master Quincy. I have that well in hand," Renfield said into the phone. He sounded like he was in a tunnel, so I figured Flynn had me on speaker.

"Fine, but get up here quick before I have to do too much explaining. I have a dead guy surrounded by a bunch of megalomaniac preachers. Leave me here too long and they'll try to resurrect his ass."

"We'll be there in ten," Flynn said, then hung up on me.

They made it in five, with a flatbed cart and a stack of black tablecloths to cover the body in, too. I loaded the metal canister and the vials of disease into a big road case, padded the vials with more tablecloths, and followed Flynn and Renny out through the service hallway. I left the empty road case on the sidewalk, and we loaded the dead psycho and his cargo into the Hummer.

"Where to now?" I asked as I slid into the passenger seat.

"Smith is still at Headquarters. We should meet up with him there and then try to figure out what the next seal is going to be."

"Oh, we already know that, Miss Flynn," Renfield chimed in.

"It's Detective, Ren. And what do you mean?"

"Well, the next Horseman, of course. We already know what he will be. The next Horseman is War."

"War?" I asked, more out of a sense of *Fuck, my days sucks* than *What did you say?*

"Yes, Master Quincy. The second Horseman rides a red horse, and he is typically thought to represent the aspect of War." Renfield pulled into the underground parking garage for Police Headquarters, ignoring the frantically waving uniform in his little guard hut.

We parked and Ren got out to talk to the agitated patrolman while I sat there for a second, trying to process.

"What's wrong?" Flynn asked from the back seat. "We stopped Pestilence, now we just need to stop War. Then we find Wally before these psychos get any further along the Apocalypse checklist, and we save the world. Come on, let's do this."

I still didn't move. I'd seen war up close and personal. Germany in 1917, then again in 1944. I had no desire to see what the physical embodiment of war looked like. *Suck it up, Q. You've lived through a lot of things you didn't like, so put on your big boy pants and go kick some ass.* I took a deep breath and opened the door.

"Let's go, Princess, we've got a war to stop." I got out of the Hummer and headed to the elevator, only to meet Smith coming out of it.

"Turn it around, kids, we've got our next target."

"Already?" I asked, reversing course for the SUV. "Can't we at least get the germ warfare out of the back seat before we go off into the war zone?"

Smith froze in his tracks. "You've got all that shit in the back of the car?" he asked, grabbing for his cell phone.

"I wouldn't call that baby tank a *car* necessarily," I said, waving at the Hummer, "but yeah. We couldn't exactly leave the dead guy in the ballroom with the anthrax, could we?"

"Are those douchebags from the CDC still fucking around in the break room? Well send them down to the garage. Tell them we've got a corpse and all their stolen germs for them to take back to Atlanta," Smith said into his phone. "No, I don't give a fuck what they do with the body. We did our job, we made it dead. They can make Soylent Green out of it for all I care. Now get them moving, we've got another situation to deal with."

Renfield walked back up from his conversation with the gate guard. "Everything all right?" I asked.

"Master Quincy, as you move along through this life you will come to understand that very few disagreements cannot be smoothed over with judicious application of twenty-dollar bills."

"You bribed a cop to let us park here?" I grinned at Ren.

"Of course not." He stiffened. "I would never do such a thing. I simply mentioned that both our superiors had a vested interest in the cargo of our vehicle, and that it might be in his best interest if he let me alert the interested parties to our presence. Then I borrowed his mobile phone, which, being the clumsy sod that I am, I dropped into a grate in the floor. Then I offered him a small token of my apology in the form of seven hundred dollars. He was so preoccupied with counting his money that he forgot all about calling his supervisor."

"Nicely done, Ren, if a little unnecessary. You are actually allowed to be here, so you could have saved your money," Smith said.

"Fear not, Agent Smith, I shall be turning in a receipt for reimbursement. My employer has not reached his current state of fiscal comfort by simply passing around cash at the drop of a hat."

"He's saying my uncle is a cheap bastard," I translated for Smith.

"I got that."

"And that you just bought that beat cop a new iPhone," I continued.

"I got that, too."

"Then what are we waiting for? I thought we had a war to stop? We should probably take your car. Mine's full of dead guy." Smith shook his head and led the way to a row of identical black Suburbans parked along the wall.

CHAPTER 10

I sat in the back with Ren, going over ammunition and weapons. I had six rounds left in my Ruger, plus two spare magazines. My Sig P226 MK25 was still holstered, with one in the pipe for 16 rounds in the pistol, plus two 15-round magazines in the holder under my opposite arm. I drew the pistol and checked the laser sight, making a bright red dot on the back of Flynn's seat.

"Don't point that thing at me, dickhead," she said without turning around.

"Oh quit your whining, the safety's on," I said, then checked to make sure I was right. It was going to take some getting used to, being around a woman who could see through my eyes if she tried hard enough. I holstered the Sig and checked my knives to make sure they were all accessible and sharp.

"You look like you're ready to take on a giant," Ren said.

"I don't know what we're getting into, but I have a feeling it won't be pretty," I replied.

"It won't. It seems that our friendly neighborhood Apocalypse cult has broken the second seal, and War is taking the form of a pissed-off motorcycle gang," Smith said from the front seat.

"Huh?" I asked.

"The local gang task force has been keeping an eye on the local Renegades MC for a while now, suspecting them of heading up a major meth distribution ring. Today they shot the surveillance detail and rode across town to burn down the clubhouse of a rival gang, the Devil's Rejects. None of the Rejects survived, but one of our surveillance team made it out of the initial attack. She said they all followed a tall man driving a red Mustang convertible."

"The red horse," I said.

"Slightly updated," Smith agreed.

"So where are they now?" Flynn asked from the passenger seat.

"They went back to their clubhouse where they sealed themselves in tight and commenced to shooting anyone who walked within fifty yards of the place. Which is a problem because there's a daycare right across the street."

"I assume it's been evacuated?" I asked.

"Can't. We tried to get a van in there, but the Renegades are better armed than we expected. They hit our van with an RPG. We lost four officers."

"So we have a bunch of psycho bikers with rocket launchers led by a mystical embodiment of the spirit of War, and if we don't stop them, they'll burn the city to the ground and usher in the end of the world, is that it?" I summed it up, as much for myself as anyone else.

"Yeah, that's pretty much got it in a nutshell," Smith agreed.

"Face impossible odds and save the world from certain destruction? Must be Tuesday," I sighed, leaning back and resting my head against the SUV's soft interior.

We pulled into a grocery store parking lot a couple football fields away from the clubhouse and got out of the Suburban. A uniform walked up to us and said, "I assume you're the government assholes the captain said would be coming."

"You got a problem, Officer?" Smith asked.

"My friend was in the van those fuckers blew up. So yeah, I got a problem with a bunch of feds coming in here and giving these bastards some kind of get out of jail free card just to get them to roll over on their supplier or whatever other bullshit you come up with."

I could see Smith take in a deep breath to unload on the kid, so I stepped forward. "You know what, Officer, you're right. Those sonsabitches shouldn't get away with this shit. And I'm here to make sure they don't. You see," I put my arm around his shoulder and walked him a little bit away from Smith and Flynn. "I'm not really *with* them. They're suits, they don't understand that sometimes you have to do bad things to bad people. And those guys," I pointed down the street at the clubhouse. "Are definitely bad people. I'm the guy that comes in to do the bad things. But we have to make the suits think all the shit we do is their idea, you know?" He nodded. "So how about you go give the asshat with the bad haircut enough of a half-assed apology to get his panties unbunched and take us inside that rolling command center where we can piss off your captain by taking over this little shit-show?"

"He's still a dick," the patrolman grumbled.

"Who, Crew-cut?" I jerked a thumb back at Smith. "Yeah, he's a total dick. But he's a dick with some authority, and that lets me get shit done."

"Whatever," the young cop said, shrugging off my arm. He turned and walked back to Smith, sticking out his hand before Smith could unload on him. "Sorry, man. Sean Nash, one of the officers killed in the van, was my training officer. He was like a big brother to me, so I'm a little on edge. I was out of line. It won't happen again."

"See that it doesn't," Smith said, and I all but heard him add the world "soldier" to the end of his sentence. *You could take the soldier out of the military, but you can't make him a spy,* I thought.

"Can we get started?" I asked. "Or do you guys actually need to whip 'em out?"

The patrolman led the way to the Mobile Command Center, and we went up the folding stairs into the high-tech RV. It was kinda like a tour bus, if you were looking to take over a small country instead of put on a rock show. One whole wall was taken up with monitors, all showing different scenes around the area, including one long-range infrared scan of the clubhouse that showed a *lot* of activity.

"Who's in charge here?" Smith asked.

A forty-ish woman with glasses and a black tactical uniform turned from the monitor she was studying. "I'm Lieutenant Ferguson. What can I do for you?"

"I'm Agent Smith, Homeland Security. I believe you got a call that we were coming?" Smith held out his hand.

Ferguson didn't take it. I admired her a little for leaving Smitty hanging. Showed serious stones. "I did, and I have to say I don't understand what jurisdiction Homeland has here. This is obviously a local law enforcement issue."

"Really? And the rocket-propelled grenades? You have a lot of those in the Charlotte metro area?" Smith asked, letting his hand drop. "This gang has obviously escalated their activities, stepped up their game so to speak. That means somebody's backing them. We want to know who."

I admired his facility for bullshit but was worried we were running short on time. "How long since you've seen any movement outside the club?" I asked a nearby tech. The skinny little guy was sitting there, his eyes glued to the monitor in front of him, trying very hard to be invisible while the people above his pay grade fought right by his shoulder.

He looked up at me and I gave him a "move it along" gesture with one hand. "It's been at least an hour since anyone's gone in or out," he said.

"We gotta get eyes in there," I said to Smith.

"What's your hurry?" Smith asked.

"The last guy was trying to infect thousands of people at one shot with a virus fierce enough to create a worldwide pandemic. I don't think the embodiment of War is going to be content with just blowing up a few local cops. Something bigger is going on here."

"Something that involves RPGs and a lot of guns," Flynn added.

"This would be a real bad time to tell me the President was scheduled to be in town today," I said.

"No, we've got no alerts like that," the lieutenant said. I heaved a sigh of relief, which quickly cut off as her eyes went wide.

"What is it?" Flynn asked.

"The First Lady is giving a speech at J.C. Smith tonight," Lieutenant Ferguson said. "We've provided some extra security, but the college was keeping her visit low-key. It's a speech to some big-time alumni and donors about HBCs."

"HBCs?" I asked.

"Historically Black Colleges," Ferguson explained. "I went to JCSU, I sometimes forget that not everybody knows all the code words."

"I studied abroad," I explained. "So I don't understand a lot about American college life."

"Yeah, he doesn't even understand March Madness," Flynn added.

"Well, Mrs. Obama will be speaking at a luncheon in about... two hours, so if you think she's the target—" I didn't hear the rest, on account of already being down the steel steps and on my way across the parking lot.

Where are you going? Flynn's voice came through my head.

Things to do, people to kill, I replied, keeping a tight lid on my thoughts.

You think you're going to just waltz in there and take out an entire motorcycle gang and one of the Four Horsemen all by yourself?

Well, I wasn't actually thinking waltz, more like a samba, or a quickstep. I pictured a heavy steel door closing and cut off the connection.

I walked back to the Suburban and Renfield. "Ren, were going at this the wrong way," I said.

"What do you mean, Master Quincy?" Renfield was screwing down a scope onto a Remington 700 rifle, getting ready to back me up, I supposed.

"We're reacting, but we need to get ahead of these fuckers. We can't keep chasing the puppets, we've got to get to the puppeteer."

"I understand the metaphor, but not exactly the plan," Renfield said.

"I need you and Flynn to find Wally. He's the key to this whole thing. If we can't get him away from the bastards that nabbed him, we have zero chance of stopping this shit."

"There is a certain logic to that, Master Quincy," Renfield agreed.

"Glad you approve," I said with a barely-restrained eye roll. It was easy for Renfield to forget that despite his fifty years of age, he wasn't really the two decades older than me he looked, but more like less than half my age. "So go back to the source and figure out where they would have taken Wally." *Flynn, meet me and Ren out by the car. Tell Smitty to stay there.*

On my way.

"And what would be the source in this situation, Master

Quincy?"

"Pretty sure that's going to be Revelation, Ren. There's gotta be something in there that's symbolic. Think like a psychopath that wants to end the world and figure out where he's taken Wally to open the Seven Seals." I kept my connection to Flynn open, so everything I said to Renfield, she got simultaneously.

"And what shall we do when we locate our missing Lion?" Ren asked.

"Then we call in the big guns," Flynn said, walking quickly up to the Suburban. "What will you be doing while we're playing Giles and Willow in the library?"

"I'll be putting on my blonde wig and doing what I do best, kicking ass," I said, turning back to the Command Center as Ren and Flynn got into the SUV and pulled out of the parking lot. I met Smith walking in my direction halfway there. "Good, I didn't want to have this conversation in there." I jerked my head toward the van.

"What's up?" Smith asked.

"Somebody in there is in on this whole mess. I don't know who, but someone is tipping the bikers off to police movements."

"How do you know?" Smith asked.

"It's the only answer. How else did they know the van pulling up outside the daycare was full of cops? The video was rolling while you were pissing on fire hydrants with Lieutenant Ferguson and there were no markings on the van. Also, no hesitation on the bikers' part. They didn't wait five seconds from the time the van pulled up outside the daycare before they opened the door and blew those cops to pieces."

"Sounds suspicious," Smith agreed.

"And something smelled wrong," I added. "You know that stinky fear-sweat that people get when they're guilty of something? That smell was all over that Command Center like the smell of Axe body spray in a frat house."

"What are you, a werewolf now?" Smith asked with a half smile.

"That's not funny." I scowled at him. "Don't ever joke about that. Werewolves are gross, man." Then I let a grin slip through to let him know I was joking. Kinda. Werewolves *are* gross.

"So what's the play? If we can't count on the police for backup, I don't know if the two of us can get in there on our own."

"Well whatever we do, we have to do it now. If the First Lady is going to be going on in less than two hours, my bet is that's the attack," I said.

"Still doesn't tell me the plan," Smith pointed out.

"I don't have much of one right now, but I'll figure it out between here and there," I said, pointing to the clubhouse.

"So your plan is you're going to walk down the sidewalk, kick down the door and shoot everybody? That's fucking insane," Smith said.

"It's also not my plan," I corrected. "I'm only going to kick the door down if it's locked, and I won't shoot anybody that doesn't try to kill me. Sound better?" I asked.

"Much," Smith said. "I'm going to go back in here and make sure that nobody accidentally shoots a missile up your ass."

"Thanks," I said. "I'm going to go knock on the door and try to kill my second Horseman. This keeps up, I'm totally getting a codename."

CHAPTER 11

It was a long couple of blocks to the clubhouse, and it felt like there were eyeballs on me the entire time. Probably because there were. I knew the cameras from the Command Center were aimed my way, and even before I got reasonably close I could see the glint of a rifle on the roof of the biker's hangout. I focused my will and muttered *"inflecto"* under my breath, pushing my energy toward the barrel of the gun. I couldn't tell if it did enough damage to the barrel to make it misfire and blow up in the sniper's face, or just bent it enough to miss. That's the trouble with magic at a distance, you can't really tell when the subtle things work. You can almost always tell when things go wrong, but you don't often get a second chance.

I was about twenty yards away from the front door when I saw a flash from the roof and heard a muffled scream. *I guess I broke it. Well, that's one I don't have to kill inside,* I thought as I continued to the front of the building.

"That's far enough," came a booming voice from inside.

I focused myself for a second and said, *"amplifico."* "I just want to talk," I lied. My spell made it so that anyone within fifty yards heard me just as clear as if I held a megaphone.

"I got nothing to say, now fuck off!" the voice replied.

By then I was at the building, but I stopped behind a solid section of cinderblock. There are plenty of handguns and assault rifles that can punch through block walls, but almost everything can punch through a window or a door, even a steel one. I decided to pause where I had a little better cover and armor up. I took a pair of titanium knuckle dusters from my back jeans pocket and focused my will on the metal. I poured my energy into the knucks, muttered, *"imitantes,"* and felt the texture of my skin begin to change. To say it was painful would be an understatement, kinda like saying Hitler was a bit of an Anti-Semite or that Mount Everest had a little snow on top. I bit back a scream as my skin tightened and became solid, shedding all the moisture and dead cells and turning into a gleaming sheath of flexible titanium. Have you ever wondered what like would be like if your scrotum ever became made of metal? Me neither, but it hurts like a motherfucker. All of a sudden your family jewels are rattling around inside a completely non-permeable tin can, and that is not a comfortable feeling.

With my new bulletproof skin on, I finished my long walk to the front door and knocked gently. Yeah, what the fuck ever, I kicked the fucking door in like the steel-plated badass I suddenly was. The door flew off the hinges and crashed to the floor several feet from the frame, taking two bikers to the ground with it.

"Avon calling, motherfuckers," I said as I drew my Sig and swept the room. It was crammed with bikers, all suddenly gone still at my apparently unexpected entry. The bartender brought his sawed-off shotgun above the level of the bar and swung in my direction, but I put two in his chest and he went down, shotgun clattering to the concrete beside him. One of the bikers shoved the door off himself and jumped up to run at me, but I put two in his forehead within half a second of his hand touching the butt of his gun.

"I'm not a cop, bitches. I don't have rules of engagement. As far as I'm concerned, every fucking one of you is already guilty, and I'm just here to execute. Now where the motherfucker called War?"

"I prefer Ares, Tin Man." I turned to see a giant leaning

against a pool table. He was all of seven feet tall and well over three hundred pounds, with a shaved head and goatee. Tattoos sleeved both arms and peeked out of the collar of his black t-shirt. He wore engineer boots, a black leather vest, dirty jeans and I could see a chain dangling from one belt loop back to his wallet. In other words, he looked like every shaven-headed biker I'd ever seen, only super-sized. He had a sword in one hand and a pistol in the other. He laid the pistol on the pool table and lifted the sword over his head, charging at me like some kind of white trash William Wallace or something.

I stepped to the side and emptied my Sig into his side and back as he passed. He stumbled, but didn't fall, and I watched as the wounds sealed and the bullets popped out, eleven in all *plinking* to the floor in quick succession. *Fuck. Well, that's going to make things a little more difficult.*

He spun around and charged me again, this time with his sword out to the side for a lateral cut. I picked up a round table and used it for a shield, dropping my shoulder into Ares' midsection. He slammed into me like a freight train, but I had myself balanced and my back leg braced, so I didn't budge. He didn't budge much either, just bounced off me with a *whoof!*

He laid into me with his sword, each blow taking huge chunks out of my improvised shield. I tried to strike back with the base of the table, but kept needing to bring it around to block. *Wait a goddamn minute*, I thought, *I'm made of fucking* metal. After his next strike, I dropped the table and landed a solid uppercut right to his chin. Ares wobbled a little, then shook his head as if to clear it, and came back with another sword cut for my head. I threw a titanium arm up and quickly realized why that was a bad idea. My skin was hardened, but the bones under it were not, and every bit of the force of the blow transferred. I felt both bones in my left arm snap, and I dropped to my knees with a scream.

"How'd you like that, Tin Man?" Ares asked.

I knelt on the floor, my left wrist in my right hand. I pulled hard on my wrist, feeling the bones of my arm slide across each other then *snap* into place. I fell forward, my forehead pressed to the floor as stars danced in my field of vision. But the arm was set and I could feel the bones begin to knit back together. In a couple of days, that arm would be good as new. I could only hope the same would be true about the rest of me.

Ares reached down and grabbed a fistful of my metallic hair, yanking me up onto my knees again. "You thought you could waltz in here with your puny little magic and fight me? I am the god of War, you ignorant mortal puke!"

"And I'm the prince of cheating, you arrogant douchebag," I said I reached over my head and poked him in the eye. He dropped my hair with a roar, and I spun around on my ass and head butted the god of War right in the balls. Time seemed to slow around me as his eyes went wide and his face bled to white, then shifted to red, then finally to purple. His sword fell from his hands and clattered to the floor, followed by the giant Horseman himself.

He dropped to his knees right in front of me, and I stood up. I reached down to him, grabbed his chin and turned it up to face me, then released his face and smashed my metallic fist into his nose, spraying blood and snot all over the floor. Ares spun on his knees, pushing himself up onto his feet and giving me a shove to create some distance. He swung wildly a few times, but it was obvious he couldn't see what he was swinging at.

I ducked his punches with ease, peppering his face and nose with stinging jabs. I kept the blood flowing from his nose and the tears flowing from his eyes while I slowly regained some use of my left arm. I couldn't make a fist, but at least I could stretch the arm out for balance, so I was less likely to topple over randomly. After half a minute of this, Ares let out a bellow and just charged me, lowering his head for a bullrush. I sidestepped him and stuck out one foot, sending the huge man sprawling through tables and chairs. He fetched up against the base of a pool table, and I almost went sprawling when I stepped on something hard and round. I looked down to find the hilt of Ares' sword under my foot.

I picked it up and felt the big claymore humming with power, obviously the focal instrument of the Horseman's magic. I felt the magic of the sword warring with my own powers, but I'd spent decades handling unruly magical toys and wrestled the sword under control in a matter of seconds.

"Put that down, Tin Man. Humans aren't meant to wield that kind of power," Ares said, circling around me slowly. I pivoted, keeping the sword between me and the temporary god of War, but this exposed my back to the rest of the bikers.

"Tell your boys that the first one to get within six feet of me gets a sword in his gut," I said.

I heard the whisper of something cutting through the air and dropped to one knee as I spun. The claymore was sharp enough to cut through flesh and bone with no trouble, and it cut one biker off at the thighs before he got close enough to hit me with the tire iron he was swinging. I didn't have time to decide whether or not the tire iron would have actually done anything to my metal head when I felt the floor vibrate with Ares' charge.

"Some guys never learn," I muttered under my breath as I straightened my legs and leapt straight up. I transferred the sword to my left hand, barely managing to hold onto the heavy blade with my busted arm as I gripped one of the building's bar joists with my right.

I looked down at Ares, tangled once again in a pile of furniture, and swung myself over to land on a pool table. "Anybody who doesn't want to die should leave right now," I announced. "This dickhead cares even less for your wellbeing than I do, if that's possible, and the cops outside want vengeance for their dead buddies. If you walk out the front door right now with your hands up, you'll probably not get shot."

One of the bikers, an older guy with a long gray beard stepped forward. "And what if we decide to throw in with Ares here and kill you?"

"Well, for one thing, I'm a lot harder to kill that it looks. And for another," I spun to my left and threw a knife, splitting the old biker's Adam's apple. He dropped like a stone, dead before he hit the ground. "I think I said it was time to go if you don't want to get dead. Clock's ticking, bitches." I didn't expect more than one or two to take me up on my offer to leave, but I certainly didn't expect the whole bunch to come at me all at once. Then I saw Ares, his eyes glowing red as he leaned against the bar and grinned.

"Have fun, boys, but be careful of the sword. It's sharp," Ares called over the sound of a dozen bikers drawing knives and brass knuckles and charging me. I leapt from one pool table to another, taking a bald head off at the shoulders as I jumped. *One down.* I hopped over a pool cue swung at my ankles and threw myself flat to the table as another one stabbed where he expected me to be. I wasn't there, and Ares' sword slid between his ribs like his lungs were butter. He collapsed, taking the sword to the floor with him, and I rolled off the other side of the table onto the floor. I felt a hammer blow to my shoulder and looked down, but there was just a small ding in my armored skin. A stunned biker stood ten feet away, holding a smoking 9mm and staring at me.

"Yeah, that's my skin, jackass," I said as I stepped over to him and buried one of my remaining knives in his gut. I angled the blade upward to pierce his heart, then spun around, using his body as a shield until I could get my back to a wall. Then I shoved the dead biker away from me and drew my Sig. I fired three rounds, and three bikers dropped. Then my head snapped back as a bullet ricocheted off my forehead, slamming the back of my head into the wall. I sagged to the floor and looked around for the shooter. I spotted him standing twenty feet away with a smoking pistol in his hand. I sighted down the barrel of the Sig but couldn't decide which one of the guys I should shoot, so I fired four times, two rounds for each of him. The guy on the left was the real one, and he dropped. I had a moment to shake my head and try to clear my vision, but it wasn't happening.

I struggled to my feet, one arm broken and throbbing, concussed and seeing double, but still titanium-skinned and getting more pissed off by the moment. Four more bikers advanced on me from the left and I lifted my left hand with a wince and shouted, "*Incendere!*"

A ball of fire the size of my fist flew from my fingertips, growing in size as the air in the bar and my rage fueled it. I continued to pour my will into the fireball until it was the size of a beach ball, then released my control of it as it hit the nearest biker square in the chest. Flames exploded from him, dousing all four thugs in a bath of flaming death and pain. They went down, rolling around like we were all taught in kindergarten. Problem is, magical fire is harder to extinguish than phosphorous. It'll burn until its target is destroyed, or I tell it to stop. And I didn't want it to stop. One biker managed to keep his feet, and he was running around like a chicken with its head cut off, spreading the fire to all corners of the bar. After a solid two minutes of running around screaming, he collapsed in a corner under a Confederate flag and died. I knelt to the floor in the smoke and confusion and etched some symbols on the floor with a knife from my belt.

The fires didn't die with the bikers, who were all gone within a minute except the one running around panicked. The fire spread to the pool tables, the bar tables, the walls, the bar itself, and before long the room was engulfed in flames. I concentrated as best I could and muttered *"purgo."* A sphere of clean air formed around my face, and I looked for Ares. He was still leaning against the bar with his arms crossed, watching me.

He pushed off the bar and walked toward me slowly. "I liked this bar. The body I inhabited caused a lot of mayhem in this bar, and I was going to use those idiots to cause even more. Now I'll just have to do it by myself. That's not as much fun. You'll have to die, of course. Not only are you fucking with my plans, but you killed all my toys. Can't have that. Say goodnight, now, wizard."

"Goodnight, fuckwit," I said, then poured my energy into the circle I'd carved into the floor. The binding circle sprang to life, trapping Ares in the center of my magical energy, which I had, in turn, tied to the earth beneath the building. There are a couple of pretty major fault lines running under Charlotte, and fault lines mean ley lines. I tapped into the magical river of power that was Charlotte's main line, and linked the spell to it. As long as the city wasn't wiped from the Earth, that circle wasn't going anywhere.

I watched Ares pound on the walls of his invisible prison for a few more seconds before I realized that I only had enough energy to keep my spells active for a few more seconds. The circle would hold forever now that it was tied to the ley lines, but my titanium skin and clean air were both about to run out. Neither of those were anything I was interested in happening while I was in a burning building.

"Gotta run, Ares. You have fun in there. Maybe, learn a trade, or a foreign language," I said, backing away toward the door. Trapped or no, I wasn't turning my back on one of the Four Horsemen of the goddamn Apocalypse. I felt the doorknob hit me in the ass, literally, and I flung the door open just as the liquor bottles behind the bar started to explode.

I got halfway across the parking lot and let my air bubble down. The smoke was still a nuisance out here, but the air was breathable. I took a few more steps and reversed the spell turning my skin to metal. Then there was a huge explosion from behind me, and the world went black.

CHAPTER 12

I woke up staring into Agent Smith's gray eyes and his grayer crew cut. "If I'm dreaming, kill me. Because you're the ugliest fucking Florence Nightingale I've ever seen."

Smith leaned back onto his heels. He was kneeling beside my head on the floor of the Mobile Command Center. "He's alive. I told you he was hard to kill." There was a strange look on Smith's face, one of the corners of his mouth was bent upward and a few of his teeth were showing. It looked involuntary, and a little bit painful. Then I realized it.

"You're smiling!" I said. "I didn't know you knew how."

"Fuck you, Harker," he said, his normal scowl returning.

"That's my Smitty," I said, heaving myself up to a sitting position. Three Smiths swum in front of me for half a second, then they snapped into focus. "Fuck, that hurt."

"What part?" Smith asked.

"The broken arm was a bitch, and the concussion sucked, but I wasn't expecting to get blown up," I replied. "So that part was pretty much no fun."

"Yeah, apparently there was a van load of fertilizer bomb behind the bar, which caught fire and blew the whole building to hell. You were under most of a wall for an hour. We figure the plan was to take his band of merry men over to the Johnson C. Smith campus where the First Lady was speaking and blow themselves up, Al Qaeda style," Smith said.

"Shifting all the attention to the Middle East, who we're already inclined to shoot at..." I said.

"Yeah, and you kill the President's wife and kids with a Quran anywhere on your person and we'll have a shooting war within the hour," Smith finished.

"Pretty good plan, frankly. It's exactly the kind of attack a terror cell would try on U.S. soil, and exactly the kind of ruse that would work. Where's Ares?" I asked.

"He's still standing out there, pissed off and stuck in that magic circle you left him in. We tried to secure him, but couldn't break the lines." Smith looked grumpy at that.

"Don't even think of recruiting that asshole. He's the embodiment of War, he lives for nothing but combat. You stick him in one peaceful little village and you'll have civil war in three hours and a nuclear incident in six."

"Sounds like my kind of guy." The corner of Smith's mouth twitched again, and I looked away. Watching that guy try to crack a joke was more painful than my last confession, which took seven hours and made three priests retire.

"Where's the sword?" I asked.

"Still laying where we found you. I wouldn't let anyone touch it."

"Good call," I said. "It does funny things to humans."

"You're human, Harker," Smith said, and I looked at him with one corner of my own mouth twitching.

"Mostly. Today's a good day to be a little something different, though." I got to my feet, checking the various hurt parts, and decided nothing was permanently damaged. My concussion was gone except for a splitting headache, and my left arm was back to at least half strength. I was covered in bruises from having a building fall on me, but I learned how to ignore bruises a long time ago, so I did. I opened the door and walked down the metal steps, looking around. The Command Center was in the middle of the street right outside where the biker bar had been. Debris was scattered everywhere, like a bomb had gone off or a building exploded. Which it had, so I figured it made sense.

The only thing still standing from the bar was a pissed-off god of War, still locked into my circle. He was a clear spot in a football-field sized blast zone littered with body parts, bricks, shattered pool tables, motorcycle pieces, and glass.

I walked over to a pile a cinderblocks and pulled Ares' sword out of the rubble. It still thrummed with power, and I felt it reaching out to me. I allowed the power to touch me, to explore who I was and what I was. I felt the power draw back at the part of me that came from Uncle Luke, and embrace the rage that ran through my human side, all the feelings of rage and loss that came from more than a century of living. I felt the magical essence of War search through my soul, and eventually decide that I was lacking. I wasn't the avatar War wanted.

"Good," I said quietly. Didn't need the local constabulary to see me talking to a sword, even a magical one. Maybe especially a magical one. "Now that we've got that settled, I need you to do something."

I walked up to the shimmering circle and stood facing Ares. "What's your name?"

"I told you, pitiful human, my name is Ares, and I am the god of War!" The giant in the circle roared, then beat on my metaphysical boundary with both fists. I felt the barrier give a little, then felt it snap back to full strength. *Shit. He's stronger than I thought.* I didn't anticipate him being able to do anything to that circle, especially not once it was tied into the city's ley lines.

"I mean what was your name before War manifested in you?" I pushed at him a little with my will, just enough for him to know I could probably pull it out of him, but that wouldn't be comfortable for either of us.

"Josh. Josh Monroe," he said, looking at me through narrowed eyes.

"Josh Monroe, I'm sorry for this. You got caught up in forces you couldn't possibly understand. Most humans can't. You became a pawn in a bigger game, and your side lost. So I'm sorry." With that I reached out with a toe and broke the circle. The second my aura touched the circle I'd cast, all the energy I poured into the circle rushed back into me, and all the energy I'd trapped from the city's main ley line poured back into the line, triggering a small earthquake. Most people wouldn't feel it, but I was at the epicenter of the quake, so it rocked me and Ares a lot harder. I knew it was coming, so I recovered my balance faster, and before Ares had a chance to gather his wits, I plunged his sword into his chest, shoving the six-foot blade through to the hilt. His eyes went wide and he looked down at the sword sticking out between his ribs.

Ares opened his mouth, but no sound came out. He just let out a small wheeze, and blood poured from his mouth as the light left his eyes. I watched as the god of War dropped to his knees and fell sideways, taking the sword from my grasp as he did. I turned around and motioned for a couple of the cops to come forward.

"Pack his body up and get it back to police headquarters. Take the sword in a separate car. Put it in a rifle case, or something, but whatever you do, *don't touch it* with your bare hands. There's a biological contaminant on the metal connected with the attack we foiled this morning. Do you understand?" They nodded, and I walked back to where Smith stood outside the Mobile Command Center.

"Let's roll. By my figuring, we've got one more Horseman to stop before we have to deal with Death himself."

"Actually, Flynn just called. They took out Famine at the North Mecklenburg Water Treatment Facility. He was going to poison the water supply for half the county."

"Nice. How did they figure it out?"

"I asked, she said something about being a detective and leaving that kind of work to her. She sounded a little smug."

"If she took out a Horseman with nothing but her wits and Renfield, then she's got plenty to feel smug about," I said. *Flynn? I sent down our link.*

Her mind came back weakly, as if she was a long way from me. *Yeah? I'm having trouble connecting. I'm on 77 heading back into town. Where are you?*

At the biker joint. Just meet us at headquarters.

Will do. You okay? You sound funny, if that makes sense.

It does. I got my egg scrambled a little, makes it hard to concentrate. I'll see you in a bit. And Flynn?

Yeah?

Nice work. Not many humans could take out a Horseman on their own.

I wasn't on my own. Renfield was with me. He's pretty impressive for a butler.

Don't let him hear you call him that. I chuckled and cut off our connection.

"She okay?" Smith asked.

"How could you tell?" I asked.

"You both get kind of a dazed look on your face when you're talking in your head. It's pretty easy to figure out after a while."

"Fair enough. But what won't be easy to figure out is where is Death going to manifest. Let's get back to HQ. I need a big map."

CHAPTER 13

I had a huge map of Charlotte tacked to the wall of the conference room and was scribbling on it with magic markers when Flynn and Renfield walked in.

"Is it Arts & Crafts time, Harker?" Flynn asked. "Because I have this awesome elbow macaroni and yarn necklace I've been dying to make."

"I'm trying to figure out where Death will manifest," I said, circling one last point on my map.

"What do you have so far?" she asked, stepping in to look at the map.

"A whole lot of fuck-all," I replied. "The last three Horsemen popped up in different places, attempted to attack more different places, and there's no pattern to any of it." I pointed to the map. I'd put pushpins in where the Horsemen appeared and attacked, or tried to. It all looked random.

"What are all these pins?" Flynn asked.

"Known supernatural actives in Charlotte. Green pins for friendly, red pins for hostile, and blue pins for the ones that just want to be left alone, like the ghost of Queen Charlotte."

"The ghost of Queen Charlotte is here?" Flynn asked.

"Part-time. Poor girl gets bounced around between Charlotte and Kew Palace just outside London. She doesn't really do anything, just hangs out wherever there are statues to her."

"Oooh, so she's stuck at the airport?" Flynn asked. "That doesn't seem very restful."

"It's not. And she doesn't know why she can't move on. Might have something to do with her jewels not being laid to rest with her, but I haven't really cared enough to go look for them," I replied.

"That's awful, Harker. You should help her," Flynn said.

"No profit in it," I said. "And since she's not hurting anybody, I figure let her haunt the airport, and the palace, and Queen Square in Blumbury until she figures out how to move on or she goes apeshit and becomes a problem. For now, there are enough red pins in my map to keep me busy for the rest of even my life."

"Good point. There seem to be a lot of things in town that don't like you," Flynn pointed out.

"Those aren't the ones that don't like *me*. That list is way longer. These are creatures or magic-users that don't like anybody, and will kill humans on sight."

"Oh."

"Yeah, so any bright ideas?" I waved at the map.

"Have you tried to cast a spell?" she asked.

"A spell to do what?"

"Find Wally. Isn't he still the point of all this? If we find him before he breaks the fourth seal, won't it all be over?"

Fuck, she's right, I thought as I swept all the notes and crap off the conference table. "Renfield, bring me Wally's overnight bag from his apartment."

"What are you going to do with that?" Smith asked.

"Well, since you two went off the reservation and killed the third Horseman instead of finding Wally, I'm going to have to break out more mojo. Watch and see," I said, putting on my inscrutable face.

Renfield hurried back in a few minutes later with a blue and white duffle with ASICs on the side and put it on the table. I started digging around in the bag, then just turned it upside down and dumped everything out onto the table. T-shirts, crumpled jeans, socks and underwear all spilled across the table. I swept all the clothes onto the floor. I opened his toiletries bag and spilled a razor, deodorant and a couple different tubes of toothpaste out. I turned the little bag inside out, then tossed it aside. I grabbed the duffel and opened the side pocket, reaching all the way down into the corners.

"Gotcha!" I said, pulling my hand out with a plain wooden box about two inches by four inches. I flipped a tiny latch on one side and the top slid open, revealing a fake cigarette. "I knew that little bastard wouldn't go anywhere without his favorite one-hitter."

"What are you going to do with that?" Smith asked.

"The same kind of sympathetic magic I cast using his blood back at the apartment. Because this is something he carried with him a lot, it will have a lot of his energy soaked into it. It's even better because it's wooden. Natural materials absorb energy better than metal or plastics. Hopefully I can get a rudimentary tracking spell off this thing. If I cast it right, maybe I can make it light up and gimme a puff whenever we're going in the right direction."

Nobody laughed. *Tough room. One little apocalypse and they get all serious on you.* I closed my eyes, focused my will on the little pipe and murmured *"Corpus ad corpus, sanguinem sanguini. Corpus ad corpus, sanguinem sanguini. Corpus ad corpus, sanguinem sanguini."* With the third incantation, I felt a tug along my magical senses pulling me off to the left. I opened my eyes and saw Flynn staring at me, her eyes wide.

"What the fuck was that?" she asked.

"You felt that, huh?" I wasn't surprised. Our bond was unusually strong, and with me throwing magic around this close to her, if she had any sensitivity at all, she was bound to feel it.

"Yeah, like something wants us to go east," she said.

"That's the tracking spell. The pipe wants to go to its owner now."

"Why didn't I feel anything when you cast the spell in the apartment?" she asked.

"I don't know for sure, but it might have something to do with the newness of the bond, or the weakness of your body. You were just recently brought back from the dead, you know."

"I wasn't that bad," Flynn scoffed. I just looked at her, one eyebrow in the air. "Was I?" she asked. I still didn't say anything. Exactly how close she was to dead was not something I wanted to discuss in a building full of mundane cops. I wasn't sure I ever wanted to discuss it, but I figured I probably wasn't going to be given a choice.

"Well, now that the spell works, let's get after this kid," Smith said. "I want four units rolling with us. Two snipers, a full insertion team—"

"No," I said. "Just us."

"What the fuck, Harker? You think you're still a solo operator? You're a goddamn government agent now, and you have the full weight and power of the United States Government behind you. You don't have to do this lone wolf bullshit anymore," Smith growled in my face.

"It's not so much lone wolf bullshit, Smitty, as it is a desire to limit the body count. How many men did you lose going after Ares?"

"Six in the botched vac of the daycare, a couple more across the op. I'd say we lost nine altogether."

"How about we handle this next one my way and we don't lose anybody?" I crossed my arms over my chest and waited.

"What's your way?" Smith asked, crossing his own arms.

I thought about making some crack about whipping them out and measuring but did the uncharacteristic thing and kept my smartass comment to myself. "Flynn drives and waits outside with your team of heavies. You, me, and Renfield go in quiet, see if we can get to the kid before the fourth seal is broken. If we can get to him, we kill the bad guys, get Wally out, and it's all sunbeams and unicorns."

"If we can't?" Smith asked.

"Then Flynn comes in with the heavies and avenges us."

"Whoa," Flynn said. "Avenge?"

"There's only two ways this thing goes down, Becks, and that's with all the bad guys dead, or everybody dead. Sorry, but them's just the facts of it."

"I told you, don't call me—"

Fuck. I saw her eyes go wide just before she finished the sentence. She was about to say, "Don't call me Becks, only my father called me Becks," and I knew it. So my mind unconsciously went back to that night in the alley and looking in her father's eyes as the last light went out of them, and right there, tied to me with a bond tighter than blood or love, was Detective Rebecca Gail Flynn. I felt all her pain come rushing up through the years in one half-second. All the milestones missed, all the father-daughter dances that never happened, all the prom dates her cop dad never scared the shit out of, all the graduations missed—high school, college, Police Academy. I felt all that loss pour through our connection as she saw through my eyes the last moments of the father she'd idolized.

She looked up at me, eyes suddenly full of tears and recriminations, and I felt the door in my mind slam shut, cutting off our connection like a light switch. "We need to talk," Flynn said.

"Not now," I replied.

"No, not now. But you better not get dead, motherfucker, because you have some serious explaining to do."

"I'll try to survive. You know, for your sake." I turned back to Smith. "Sound like a plan?"

"What the fuck just happened?" the agent asked. I looked over at Renfield, who gave me the tiniest shake of his head. He was right, Smith didn't need to know anything about Paul Flynn's death and my promise to him.

"Remember that connection you made me forge to Flynn's soul?" I asked. Smith nodded. "We just had a whole argument, without ever having to yell at one another. It's not really satisfying, but it's better for the crockery. Now, the plan?"

"It's fine, but why is he coming with us instead of Flynn?" Smith pointed at Renfield. "I don't like involving civilians in my operations."

"And ordinarily I would applaud that effort and go home straightway, but this endeavor requires certain skills which I possess that I daresay would escape most, if not all, of your men," said the dapper little manservant.

"He means he can pick any lock ever made and move like smoke," I said.

"I do have certain skills in that regard." Ren tipped an imaginary hat.

"So whattaya say, Smitty? We rollin' or not?"

"Might as well try it your way, since it worked so fucking swimmingly with Ares," Smith said, then turned and started walking to the front door, where Ren had left the Hummer parked. We climbed in, Flynn behind the wheel, and headed down Elizabeth toward Kings. Following the marijuana-beacon, we turned left on Central and followed it down past Eastway toward Albemarle. The beacon started shifting right after we crossed Eastway, and pulled hard right onto Norland. I motioned for Flynn to park in a school parking lot, and we got out.

"Of course," I said, staring across the street at the cemetery. "If you're going to raise Death, why not start with a bunch of dead people?"

CHAPTER 14

The cemetery was pristine, with rolling hills of freshly-mown grass and not a soul in sight. There was a green tent still standing from a recent interment, but all the holes were filled and all the heavy equipment was gone. Fresh flowers dotted some of the nearest graves, and a few tiny plastic flags fluttered in the light breeze. I didn't really need the one-hitter in my pocket pulling me toward the small chapel in the center of the graveyard; the fact that the only two cars that weren't government-issued in the entire place were parked outside of it was clue enough.

Smith and I walked side-by-side to the front of the building, with Renfield hanging back a little and keeping an eye open for trouble coming up behind. I saw the goon standing by the door before he saw us, and I drew my pistol, keeping it down by my leg and dropping a step behind Smith as we approached.

The goon saw us and stepped forward, holding up a silver shield. "Sorry, folks, this is an active crime scene. You can't go in there."

We were still a good ten yards away, so I pretended not to hear him. "What was that, Officer?" I yelled, putting one hand up to my ear.

The goon took a few more steps forward and we closed to about fifteen feet before he repeated, "You can't be here right now, there's been a murder. You'll have to come back later."

"A murder?" I asked, then raised my gun and shot him in the left eye. He dropped like a stone, the back of his head turning to a mess that resembled nothing more than a raspberry cobbler.

Smith stopped in his tracks and spun to face me. "What the

actual fuck was that about, Harker? That was a human, not a monster! You can't just go around shooting people for no reason!"

I didn't stop walking. "No reason, Smitty? He's helping to open the *seven fucking seals*. I think that takes him right off the Dalai Lama's Christmas card list." I was at the door and tried the handle. It was every bit as locked as I expected it to be. "Renfield, take care of this before I blow it up." I gestured at the door.

"I don't believe the Dalai Lama sends Christmas cards," the slight man said as he knelt before the chapel doors.

"That explains why I've never gotten one. And here I thought he didn't like vampires. I feel better now. Thank you, Ren."

"Happy to help, sir." He pulled a small leather case out of his pocket and slid a couple of thin metal rods out of it. He manipulated the rods within the lock for a few seconds before I heard a tiny *click* and the cylinder rotated. Renfield stood up, put away his tools, and motioned at the door. "After you, sir."

I turned to see Smith standing on the bottom step fuming. "You wanna bitch at me some more or you wanna go save the world?"

"I'm thinking," he growled.

"Well, you think about it, and I'm going to go in here and see what else needs killing."

"Master Harker?" Renfield tapped me on the shoulder.

"Yeah, Ren?"

"There seems to be a certain odor emanating from the building."

"Yeah, you'll have that where they bury lots of people, Ren." Then I smelled it. "Shit," I said under my breath.

"No, Master Harker, I don't believe that's the smell," Renfield said.

"Stay here, Ren. No matter what, you stay here," I said and

turned to the door. Then I thought for half a second and turned back. "Scratch that. If it all goes to shit, you get Detective Flynn out of here. It won't do any good long-term, but it might give her a few extra hours."

"I don't think I understand, sir."

"Yeah, and I'm sorry about that, Ren, but I don't have time to explain. And we won't be going in stealthy anymore, so you should stay up here where it's safer. Smith, come with me. We've got a lot of bad things to kill."

"I don't think I can trust your judgment on what needs killing, Harker. That man back there—"

"That man allied himself with creatures that are working on opening a portal to Hell right under this church, right fucking now. So that put him on the 'Bad Guys' list. And I don't believe in rehabilitation, Smith. I see big nasties, I put them down. And there's some serious big nasty going on here today, I can smell the brimstone all the way up here. So can we please haul ass before they break the fourth seal and unleash Hell on Earth?"

I pushed through the door and went into the chapel without looking to see if Smith was following me. I opened up my Sight as I crossed the threshold and almost went mind-blind with the force of the magic hammering against me. The inside of the little church looked about like those places do, with half a dozen rows of pews split by two aisles leading to a small pulpit with a clear space in front for a casket. There was an electric organ off to the right of the pulpit, and a font of holy water off to the left. Light from a dozen or more stained glass windows depicting events in the life of Christ sent a crazy-quilt of colors dancing around the room, and a rose window in the small choir loft shone white light through a huge dove onto the communion table down front.

And laid out on the communion table was a man I assumed

was the priest. At least that was my guess based on the robes. I couldn't have identified him by anything more than his teeth or DNA because his face was missing. So were his hands and a fair amount of the flesh from his torso. His organs were laid out on the table in front of him, like some kind of twisted sacrament, and a goblet full of a thick red liquid sat beside his head.

The body glowed red to my Sight, and the smell of brimstone became so thick I could almost taste it as I drew near. I holstered my gun and knelt by the body. Something gold glittered from within his abdominal cavity, and I looked closer. I took a deep breath and reached into the priest's body, wrapping my hand around the object and pulling it free with a squelching sound. I reached down and used his robes to wipe the crucifix free, then wiped my hands. I set the crucifix on the table by his head and stepped over to the font. I dipped my hand into the holy water and leaned over the priest's body. I dabbed a little holy water on his forehead and closed my eyes.

"*Per istam sanctan unctionem et suam piissimam misericordiam, indulgeat tibi Dominus quidquid,*" I whispered.

"You know it's supposed to be olive oil, right?" Glory's voice came from behind me as I knelt by the body.

"Yeah, and it's supposed to happen before he's dead, too. But I figured it couldn't hurt."

"And you're not opposed to covering your fists in holy water before you try to find the steps down to wherever the ritual is taking place, either."

"That thought had crossed my mind." I turned and looked at Glory. She was wearing Smith's body, and it was really disconcerting to hear the angel's voice coming from Smith's grizzled face. "Glory, I need you to do something for me."

"I'll try."

"If this all goes to shit, get Flynn out of here. Get her to her mother's, or church, or somewhere. But get her as far from here as possible."

"Why Harker, I'd almost think you care about this girl," Glory said, and I saw a little smile on her face.

"I made a promise to her father. And I keep my promises." I leaned over the font of holy water, preparing myself for the coming battle.

"That you do, my reckless ward. That you do indeed." I watched Smith's eyes go blank, then watched his consciousness take control again as Glory left him.

"What the fucking fuck was *that*?" the agent asked, turning around looking for whatever had just been in his head.

"You, my dear Smitty, have just been touched by an angel. Now let's go downstairs and kick some ass," I said, pointing to a thin door behind the organ.

CHAPTER 15

The first thing I noticed when I opened the door to the stairwell was the stink. Brimstone—real, unfiltered, straight-from-the-bowels-of-Hell brimstone—is way stronger than sulfur. It's like sulfur on steroids, with a dash of blood and rot mixed in. And it was brimstone I smelled. Even without my Sight, I could tell there was some serious mojo being thrown around downstairs, and it wasn't anything good for anyone. The chanting in Enochian was another dead giveaway. The language of angels wasn't something to be thrown around lightly, and anyone willing to play with that shit under a slaughtered priest was definitely working against the common good.

Smith and I crept down a narrow stone staircase, pressing our backs to the wall opposite a row of flickering torches that cast long shadows ahead of us. The chanting grew louder as we moved closer, and I began to be able to pick out a few words here and there. None of them were words that I wanted to hear in an occult ritual—things like "devourer," "ravager," "destruction," that kind of light-hearted little ditty.

I held up a finger to Smith and he froze. I opened my Sight and pushed my will outward from myself, using my Sight to peek around the corners and get a sense of what was ahead. I got a feeling of rage, pain, and fear and pulled my Sight back in as a dark consciousness locked onto mine.

"We've been made," I whispered to Smith as I stepped off the wall and strode openly into the room. What had once been a storage room for communion candles and decor for the multiple denominations the chapel served had been turned into a collage out of a haunted house or a horror movie. It was so over the top it would have been funny if there hadn't been a terrified black kid bent backward over an altar stripped to the waist with Enochian symbols drawn on his chest in blood.

The pulpit had been a pair of file cabinets in a former life, covered with red velvet and with Wally tied to it. There were black candles scattered all around the room, probably fifty or more of them. Black fabric draped every wall, and half a dozen men and women in black robes and golden goat masks surrounded the altar. They all looked up when I walked in, and their chanting trailed off to silence.

"Hi kids, how's it hanging? Gonna raise a little hell?" I asked, stepping up to the altar and putting a hand on Wally's chest. I also made it a point to step across the huge circle drawn on the floor around the altar and drag my foot through the lines, breaking the circle and disrupting any protection it may have offered the idiots outside of it.

"You cannot stop the Acolytes of Armageddon, fool! Leave now before we smite you down!" the goat-head nearest Wally's right shoulder bellowed at me.

"You know I'm standing right here, pal. No need to yell. Or do these things make it hard to hear?" I reached out and yanked his goat mask off and threw it over my shoulder. A Rick Moranis look-alike, horn-rims and all, goggled at me from inside his cavernous black hood and robe. "Is that better? Can you hear me now?"

"You can't interrupt the ritual!" Moranis bleated at me. "We've already begun summoning Death incarnate! He whose arrival will signal the oncoming Apocalypse! The sacrifice must be completed!" The little dude stretched out his right arm and jabbed a curved dagger downward toward Wally's chest. I gave the kid a shove and he toppled over, homemade altar and all. The nerd with the knife staggered forward and I stuck out a leg, sending him sprawling. He tumbled into a heap at Smith's feet and his knife slid across the floor.

"Where did you guys find each other, Henchmen-R-Us?" I asked. "'Cause I was way more worried about the thug you left guarding the door. *This* is your fearless leader? He couldn't summon a cheeseburger at McDonald's, much less bring about the end of the world."

"You're right, Mr. Harker. Eric was simply a cog in my machine. He was never intended to be the leader of anything, merely a distraction for meddling do-gooders."

"You mean like *moi*?" I pointed at my chest.

"I mean exactly like you. I thought if you decided Eric wasn't a threat, then you would probably do something brash and stupid, like break the containment circle and free our Dark Lord."

"What do mean…oh fucksticks." I turned to see Wally getting up from where I'd toppled the altar. There was no hint of the enthusiastic but addled stoner I'd met the night before. Standing in front of me with his eyes gone completely black was Death himself. Power rolled off him in waves, and I felt it even without using my Sight.

"Mr. Harker, I must say that I am pleased to finally make your acquaintance. You have sent so many to my realm, I feel as though we are old friends." Wally/Death raised his hand and the two goat-heads nearest him dropped to the floor. "Ahhh, they were full of life. Delicious, but you know that, don't you, Mr. Harker?"

"It's been a while since I ate my meals *tartare*. Trying to live in civilized company nowadays. You know how it is."

"No, I don't. And I suggest that if you wish to continue

breathing, you stop moving toward your gun, Agent Smith. Or whatever they are calling you now." I turned my head a little and saw Smith put his hands up.

"That's nice. Just stay there for now. I'll let you know when it's time to die."

"So what's the plan?" I asked. "You gonna go up out of here and kill everybody, is that it? Gonna wipe the Earth clean as a baby's butt? Bring about the end of the world? Without Wally, you can't open any more of the seals, can you?"

"With Death at my command, I won't need to open any more —" The lead goat-head cut off in mid-soliloquy, dropping to one knee, then falling face-first to the concrete. He pressed one hand into the floor and flopped himself over, ripping at his mask. I watched his face turn red, then purple, then move right on to black as the life poured out of him into Death's upraised left hand.

"Let me guess, you have altered the deal, and I should pray that you don't alter it further," I said, frantically scrambling around in my brain for anything that would get me out of this mess. Wally was gone, as far as I could tell, possessed by the spirit of Death, just like the other Horsemen.

"Exactly. Now, Mr. Harker, are you going to get out of my way and let me pass, or are we going to do this the hard way?" Death asked.

"I only really know the hard way, sorry." *Flynn, you there?*

On the stairs. He hasn't seen us yet.

Us?

Renfield wouldn't let me come alone.

That's probably good. You're going to have about half a second if I do this right, a lot less if I screw it up.

I got this. All you need to do is piss off the most badass of the Four

Horsemen enough to drop his guard for a second.

That's kind of my specialty. I wasn't one hundred percent on exactly what Flynn had in mind, but from the images in her mind it involved Renfield, a sniper rifle, and me maybe dying. I was good with two out of three.

Death hadn't moved, just cocked his head a little to the side. "What are you plotting, parasite?"

"Now that's just rude," I said. "Stuff like that really hurts, and it makes me want to poke holes in your meat suit." I drew my Sig and leveled it at his chest.

"You won't shoot. You like this mortal and think there's some chance of saving him. You'd never—" Death's character assessment was cut off and proven wrong as the 9mm round slammed into his chest, followed by two more in a tight grouping. He staggered back, then smiled at me. I hate it when the bad guys smile; it always means things are about to get painful for me.

Death waved a hand, and three misshapen chunks of lead and copper slowly wiggled their way out of his chest and *clinked* to the floor. "That was anti-climactic. My turn." He stretched out a hand, and I felt my life force begin to drain away. I started to go weak, then my vision started to dim, then feeling started to fade in my extremities. I fought to stay on my feet as the blackness crept over me, clinging to consciousness by a thread.

Drop, jackass! I heard in my head. I fought harder, struggling against the weight of Death's life-draining power.

Fall down, you moron! Flynn's mental "voice" hit me like a slap across the face and I realized what was happening—she was feeding me her life force to keep me alive, but she was running out, and I was screwing up the plan. For the first time, I saw the whole thing unfold in front of me and dropped to my hands and knees.

A loud *crack* split the air inside the room and Death's head snapped back. His hold on me vanished as his attention was diverted, and I felt my energy rush back along our severed connection. I fed some back down the line to Flynn and stood up, pulling a flask out of my back pocket. I unscrewed the lid of the flask and threw the whole thing at Death. It hit him in the chest and toppled over, covering him in holy water.

"Ego te demonium in inferni profundos abyssos expello," I said, pushing my will outwards and enveloping Death in my will and the power of the holy water. I could feel the Horseman fighting me, struggling against the incantation as I repeated the words again and again, increasing volume until I was yelling at the top of my lungs. I felt him begin to break free when out of the corner of my eye I felt more than saw a slight figure dash past me and tackle the avatar to the ground.

Renfield reached beneath his shirt and pulled out something shining on a golden chain. He pressed the necklace to Death's forehead and bellowed, "In the Name of God, the God of Yisrale: may Michael be at my right hand, Gabriel at my left, Uriel before me, Raphael behind me, and above my head, the presence of God. I command you to *begone!*" With a crack of thunder that almost split my eardrums in the confined space, a blinding light flared out from Renfield's hand, then all was still.

I stepped forward, my gun trained on the bodies on the floor, but everything looked moderately normal. Renfield was on his knees, hunched forward and either sobbing or retching, or maybe both. I couldn't really tell. Beside him lay Wally, all hint of Death's possession gone and the happy-go-lucky dreadlocked college kid restored to his very mortal glory. Wally lay there with his eyes closed and a tiny smile on his face. For a second I waited for him to wake up, then I saw the round hole in the center of his forehead, and I dropped to one knee.

I put an arm around Renfield's shoulders. "I'm sorry, buddy. The first one is always the hardest. But you did good, Ren. You saved a lot of lives today."

"That doesn't help," the kind-hearted little man said, sniffling. "We were supposed to save this one."

"No," I said. "We were supposed to stop the end of the world. And that's bigger than any of us. Bigger than all of us. And that's what you did. You saved us all. What was that, anyway?" I pointed to the necklace he was white-knuckling.

He opened his hand to show me the Star of David lying in the palm of his hand. "It was an ancient Jewish ritual of banishment."

"I didn't know you were Jewish, Renfield."

"There's more to me than meets the eye as well, Master Harker," Renfield said, struggling to his feet. "Now, should we being cleaning this...?"

"No, I've got that covered," Smith said. "Harker, you never told me your butler was a wizard."

"I'm not," Renfield said, clearing his throat. "I am neither a butler nor a wizard. I am an executive assistant, and I have many skills in many areas. Some of them I choose not to disclose until they become needed."

"Well, Ren, I'm damn glad you decided to disclose this one today. Let's get out of here before the press shows up and I have to mojo a dozen asshole reporters," I said, walking to the stairs. Flynn sat on the stairs and I held out a hand to help her up.

You okay?

I'm not sure yet. You have a lot of explaining to do.

True, but I'm not going to do it in front of Smith, and I'm not going to do it without alcohol. So if you want answers about your dad, you'll have to come with me.

Fucker.

True enough.

She reached up and took my hand, and we walked up the stairs into the daylight.

EPILOGUE

The sunset painted the sky with broad strokes of red, orange, and purple, with a single white contrail slicing over the city as I stepped out into Uncle Luke's backyard. The scene looked like something out of a twisted Normal Rockwell painting—Renfield in a fresh suit identical to the tattered one he'd left the cemetery in, a crisp white "Kiss the Chef" apron wrapped around his middle as he turned steaks and potatoes on Luke's thousand-dollar extravagance of a grill, the most frivolous purchase in the history of cooking devices. Smith stood beside him, offering advice on how and when to flip the steaks, which Renfield promptly ignored. Smith's own steak was already steaming on a plate, one half step past *tartare* in prep and stewing in a plate full of juices.

Luke stood on the porch glaring at the last rays of sunshine as they retreated across the yard from him, their poisonous golden light fading into a more welcome blue and lavender-hued evening. I stood next to him for a moment, looking out across the yard at more activity than the home had seen since Luke and I moved to Charlotte decades ago.

"Looks like a strange family picture, Uncle," I said, passing him a bottle of dark red liquid I brought out from a cabinet in the kitchen. Luke liked his dinner room temperature, but that made storage a bitch. But after a while we'd determined the right mix of anticoagulants to keep blood fresh for at least a week, so he could hunt less frequently and stay in one place longer.

"Well, we have always been a strange family, Quincy," the king of the vampires replied with a sigh. "I wish your parents were here to see this. They always worried that you would grow up twisted by my influence."

"Luke, I can't say that I'm well adjusted, but I'm pretty sure it's not your fault. I've done plenty of twisting all on my own." I patted him on the shoulder and walked across the yard to where Flynn sat on a two-seater swing.

I put the plastic grocery bag on the seat beside her and sat down. I pulled an Olde Mecklenburg Dunkel out of the bottle and pried the top off with my pinky finger. Flynn reached in and took out a bottle of Olde Meck Copper and tilted the neck towards me.

"These aren't twist-tops," she pointed out.

"I'm a super-hero, it comes with some perks," I replied as I used my finger to pop open her beer. We sat there in silence for a few moments, drinking and watching the Ren and Luke cooking show. I finished off my beer and opened another.

"You know that's a winter brew, right?" Flynn asked.

"I spent a lot of time in Germany, where they invented Dunkel. I get to drink it whenever I damn well please."

"How did my father die?"

"That's all the small talk we're going to do? You're drinking beer out of season, then right into the heavy shit?"

"I'm not looking for foreplay, Harker, I want information."

"Are you sure you want *this* information, Rebecca?"

"I need to know."

"Let's start with what you remember, what you were told."

She took a deep breath and I could see her focus, put herself back in the moment. "I was ten. It was late, past my bedtime, but I stayed up late to wait for Daddy. Mom and Dad let me do that on Fridays because it wasn't a school night. Mom was asleep on the couch, so I had turned down the TV really low so she wouldn't wake up. I was watching Nickelodeon because grown-up TV was boring. I knew something was bad when the doorbell rang.

Nobody had ever rang our doorbell that late before. I opened the door and two policemen were standing there. One of them I knew; it was Uncle Robert. He wasn't really my uncle, but he was my dad's partner. His face was all red, like he'd been crying, and when he looked down at me, two big tears rolled down his cheeks. The other man was older, skinny, with a lot of medals and things on his uniform. I didn't know him then, but he was Chief McFrayn, the Chief of Police. Once he saw me, he knelt down in front of me and asked to see my mom.

"'Is my daddy dead?' I asked him.

"The skinny man knelt there staring into my eyes for a long time, then he said 'Yes, darling, he is. A bad man killed your daddy, but your daddy killed the bad man, too. Your daddy is a hero.'"

I sat next to Flynn while she told the pieces of the night that she remembered. It was standard disjointed little-kid memory stuff, pieces here and there. When she finished, she knocked off the last of her beer and handed me another one to open. "Your turn, Harker. What happened to my father? They wouldn't let us have an open casket, said it would be too hard for me to handle. Why wouldn't they let me see my father's body?"

"Because there wasn't enough left to see," I said simply. "The initial vampire attack drained most of his blood and his essence with it. But the vamp that attacked your father was a newborn, and insane to boot. So after she was full, she took a few minutes to play with her food. By the time I got there, your father was just barely hanging on."

I remembered it like it was yesterday. The light mist making everything slick, the newborn vamp running out of her master's lair, flush with new power and starving from her rebirth. Her maker laughing at his insane progeny and daring me to do something about it. I'd been hunting him for weeks, following a trail of bodies across the South as he bounced from Atlanta to Charlotte to Knoxville to Memphis back to Atlanta, then to Charleston and back up to Charlotte. I finally cornered him on the top of the Bank of America parking garage, catching him as he snacked on a violinist for the symphony who was just a little too slow getting her car unlocked. He drained her in front of me, then opened his wrist and dribbled just enough of his blood down her dying throat to turn her, but not enough to satisfy the new urges she didn't understand. She sprang back to life, desperate for blood, and ran at me.

I fought her off and put her through the windshield of a parked truck. I hoped that would keep her out of the way until I dealt with her maker, but no such luck. I turned to face him and heard the truck door open behind me, then listened to her feet dash away through the garage.

"What's it going to be, Hunter? You going to fight me, or chase down the murderer I just turned loose on the city? You know she's going to go kill someone. She can't help it. But you can. You can stop her. All you have to do is let me go."

I couldn't. I'd chased this maniac for a month and a half up and down the East Coast. There was no way I was going to let him go. The city would just have to fend for itself for half an hour.

"And in that half hour..." Flynn said.

"Yeah. In that half hour, there was an altercation at Mythos, a dance club that used to run downtown, and your dad and his partner were called. When they arrived on the scene, your father noticed a severely intoxicated woman in the neighboring parking garage. He sent his partner, your Uncle Robert, into the club to see what the call was about while he tried to help the woman. She turned out to be the newborn vampire, and she attacked him with a savagery that you can only imagine. He was not only killed, he was horribly mutilated. There was no way a child's last memory of her father should be that."

"Where were you?"

"Two blocks away. If took me less than fifteen minutes to destroy the vampire and track down the newborn. But it was too long. She was kneeling over your father's body when I got there, and she came at me again. This time I decapitated her with one swipe of my katana. I mentioned this was the 90s, right? Long coats and katanas seemed somehow in keeping with the decade. Anyway, I killed it and checked on your dad. He was almost gone, but with his dying breath he made me promise to look after Becks for him. So I have."

"You have what?" Flynn asked. Her eyebrows were crawling high into her hairline at this point.

"I've been around every major event in your life, Detective." I opened my mind and let her see the memories I carried—her high school graduation, college commencement, Police Academy graduation, her first collar, more bad first dates than she even remembered having, and a couple of embarrassing karaoke moments with other cops in her precinct.

"You've been…"

"Keeping a promise."

"Spying on me!"

"It was never like that, and you know it." And she did, we could feel each other through our link and she knew that I was telling the truth. There was never anything prurient in my skulking. I was just keeping a promise to her father.

"When were you going to tell me?"

"When I had to. It was going to come out eventually, with us working this closely." I sat there, watching her out of the side of my eye. We rocked back and forth on the swing for several minutes, her not speaking a word to me.

"Thank you," she said at last.

"For what?"

"For being with him at the end. All these years, all I knew was that a bad person killed my daddy, and his partner was okay. I assumed he died alone, and I didn't want that."

"I was right there, his hand in mine."

"Good. Thank you."

I didn't say anything else, just sat rocking beside Flynn as the smell of cooking drifted over the darkening lawn.

HELL ON HEELS

A Quincy Harker, Demon Hunter
Novella

CHAPTER 1

I was headed home after a particularly disgusting exorcism when my cell phone rang. I took a minute to find a dry spot on my jeans (the back of the knee is good for this, no matter what you do, unless you're absolutely submerged, you usually stay dry there) and wipe off my hands before I answered.

"I'm tired, dirty, sober, and pissed off, so what do you want?" I growled into the phone.

"You have the sweetest phone voice," said Detective Rebecca Gail Flynn of the Charlotte-Mecklenburg Police Department, currently on special assignment to the Department of Homeland Security's Paranormal Division, a division that didn't officially exist. "How quickly can you get over here?"

"Where is here?" I asked. "Because if it's your apartment and you've got the jacuzzi running, the answer is fifteen minutes. If it's police headquarters, the answer is at least two hours."

"Let's try putting those two together and getting you to HQ in fifteen minutes. We've got a bad one," Flynn replied.

"You *think* you've got a bad one. I've still got most of a bad one splattered all over my clothes. I'm going to have to bill these people for a new pair of shoes, at the very least. Do you have any idea how much food a person can eat when they've been possessed by a gluttony demon for a week? And do you have any idea what happens to that food when the demon is exorcised?"

"That's a no on all counts, Harker, and I don't give a shit. Just get your ass over here. You can shower in the locker room, and I'll get you something to wear."

"No dice," I replied. "Meet me at my apartment in twenty.

I'll leave the door open." I hung up on her protests and slid the phone into my pocket as I walked to my car. I tossed my exorcism bag into the trunk of my old burgundy Accord and shrugged out of my leather duster. It was a little ostentatious, but it looked the part of a wizard a lot more than I did, and it kept me from getting completely covered in puke on gigs like this. I emptied the pockets, then left the duster laying on top of a bush for the next homeless guy to find. Then I grabbed a towel from the trunk and wiped myself down as best as I could. I put another towel on the seat of the car and headed home to clean up, mentally tallying up the cost of the new wardrobe so I could add it to the client's bill.

I was lathering up for a second scrub-down when I heard someone enter my apartment. "If that's Detective Flynn, I'm in the shower. If it's my order from Playmates R' Us, I'm in the shower. If it's anyone else, fuck off!" I called from the open door of my bathroom.

"Playmates R' Us?" Flynn asked as she came in and leaned against the counter.

"A man can dream," I replied, rinsing off and reaching down to turn off the water. I pulled the curtain back and grabbed a towel from the rack, a little disappointed that Detective Flynn had decided to give me my privacy. I wrapped a towel around my waist and stepped out into the bedroom. Flynn was sitting on the end of my bed, looking impatient.

"Where were you, Harker? Your clothes smell like shit," she said, kicking the pile of puke-covered clothes even farther away. I had them all piled up on a towel to be taken out and burned. Days like this it was a damn good thing I have a rich uncle.

"Puke, actually. That's the remnants of about thirteen pizzas and a gallon or two of ice cream, by my best guess."

"What were you doing, teaching Ouija lessons to sorority girls?"

"That's not a bad idea, and probably a fuckload cleaner than this gig. No, I was exorcising a fifteen-year-old bulimic who had suddenly started eating her family out of house and home. Seems Little Miss Size Six wanted to be Little Miss Size Two and found a spell on the internet that promised to help her lose twenty pounds in a weekend. It was really a spell to summon a gluttony demon into the caster's body, so she was well on her way to eating herself to death by the time her parents called me in."

"That's disgusting."

"That's not even the disgusting part," I said.

"No, I mean a fifteen-year-old girl who's a size six thinking she's fat. What the hell is this world coming to? I'm a size twelve and I think I look pretty good."

I dropped my towel and opened the dresser for some boxers. "I'd have to agree, Detective. Looks like everything's in the right places to me."

"Oh for God's sake, Harker!" Flynn exclaimed, covering her eyes.

"What?" I asked, then looked down. "Sorry," I said. "Raised in Europe, remember? All your American hang-ups about being naked kinda missed me."

"I thought you grew up in Victorian England?"

"Edwardian, to be precise," I called out. "I was born in London in November 1896, but by the time I could remember anything, what you call the Victorian period was over and we were much more Continental."

"But you still didn't run around flashing people!"

"Meh, it was more of 'do what you like, just don't scare the horses.' We did whatever we liked in private and with close friends, but we were much more reserved in public."

"Well, as far as you being naked is concerned, let's keep it a little reserved. We're not that close friends."

"What's wrong, Detective? See something you like?" I turned to her and flexed a little, showing off my abs. It would probably have been more impressive if I had abs, but exercise was never a strong point of mine. When you come by your superhuman strength the old-fashioned way, by having a vampire bite both your parents and muck about with your DNA before you're even conceived, you don't sweat the gym membership too much.

Flynn ignored me, so after a few seconds I pulled on a pair of black jeans and a black t-shirt. I sat next to her on the bed, pulled on a pair of socks and started lacing up my Doc Martens. The all-black ensemble was a little pretentious, but since I only owned black jeans, black t-shirts, and black boots, it certainly made dressing for work easier.

"So what's the deal? I'm pretty sure you didn't come here just to ogle me as I scrubbed chunks of puke out of my hair," I asked.

"I think there's a vampire on the loose in Charlotte," Flynn said.

"Yeah, his name's Dracula, but he'd really rather you just call him Luke. Or even Mr. Card."

"I'm not talking about your uncle, asshole. There's another one."

"Impossible," I said, standing up. I dug my phone and wallet out of my pants and tied the towel around the bundle of disgusting clothes. I dropped it onto the tile of the bathroom, figuring at least then it wouldn't soak into the carpet.

"Why is it impossible?"

"Because my uncle lives here, and he doesn't like other vampires. He barely tolerates me, and I'm his fault, for Christ's sake. No way would he let another real vampire run free in Charlotte." I held up a hand. "And before you even say it, there is also no way a vampire could operate within a hundred miles of here without his knowledge. He knows these things. It's kinda creepy, but he does."

"Then either he's gotten sloppy, or we've got something else feeding on humans that looks an awful lot like a vampire."

"And how do you know what a vampire attack looks like, Detective? If I recall correctly, the veil was lifted for you just a few months ago, and before that you had no idea that the monster under your bed was real."

"What do you mean, the monster under my bed was real?"

"There are monsters under children's beds. Or at least, there are a lot of times. They're little guys, almost completely harmless unless they eat too much. They're called gurties, and they feed on dreams and imagination. And what better place to find that than in a kid's bedroom? So they live under the bed, and usually there's no problem."

"Usually?"

"Yeah," I said. "Every once in a while they eat too much, and the kid turns nuts. Did you know having your dreams taken away from you could make you crazy? Well it can, and when it does, I go kill the gurty and the kid goes into therapy."

"What happens to the kid?" Flynn asked.

"Nothing. I can't rebuild devoured dreams; once they're gone, they're gone. All I can do is make sure the gluttonous little bastard doesn't do it to anybody else. But you were saying something about a vampire?"

"Yeah, there have been three bodies discovered in the past three nights, all with similar wounds, and all of them completely drained of blood."

"In populated areas?"

"Nearby. One in the alley between the library and Spirit Square, one in the parking deck across from the Blumenthal Center, and one behind the pizza joint in NoDa." She named two Uptown locations and one spot in the trendy arts district just north of Uptown.

"Those are way outside Luke's typical hunting grounds, and besides, he doesn't drain his victims completely. That's how..." My voice trailed off. "You said three bodies in three nights?"

"Yeah? Why?"

I was already out of my bedroom and into the living room. I slid my Glock holster onto my belt and grabbed two silver stakes from a wood block in the center of the dining room table. Leave me alone. They're pretty and when arranged right, look like some kind of funky centerpiece instead of a home defense system. I stopped at the door. "You coming?"

"Where are we going? And what's got you in such a rush?"

"It takes anywhere from one to three days for a vampire to rise. Vampires are made by completely draining a living victim. If these people really were attacked by a vampire, and if the first victim was found three days ago, then your coroner is in for a surprise right about—"I never finished my sentence. Both our cell phones rang at the same time, with the same Caller ID—Smith.

"You drive," I said to Flynn as we left my apartment and ran down the stairs. I pulled out my phone and pushed the green button. "Go ahead, Johnny." John Smith was no more our supervisory agent's real name than mine was Santa Claus, but I let him have his little illusions.

"Get down here right away, there's—"

I cut him off for a change. "A vampire outbreak at the morgue. You've got three, maybe more, baby vamps that just woke up and are hungry as hell. Have they killed anyone yet?"

"No, the Assistant M.E. saw the bag moving, opened it, and freaked out. He slammed down the quarantine shields quicker than you can say 'ebola'."

"Good thinking on his part," I said. "We're on our way, be there in five." I could have run from my place to the Medical Examiner's office in less than five minutes, but this exercise wasn't about me, it was about Flynn, so I slid into the passenger seat of her Homeland Security-issued Suburban and buckled my seatbelt.

"How did you know these were vampire attacks, Flynn?" I asked as she put the SUV in drive and screeched out of my parking garage. I was hoping for something easy like pinpricks in the neck, or pale skin, or something that I could rationalize away.

"I don't. Not really, but what else drains the blood from its victims and leaves the bodies perfectly posed?"

"What do you mean, posed?" I felt a chill run down my spine at her choice of words. I really didn't want to hear the next few words out of Flynn's mouth, but I had to.

"All three bodies were left out in the open, where they would be found quickly. And each body was fully dressed, eyes held closed with silver dollars, and their hands folded across their chests."

"Holding a single red rose?" I asked. My voice was very quiet, but Flynn's head snapped around to stare at me anyway.

"How did you know that? I didn't tell you that. Are you doing that see through my eyes thing again?" Her words came out in an angry tumble, and I held up a hand to stop her.

"No, it's nothing like that. I knew there was a rose because I've seen these kills before, and there's always a rose."

"Wait, you've seen these before? Are you telling me these people were killed by someone you know?"

"Yeah," I said. "I know who killed those people. And I know what he wants."

"Who?" Flynn asked. "What does he want?"

"His name is Augustus James Renfield, and he's here to kill Dracula."

CHAPTER 2

"What?" Flynn asked.

"Gus was the first Renfield. He was a good manservant for a long time, and Uncle Luke promised to turn him after his term of service was over. Unfortunately, as the years went by, Luke realized that most people aren't meant to live forever, so when the time came to turn Gus, Luke refused to do it.

"Gus was batshit crazy, you see. Not the cute kind of crazy they show in the movies where he eats flies, but the fucking scary kind of crazy, where he eats eyeballs. He worked for Uncle Luke for twenty years until he finally went completely around the bend. When Luke fired him, he came calling demanding to be turned. Uncle Luke refused, and Gus stormed off, promising to be back.

"He kept his promise. He came back the very next day, when the sun was up, with stakes. But he didn't know that I was around, so when he went down to the basement to add a little oak to Luke's diet, I beat his ass and sent him packing. We thought he died of natural causes until a couple decades later when we ran into him in Vienna. He was snacking on a tenor out back of an opera house when we found him.

"I don't know where or when he found someone to turn him, but he did. He was a full-on vampire and strong as hell. He beat me to a pulp and went toe to toe with Luke for a couple minutes before he bolted. The next morning we found the tenor on the doorstep of the apartment we were renting, his eyes closed with silver dollars and rose in his hands, folded neatly on his chest."

"Holy shit" was all Flynn said as she turned into the coroner's office parking deck. She straddled two compact parking spaces with the Suburban and got out.

I slid out after her. "You just gonna park like a dick?" I asked.

"I'm the government. Anybody doesn't like it, I'll send them to Gitmo." She never broke stride, just walked straight to the elevator and pushed the button.

I got there just as the doors slid open, and I pressed "G."

"How crazy is this guy?" Flynn asked.

"Makes me look well-adjusted," I said.

"Fuck. Okay, so super-crazy."

I laughed a little. A very little.

"How strong?"

"I can't get close to his raw strength. He's got nothing on Luke, but if he gets me in close quarters and I don't have anything ready for him, it's going to be a bad day for me. That reminds me." I pulled out my cell phone. One bar. I stared at the screen until the elevator doors slid open and I stepped out into the Coroner's Office lobby. The morgue shared a lobby with about half a dozen other esoteric and often messy government offices, like the pistol permit office, the place where folks buy their garage sale licenses, and the office where they process protests to tax valuation. But the lobby was nice, and I had perfect cell reception.

I pushed one of my speed dials and held the phone to my ear. After three rings, a cultured male voice answered. "Card residence. How many I help you?"

"Ren, it's me," I said into the phone.

"Master Quincy, how good to hear from you. Will you be joining us for dinner this Friday? You know your uncle loves to —"

I cut him off. "Ren, I need you to wake Uncle Luke. Follow emergency protocol Pitchforks and get him out of the house.

Right now."

"Master Quincy?" Renfield sounded confused, and I didn't blame him. We hadn't used the Pitchfork protocol, named after the final scene in *Frankenstein*, in years.

"This is not a drill, Ren. My uncle's safety is in your hands. Execute Pitchfork, right the fuck now."

"What do I tell him when he asks what the threat is?"

"Tell him it's your granddad," I said.

"I'm sorry, Master Quincy, I don't understand. My grandfather is long deceased and had no quarrel with…" I could almost hear Ren's eyes go wide as the realization dawned on him.

"Exactly. The first Renfield is in town, he's killed three people already, and I'd bet dollars to doughnuts that Uncle Luke is the top of his hit list. Now get Luke somewhere safe and gear up for a fight. I've got some leads to follow up downtown, then we'll come collect you and send this rat bastard to Hell where he belongs!"

I hung up on Ren's assurances that he would handle everything, and looked over to where Rebecca was waiting for a main elevator going down. I took a couple of steps in her direction, then started to run. I passed her at a full sprint heading for the stairs.

"Come on!" I yelled at her.

She didn't hesitate, just drew her sidearm and ran after me. "Why are we taking the stairs?" she shouted at my back.

"Remember that whole super-hearing thing?" I asked over my shoulder. I got to the fire stairs and almost ripped the door off the hinges.

"Yeah, I remember. You hear something?"

I nodded, starting down the stairs. "Yeah, the screaming's already started."

The screaming was going on in earnest by the time I made it

to the morgue, having left Flynn a couple of floors above me on the stairs. I kicked in the Plexiglas quarantine doors, silver stake in hand, and froze. Instead of there being one newborn, starving vampire in the room, there were at least two, and from the looks of the shaking bag on the exam table to my right, about to be more.

I didn't waste time, just jammed the silver stake through the bag and in the rough area of the heart of the creature trying to get out of the bag. Silver covers a lot of sins when dealing with supernatural creatures. With vampires in particular, it lets you miss the heart by a couple of inches and still kill the thing. The bag went still, and I pulled the other stake from my belt. One vampire was stalking a human across the room, who I assumed was the coroner. He wasn't moving, and the vampire wasn't in a hurry, so obviously this one had already learned how to mesmerize its prey.

Fast learners. That's never good. The other vampire was standing in the center of the room, smiling at me. It had none of the hallmarks of a newborn. No red eyes, no confusion on its features, no blood running down its mouth from the first time the fangs break through the skin. Apparently that's painful and involved some pretty significant restructuring of the jawline. I don't have fangs, and I've never spent enough time close to a vampire's mouth to notice.

Flynn burst into the room just about the time realization dawned on me. "Becks, get out of here!"

"Oh fuck, Harker, I just got here," she panted. I forget that normal humans, even slightly magically enhanced humans, get a little winded after four flights of stairs at a dead run. "Can't I just shoot one of these bastards before I go?"

The answer was obviously "no" since as soon as she got the

words out, the vamp in the center of the room flew into action. Not quite literally, but almost. He moved with inhuman speed, vaulting over the exam table and sprinting at Flynn. This put him headed right past me, and he apparently hadn't heard of me, or what I can do.

Like match him almost speed-for-speed. He was headed past me for Flynn at a dead run, faster than a human eye could follow. Lucky for Rebecca Gail Flynn, I'm a little more than human. I stuck my right arm out and delivered a clothesline that would have made Nikita Koloff proud. The vampire turned completely over in midair before landing on his belly in the middle of the morgue. I jabbed down with my other stake, but he rolled out of the way and sprang to his feet before I could strike. This put my face at the unfortunate level of his knees, and he took a second to introduce me to his right knee with extreme prejudice.

I flopped flat onto my back, then nipped up onto my feet in a move I'd perfected watching Sunday afternoon Kung-Fu Theatre as a child. Okay, as a seventy-year-old, but a very spry septuagenarian. Vamp threw a punch that was intended to cave in my face, but I sidestepped and swung an elbow that would have crushed his throat if it had connected. He grabbed my arm and flipped me. I used my superhuman agility to land on my feet and kick at his balls. He slipped out of the way and slammed down on my knee with both fists. There was no way I could ever beat him fair and square, so it was probably good for me my moral compass broke in the 1920s.

Becks, you got silver in your pistol? I asked over the mental link that Flynn and I shared. I tried to stay out of her head as much as possible to give her privacy. She tried to stay out of my head even more because my head is a very disturbing place. But this time I needed backup, and she was all I had. Well, her,

her marksmanship medals, and sixteen rounds of silver-tipped ammunition.

Yeah, I swapped out mags on the stairs.

Good. Wait for the opening.

The vamp and I exchanged punches, blocks, parries, and kicks for what felt like at least half an hour, which probably meant a minute and a half, then I overextended with one punch. It was an error of a millimeter or less, but it was all he needed. He leaned back out of the way of a devastating right cross, then grabbed my arm and pulled me past him onto a nearby exam table.

Now! I shouted to Flynn mentally as I switched targets for a second and turned my dive into a roll, flipping over the table onto my feet and throwing my second and last silver stake across the room at the third vamp. The foot-long hunk of sharpened silver went into the vampire's head right behind and below the right ear, *crunching* through the skull and burying itself into the monster's brain and severing the spinal cord. It dropped like a stone at the coroner's feet, who took a good look at the critter before him, threw up, and fainted dead away.

With two less vampires and one less human to worry about, I spun around and saw Flynn locked in a contest of wills with the last vampire. He had her gaze; you could almost feel the force of her will struggling not to be overcome by the powerful vampire's suggestion. I decided that while Flynn had a hellacious amount of willpower, this wasn't the night to make her go toe-to-toe with the varsity squad of monsters. I picked up a metal bowl from a nearby table and smashed it into the side of the vampire's head with a loud *bong*.

The vampire turned to me and smiled. "Is that the best you could do, human?"

"Boy, do you have the wrong city," I said with a grin. "All I needed to do was distract you. She's gonna—"

I never got a chance to tell him what Flynn was going to do because she commenced to doing it the second the vamp's eyes swung back in her direction. She put three in the creature's chest, dropping it to the ground instantly. Then she took a few steps forward, lowered her weapon to the ground, and put two more in the vampire's head.

She looked up at me with a shaky smile. "Thanks for the save."

"No problem. You know I got your back."

"Yeah, but what was all this?" She gestured around the room at the three dead vampires.

"I don't know. They shouldn't have turned this quickly. Not all of them, anyway. Something weird is going on here, and I think we might have a bigger problem than just a pissed-off Renfield on our hands."

CHAPTER 3

"I'll have to give you an A-Plus for understatement on that one, Harker." Agent John Smith's voice came from the doorway to the morgue. He looked like every federal agent in every cop movie, except his suit had razor-sharp creases, and his salute was snappy and tight. His salt-and-pepper hair was buzzed close to his scalp, and the wrinkles around his eyes would have been called smile lines on anyone else, but on Smith you could tell those were lines caused by a man who's stood on many a hill surveying the forces arrayed against him.

"You know something I don't know, Agent Johnny?" I asked. I kept playing with different variations on his fake name, but he never cracked, no matter what I called him.

"I know a great many things you don't know, Harker, but I don't know shit about these guys. As far as I knew, they were human a couple of days ago. Obviously, that wasn't the case."

"Obviously," I agreed. I turned to the coroner, who was just getting to his feet. "Are you okay to be in here? Because a lot the things we deal with can seriously fuck with your worldview."

The white-haired man just laughed at me. "Son, I've been dealing with the aftermath of man's ill treatment of other men for thirty years. If there's anything left under heaven that can shock me, I can't wait to see it."

"I'm afraid that will have to wait another day or two, sir," Smith said. He flashed his badge at the coroner, who gave it a once-over and nodded. "I'm John Smith with Homeland Security, and this is my scene now."

"It can be your scene all you like, Agent Smith," the doc said, wiping his wire-rimmed glasses on his lab coat. "But this is my morgue, and these are my dead bodies." He gestured at the vampires, who were now scattered all over his morgue. Unlike on television, real vampires don't turn to dust when they're killed, unless they're really, really old. Or burned by the sun. Massive sunlight exposure will cause them to burn up and turn to dust, but it's not instant, and it's very smelly. Not something you want to be around.

"Fair enough, Doctor...?" Smith raised an eyebrow.

"Strunin. Doctor Jacob Strunin, Chief Medical Examiner." He extended a hand, and Smith shook it.

"Okay, Doctor Strunin. You are hereby deputized into the Department of Homeland Security, Paranormal Division, under my direct supervision. Please understand that revealing any information that we uncover as part of our work here will result in your immediate arrest for treason, which I will prosecute to the fullest extent of the law. Do you understand me?"

I watched the little doctor's face pale, then he stood up straight, nodded his head and said, "I understand. Now can we get down to the business of figuring out why these dead people just tried to kill me?"

I laughed and walked over to clap the little doctor on the shoulder. "That's the spirit, doc. But these aren't dead people. Hell, they're not even people!"

"What are you trying to say, Mr.- um, I'm sorry, I didn't catch your name."

"Harker. Quincy Harker, Demon Hunter, at your service." I gave him my most florid bow, but my courtly manners left something to be desired, and I had to grab onto an exam table to keep from falling on my ass in the middle of the morgue.

"Well, Mr. Harker," the doctor said, obviously holding back a laugh at my expense. "What are these bodies if not people?"

"Doc, these are vampires." I waited for the inevitable, but it didn't come. He just knelt by the nearest corpse and peeled back the top lip.

"Hmmm... There are definitely extended canines. That seems to validate your theory." He pried open an eyelid and poked at the eyeball. "The vitreous fluid seems thick, almost viscous. I can't prove that they are vampires without a more complete workup, but there's also nothing proving they are not vampires. So, we have vampires in North Carolina. Who knew?"

I raised my hand, but that's as much because I'm a huge smartass than as anything else. "I was pretty much aware of it."

The doc shot me a dirty look. I ignored it because that's what I do. He knelt down again and started poking at the vampire corpses. "What are the odds that these guys are going to get up and come after me again?" he asked, not moving back at all.

"Zero," I assured the man. "We staked them with silver. Destroying the heart gets rid of the blood reservoir, and silver is supremely poisonous to vamps, so it's kind of a double-whammy."

"Hmmm..." Strunin murmured. "So that old wives' tale is true, what about the others?" He looked at Smith, who jerked a thumb at me as if to say I was the resident expert. Which I suppose I was, living most of my life with a vampire.

"Running water, not a thing. Scattering rice in front of one, not a thing. Garlic—there's actually an interesting story there, but let's just say that Bram Stoker had a thing against Italian cooking and we'll leave it at that. Garlic does nothing. Holy Symbols can burn, but it's because they're usually made of silver. They don't reflect in old mirrors because mirrors used silver backing. New mirrors aren't a problem. What else? Oh yeah, sunlight is definitely a thing; it'll crisp a vamp in seconds. They can get drunk off drinking blood from a drunk person, but most drugs don't affect them, oddly enough. They don't eat or drink, and they can't really turn into a bat or fog. But as you saw, they can bespell you, so don't look one in the eyes unless it's a vampire you know and trust. And let's face it, unless you're me, there probably aren't very many vampires you know and trust."

"And this rule doesn't apply to you because?" It was almost funny, watching him put two and two together and get five. I saw him think back to the introduction, then back to the first time he read *Dracula*, either in Classic Comics or the whole novel. Or worse, saw one of the movies. But I saw him recognize the Harker name, try to rationalize it with the age of the man in front of him, and eventually give up.

"Jonathan Harker is a character in *Dracula*," the stunned doctor said.

"I called him Dad," I said. "My parents were fairly important to that book."

"But...how *old* are you?"

"Older than I look, and let's leave it at that. I'm not immortal, like Uncle Lu-, like Dracula. But I age very slowly. And I know a few things about vampires, and one of those things is that these vampires are real-dead. Like forever dead. Almost like human dead, except without all that annoying bleeding."

"So we know what killed them, which is to say you," Strunin said. "And we know that they were vampires, so what am I looking for in my examination."

"Nothing," I said. "You're not doing the examination. I am."

"Excuse me?" The doctor took off his glasses and polished them furiously on his lab coat. If he polished those lenses any more, he'd wear a hole in them.

"We aren't doing a medical examination, Doc. We're looking for other clues. Like you said, we know what killed them. Silver poisoning. Now we need to learn as much about them as possible." I reached down and hefted the nearest vamp onto a nearby exam table.

"Like this guy," I said. "We know he's European from his hair gel. I can smell it, and it's a kind only found in France. They don't even ship to the US because they're French, and 'fuck you' is the motto of France. His nails are done, so he comes from money or is old enough to have learned to appreciate a good manicure. His shoes are recently shined, so I would guess he flew in within the past week."

"And you know this because?" Flynn asked.

"I've lived in this town a long time, and the only place I've found to get a good shoeshine is the airport. And this shine is just a few days old." I pried open the dead vampire's mouth and peered inside. I pulled a tiny flashlight out of my pocket and shined it inside the mouth.

"Well, we know he's old," I said, closing the mouth.

"How do we know that?" Doc Strunin asked.

"He's got most of his teeth, which means that he lived probably no earlier than the eighteenth century, but his dental work is friggin' terrible, so he was turned no later than 1850."

"So you're saying that my twenty-first century murder victim is actually an eighteenth century vampire?" Flynn asked.

"That's what it looks like, detective," I replied. "Seems that these were decoys Gus sent in to lure Uncle Luke out into the open by making him think there was a new vampire in town. Now, where would we find a bunch of eighteenth-century relics in Charlotte?"

"I have no idea," Flynn replied. "I thought we bulldozed

anything over thirty years old."

Just then Flynn's cell rang. She answered it at the same time that Smith reached into his jacket and pulled out a vibrating phone. The phone on the coroner's desk lit up, and I felt left out because nobody was calling me. I had the mental connection between Flynn and me locked down as much as I could, but I still felt the spike of anxiety, excitement, and fear at whatever she was hearing. Everyone hung up at about the same time, and I looked at each one in turn. Flynn looked a little flushed, and I could feel the blood rushing in her veins. Smith looked like a rock with salt-and-pepper five o'clock shadow, and Strunin was pale, with a couple of little beads of sweat popping out on his forehead.

"Let me guess, another corpse?" I asked.

"Looks like a vampire attack," Smith confirmed. "Parking deck at The Green downtown."

"The one under the hot dog place? I know it. What level?" I asked. I checked the magazine in my Glock and made sure I'd returned my silver stakes to my sheaths.

"Bottom floor," Flynn said. "I'll drive." She started for the door, keys in hand.

"No way," I said, not moving.

She froze in mid-stride and spun back to me on one heel. "What?"

"You're not going," I said. I watched the red start at her neck and creep upwards and knew there was an explosion coming.

"Why in the ever-loving fuck would you think I'd let you go by yourself?" She bit off each word with an almost audible click of her teeth.

"If this is Gus, you can't hang with him. You do pretty well against regular vamps, and if it's a fledgling, I'm not worried at all unless you come down with a terminal case of the stupid. But

Gus is a badass. He's shared blood with every old vampire he can find for over a century, and he gets a little bit stronger each time. He's faster than me, smarter than me, and so much stronger than me it's not even funny."

"So what makes you think you can beat him?"

I held out my right hand, palm up, a little over waist high, and focused my will. "*Solis Ortus!*" I shouted, and a ball of light coalesced in the air above my hand, growing brighter and brighter until we all had to look away.

"*Eclipsis!*" I said, and the light dispersed. "I have a few other tricks at my disposal that might make vampires uncomfortable," I said. But I can only focus on two or three things at a time. I can fight Gus and cast spells at the same time, but I can't pay attention to keeping you alive while I do it, and Gus will know it. So please, just stay here and let me do the heavy lifting."

"Can I at least go to the safe house and wait with Ren and Luke?" Flynn asked.

"You can. He can't." I gestured at Smith. "No offense, but Uncle Luke still kinda thinks he's a sovereign government. He doesn't like being reminded that there are people who outrank him in this country."

"Fair enough. I'll stay here and run point on the investigation into these dead vamps' clothes. I'll find out everything I can about who they were and what brought them here. If it's your friend Augustus, maybe they can give us some insight into his plans."

"Sounds like a deal. Now I'm gonna jog over to Matt's Chicago Dog and take care of a little vermin problem in their parking garage."

CHAPTER 4

As always, *The Girl from Ipanema* was playing in the elevator as I rode down to the bottom of the parking garage. I don't think I've ever noticed a different song in an elevator. I don't know if it's just the song that elevator people use, or if I notice that song because it's so annoying, and other songs don't bug me, so I ignore them. Either way, I stepped out into the garage humming *Ooh...but I watch her so sadly*, and almost missed the sound of shoe leather on concrete that told me my target was somewhere off to my left.

I took a handful of marbles out of my jacket pocket and gripped them tightly in my right hand. I brought my fist up to my mouth and whispered *"Lumos"* into my closed hand. I cracked my grip just enough to let the light stream through my fingers for a second, then closed my fist again.

I walked down the ramp, trying to look innocuous and vapid, like any other yuppie trying to find his SUV or mini-van, or crossover, or whatever it is yuppies drive. I'm not a car guy. I have a shitty Honda Accord and an old Harley that I keep at Luke's. I heard the scuff of shoes poised for a leap as I turned the corner into the lowest level of the garage. I tensed, then dove forward into a roll as my attacker sprung for me.

I was rewarded with a surprised gasp, then a heavy *thud* as the vampire crashed into the side of a parked car. I spun around and flung my fistful of glowing marbles out in front of me. Immediately half a dozen little balls of sunlight flew into the air and hovered a little over head height, banishing all the shadows in the garage and leveling the playing field pretty quickly. I saw the vampire, a man turned in his thirties or forties, dressed in contemporary clothes, spin back toward me and launch himself at me again.

He was fast, but I was expecting his leap. I dove under him, staying low to the ground to avoid his claws and fangs, then popped up to my feet five yards away from the pissed-off vampire.

"I'm going to drink you dry and burn your carcass, human," the vampire hissed.

I grinned at him and said, "Human? Somebody's been feeding you bad information, friend." He came at me again, staying on his feet this time, just using his speed to close the distance between us in half a second. He slashed at my throat with his razor-sharp claws, but my throat wasn't there. I dropped straight down to one knee and let his hand pass harmlessly over my head. Then I stood up, throwing my entire body weight behind an uppercut that should have taken his head off and ended our little encounter right then.

Except it didn't. I heard a loud *crack* as his jaw broke, and he staggered back a few steps, but then he cracked his head from side to side and grinned at me. He grinned and my blood ran cold because that was the smile of a man who knew he had the upper hand and was just there to toy with me.

"This is going to be fun," he said, and while I disagreed pretty vehemently, I didn't argue because I was too busy drawing my Glock and emptying the magazine into the vampire's center mass. I put sixteen silver-tipped rounds through that bastard and he didn't go down.

"Silver?" he asked. "I like silver. He ripped open the top three buttons on his shirt to show me the silver crucifix hanging around his neck.

Fuck. I'd seen vampires that weren't bothered by holy symbols. Hell, Luke kept crucifixes hanging all around his place, but I'd never seen one able to touch silver with his bare hands. Either this guy was super old, or somebody'd figured out how to build a better bloodsucker. Either way, I was not a fan.

I barely got my nose out of the way of his next punch, and I snapped out of my reverie pretty damn quickly. He came at me with punches, kicks, roundhouses, jabs, and some wild-ass chops that I couldn't tell came from watching too much Kung-Fu Theatre or too much Ric Flair. Either way, I knew he'd cave my ribcage in if I let him connect.

I tossed my gun at his face and used the momentary distraction to draw my silver stakes. Even if silver didn't hurt him, getting a pointy thing in the chest will ruin pretty much anything's day. He batted my pistol out of the air, and I slashed out at him with one stake. He blocked my cut, and it felt like I'd just wrapped my arm around a lamppost, backward. The stake clattered out of my now-numb left hand, and he grabbed the front of my shirt.

The vampire drew me to him, his fangs extending as he leaned in to bite me and drain my life force. I flailed a little, battering uselessly at his face and shoulders, then I slumped in his grasp, awaiting my fate. His face got to within inches of mine, and I could smell the stench of the grave on his breath.

Just before his fangs broke my skin, I held up my last marble and whispered through my abused vocal chords, "*Solis Ortus!*"

Several things happened at once. The grip on my throat loosened as the vampire gave me a strange look. The marble floated between us and burst into light like a miniature sun, and the UV rays burned part of my assailant's face off. He jerked back, smoking like the crowd at a Dave Matthews concert, and turned to run. I left the marble-sized sun floating and took off after him.

He was fast, but he ran like I'd melted an eye, which I found out was true when I caught up with him.

I yanked him around, and he used his momentum to follow through with a punch that knocked me back a good ten feet. If I hadn't let myself roll with it, he probably would have broken my jaw. As it was, he just turned to run again. I stood halfway up the ramp and watched his feet as he turned the corner and started up the next level. I focused myself, drew in my will and murmured, "*Constringo.*" I sent my will out with a gesture, and the fleeing vampire's ankles snapped together as if tied by a rope. I found him struggling to stand halfway up the Level 2 parking ramp, one eye turned to black goop, half his face a charred mass of smoking flesh, and part of his mouth burned away revealing one fang.

"What are you?" he asked as I stepped up beside him.

"I'm your worst fucking nightmare, asshole," I said, dropping to one knee with all my weight on the stake in my hand. I *crunched* through his ribcage and pulverized his heart with the silver point. Then I reached behind my back and drew a silver-plated kukri. I used the big curved knife to decapitate the vampire, then I dragged his corpse out of sight. I put his head on his stomach and turned to find his victim, hopefully before it was too late.

I quickly scanned the area where we fought and found nothing. So I started the laborious car-to-car search, walking every inch of the parking garage. As I walked, my mind flashed back to another parking garage and another search that ended a lot worse than I hoped this one would. I was chasing a newborn vamp through downtown and it had just been spotted in the Seventh Street Station garage near a nightclub called Mythos. It was the hottest thing downtown at the time with people lined up out the front entrance trying to get in and lined up around the back entrance grabbing a quick smoke, ducking out to puke when the night got too heavy, or slipping off into the shadows for a little illicit activity.

I remembered the thump of the music driving my footsteps as I heard the gurgle of a life passing through a shredded throat. I turned a corner and the vamp looked up from its meal. That blood-smeared face has stayed with me for years—the blank, animal look, all humanity gone, nothing inhabiting the creature but hunger like a living thing. The beast dropped its prey and came at me, but a baby vamp hasn't been a match for me in decades. I dropped it with two silver throwing knives then took its head with a ridiculously long sword I carried because it was the 90s and I wanted to be the third MacLeod on *Highlander*.

I was too late for the victim, though. I remember running to him, but his throat was nothing more than a mess of flesh and blood. He pressed something into my hand, and I saw it was a school picture of a little girl, a little brown-haired girl who would end up a central character in my own story. I knelt beside him, then turned myself around and sat with his head in my lap. He stared up at me, brown eyes full of fear. Not for himself, but for his daughter, left alone in a world that didn't take care of little girls without fathers. I promised him that I'd look after her, wiped the sweat and blood from his face, and held him while he died.

When the light had left his eyes, I reached down into my lap and snapped his neck to make sure he wouldn't come back. The last thing that little girl needed was her father knocking on her door in a few days asking to come in for a snack.

All these things rolled through my mind as I searched the parking garage for this vampire's victim. I felt Flynn behind my eyes as I peered into cars, trucks, vans, stairwells and elevators.

"No comment, Detective?" I asked the air. I knew she could

hear me if I just thought my questions, but this felt better to me somehow.

I don't know what to say. You told me you were there when he died. You told me he asked about me right before he went, but the whole thing about breaking his neck...I never knew that.

"I didn't think it important until now, but I figured it might come up, so I decided to go ahead and tell you."

I'm glad of that, and I'm glad you did what you did, it's just...I don't know, Harker, what am I supposed to feel?

"Love, if I had any idea what a woman was supposed to feel about anything, I'd have a fucking lot more second dates!" I laughed and then froze. Something wasn't right about the echo. Something else was — *there!* "Found you!"

I ran over to a dark blue Prius with its driver door open. A young woman was lying in a pool of blood by the car's front wheel, her neck shredded and her purse and keys lying on the ground next to her. She was trying to breathe, but there wasn't enough of her throat left to hold the air in.

"Goddammit," I muttered, flashing back again to that other parking garage so many years ago. I knelt beside the woman and pulled her into my lap. She didn't have the strength to resist; she just lay there staring up at me with terrified eyes.

"Don't worry, miss, it'll be fine. I'm with the police, and help is on the way." I said all the reassuring things, all the lies that I hoped would make her feel a little better, but she just stared at me, a frightened woman who no longer had the vocal chords to speak with while she drew her last few breaths.

Her purse caught my eye, and I reached into it, pulling out her wallet. "I'm not going to rob you, darling, I just want — there it is, here we go." I opened her wallet and pulled out her driver's license. "Alright, Suzanne Jonas, you can relax. We'll be able to get in touch with your parents and tell them what happened." She relaxed visibly at my words.

"Do you have a husband?" She shook her head. "A boyfriend?" Another head shake. "A dog?" A weak nod. She was fading faster. "I'll take care of the puppy, Suzanne Jonas. I'll make sure it's cared for and that your parents know that you loved them very much." A tear rolled down her face, then she let out one long, ragged breath, and was still.

I knelt there, holding her body as it slowly went cold, thinking about all the people I'd watched die over the years, and the ones that I'd killed myself. The count was a lot higher than I liked in both categories, and every face flickered across my memory as I knelt in Suzanne Jonas' blood in the parking garage. Then I took a deep breath, squared my shoulders, and snapped her neck to make sure she stayed dead.

Do you just do that to everybody you watch die? Flynn's voice was snotty inside my head, but I let it go. I knew where she was coming from, and I didn't have the energy to fight anyway.

"She was drained. I had to make sure she didn't come back. She was a nice lady. I didn't want to have to kill her tomorrow."

"Don't worry, monster," came a woman's voice behind me. "You won't be around tomorrow to kill anything."

CHAPTER 5

I turned to see a petite woman in her twenties pointing a crossbow at me. A crossbow, of all things? I had just about enough time to wonder if this was an *Arrow* rerun before she pulled the trigger, and the bolt leapt at my chest. I dropped the corpse and sprang out of the way, letting the broadhead bolt sink into the Prius's tire instead of my ribcage.

"What the hell, lady? Didn't your parents teach you not to shoot at strangers?" I said. My mystery assailant was nowhere to be seen. I guessed she was off somewhere reloading. That's the worst thing about crossbows—nobody's made a semi-auto version of them yet.

"They taught me not to take candy from strangers and not to let vampires live to see another sunset." The girl's voice came from near where she'd been standing. I hopped over the roof of the BMW she was hiding behind and tapped her on the shoulder. She spun around and nearly buried a knife in my leg, but I was a little too quick for her. Which meant she was ridiculously fast for a human. I'd better watch out for this one.

She darted away again, but I got a little better look at her this time. Black tights with leather chaps, good for flexibility and protecting the knees. Black hoodie with what looked like a bulletproof vest under it, and if she really knew anything about hunting vampires, I'd bet she had a chainmail choker or something of the like under that hoodie, too.

I revised my earlier guess at her age downward after I looked at her for more than half a second, deciding she was probably in her early twenties. Auburn hair snaked out from under the hood, and her features were Western European, speaking to maybe Germanic or French heritage. She had a big damn knife and a crossbow, and I wasn't in too much of a hurry to see what else she was packing, weapons-wise, but I also wasn't just going to run away and let a psycho with a fetish for pointy things run around my city.

I stopped at the end of the car, focusing to hear her movements. She was smart enough to stay still when I was trying to track her, but she wasn't enough of a pro to control her breathing. I could hear the little panting of her breath a couple of cars over, so I crept backward the length of the car and then crab-walked sideways. She was kneeling behind the tire of an SUV, listening hard for me. *Hate to disappoint you, kid, but I've been skulking around places I wasn't welcome since long before there was such a thing as a parking garage.*

"You want to tell me why you want to shoot me, or should I just go ahead and get that paternity test?" I said. The girl whirled around, but her reflexes were far better than I expected. She fired a new bolt dead at my chest, forcing me to throw myself backwards to keep from getting skewered. Then instead of running again, she leapt at me, knife drawn. I scurried backward to keep her from slicing off anything I really value with the knife, but she just kept on coming.

I finally landed a solid kick to her face that left her on hands and knees for a moment, shaking her head like a bulldog that finally caught a car. I took the opportunity to scramble to my feet and draw my ASP extendable baton. I left my Glock holstered. I didn't want to kill the kid; I just wanted her to stop trying to kill *me*.

"Hey honey, can we talk?" I asked, keeping the baton low in front of me.

The girl tossed her crossbow away behind her and slid her

knife into a sheath on her hip. I stood up a little straighter, relaxing as the hostilities seemed to be lessening. Until she reached behind her back and pulled out a pair of escrima sticks and came at me in a whirling dervish of metal-tipped wooden pain and suffering.

Escrima sticks are those two-foot long wooden sticks that you see Filipinos use in martial arts movies. They're used in arnis, the national martial at of the Philippines, and they're absolutely lethal in the hands of an expert. This girl was an expert because once she got moving, nothing in the world was getting through the spinning barricade of pain she was wielding. I blocked a couple of strikes with my ASP, took a couple of brutal shots to the forearm and thighs, and managed not to collapse whens she scored a solid hit on my left knee.

"Ow, goddammit!" I yelled. "Would you fucking *quit* that?"

To my complete shock, she did. She froze for a minute and stared at me, then came at me again. I backed away, blocking and parrying as well as I could with one bum knee, but finally got frustrated and flung my ASP at her head to try and gain a little space. She ducked, and I hopped over the back of a Mercedes, setting off the car alarm and adding even more noise to our little scrap.

I took advantage of the momentary confusion to focus my will and draw a deep breath. When my attacker came around the end of the car and started at me again, I flung a handful of dust at her and said, "*Somnos.*" She took in a face full of dust, sneezed once, and fell face-first onto the concrete floor, dead asleep. Her escrima sticks clattered to the floor beside her and rolled under a nearby pickup.

"Nighty-night," I said under my breath. A face full of sleep spell was enough to keep a full-grown man out for eight hours. It should have been enough to keep this little slip of a girl knocked cold for twelve or so. So imagine my surprise when I rolled her over and she kicked me square in the family jewels. I toppled over, pinning her beneath me, and just wrapped my arms around her thrashing form. I'm not the biggest guy, but I had at least a hundred pounds on her, and even with my agonized balls, I had enough presence of mind to bear hug the little assassin and not let her go.

She fought like a wildcat, kicking and flailing and biting at me, until I head-butted her in the nose one good time. I heard a wet *crunch*, and blood started to pour from her nose. Then she shifted gears from trying to get loose to kill me, to just trying to get away.

"Hold still, dammit, I don't want to hurt you!" I said once I got my breath back a little.

"Go fuck yourself, vampire!"

"I'm not a vampire, jackass! I killed the vampire. It's the next floor down."

She froze at that, then pulled back a little from me. She looked at my face and said, "Show me your teeth."

I gave her my best disarming smile, which admittedly looks like I'm going to murder someone, especially when I make it a point to show off my not-exceptionally-pointy incisors. "Satisfied?"

"Not even close, but I guess you're not a vampire. You wanna get off me so we can talk about this, or you just gonna dry-hump me in the middle of the garage?"

I let her go but drew my Glock and aimed it at her leg. "You touch those fucking sticks again and I'm going to shoot you in the kneecap. I am not in the mood to fight you any more tonight, so I'm just going to end this shit right here and now. You understand?"

"I got you," she said. I watched as she reached up and with a quick jerk to the right and gout of bright red blood she set her nose back in place. "Fuck! That really hurts." She glared at me.

I didn't bother with sympathy because I typically don't have any. "It's not nice to kick people in the balls. Bad things happen to people who aren't nice, like broken noses."

"Sorry about that. I thought you were a vampire."

"Yeah, about that," I started.

She held up a hand. "Not here. Or at least not yet. We need to deal with these bodies before the police get here. Then we need to be someplace else, *fast*. I don't know why nobody's called it in, with all the noise we were making, but I'm not going to look a gift horse in the mouth. Can you get the vampire up here? If we put both bodies in the trunk of her car, then it'll be easier to get rid of everything."

She started to stand up and I grabbed her arm. "Hold up there, speedy. First off, a Prius does not have a two-corpse trunk. They don't even make cars anymore with two-body trunks. We'd need to steal an SUV at least. But it's not a thing. The cops aren't coming. They've got the elevators and the automobile entrances blocked off, and men on all the stairwells waiting for me to give them the all clear. So we don't have to worry about the authorities showing up because I am the authorities." And boy, did that ever feel weird to say out loud.

She looked at me with a raised eyebrow and I sighed. "I'm going to reach into my back pocket. Don't try anything stupid or I will shoot you, okay?"

She glared at me, a sullen scowl that made her look even younger. "Okay."

I pulled out my wallet and flipped it open to the badge and photo ID Smith insisted I carry. It listed me as a Special

Consultant, Department of Homeland Security. It also listed my name as Quince Goddamn Harper because that's what I told the woman at the ID office when she asked me for the fourth time. My photo was accurate, but unflattering, as I was giving the finger to the camera and rolling my eyes when it was taken. Smith kept pestering me to get a new one, but I was putting it off until the mostly deaf and completely illiterate woman responsible for typing my name incorrectly three times in a row retired.

"This looks like you printed it at home on your inkjet," she said, tossing the leather bi-fold back to me.

I snatched it out of the air and tucked it back in my pocket. "That right there should be proof enough that it's real. If I were going to try and fake a government document, I'd likely do a better job than they could manage."

"Good point. Now what? We leave her here and do what with the vampire?"

"There's nothing else to be done with the vampire, he's forever-dead."

"So what, we just leave?" She asked.

"No, now we go find a place with really, really cold beer and you answer a few questions for me, starting with who you are."

"I'm all for a beer, but you might need something stronger when I tell you the truth about myself. It's a little hard to believe, even for somebody who hunts vampires."

"Why not try me, then we'll head to this little joint called Valhalla. It's just a couple blocks from here and they have fish and chips that are almost good enough to deserve the name."

"Sold," she said, holding out a hand. I shook it and she looked me straight in the eye as she continued. "My name is Gabriella Van Helsing, and I'm the great-granddaughter of the man who killed Dracula."

Well, fuck. I heard echo through my thoughts as this news registered with Flynn.

My thoughts exactly, I thought, then went rapidly in search of that beer.

CHAPTER 6

I walked a couple of steps behind Gabby, as she told me to call her, and pulled out my phone. I sent a quick text to Ren saying nothing more than "911 - Van Helsing in CLT. 911!" Then I sped up to catch the trim woman, noting briefly how nice the view was from the back. For a cold-blooded killer sworn to destroy part of my family, she had a really fantastic ass.

"So you're a descendant of the Van Helsing from the movie, huh?" It was all I could do to not append "that fat shite" in front of "Van Helsing." That's the only way I've ever heard the name, after all.

"Yeah, he was my great-grandfather. I never knew him—he died long before I was born." I knew that was true, since she didn't look to be any older than her early thirties, and besides, I'd been in the room with her grandparents when old Abraham died in 1906. Old Abraham had always been kind to me, with his thick beard and funny accent, even if he did always ask me questions about Uncle Luke. Mother and Father made me promise to never tell Abraham about Uncle Luke, so it was in complete ignorance of his old nemesis standing right outside the window in the snow that Abraham Van Helsing, legendary vampire hunter, passed in the wee hours of the morning. He was surrounded by his son and daughter-in-law, my parents, the other survivors of the hunt on Dracula, and me.

I watched raptly as the old man's breathing became labored, then rattled to a stop sometime in the darkest hours of the night. I watched Abraham, I watched my parents for clues on how to act, I watched his family, and every once in a while I went to the window and stared out at Uncle Luke.

Luke stood on a small hill almost a hundred yards away from the window, unmoving. It's in the stillness when vampires look least human and more like the dead things they really are. Luke stood for hours, never moving so much as an eyelid as his old adversary railed against the dying of the light. I looked out the window one last time after they pulled the sheet up over the old man's face, and Luke raised his hand, as if in tribute, then disappeared. I didn't see him for months after Van Helsing's death, and when he returned, there was a new shadow in his eyes, a new tone of melancholy in his voice.

"Hey, you okay?" Gabby's voice snapped me back to the present. "Is this the place?" she asked, gesturing to a heavy wooden door with antique hardware. The wooden sign above the heavy door read, "Valhalla."

"Yeah, this is it," I said, pulling the door open for her. We entered a low-ceilinged pub with dark wood and about a dozen beer taps. The place was almost full, but the noise level was surprisingly low. We took a booth in the back, and I ordered a double shot of Johnny Walker Black and a beer back.

"Jesus, Harper, go easy on that stuff. I don't want to have to pour you into a cab," Gabby said.

"I've got a quick metabolism," I said. Our drinks showed up almost immediately, and I slammed my scotch and motioned the waitress to bring me another. I knocked back half my beer in one long pull and waved a few fingers at the vampire huntress. "Okay, tell me a story, Miss Van Helsing, if that's even your real name." I knew it was her real name long before she pulled out her own wallet and slapped her ID down on the table. There was no mistaking her grandmother's eyes, and her great-grandfather's cheekbones, and the fire in her eyes that was all hunter. She was going to be a serious problem.

"This might sound a little far-fetched, but you handled yourself back there like somebody who's seen a thing or two outside the ordinary, so maybe you'll be able to handle it." I managed not to snort my beer at the understatement, which I considered an enormous accomplishment, especially with Flynn laughing her ass off inside my head.

You're so fucked, Harker. It's like she's you, only with boobs!

I hadn't noticed her boobs until that point, so I took a moment to rectify that oversight. Not bad. Pert, like her ass, and her smile, which fell off her face as she caught me staring at her chest.

"My eyes are up here, asshole."

"That's not what I'm looking at, love. I mean, they're nice and all, but they're not exactly what's holding my attention right now. That amulet, where did you get it?" She pulled a gold chain and the rest of the piece of jewelry came into view.

"My father gave it to me when it became obvious I wasn't going to follow his footsteps and stay the hell away from the family business. It belonged to—"

"Van Helsing," I said, the words soft. I remembered it dangling from the old man's hands as he spun it in front of the firelight to entertain a chubby-cheeked little boy. I could almost hear his accented voice talking to my mother. *Now, Mina, I know he seems like just an ordinary little boy, but ve must take every precaution to make sure he grows up and remains ordinary. Mein Gott, child, just think what changes that monster may have wrought upon you and Jonathan in your time under his thrall!*

It wasn't until much later that I realized he was using the amulet to see if I felt its power, to see if I was attracted to magical things. I wasn't, not then. It wasn't until much later, long after old Abraham was dead and buried, that my talents manifested.

"Yes, how did you know?" Gabby asked, her face suddenly a mask. I could feel the tension rolling off her in waves. Every nerve tight as a bowstring, she was ready to bolt at a moment's notice.

"I...I saw it in a book, I think. A photograph, or maybe an illustration. It's how he warded himself from Dracula's mental powers, right?" I put on a face of an enthusiastic fan, burying the level of my interest.

"Yes, exactly!" she said, clapping her hands a little. "It allows the wearer to resist magical spells and abilities. I'm not sure why it worked on your knockout dust, though. It shouldn't have any effect on biological or chemical agents."

"Maybe it's because I bought it at a Chinese herb shop. The lady at the counter insisted it was ground up unicorn horn and was good for helping others sleep, or for keeping part of me awake, if you know what I mean."

"Oh great, so I got knocked out by a dose of Viagra? Brilliant." Yeah, but that was a lot easier than telling her she got knocked out by a spell cast by the nephew of the man her entire family was dedicated to destroying.

"So what brings you to Charlotte?" I asked. "I'm guessing it's not a gig at one of the banks, like most people."

"I'm hunting a master vampire. I picked up his trail outside Boston, and I've been chasing him down the east coast for the past nine months. He never stays more than a couple of weeks in any city, and he's usually fastidious about his kills. This is the first time he's used lackeys and the first time he's turned anyone. I don't know what caused the change in MO."

"Power," I said simply.

"Excuse me?" Van Helsing asked.

"He's been building a power base. He started in Boston

because that's where the seat of vampire government in the US is. Or was. My guess would be that he killed all the members of the council and just installed vamps loyal to him in their seats. Or he just killed people until they all started agreeing with him."

"You talk like you know this guy." She looked at me over her beer, some local brew called a Jam Session. I hate cute beer names, but it's a decent brew.

"I know vampires. Consensus-building isn't exactly on their resumes."

"And how do you come to know so much about vampires, Mr. Harper?" She was still using the misspelling typed on my badge, and as long as it kept her a couple steps away from Uncle Luke, I was happy to keep her a little confused as to my real identity.

"I don't know if you noticed the small print on my badge or not, but I'm a part of Homeland Security's Paranormal Division. We're kinda like The *X-Files*, but without the skeptics. I hunt down things that go bump in the night, and I make them stop bumping. Vampires are one of the most common supernatural creatures, and unlike witches and most weres, they don't just want to be left alone to dance naked under a full moon. They eat people to stay alive, and that's also how they make more vampires, so I have a professional interest in vampires."

"But what's your story, Harper? Nobody graduates from college and wants to be a vampire hunter. It's personal. It's always personal. My family has been in this business for over a hundred years, why are you doing it?"

"A vampire attacked my mother. My father rescued her, with some help, but he lost a good friend and got a little chewed in the process. So I grew up knowing that there were bad things out there and that sometimes good people have to stand up against them." More half-truths. If I get much better at this, I might rethink my personal ban on marriage.

"So now what, Mr. Secret Agent Man?" Gabby asked.

"Now I think the best solution is for you to let us handle this. We've got plenty of resources and plenty of experience. We can take care of one vampire, even if he is powerful."

"But it's not just one vampire," she protested. "You saw that tonight. This guy's got minions, and that means he's organized and might be making a move on the local vamp boss. Do you have any idea who that is?"

"We do. We've actually got a relationship with him and have used him as a resource from time to time."

"God, the government really will get in bed with anybody. But I guess the devil you know, and all that. But if you think I'm leaving just because you pat me on the head and send me on my merry way, you've got another think coming. I've been chasing this bastard for months now, and the only way I'm leaving Charlotte is with his heart in a box. Figuratively speaking, of course. I don't actually carry vampire hearts around in a box. Oh, hi!" She turned to the waitress, who was standing by my elbow looking both shocked and a little queasy at the talk of vampire hearts.

"Do...you two know what you'd like to eat?" the poor pale woman asked.

"I'll do the fish and chips, please," I said.

"I can do the same. You have malt vinegar?" Gabby asked. The waitress pointed to a bottle on the table and turned to beat a hasty retreat.

"You guys order enough for three?" asked Detective Flynn as she passed the waitress en route to our table. "Detective Rebecca Flynn, Charlotte-Mecklenburg PD." She held out a hand to

Gabby, who took it. Gabby looked back and forth between the two of us, eyebrows crawling to the ceiling.

"I'm on temporary assignment to Homeland Security as Q's partner," Flynn explained. She turned to me. "Cleanup is done with the garage, and Smith wants to debrief you back at HQ as soon as you're done with your date night. His words, not mine."

"Oh good lord, Becks, it's not a date! She's cute enough, but for Christ's sake, I'm old enough to be her father!" And that was just how I looked. I was really old enough to be her great-grandfather. "But I'd better go ahead and boogie. You can fill Miss Van Helsing here on everything we do at Homeland Security, and she can give you all the information she had on the new fang-boy in town. I'll go make nice with the boss, and y'all have a nice kibbutz."

I left the two women waiting on their fish and chips, something I truly regretted missing out on, and hauled ass back to my car, parked on the curb out front of The Green garage. I hopped into the Honda and smoked the tires pulling out into traffic. I had to get to Uncle Luke and find a way to get him out of town. There was a new Van Helsing in town, and the last thing in the world I needed was a rematch of Stoker's novel in the streets of Charlotte.

CHAPTER 7

"I'm not leaving" was Luke's response to the news of Gabriella Van Helsing's appearance. "I won't let that fat shite's granddaughter run me out of the city I love, especially when that ungrateful bastard Augustus is in town."

"I'm not saying she should run you out of town, Uncle Luke. I'm just saying that this would be a great time for that New York vacation you've been talking about for the past decade or so. You haven't even seen Times Square since it went all Disney! You'd barely recognize the place. And Broadway! You love the theatre."

"Oh yes, Quincy, I'll jet off to New York and watch some has-been television 'actor' in a stage version of a mediocre movie because that's what passes for original art these days. No, these fools think they can just waltz in here and take over my city? Well, they've got another think coming!"

"I think only one of them wants to take over the city. I think the other wants to kill the one who wants to take over the city. And every vampire, like, ever. So, by extension...you," I said. "Ren, would you help me out here?"

"I'm sorry, Master Quincy, I must agree with the Count's assessment of these circumstances. The only acceptable response to a threat from an outside force is to destroy the threat. Abandoning our city and our responsibilities to it simply is not an option."

"What responsibilities?" I asked. "You drink people, and every once in a while you bail my ass out of jail or something else stupid that I've done. And I have the whole federal government to do that now! So I'm good. And we can find people for you to drink in Atlanta, or Nashville —"

"I hate country music," Luke cut in.

"Then Memphis! Whatever. Please, Uncle Luke, just take a couple weeks and vanish while I deal with Gus and little miss Helsing. I'll get everything straightened out and you can come home, I promise." I reached into my pocket and grabbed my vibrating phone. The screen read "Flynn," so I swiped my finger across it.

"You've been talking to me inside my head all night and *now* you decide to call? What's up?"

"The whole head-to-head thing was giving me a headache. Where are you?"

"I'm at Luke's, trying to get him to leave town for a little while. You?" Our bond allowed me to see through her eyes so I didn't really need to ask, but I was trying to respect her boundaries. It was hard, something about old dogs and new tricks, but I was getting there.

"I'm on my way home for a little sack time. I left your girl at the Hyatt House downtown. She's registered under the name Mary Jane Watson."

"Like in *Spiderman*?"

"Apparently she's a comic book nerd and a vampire hunter. Who would have guessed?"

"I suppose the two go hand in hand. What's the plan?" I asked.

"Like I said, I'm going to sleep for a while, then get back at it in the morning. By then forensics will have everything from your dead vampires and we can try to figure out where this guy is operating out of. Then if we're lucky, we can stage a daytime raid."

"You know that doesn't really matter, right? Vampires don't really sleep all day. Luke sleeps because he prefers it to the reminder of being stuck indoors, but he can function in daytime just fine if he has to. And I bet a SWAT team breaking down the door qualifies as 'has to'."

"Well, shit, then. I guess I'll just let you go first, then. Meet me at the station at 10. We'll see what we can dig up on Augustus' location and make a plan from there."

"Deal. I'll see you there." I pressed a button on the screen and slid the phone back into my jeans.

"So you and your little human think you're going after Augustus Renfield on your own? Are you delusional or just stupid?" Luke asked.

"Not the first time you've asked me that question, Uncle. And not the first time I've ignored it. Can I crash here for the night? Between fighting vampires in the morgue, fighting vampires in the car park, and fighting a vampire hunter, I'm beat."

"You must be tired, Master Quincy," Ren remarked.

"Why's that?"

"You called it a car park. You never let your British show unless you're extremely tired, or around a bunch of Englishmen."

I chuckled. "Or drunk, Renfield. I get very British when I drink, too." I went upstairs to my room and stripped down for a shower. After a long shower under steaming water, I lay awake on top of my sheets thinking for a long time.

Seeing Gabby Van Helsing brought back a lot of memories and sent my thoughts spinning down corridors in my mind that had long been deserted. I flashed back to that night watching old Abraham pass on; I remembered birthdays and Christmases with his family, then more birthdays and Christmases with just my family, then the one Christmas we had between my mother's death and my father's passing. I remembered burying my parents, my brothers, every friend I ever had. It was a melancholy parade of funerals that marched across my memory until the sun rose and I got up to take another shower and meet Flynn.

I had just pulled on my black jeans when there was a knock at my door. "Come in."

Renfield opened the door and stepped in with a glass of orange juice. "Good morning, Master Quincy. I brought you some juice."

"Thanks, Ren, but I could have gotten it myself. I'm heading down in a few minutes anyway."

"I understand that, sir, but I wanted to ask you something first. Something...of a personal nature."

"Something you didn't want my uncle to hear you ask me," I clarified.

"I don't want you to think I'm keeping secrets from him, sir, it's just that..."

"Go ahead, Ren. I'm something of an expert on keeping secrets from Uncle Luke. I know you'd never do anything to endanger him."

"Of course not, it's nothing like that. It's this new vampire, sir. I'm worried."

I looked at Ren. He didn't look worried, but he never did. Renfield was the most unflappable human being I'd ever met, and I'm really old, so I've met a lot of people. "What are you worried about, Ren?"

"He's scared, sir."

"Luke?"

"Yes, sir. It took me a little while to recognize it because I've never seen the symptoms, but he's honestly frightened of this vampire and his challenge."

I sat down on my bed and started lacing up my Doc Martens, noticing that Ren had not only shined my boots in the few hours I'd been asleep, he'd also replaced the worn lace in my right boot, emptied the pockets of the jeans I'd been wearing, put all that crap on my dresser, and either bought me a new duster or just pulled one from a magical leather duster supply he has somewhere in Luke's house.

I thought about what he said for a minute, then looked up at him. "I don't think he's afraid that Gus will hurt him, or kill him, or somehow win. I think he's afraid that he's actually going to have to do something about Gus once and for all. That he's too far gone to save, and there's no more last chances. I think that's the thing he's most afraid of — that he's going to have to destroy someone he once cared about quite a bit."

"He really is a soft touch, isn't he?"

"For an undead monster who lives by consuming the life force of others, yeah, he's a real teddy bear."

"I don't find that funny, Master Quincy," Ren sniffed.

"I wasn't joking, Ren," I let my voice get hard. "I know you think you know Luke. I know that right now you do know him better than all but two or three people in the world. You know what he likes for breakfast, how he likes his blood mixed with a little cabernet so he can pretend to be human, what TV shows he prefers, even what period of art he really cares for. But you've got to understand, underneath all of that is a hard-core motherfucker who did not become the thing mother warned their children about in Eastern Europe for decades by handing out candy canes at the Christmas parade.

"When he wants to be, when he *needs* to be, he can drop all that 'Uncle Luke' bullshit in a hot second and turn into Count Motherfucking Dracula, Vlad the Goddamn Impaler, Lord of the Undead and One Hundred Per Cent Baddest Son of a Bitch on the Planet. If you forget, ever, for even a second, that your employer can rip your heart out of your chest with his bare hands and drink the blood from it while it still beats hot in his palm, it may be the last mistake you make."

"You don't think he'd hurt me, do you? I've been nothing but loyal and faithful."

"And as long as that's the case, you'll never have a problem. But Gus? He turned on my uncle. He felt betrayed, and betrayed Luke in turn. So no matter how much it pains Uncle Luke to do it, he will bring down hell upon the head of Augustus Renfield, and God help anyone who gets in his way. Because this ain't no movie BS. This is the real deal, and Dracula is gonna get biblical on a motherfucker. That's what you've been noticing. It's not fear. It's regret moving into resignation at the knowledge that after all the time and all the second chances, he's going to have to solve Gus for good."

CHAPTER 8

I first met Augustus in Paris after the war. World War II, that is, which is the only war Paris has known in my lifetime. I had spent some time in the end of the war working with the French Resistance, and I was making my way back to my apartment late one night when I heard a muffled scream from an alley.

I ran into the alley, which might have been more of a stumble given the amount of good French wine I'd consumed, and saw a gaunt man holding a woman against a wall. To most normal people, I'm sure it looked like they were making out. But I knew the difference between two people kissing and one person drinking blood from another's neck.

"Merde," I muttered, and ran down the alley. I picked up a piece of lumber lying on the ground by a wall undergoing repairs and swung it hard across the vampire's shoulders. The board broke into two pieces with a resounding *crack*, and I shook my hands at the sting.

The vampire slowly drew himself up to his full height and turned to face me. "That was very rude," it said. "I don't abide rudeness during my meals." The face he turned to me was an almost normal face, except for the pallor. He had mousy brown hair that parted on one side and hung down a little too long in the front. He wore a brown tweed suit and a striped shirt, and there was just a hint of blood on his brown bowtie. His features were preternaturally narrow, with cheekbones reaching almost to his hairline and the sunken cheeks of a man who hadn't fed in months. But there was no shortage of food in Paris after the blitz, what with the orphans and widows and homeless.

He reached out and took my shirtfront in his hand, and I marveled at his fingers, the longest and boniest appendages I'd ever seen. He pulled me to him and locked gazes with me. "I think you shall become my meal since you interrupted this one. She'll never taste the same."

He turned his attention to the young woman he'd been drinking from when I happened by. "Goodbye, my dear." He then flicked out his other hand and ripped her throat out, without ever losing his bemused, slightly surprised expression. Her eyes went wide, and she opened her mouth to scream, but it's hard to do more than gurgle with your vocal chords ripped out. She collapsed against a wall, crimson pouring down her bodice and covering her body as she died.

"You bastard," I growled. "You could have fed from her without killing her."

"I could have," he agreed, "but why? She was food. I was finished with her. Wasteful, I admit, but I don't believe she would remain fresh in this heat."

He still had a grip on my shirtfront, but it was loose in his fingers. I reached up to knock his hand away, but he caught my wrist in those skeletal fingers and shook me, hard. My head whipsawed back and forth, and my wine threatened to make a surprise appearance all over this vampire's dandy bowtie.

"What are you doing here, human? Do you blindly rush into death often? I would expect that to be a poor choice."

"Human is only part of the picture, vampire. I'm a little more than you're accustomed to," I said, pulling my wrist free and lifting him off his feet with a short uppercut. Gus staggered back a few steps, giving me all the room I needed. Or so I thought. I charged him, my shoulder low to catch him under the ribs and smear his accent all over the opposite wall.

Except he wasn't there. He spun out of the way faster than anyone I'd ever seen, and I learned to fight dirty from friggin' Dracula. He landed four quick shots to my midsection, and I heard a sharp *crack* as each punch landed, signaling a cavalcade of broken ribs and pain for me.

I dropped to one knee, the pain in my ribs making breathing all but impossible. I felt the whistle of a fist through the air and rolled to one side, barely avoiding the double-fisted blow that would have broken my neck. I looked up into the mad face of my attacker, and there was something strangely familiar there. He stomped down, and I caught his foot with both hands and shoved him backward. He toppled over onto his back, and we both leapt to our feet. We threw punch after punch, faster than any human could ever punch or block, but it took less than a minute for the pain in my ribs to sap the strength from my blows and the speed from my blocks.

I was just a hair too late getting my arm up, and he flicked out a jab that caught me flush on the point of the chin. I saw stars, birds whirling around me head, the whole bit as I sank to my butt in the alley. He stood over me, droplets of blood-sweat beading his brow.

"What are you?" he asked. "You're right, you're not human. Or at least not completely. But you're not a vampire, nor a were of any type I've encountered."

"What he is, Augustus, is my nephew. And thus off-limits for your appetites." Uncle Luke's voice came from the mouth of the alley. I have never before and rarely since been so happy that my uncle, the blood-sucking Lord of the Undead, has an overprotective streak. I peered past Gus to watch Luke stride down the alley, his raincoat billowing out behind him like the long cloaks he favored in the movies. He stopped about ten feet from us, just out of leaping range for his psychotic former manservant.

I caught a flicker of movement out of the corner of one eye and turned my attention back to Gus. I drew in a sharp and extremely painful breath at what I saw. Where he used to look like a harmless, if a little lecherous, skinny man in a boring suit, now his eyes were wild and rolling in his head like a dog caught in a bear trap. More bloody sweat poured from his brow, the crimson staining his shirt collar. Something, I couldn't tell what—fear, rage, excitement—vibrated through him like electricity.

"You!" the gaunt man hissed at Uncle Luke.

"Me," Luke replied calmly. "I see you found some measure of control over your abilities and have made something of a life for yourself. I am glad. I never wished you ill, Augustus. I just didn't think this life was the best for you."

"You didn't want the competition, *Sire*. You didn't want anyone else to taste the power, the sweet, sweet power that comes with the blood. But I did, yes, I have drank from the spring of eternal life and I have felt the power run through my veins! And now you can't stop me, *Sire*. No one can stop me!"

He sprang at Uncle Luke, all gangly arms and claw-like fingers, like some crazed spider flying through the alley. Luke simply swung a hand up and slapped him out of the air. Gus bounced off one brick wall and then crashed to the broken cobblestones, writhing. Luke reached down and helped me up, then opened his wrist with a thumbnail.

"Drink," he said, thrusting his arm at me.

I gaped at him. I'd drank from Luke before, but only when mortally wounded. This was painful, but nothing life threatening, so I didn't understand why he was so insistent.

"Drink, Quincy," he repeated, his voice an urgent hiss. "Drink, then run. Augustus is powerful and completely insane. He will have no restraint, and now that he knows we are close, he will destroy you if given the opportunity. You must heal, and then you must return to our quarters and pack our things. If I do not return by sunrise, flee. I will find you."

I drank, taking in the stolen life force of Dracula himself. Drinking blood is gross, let's start there. It's coppery, thick, and nasty shit. And I only know this because of some ill-conceived experimentation Uncle Luke and I did in 1918, after both my brothers died in the influenza epidemic that killed a good portion of, well, the world. We wondered why I could visit them and not even get sick, and then it occurred to Luke that I hadn't really aged much in the past few years. I was twenty-two and still looked fifteen, a useful trait with the ladies, less so when drinking in bars. They weren't all that strict, but the more I looked like a little kid, the less likely I was to get served from the top shelf.

Anyway, drinking human or animal blood is nasty, but drinking vampire blood? Let's just say I understand how people fall under the thrall of unscrupulous vamps. It's like the very best red wine, but sweeter, and the rush you get is like no drug I've ever tried. And I've tried pretty much every drug that can be created without a chemistry set, and some that can't.

I let the warm liquid flow across my teeth and down my throat, feeling my ribs knit back together, all my bruises fade, and even feel a little indigestion clear up. The cut on my chin from shaving that morning even healed in seconds. I tore myself free from Luke's arm with a profound sadness and feeling of loss. I licked my thumb and ran it over his wrist, using the magic in my spit and his blood to heal the wound.

"Now go," he said, wiping his arm dry against his cloak.

I turned to do just that, but it was too late, Gus was on us again, and this time he was equally intent on killing me as he was destroying Luke. But he couldn't handle both of us at top form—not many things can, honestly. He charged me, rightly considering me to be the weaker of the two threats, but I was well into my magical studies by that point, so I focused my will and said "*Ventos!*" I flung my hand in his direction, and a whirlwind picked up every piece of debris in the alley and pelted him with it.

It was a petty distraction, of course, but I just need to get him to close his eyes for an instant. He did, and I dropped the spell. Luke didn't run by me, he didn't leap past me, he jumped over me in a flying kick and took Gus square in the chest.

"Run!" Luke shouted at me, but I didn't. Why bother, right? We had this guy dead to rights now that we were healthy and working together, didn't we?

Well, no. Luke's kick caught the off-balance Augustus square and knocked him flat, with Luke rolling through to come up on his feet at the other end of the alley, but Gus popped right back up with not so much as a scratch on him and dove for me, his fangs out and aiming for my throat.

I flung up a hasty shield spell, just enough to slow him down for a second or two, but that's all Luke needed. He grabbed Gus from behind and smashed his face into the cobblestones at my feet.

"Run, damn you, or I'll never be able to concentrate!" Luke yelled at me. This time I did as I was told—I ran. I hauled ass back to the small apartment house where we had three rooms, and I woke up the current (and brand-new) Renfield.

The poor guy hadn't yet gotten used to being up all night and sleeping a few hours here and there during the day, so he was in his nightshirt when he answered the pounding on his door.

"Master Quincy? What is wrong?" he asked through bleary eyes.

I said one word, the one word that ever since Luke and I belly-laughed our way through *Frankenstein* had meant "pack all our shit and be ready to move." I looked at Renfield, and I said, "Pitchfork."

He goggled at me for a moment, then he drug up "Pitchfork" in his memory, and his eyes got wide. I reached out and caught the lamp he nearly dropped as he turned to go back into the room.

"Renfield, are we clear? We are Pitchfork."

Renfield turned to me, all signs of sleepiness gone from his face. "Indeed, Master Quincy. We are Pitchfork." Then he turned back to his room and started packing. Luke made it to the apartment just before sunup, and Renfield and I loaded him into the limousine we had specially prepared for just such an occurrence. It had a separate passenger compartment for Luke that was completely light tight, as well as a regular compartment that was big enough for two other passengers. Renfield drove, and I started the journey back in Luke's compartment with him.

"You look like me after that five-day bender in Berlin back in 1926," I said.

"Yes, that was quite a time you had. Who knew that you would celebrate your thirtieth birthday by getting in a fight with six Germans, three Austrians, and one random Italian woman who just happened to be walking by at the wrong moment?"

"In my defense, I was drunk at the time," I replied.

"If I recall correctly, nephew, you were drunk for the entirety of 1926," Luke replied, smiling. He winced, putting a hand to his split lip.

"It was an experiment. I wanted to see what would happen if I got drunk every day for a whole year."

"And what were your findings?"

"I found that it takes a lot of money to get me drunk, and I don't get fat like normal people. So I got drunk a lot, and I got very poor very quickly. I don't recommend it as a lifestyle. Nor do I recommend doing battle with incredibly strong vampires in alleyways. Who was that beast?"

"That was my old manservant, Augustus Renfield."

"The one who...?"

"Yes, the one from the book. There were a few things incorrect in the story, of course."

"Of course. It mentions the fact that you're dead, after all," I agreed.

"Well, I am dead, but not forever dead as Stoker implied. And Renfield was not always a madman, but he certainly became one after many years in my service. I believe your aunts may have had something to do with that."

"You never talk about them," I observed.

"They were a mistake. I do not enjoy discussing my mistakes."

"A mistake you made three times." I might have taken a little too much joy in twisting the knife, but Luke so rarely showed any self-doubt or vulnerability, I couldn't resist.

"Well, it takes a certain amount of experimentation to prove a theorem. I had to know that all three of them were mistakes, you see." He gave a little half-smile, and it made me feel better that he was still capable of laughing at himself.

"So this Renfield, the original. What's his problem?" I knew by the twitch under his eye that I had hit on a sensitive subject, but I wasn't about to let go. "Go on, Uncle. He almost killed us both tonight, I deserve to know about him."

"I promised him eternal life in exchange for three decades of service. The same offer I make to all my valets. Most of them realize after only a few years that they are not cut out for service to one such as myself and do not last the term, or they realize that there is a great deal more "forever" than "living" in living forever, and they choose a generous mortal severance instead. Augustus came to neither of those conclusions. He fixated on becoming like me, becoming one with the night, until it drove him quite mad.

"He was mad long before his term was up and could not fulfill his terms of the bargain, so I was under no obligation to turn him. He did not see things quite that way and escaped from the asylum, insisting that I give him The Gift. I refused, and he ran away."

"Until today?" I asked.

"Oh, but I wish it were so," Luke replied. "He returned to England some years hence, already one of the undead. And the power he had! He was the strongest of us I had ever seen! I know not how he grew so strong, but I believe it is from drinking the blood of many elder vampires. As you know, there is power in the blood, and the older the vampire, the more power there is to be found. Augustus found that power and returned to England to destroy me. I could not vanquish him and keep those I cared about safe, so I returned to Transylvania, in part to escape, but mainly to do battle on familiar ground. Van Helsing went with me, as did Holmwood, and your father, leaving you the man of the house to look after your brothers and mother."

"I remember that trip," I said. "I was eight or nine. I never knew where Father went, only that we had to get dressed up when he came home and that Mother cried a lot that summer."

"She wept for Arthur Holmwood, who Augustus killed with his bare hands. It was likely to his funeral that you went upon your father's return. She wept in fear of repercussions from our visit, for although we thrashed Augustus soundly, he escaped before we were able to mete out a final, killing blow. But we did defeat him, and we imprisoned him within my old castle there, hopefully until such a time that he either died of hunger or found himself somehow and became less of a danger to others."

"Apparently neither of those things happened," Luke said, staring out the black windows at a history only he could see.

"Apparently not," I agreed. "Now what?" I asked.

"Now we find out where he sleeps and we kill him at high noon, when his power is at its lowest point."

"That's a plan I can get behind," I said. "You get some rest, we'll be at the safe house in an hour." I slid between compartments and directed Renfield to one of our many boltholes around the French countryside.

CHAPTER 9

"Obviously, we didn't kill Gus. We couldn't find his lair, so after several days of searching, we left Paris and worked very hard to forget about him." I finished my little tale and stood up, ready to go out and face the day. Or at least face police headquarters, where I was overdue to meet Flynn and Smith.

"Until last night," Ren said.

"Until last night," I agreed. "Look, Ren, I don't know what to tell you about Gus. He's the only Renfield my uncle's ever had that went cuckoo, and maybe he was a little nutso before Luke took him on. But it's not like it's a thing, people that work for Luke going crazy and getting turned into über-vamps. So if you're worried about that…"

"That's not it at all, Master Quincy. I merely wanted some background on the man so that I might better understand the monster he's become. If I understand him, I'll be better prepared to fight him should he attack us here."

"No!" I said, a little more vehemently than I intended. "Gus is bad juju. If he comes after you here, do not engage, just get the hell out. Luke can take him if he's rested and Gus doesn't get the drop on him, and if he doesn't have to worry about anyone he cares about becoming collateral damage. That's one thing that kept him from going full out against him back in Paris—he was worried I'd get caught in the crossfire somehow. So if he comes here, get to safety, and call me as fast as you can."

"What will you do?" Renfield asked. "You've already said you can't beat him."

"In a fair fight, I can't. I don't stand a chance. He's faster, stronger, and can withstand way more punishment. Good thing for me, I don't fight fair." I patted Ren on the shoulder and stood up. "I gotta roll. Becks and Smith are waiting for me at headquarters. I'll be back at dusk to put my head together with Luke and plan tonight's hunt."

"I'll take care of him while you're away," Ren said.

I looked at the sincere little man, all creases and quiet competence. "I know you will, buddy."

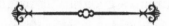

By the time I grabbed a nasty fast food biscuit and kickstarted my system with a jumbo soda, it was 10:30, so I was almost an hour late when I strolled into the conference room we'd appropriated from the Charlotte-Mecklenburg Police Department. I stopped dead in my tracks at the sight of Gabriella Van Helsing standing next to Flynn, both in pant suits and sensible shoes that screamed, "I'm a government agent and I have at least one firearm hidden under this suit jacket."

"What the flying green fuck is she doing here?" I asked as I sat at one end of the table. It wasn't a power thing, it was just closer to the outlets and I needed to charge my phone. I plugged the electronic everything into the wall and put my keys next to it. I left more phones in stupid places until I started putting my keys next to them. That way I can't leave without getting my keys, and I see my phone under them.

"Ms. Van Helsing is on detachment from the Federal Bureau of Investigation, here to explore the possibility that the deaths we've experienced are part of a larger pattern, a serial killer that has been working the United States for nearly sixty years." I couldn't see enough in Smith's eyes to see if he knew her cover was bullshit or not, so I went along with it.

"That's nuts," I said. "How could one killer operate for so long without drawing attention to himself? I'm sure what we've got here in Charlotte is an isolated incident. You can stay if you like, and help us with our investigation, but let's not be thinking that this a great time to push the yokels aside and make a name for yourself, because it's not."

"I assure you, Mr. Harper, that is the last thing I intend to do. As a matter of fact, as a gesture of goodwill, I brought in all the data from the Bureau's geographic profile. It shows the most likely location for this bloodsucker's safe house to be somewhere between Fifth Street and Eighth Street on College. Do any of you know of any abandoned building in that area?"

"Not really," Smith said. "That's right in the heart of Uptown. I mean, I suppose there are some hidey-holes around Discovery Place where he could build a nest, but I can't imagine anything would really be private enough."

"The Carolina Theatre," I said. Everybody turned to look at me. "Oh come on, folks. It's right there in the center of the profile zone, and it's been abandoned forever. It's perfect. It even has the vampire-ready architecture. If he's anywhere downtown, that's where he'll be."

"Abandoned theatres do tend to make excellent hideouts," Van Helsing agreed. "Particularly if there are any Deco or Gothic features, many older vampires will feel very much at home there."

"I've never been inside the place," I said. "But from the pictures I've seen, it's currently decorated in Early Decay. But it was big-deal Vaudeville-style theatre back in the day."

"Then that's our most likely spot," Van Helsing said. "We should launch our assault soon. Vampires are perfectly capable of functioning during daylight hours, but they are weaker, and exposure to sunlight is fatal to their kind."

"So if you find yourself in a pinch, break a window," I said. "What's the team?" I asked Smith.

"Just the four of us," he replied. I raised an eyebrow. "We don't have enough men trained in dealing with supernatural threats. We learned that the hard way dealing with War a few months ago. And since I'm in no hurry to throw perfectly good men away, I thought we'd skip the suicide mission today."

"Makes sense," I said. My scrap with the incarnation of War itself wiped out two street gangs, one biker gang, and a dozen very brave and very unprepared police officers.

"Let's load up. We should be able to do this in one Suburban," Smith said.

"There are four of us, Smitty. We could do this in a Hyundai." I followed him down the hall and we boarded an elevator. A couple floors later, the doors opened up into a parking garage full of all-black SUVs and sedans. We piled into a Suburban and rolled out of the underground garage, blue lights flashing. It was a little anticlimactic that there was no traffic in the middle of the day and that our ride in the urban assault vehicle was only about six blocks, but sometimes when you work with the government, you've got to do things the government way.

I strapped into the passenger seat and sent a little mental "knock knock" back to Flynn, who was sharing the backseat with Van Helsing.

Yeah, what's up, Harker?

Harper, I corrected. At least for today. The chick next to you isn't FBI, she's —

Flynn cut me off. *I was there, remember? At least part of the time. I know who she is. But why hide your name? It's not like the connection is that obvious.*

It would be to her. I knew her family growing up. There's a chance there might be old pictures of me around. I'd like to keep my ID hidden unless it's absolutely necessary. And the how? My badge printed wrong, remember? The stupid woman down in HR who can't do anything right except file enough discrimination complaints every year that everyone's terrified to fire her? She strikes again. But this time she may be useful.

That would be a first. Fine, I won't do anything to blow your cover, but you're on your own with Smith.

Yeah, that was a whole different issue. But before I got a chance to communicate anything to our boss, we were at the theatre. The only thing to indicate there had ever been a Carolina Theatre was a blue neon sign running up one wall. Every other indication that the building we were looking was anything other than the backside of a bank or warehouse was gone. I walked up to a side entrance, but it was locked.

"Anything?" I called to Smith, who had gone over to the small door in the front of the facade.

"No. Locked up tight."

"The alley it is, then," I said. I motioned for him to head my way and turned to see Flynn and Van Helsing walking toward me. Flynn tossed a pile of metal at me, and I snatched it out of the air. I turned it over in my hands a couple of times, then looked at her.

"Ummm, thanks, but I'm not into the whole bondage thing," I said.

She took the thing out of my hands, shook it once, undid a clasp, and tossed it around my neck. Once it settled into place, she tightened one strap around my throat until I croaked and yanked down on it, hard, then she relaxed her grip and fastened it into place. I reached up and patted my neck, now protected by a chain mail neck guard that ran from just under my ears to my collarbone.

"Good thinking," I said.

"Kevlar's great, but this is definitely a job where being wrapped in sheets of metal is preferable," she replied.

"Yeah, I don't know many vampires that pack pistols, but a mouthful of metal is a good way to ruin a vamp's day," I agreed.

"Especially since it's been doused in holy water and brushed with silver oxide."

"Holy water, huh?" I asked. "No wonder it burns a little." I grinned at her and started down the alley. Flynn was right behind me, with Van Helsing following her. Smith had rear guard, covering the alley behind us with his Mossberg full of silver shot.

I put an ear to the door but heard nothing through the reinforced steel. I turned to Smith. "Who brought the key?"

He moved past me to the door and pulled a spool of det cord out of his backpack. In less than a minute, he had a line of explosive running the length of the door's hinge and wires connected to a handheld detonator.

"Let me try something before we completely give up on the element of surprise," I said. I knelt in front of the door and pretended to fiddle with a set of lock picks. All I really did was put my head close to the lock and whisper, *"Aperio."* The lock clicked open and I pushed the door inward. Blackness yawned before us as I peered into the abandoned theatre.

I stepped through the doorway first, flicked on my red-lensed flashlight, and all hell broke loose.

CHAPTER 10

The second I clicked on the light, I heard a creak on the wooden floor off to my right. I swung the light in the direction of the sound and almost dropped the flash at what I saw. There must have been two dozen vampires on the stage, all rising from a sleeping position and turning their attention to the door.

"Guys, we have a situation here," I said. I drew half a dozen glow sticks from my back pocket, cracked them all at once, and threw them as far around the room as I could. "Get as much light in here as you can, and go back-to-back. There's a fuckton of fangs in this room, and none of them look happy to see us."

Flynn, Van Helsing, and Smith all charged the room at that point, Smith firing a white phosphorous flare out into the gutted auditorium. A section of rotted flooring immediately caught fire from the sparks, adding to the illumination, but also pouring smoke into the sealed room and starting a bonfire in one of Charlotte's last standing historic landmarks.

I glared at him. "Was that really a good idea? Flares? Indoors? Didn't your mom ever tell you not to set off fireworks in the house?"

"Seemed like a good idea at the time," he replied. "Isn't that what you always say when you do something stupid?"

"Shut up, Smitty," I growled and leveled my pistol at his head. He dropped to one knee, and I put two in the head of the vampire that was coming up behind him. Smith, in turn, pulled the trigger on his shotgun and literally cut the legs off a vampire charging in from my left. I stomped on the monster's neck with my boot, breaking its neck and rendering it forever dead.

I heard pistol fire from behind me, but I couldn't spare a thought for Flynn and Van Helsing because three vampires converged on me at once. Or at least they tried to, but since they had obviously never fought together, it didn't go well for them. The one that got the closest fastest ended up in my grasp, and I spun him around to block a huge punch from an overgrown vamp coming at me head on. He hit the first vampire so hard in the head that the creature's skull exploded. I dropped my undead shield and put four in the big beast's chest, but that was only enough to bring it to its knees.

Then the third beast had me. It caught me from the right in a flying tackle, which is always a bad idea. Any time you leave your feet in a fight, bad things can happen. In this case, the bad things happened to me, as the vamp drove me into the stage floor and then stood up to stomp my ribcage in. But just as it lifted up its foot, the pain kicked in and the vampire looked down at its chest. The chest with a silver stake poking out of it. When it tackled me, I managed to roll around and draw one of my stakes before we landed, then staked the bastard when he landed on top of me.

I yanked the stake from his chest, he dropped, and I turned to jab the stake through the eye of the giant vamp I'd left on his knees in front of where I'd once stood. Except he wasn't there, he was stomping across the stage at the girls, who were shooting everything in sight but not killing nearly enough. They had four or five vampires around them, plus the big boy. Smith wasn't doing much better. He'd dropped his Mossberg and drawn a katana, which I'd never seen before. But the numbers game was getting to all of us. Even with my few seconds' reprieve, I still had half a dozen bloodsuckers all converging on my position and very little idea what to do about them.

"He's mine," came a voice from the balcony, and I looked up to see Gus swooping down from fifty feet away. That bastard always knew how to make an entrance. He glided down to the stage, an honest-to-God *cape* billowing out behind him, landing on one knee about ten feet in front of me. His vampire minions backed away, leaving an alley for him to approach me. He stood and swept his cape back off his shoulders, letting it flutter behind him like a black velvet banner. He walked toward me, almost stalking, his polished black riding boots echoing across the stage.

Everything stopped in that surreal moment. All the other fighting stopped as his henchmen watched our confrontation. He was playing the role of the Master Vampire to the hilt, and I knew exactly where he learned it, He had Uncle Luke's shtick down cold, from the cold glare, to the shoes polished to a mirror gloss, all the way to his hair plastered tight to his skull with more product than a Lady Gaga concert. He stopped in front of me and looked at me, a little smirk curling up one corner of his mouth.

"Did you actually think you could beard the lion in its den, little man? In what world are you strong enough or smart enough to best me?"

I kept my voice low but looked him straight in his cold gray eyes. I wasn't afraid of his mind control powers; I'd been training with the OG boss vampire for a hundred years. I locked gazes with him and said, "If you leave Charlotte right now, I won't hunt you and you can keep your pitiful little pseudo-life for as long as you like. But if we throw down, I'm not going to stop until you're true dead and I've scattered your remains at sunrise over Freedom Park. You got me?"

He snarled and reached out with his left hand, grabbing me around the throat and picking me up one-handed. "You insolent fool, you dare to threaten me? I should snap your neck right now!" His face grew mottled with rage and his grip tightened. Just like I'd planned.

The problem with picking someone up by the throat is that you have to lock your elbow to do it with any touch of aplomb. And with your elbows locked and held straight out in front of you, your elbows become vulnerable to all sorts of nasty things. Like people smashing you in the elbows and dislocating both of them in one sharp blow.

So that's exactly what I did to Gus. I reached up and punched him on the back sides of his fully extended elbows. There were two loud *snap* sounds, and he dropped me, screeching in pain. I hit the floor and rolled, coming up with my pistol back in my hand and putting silver-tipped hollowpoints in the chest of the three nearest vampires. My gun clicked empty, so I drew a pair of silver stakes from the back of my belt and went to work.

I was a whirlwind of silver and smartass comments, taking out half a dozen vampires in half a minute. The vampires covering Flynn, Van Helsing, and Smith all turned to look at the carnage I was creating, and all became part of carnage. Flynn and Van Helsing took out two vampires each, and when I turned to see how Smith was doing, I watched him pull his hand back through a gaping hole in a vampire's chest. I gaped at him, but he just held a single bloody finger to his lips. He spun on his heels and grappled at another vampire, and my attention returned to the undead murderer at hand.

I looked down at Gus, who was still working on getting his elbows back into alignment. I stepped forward and put a foot on one of Gus' ankles. "Stay still, asshole," I growled down at him.

He looked up at me and said, "I'll have your soul for breakfast for this insult, H—"

I cut him off, still trying to avoid Van Helsing figuring out my name. "You won't do shit, Gus. You'll either run now with your tail tucked between your legs like the good little butler you really are, or I'll rip those useless arms off your body and beat you to death with them."

He glared at me. "You don't have the stones, boy." His voice was low and dangerous, and I could feel the hate rolling off him like steam. He bent over, stomped on the fingers of one hand, then pulled until his elbow popped back into place. He swapped arms, repeated the process, then stood up, flexing his newly-restored arms. I could see the pain in the beads of sweat dotting his forehead, but he never let it touch his face.

"I believe the question is, is that the best you've got?" he asked as he charged me. I dove to my left, landing in a roll and coming up with my hands already spinning a warding spell. "*Murus!*" I said, pouring my will into the words.

Gus slammed into my hastily drawn circle, then pounded on it as he howled in rage. "You cannot defeat me, Quincy Harker! I will never let you leave this place alive!"

He was looking more and more correct as Smith's flare continued to burn and catch more segments of the audience seating on fire. I looked out to see most of the audience chamber engulfed in flames and smoke roiling across the entire building. The vampires didn't care, of course, but my human companions and I were starting to have a rough time breathing.

I looked up at the ceiling and the fly grid, some eighty feet above the stage. All old wood, it was ripe to catch fire and come down on all of us in a heap of burning wood and death. I focused my will, opened a tiny hole in the top of my dome, thrust out my hand and yelled, "*Foenestra!*" I unleashed my magic in a tight beam, focused down to a two-foot circle, and blasted a hole through the grid, all the rigging, and the roof of the theatre. All the debris flew up, and so did the smoke.

The air cleared almost instantly, but what goes up, must come down, in this case in the form of chunks of four by four and nails.

"Heads up!" I yelled, running full tilt for the side of the stage out of the drop zone. I watched Smith reach up and bat a chunk of wood out of the air, then turn right back to beating a vampire's face in, and saw a two-foot length of lumber pin one vampire to the floor, coming down straight through its neck and knocking him flat. The wood missed his heart, brain, and spine, so he just lay there writhing like a bug in a kid's science project.

I heard a scream and turned to see Van Helsing lose her footing and go down in the center of a circle of vamps. Flynn tried to get to the fallen slayer but found herself surrounded. I turned to run across the stage to help the women, but Gus was on me in an instant. He grabbed the back of my coat and pulled me back to him, wrapping me up in a full nelson and effectively immobilizing me.

"Watch, Harker," he hissed into my ear. "Watch as my minions tear your friends limb from limb. Watch as we destroy even the faerie, with all his strength and magic." He turned me to look at Smith, who was hard-pressed by a cluster of four vampires.

Faerie? Smith? It made a certain amount of sense, but I couldn't think about that just then. I had to come up with something, and fast, or all my friends, and Van Helsing, were going to be a vampire buffet. I struggled against Gus's grip, but he held me tight. I thrashed and heard a sharp hiss as a beam of sunlight from the hole in the ceiling danced across the back of his hand. A thin tendril of smoke climbed from the back of Gus's hand, and I saw my out.

I looked up, focused my will, and shouted, *"FOENESTRA!"* at the top of my lungs. Power flew from me, scattered without the focus of a gesture, and blasted through the wooden grid and the rest of the ceiling. Wood, brick, and steel flew upward from the roof, falling outward onto the surrounding streets and alleys, but that couldn't be helped. As the dust cleared, sunlight streamed into the theatre from the new twenty-foot skylight I'd created, and vampires burst into flames all around the stage. Gus dropped me like a hot potato and ran for the shadows, but most of his minions weren't so lucky. The four around Van Helsing died almost instantly, and three of the ones surrounding Flynn met the same fate. The few survivors scattered to the shadows and the dark places under the theatre, but we were in no shape to pursue.

Gus stopped in front of a stairwell leading down into the bowels of the building, glared at me across the stage and shouted, "This isn't over, Quincy Harker! I'm not done with you, or your 'Uncle' Vlad, either!" Then he turned and ran down into the safety of the theatre's catacombs.

I turned to see Gabriella Van Helsing standing less than ten feet away from me, a nickel-plated Colt 1911 pistol leveled at my head and a scowl on her face. "Just what did he call you?"

CHAPTER 11

"Go ahead, Agent *Harper*," Van Helsing said. "Tell me your name again." The Colt didn't waver, not even a little. Pretty impressive for a slight woman who had been getting the shit beat out of her by vampires less than two minutes before.

I sighed and took the gun from her. It was a lot harder than it should have been because she's really strong and fast. For a human. But since I'm not exactly human, it still wasn't that hard. I ejected the magazine, cleared the chamber, and handed it back to her.

"Point that thing at me again and I'll slap the taste out of your mouth," I said. "I usually don't hit women, but you're better armed and a better fighter than most men, so I'll make an exception if I have to." I took a deep breath. "My name is Quincy Holmwood Harker. Yes, I am that Quincy, born from that Jonathan Harker and Mina Murray. I am the apparently immortal or at least stupidly long-lived son of two parents that Dracula fed on, shared blood with, but didn't turn. That does something to your DNA, we're not exactly sure what."

"How old are you?" she asked.

"About a hundred-twenty," I said. "And yes, I knew your great-grandfather. He was very nice to me when I was a little boy. He let me pull on his beard and gave me sweets when my parents weren't looking. Visiting with him was one of the bright spots of my childhood."

"What kind of monster are you?" she asked. At least she put the gun away.

"I don't think I am a monster," I said. "I'm not a vampire,

a were of any flavor, or a demon. I guess you could call me a wizard if you felt the need, but I guess I'd prefer the term magic-user."

"You lied to me," she said, and the betrayal in her eyes hurt more than the bruises Gus had left.

I tried to weasel out of it, but I knew it was useless. "Technically, I didn't lie to you. My ID badge was misprinted, and I just didn't correct you."

"You're an asshole," she hissed.

"No arguments there," Flynn chimed in.

"Not helping," I said.

"Not trying to," Flynn said, and I could feel her grin through our mental connection. Having a hitchhiker in your head pretty much always sucks, but it sucks worse when the hitchhiker is an insufferable smartass.

"You're a monster," Van Helsing growled, and I could feel the situation slipping away from me.

"I'm not a monster, I'm a guy. We're all assholes, and we all lie, but that doesn't mean you have to do something stupid." I held out my hands, palms out, trying to calm her down. I had my usual level of success in calming down angry women, which is to say none.

"You lied to me to keep me from know what you were, and now I find out that not only are you part vampire, but the bloodsucker that my great-grandfather thought he'd killed all those years ago is alive? What am I supposed to do about that?"

"That's really two questions," I stalled, trying to come up with one, much less two, valid answers. "About the me lying to you thing, I've always been a big fan of forgiving and forgetting, personally."

Flynn barked out a laugh. "You're still mad at your uncle for bespelling the 1919 White Sox into throwing the World Series, and that was almost a hundred years ago!"

"Not helping," I said. "Besides, there are forgivable sins, and then there's baseball. You don't mess with baseball. Anyway, you can forgive me or not; that's your call. But about the other thing—about Count Vlad Dracula still being alive regardless of what Stoker put in his little bedtime story? That's nobody's fault but Stoker's. Not even your grandfather."

"Great-grandfather," she corrected.

"I know, but I feel old enough already, so we're going to skip that part if it's quite all right with you. Look, Abraham knew that Luke wasn't dead. He even knew that Luke was there when he died."

Her eyes widened briefly at that, then narrowed in suspicion. "How would you know that?"

"Because I was standing at the foot of his bed when he waved out the window at him. Your grandfather, Abraham's son this time, would never invite Luke in, so he stood out in the snow and watched through the night as we kept vigil. They were never friends, but there was an understanding at the end between hunter and vampire."

"And what if I think you're full of shit? What if I decide to go after your uncle anyway?"

"That would be a very bad choice," I said.

"What, you think he'd turn me? I'm not afraid of living forever."

"Says everyone who's never tried it," I said. "Get back to me in seventy years or so and let me know how it's going. But that's not the point. I'm not the least bit afraid of Luke turning you. He hasn't turned anyone since my mom's best friend Lucy. Nowadays he'd just kill you."

"Others have tried," she shot back.

"Fine, then. Don't forgive me and work with us to take down the vampire that's an actual threat to the people of this city. Stay pissed and go after Luke, you know, the vampire that the whole genre is based off of. He's taken down more vampire hunters than I've gotten lap dances, and let me tell you, that's a pretty big number."

"Fuck this, I'm going after him." Van Helsing started to storm out the door, but Flynn got in front of her.

"Look, Gabriella, let's all just take a minute to dial it down…" Flynn took her by the arm, and the vampire hunter shook free and gave Flynn a hard shove.

"Bitch, don't you put your monster-loving hands on me!"

"You'd better think twice about calling a police officer a bitch in this town, or you'll find yourself brought up on charges for impersonating an FBI agent, *bitch*. I checked your backstory, and it's thinner than Harker's last excuse for being late."

"Hey! Whose side are you on?" I asked.

"Shut your pie hole, Harker," Flynn snapped. "And you, miss high-and-mighty vampire hunter, I'm telling you as the local law enforcement that any harassment of our citizens, including Mr. Lucas Card, major donor to the Policeman's Charity Ball and the funds for families of fallen officers, will be handled with extreme prejudice."

"I'm feeling pretty damned prejudiced right now, why don't we just settle this shit? I kick your ass, I'm free to do whatever I like to Dracula. You kick my ass, I leave town and forget I ever heard about Lucas Card." She assumed a fighting stance.

Flynn mirrored her and nodded. In a matter of seconds, the whole mess had escalated from me pissing off another pretty girl to a pair of badass women about to throw down in the middle of a theatre full of recently-ashed vampires. I was looking around for the popcorn vendor when Smith stepped between them.

"Cut this shit out, NOW," he said, in a voice that was a cross between a drill sergeant and middle school principal. He held out one arm to each woman, muscles bulging beneath his tactical uniform. But nobody was looking at his arms. We were all focused on his eyes, which had flashed to a deep yellow, like a big cat's. His pupils were vertical and oval, and his eyes seemed to glow with an inner light. Flynn took a step back, as did Van Helsing.

"What the fuck are you?" Van Helsing asked the question that was hanging in the air.

"Pissed off is what I am," Smith replied. "I'm pissed off that my squad can't get along for the time it takes to clear one building and make sure that there are no more vampires running around. I'm pissed off that there was a vampire nest in the middle of my city, and I'm pissed that the so-called Master of the Vampires either didn't know about it or didn't care enough to do anything about it. You got any other questions?" He turned his full attention to Van Helsing, but she didn't flinch.

"Yeah," she said, right up in Smith's face. "What. The. Fuck. Are. You? Did I say it slow enough for you that time?"

"I heard you the first time. I just ignored you because it's none of your fucking business. Is that clear enough?"

"Yeah, it's clear that this whole team has been infiltrated by monsters, so you won't be any fucking good at stopping them. I'm better off on my own." She turned to go. I cut her off at the door.

"Don't do this," I said. "Hang with us. We're not monsters. Okay, I'm not. I don't know what the hell Smith is, but whatever it is he turns into, it can't be much worse than mid-level government functionary, can it?"

She laughed at that, and I reached out and touched her arm. "Look, I'm sorry we lied to you about some stuff, but I've got some people to protect, so I can't go telling all their secrets, you know?"

"I get it," she said. "I understand why you did what you did. I've just gotta go process. I mean, it's not every day that you find out a whole branch of the government is run by monsters." She pushed past me to the door and walked out into the daylight.

Smith stepped up beside me. "Wait 'til she finds out about the Supreme Court." I gaped at him, but he just gave me a smile.

CHAPTER 12

Despite blowing most of the roof off of the old theatre and letting the sunshine in, as the song goes, there were still a *lot* of places for vampires to hide in the Carolina Theatre. And after hearing the ruckus we caused upstairs, none of them were very eager to come out and tangle with us. Which is usually fine, because I'm a live-and-let-unlive kinda guy most of the time, but in this case, we spent the rest of the day combing the theatre for stragglers and clues as to where Gus would go to hide or what he had planned next.

It was early evening when Smith, Flynn, and I reconvened on the stage to go over what we'd learned. We sent all the other agents home and gathered around a table I dragged out from some backstage office. I dropped the few clues I'd picked up throughout the day onto the table, but it didn't amount to much. I had a couple of takeout menus, a listing of upcoming Broadway and Symphony shows coming to town, and a course catalog for Central Piedmont Community College. I was pretty sure most of that stuff had been left by the last people to rent the theatre, since I didn't see Gus as the type to take night classes in Japanese or try the best new place for Pad Thai, especially since vampires can't process normal food.

Smith hadn't fared any better, picking up a few parking stubs and collecting wallets from the vampires we staked and beheaded. If their IDs weren't lying, none of the vampires from Gus's crew were local, which meant he was traveling in something big and with a light-tight cargo compartment. That narrowed down his parking solutions pretty dramatically, so Smith got on the phone and started calling long-term lots that were big enough to handle that type of vehicle, and Flynn opened her laptop and started looking up parking citations for oversized vehicles in the past couple of weeks.

I had nothing, so I sifted through papers aimlessly for a few minutes, then started scouring the floor for clues from our earlier fight. I don't know what I thought I was looking for, but I found a whole lot of nothing.

A few minutes after the last rays of sunlight stopped flickering through my impromptu skylight, my cell rang. I looked at the display and swiped my finger across the screen. "What's up, Luke? Met up with an old friend of yours today. Boy, that Augustus, he's got more issues than Reader's Digest."

"Quincy, while I often do not mind you borrowing my manservant for your little forays into mortal law enforcement, I must ask that if you are not going to have him home in time to prepare my breakfast, please leave a note. It is only common courtesy, after all," my uncle's cultured voice came through the tinny speaker crystal clear, pissiness and all.

"What are you talking about, Unc?" I looked around the stage just to make sure, but nope, no Renfield. Just like there hadn't been a Renfield there all day.

"Where is Renfield, boy? I just woke up, I want my breakfast, and I am without my manservant! Are you being deliberately obtuse, or is it a natural state?"

"Don't get bitchy, Uncle, I don't have your butler. I haven't seen Ren since I left the house this morning, and I haven't heard anything out of him all day. Did he go out grocery shopping or something? I know it's low on your priority list, but he has to eat, and he keeps a few things around the house for me, so maybe he went shopping."

"He did. Much earlier. There is a new six-pack of that beer you like in the refrigerator and a receipt on the counter from before noon. No, he's not out shopping. And he never stays out past dark without a very good reason."

I started to feel a sick feeling in my stomach. "What reason would be good enough?"

"What are you talking about, boy?" Luke tended to call me "boy" when he was upset. Some things you just learn to live with when dealing with monsters that are hundreds of years old. "Boy" was one of those things.

"I'm saying has he *ever* been gone when you woke up before? For any reason?"

Luke paused and took a deep breath. After what felt like forever, he answered. "No. He hasn't. Quincy, do you think something is wrong? Had something happened to him?" I gotta give him credit, Luke sounded legitimately worried. In that moment, he sounded more human than I'd heard him sound in years.

"I don't think something happened, Uncle. I think *someone* happened," I replied.

"Augustus," Luke said.

"Augustus," I agreed. "After we thumped him here, I bet he went to your place and decided to hit you where it would hurt the most—threatening the people who rely on you for protection."

"That son of a bitch!" Luke exploded, and I pulled the phone away from my ear. Smith's head whirled around, and I dialed in my suspicions about him a little further. "I'll destroy him once and for all. If he's harmed a single hair on that man's head, I will tear him apart with my bare hands!" I held the phone further away from my head as Luke ranted. Super-hearing comes in handy a lot of the time, but when people are yelling into a cell phone, it turns every conversation into an argument.

"Luke," I said, but he ignored me. "Luke!" I shouted, and he fell silent.

"Don't do anything crazy," I said. "We're on our way."

I turned to Flynn. "You get that?" I asked.

"Yeah."

"Explain it to Smith while I pull the car around front. Grab all our weapons and be ready for some superior cover-up work in tomorrow's paper if we find the bastard," I said, turning to the door.

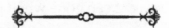

Two minutes later we were speeding down Seventh Street headed toward Luke's house. We turned right off the main road into Luke's neighborhood, then left into a housing development.

"I still can't get over Dracula living in a housing development," Flynn said as a cavalcade of nearly identical split-level houses circa 1964 rolled by outside the windows.

"It wasn't a housing development when he built here. It wasn't even Charlotte when he built here. I'm sure if he'd known the city would actually grow into something, he would have stayed far away. But he likes it here, so we stick around."

"What about you, Harker?" Flynn asked. "Do you like it here?"

I looked over at her, but there was none of the normal mocking in her eyes. I thought for a moment, then said, "Yeah, I like it here. I've lived here longer than I've lived anywhere as an adult, so it feels as much like home as anywhere that's not London. And even London doesn't feel much like my London anymore. There have been a few changes in the last hundred years or so. Charlotte's a good place to live, and there's enough turnover in the population that I can change apartments and names every ten years or so, and as long as I don't go back to my old hangouts, I don't get outed too often."

"How long have you been here?" Flynn asked.

"Well, Luke's been here in one name or another for a lot longer than me, but I got here in the seventies. If I had to live in America during those years, I was at least going to live in the South where bell bottoms weren't quite as big as some places." I chuckled, then grew focused. "We're here. Smith, I need you to take the back entrance. Can you handle it solo?"

"Kid, I was breaching doors when you were still trying to figure out how tie your shoes."

"I rather doubt that since I learned to tie my shoes at the turn of the century. The twentieth century." I parked the Suburban in the driveway and headed for the door. I took the front steps two at a time and hit the door at a run. Good thing for everyone Luke had it unlocked.

He was waiting for us in the living room. Smith joined us a couple of minutes later, shaking his head.

"No sign of anything out back," he said.

"Luke, what do we know?" I asked.

"We know that rat bastard Augustus had kidnapped my Renfield and is using him for bait to lure me out. We know that I'm going to find him and do largely unpronounceable things to him that wouldn't be possible if he weren't an undead monster. We know that you're standing between me and the front door, thereby impeding my ability to kill Augustus and get my manservant back."

"We know that you have voicemail," Flynn cut in.

"What?" Luke whirled around. "I have voicemail?"

"That wasn't Luke asking if anyone left him a message," I

translated. "That was Luke admitting he had no idea there was an answering machine."

"True enough," my somewhat technophobic undead monster uncle agreed.

Flynn pressed a button on the console beside the phone and a tinny voice informed us that we had one message.

"Hello, Count." Augustus' voice came through, a little scratchy for the recording, but there was no question who it was. "I have something of yours. I believe you'll want it back. Did you actually believe this simpleton could replace *me*? This human fool doesn't have the power to light a candle, much less destroy the Lord of the Undead. But that's what I'm going to do, Count. Or should I call you Vlad, now that you're landless?

Regardless, meet me at the bandshell behind SouthPark Mall at midnight. That will be a lovely place to settle our differences. Oh, and bring the Harker brat. I might have something for him, too." The recording clicked off and we all looked at each other.

"How does a European vampire from the nineteenth century even know there's a bandshell behind SouthPark? How does he even know there's a SouthPark?" I asked the room.

"It means nothing to Augustus, but the location is significant to my current Renfield. He was an oboe player in the symphony before I brought him into my employ," Luke said. "But that matters little at this point. All that matters is rescuing Renfield and destroying that psychopath Augustus once and for all."

"Hold your horses, Luke," I cautioned. "You know I'm usually the last one to argue for discretion as any part of valor, but I've got an idea."

"I know that look," Luke said. "Ever since you were a child, you got that look on your face whenever you were about to do something you thought was clever. It usually ended up with you crying and blood streaming down your face."

"That's kinda the plan here, too, Uncle, except I don't plan on doing the bleeding and crying this time," I said with a grin.

CHAPTER 13

We pulled up to the rear of SouthPark Mall in two cars. Me and Luke in his Mercedes coupe, and Flynn and Smith coming in from the opposite direction in a black Suburban. We had little chance of fooling anyone who was paying even a little attention, but it was worth a try. Luke and I started the long walk across the grass down to the bandshell while Smith and Flynn walked in from the side.

The bandshell at SouthPark Mall was built when the Symphony and mall management got tired of building temporary staging for the Summer Pops series. So they got together and built a little stage with a curved roof out on a little island behind the mall. In the summer, yuppies and music lovers of all stripes bring lawn chairs and sip wine while listening to the Symphony. It's a nice little gig, and now every time I tried to pick up a chick at a concert, I'd think of Gus. One more thing for the asshole to answer for.

I saw the scrawny rat bastard from a hundred yards away, and judging by the low growl he let out, I knew Luke saw him too. He was standing near the front edge of the stage, right smack in the middle. A few feet away, he had Renfield tied to a chair, and even from a distance, I could tell the man had been beaten, and badly.

We stopped just on the mall side of the moat in front of the stage. Twenty feet of water separated us from our prey, but he either thought it was too far for me to jump, or counted on his ability to kill Renfield before Luke could run the bridges at the side of the stage.

"So glad you could join us, gentlemen," Gus said when we

came to a halt.

"Augustus, I command you to release my manservant at once!" Luke commanded, and suddenly I saw the vampire that kept an entire countryside cowed before his power. Every inch of cultured businessman was gone, and left standing beside me was a man who expected his every whim to be obeyed, and woe betide the fool who crossed him.

Gus laughed. He actually had to step away from the edge of the stage to keep his balance, he was laughing so hard. "You impotent old fool," he sneered. "You actually think you can still command me? I, who have not only grown greater than I ever was as a human, but I have evolved into the pinnacle of the Nosferatu!"

"Vampires who refer to our kinds as Nosferatu are invariably assholes," Luke muttered to me. I turned to him in shock. "What?" he asked. "You don't expect me to *listen* to this douchebag, do you?"

"No, but I didn't expect you to know the proper use of the term douchebag, either." I drew my Glock from a shoulder holster and shot Gus in the throat. The report echoed across the expansive lawn, and blood spattered all over the stage. Gus dropped but sprang to his feet almost immediately.

Bad news for him was that twenty feet was less than my standing broad jump, and that Luke was faster than he expected, so when he hopped back to his feet, we were standing directly in front of him. He made a few gasping noises, spraying bloody mist across the stage.

"What?" I asked. "I'm sorry, Gus, I can't hear you." I broke up laughing at my own joke, which just served to further enrage the pissed off and newly perforated vampire before me. I holstered my largely useless pistol and got ready for a fight. Luke slid over to the side to position himself between Gus and Renfield, then when Gus charged me, Luke set to work untying Renfield. Everything was going according to plan.

The only problem was that the plan consisted of me going toe to toe with a powerful vampire for long enough to get Ren to safety, preferably without getting dead. Gus dove at me first, so I caught him by his lapels and rolled backward, placing two feet into his gut and flinging him over my head into the moat.

He leapt back onto the stage with a little splash, and I hopped to my feet to meet him. He sprang at me again, not giving me enough time to get a spell ready, so I sidestepped his charge and punched him in the back of the head as he went by. He sprawled on the stage but was back up in an instant. This time he was more cautious, stalking me, feinting a jab here and there. He was consciously ignoring Luke and Ren, which set off alarm bells to me. Then I heard a rustle from above, and it clicked into place. I put everything I had into one massive punch, which took him right on the cheekbone. Gus's head snapped to the side, his whole body spun with it, and he dropped once again to the deck.

"Luke!" I shouted. "Look up!" He paused in walking Renfield across the bridge to the lawn and looked up. The entire roof structure was covered with vampires, staring down at us, just waiting for the right moment to strike.

Apparently, when I noticed them was the right moment because a good three dozen vampires dropped to the stage around me. The nearest half dozen or so vampires to me got a rude awakening when they landed because decking Gus gave me just enough time to focus my will on the Zippo lighter I carried, shout *"FRAGOR!"* at the top of my lungs, and jump straight up into the rafters the vampires just fell from.

A fireball ten feet in diameter erupted from the Zippo,

engulfing the nearest vampires and turning several of the older ones to dust instantly. The fresher vampires, the ones turned more recently, burned more like humans, except they turned completely to ash when they died. I dropped from the ceiling onto the back of another vamp, snapping its neck like a rotten branch.

That only left thirty vampires plus Gus to go. I glanced over to where Luke almost had Ren over the bridge to the relative safety of the lawn, then turned my attention back to the horde of angry and slightly singed vampires surrounding me. I drew my Glock and put rounds in the chests of the four nearest vampires on my right side, and they dropped like stones. A silver-tipped bullet in the throat won't do much more to Gus than piss him off for a while, with an added side of shutting him the hell up. But to a new vampire, a silver bullet through the heart turns them to real dead real fast.

Four bullets wasn't doing much to get me out of harm's way, so I breathed a sigh of relief when rifle shots rang out from the left side of the stage.

We're in position, Flynn's voice came across the mental link we shared, and for a second I had the weird double vision where I saw through my eyes and hers as well, but I shook my head and dialed it back a little. Flynn and I usually keep enough of a conduit open to each other that we know when one of us, usually me, is in trouble, but sometimes you just don't want to see life through the other person's eyes. On the other hand, I learned the hard way that my nicknaming her EMT boyfriend Black Superman was pretty damned accurate.

Flynn and Smith were set up in mini-sniper perches on the lawn behind a little grassy knoll with Remington 700 rifles just casually blowing the heads off vampires. Stoker never mentioned that a high-powered rifle round is better than a stake, but I guess he also never fired a really powerful, accurate weapon before. Some of the vampires turned to run up the hill at Flynn and Smith, but they barely made it onto grass before they were taken out with headshots.

I emptied my Glock and pitched it onto the grass behind me, flung one more fireball that took out four vamps, then went hand to hand with the last few vampires until the platform was littered with bodies. I stood in the center of the stage, panting, with blood dripping from my hands, staring upstage at Gus. His throat had healed, but I knew what repairing that damage took out of him. He stepped down toward me, then looked me up and down from ten feet away.

"There's more to you than I expected, Quincy Harker," Gus said with a sneer.

"That's what your mom said when I left her this morning," I replied. I don't care if I live to be a thousand, which is unlikely given my mouth, but I will never get tired of "your mom" jokes.

Gus looked perplexed for a moment, then his eyes narrowed and he bared his fangs in a terrifying grimace. Terrifying, I'm sure, if you don't get to see Dracula in his old man boxers far more often than anyone would like. After that, I'm hard to scare.

Just before he charged me, Gus's eyes went wide and a crimson stain bloomed on his shirt. A slender piece of wood ripped through the front of his clothes, and Gus dropped to his knees, revealing a smiling Gabriella Van Helsing standing behind him with a second stake in her left hand to match the one buried in Gus's back. I stepped forward, then looked at Gus again, wondering why he wasn't toppling over like a good dead vampire.

That's when I got a better look at the angle of the stake, and my blood froze. "Move!" I shouted to Gabby, but she just looked at me. "You missed the heart! He's playing possum!" I yelled, and Gabby went white.

Gus hopped to feet, reached behind his back, and wiggled the stake free. "Ouch," he said. "That got stuck on some ribs. For that, I'm going to make this hurt. A lot." He flung the stake at Gabby, who knocked it out of the air, but left herself open to Gus's first punch, which would have been Gabby's last if it had landed. I poured on the speed and caught the vampire's arm before he could crush Gabby's face, then found myself far closer to Gus than I really wanted to be.

He had my throat in one hand, then his left hand flashed out, moving faster than anything I'd ever seen before, and he pulled Gabby in close to both of us.

"There are some three-person scenarios I've considered with Miss Van Helsing," I admitted, "but sorry to say, Gus old boy, you weren't in any of them."

"It's long past time someone silenced your insolent tongue once and for all," Gus hissed, spit and a little bit of blood from his nearly-healed throat splattering across my face.

"While I often agree with that sentiment, Augustus, the time for that is not now, and the place for that is not yours." Uncle Luke's cultured voice rolled across the bandshell and everything stopped. Gus and his minions froze, Flynn and Smith stopped shooting things, and even the urgent alert from my bladder stepped it down a notch.

Luke continued, stepping to the center of the stage. "Release my nephew, Augustus. Release my nephew and let us settle this like we should have many decades ago, like men."

"We are not men any longer, Vlad! That's what you've never accepted! We're not men and never will be again. And while you long for more time as a human, I revel in my greatness! I accept my superiority and thrive in it, like you never have! And when I destroy you, I shall rule over all the world!"

"You shall die, Augustus," Luke said, and I could hear the disappointment in his voice. "You shall die, and I shall be the one to do it."

And then, it was *on*.

CHAPTER 14

The last time I saw my uncle really throw down was in Tibet in the 1920s. We were wandering the Himalayas looking for enlightenment or some such crap, when we came across a band of particularly territorial yeti. Their clan leader challenged Luke to single combat, one of those "win and I won't rip your arms off" kind of challenges. It was very ceremonial, and when Luke drew first blood, we were welcomed among the clan with drinks and roast moose.

This was nothing like that. This was like a ballet set to Rob Zombie where all the dancers are psychotic mass murderers tweaking on crystal meth. It was easily the most terrifying thing I've ever seen, and I've summoned Japanese sex demons for kicks. Luke and Gus flew at each other, and I mean that literally. They each took about two steps, launched themselves into the air, and crashed together a good twelve feet in the air. They spun around and around in midair, grappling for an advantage and tearing into each other's biceps with their nails. Neither one would release their grip, so they spun around a couple of times, then crashed to the stage and rolled over and over, each man trying to gain purchase on the other.

After a few seconds of struggle, Gus pushed off backward to get some space. His black shirt hung in rags from his arms, and blood streamed from a dozen little cuts on his upper arms. He ripped the rest of his shirt off and threw it behind him, and I saw more ribbons of blood running from little cuts all over his torso.

Luke was in about the same shape, and he shrugged out of his suit jacket and tore his white dress shirt away from his body, reveling dozens of little holes in his arms where the other vampire's claws had scrabbled for purchase. Luke shot Gus a nasty grin and leapt for him, covering the twenty feet that separated the two vampires in a single leap. Gus braced for impact, and caught Luke with a solid punch to the chest. A *crack* echoed across the stage as Luke's impact broke ribs, and he grimaced in pain.

Luke hung in there, though, with the increased pain tolerance that comes from living through the Industrial Revolution. And being a vampire. He wrapped his hands around Gus's neck and started to squeeze, the muscles of his arms standing out in ropes. Gus hammered on my uncle's arms, but Luke was too strong. I knew there wasn't much to be gained from choking Gus, but crushing his throat looked like a good start. Gus got his hands in between Luke's arms and broke the hold, but Luke ripped a chunk of newly regrown throat out when he let go.

Gus kicked Luke off him and clambered to his feet. Luke did some wild vampire ninja flip thing and landed on his feet, then spun around to kick Gus in the jaw. Gus responded with several quick punches to Luke's face, then landed a huge roundhouse on Luke's jaw. Luke spun around, and Gus hit him several more times, staggering Luke. Luke ducked the next punch and lashed out with a kick to Gus's knee, toppling the other vampire. Luke stood, then stalked over to where Gus lay writhing on the floor, holding his leg.

He reached down, pulling Gus to his feet by his hair, then drew back his hand for a killing strike. His hand was different, transformed into something I'd never seen on Luke. It was more claw than hand, with elongated fingers and nails that curved into claws. His hand flashed down, but Luke wasn't as hurt as he seemed, because he got his own claws up to block, and broke free of Luke's grasp. Gus took a step back, measuring Luke, and I got my first good look at them both in their *Nosferatu* form.

When vampires are injured, or starving, or hurt badly, all vestiges of humanity fall away and their monstrous nature is revealed. Luke's face became very bat-like, his fangs were extended, and his hands were crooked into claws. Gus looked more cat-like, but similar, with arms elongated and his fangs very pronounced, Gus sprang at Luke, but instead of trying any funny moves this time, Luke just stood tall and snatched the oncoming vampire out of the air, then slammed him onto the stage floor.

He slammed Gus into the floor, then picked him up and smashed him into the floor again. He repeated the process a third time, and this time when he picked Gus up, the other vampire hung limp in his grasp. He bashed him face-first into the wooden stage a fourth time, then he lifted Gus over his head, brought the thrashed vampire down across one knee, and snapped his spine like a rotten twig. The *crack* sounded across the bandshell, and Luke let the body fall to the floor. He stood over his old adversary, then with a long sigh, he reached down and ripped Gus's head from his shoulders.

Luke stood, holding Gus's head by the hair, and stretched his arm high over his head. "Does any other dare challenge the Dracula?" he shouted, and his voice rang through the night. All Gus's minions looked from one to the other, and I knew in my heart of hearts that it was over, that we were done with Gus, that Luke could switch back into this über-civilized form, and we could all go home.

Gus's minions weren't that smart. They rushed Luke. Eight young and brutally stupid vampires against one old vamp who had just been through the fight of his life. They probably thought it would be a cakewalk, that they'd knock off a legend and be the hot new stuff on the bloodsucker scene. They didn't have a fucking chance.

Luke ripped the first one's arm off and literally knocked him out with it. No shit, he caught the punch the vamp was throwing, put one hand on the creature's shoulder, and gave a hard yank. He pulled the vampire's right arm off, gripped the wrist like Babe Ruth, and hit the stupid bloodsucker across the face with his own arm. The vampire toppled back and laid flat on the stage, his unseeing eyes staring up at the lighting rig. Two more descended on Luke immediately after, and they fared no better. A single hard punch from Luke pulverized the heart of the first vampire, and the next fledgling died when Luke knocked him down and smashed his skull flat with one stomp.

Two of the five remaining vampires chose discretion as the better part of valor, but Smith put a .308 round in each of their heads from fifty yards. That wouldn't kill them, but it would keep them down long enough to decapitate.

One turned to me and smiled, obviously thinking that a human would be a better option. I smiled back at him, put a hand on his chest, and whispered, "*Fuego*." He looked puzzled for a moment until his clothes burst into flames. He almost made it to the moat before he was completely consumed. The last two vampires went at Luke together, and it went about like everyone, including the two idiots, expected. Luke twisted one of them around until he could look at his own ass and punched the other guy so hard in the chest his heart exploded out the back of his ribcage.

I looked around the bandshell, silent except for the sound of blood dripping from the rafters and a few cicadas chirping in the distance. "Well, I'm glad that's over. It is over, right, Luke?"

I turned to see Luke and Van Helsing standing toe to toe. Gabby had a pistol in her right hand and a silver stake in the other. Luke had nothing in his clawed hands except blood and bits of dead monster. Gabby gave up half a foot in size and wasn't fueled by magical mystery fighting mojo, but she also hadn't had the shit beat out of her by a super-vamp in the last five minutes, so the scrap was looking pretty even.

"This is not how my night ends, people," I said, walking to the two of them. I stopped a couple of feet away, then glared at Luke.

"Uncle, it's time to look human again. You're making the company nervous."

"The company wants to kill me, Quincy." The fangs made everything Luke said extra-sibilant and menacing. There were times that was a good thing. This wasn't one of them.

"A lot of people want to kill me, Luke. Hell, half the time my own partner wants to kill me! You can't hold that shit against people, or you'll just spend all your time worrying about who wants to kill you today."

I don't want to kill you nearly as much anymore, Flynn's voice came from inside my head.

But admit it, you spent years wishing I'd just drop dead.

Oh yeah, like the first several years I knew you,

"Don't worry, vampire, after tonight we won't have anything to worry about because you'll be dead, and I will have finally honored my great-grandfather's legacy."

At Gabby's words, something snapped in Luke's eyes, and for once in my life, it snapped in a good way. In the matter of thirty seconds, his hands returned to normal, his face returned to normal, and his fangs withdrew, cleaning up his speech a lot. It's hard to speak clearly with spikes hanging out of your mouth.

"You really are Abraham's granddaughter?" Luke looked at Gabby, really *looked* at her for the first time. He reached out with one hand and touched her face. Gabby froze, her eyes wide as the leading figure in her childhood nightmares stroked her cheek with the back of his knuckles.

"Great-granddaughter," she whispered.

"No matter," Luke said. "I see it. I see it in your eyes. The fire, he had that same fire you have. Whenever Abraham saw something he wanted, he got that fire in his eyes. He looked at me the same way you look at me now. Not like something to fight, like something to overcome. I am not your challenge, young Van Helsing. You are your own challenge. You must win your own battle before you can ever hope to vanquish me."

Gabby's hands twitched, her finger tightened on the trigger, then relaxed. Tightened, then relaxed. I gathered my will, readied a spell that would throw up a barrier between the two of them, then let out a breath I didn't know I was holding when Gabby stepped back and holstered her pistol.

She turned to me and tossed me the silver stake. "I think this is yours, Harker."

I caught it on the fly and stuck it through my belt. "Thanks. We all gonna be cool now?"

"Once your uncle tells me why he let my great-grandfather go to his deathbed thinking he'd won."

"Because he had won, young Van Helsing. He had cost me my latest minion, my latest two brides, and my home. The only thing he hadn't managed to do was kill me."

My blood ran a little cold at Luke's admissions. He was talking about my parents as his bride and minion, which freaked me out more than a little.

Luke kept talking, and I kept shutting up. Gabby was getting more ancient history out of Luke in minutes than I'd gotten in a century and change.

"I became a different man after my encounter with Abraham

and Quincy's parents. They showed me that I could no longer behave as a feudal lord, as I had for centuries. From watching them and learning from them, I realized that the world was changing quickly, and I would no longer be able to stand apart from it as an overlord, but must drift outside the world, in its shadowy places. I believe your grandfather was unwittingly responsible for my survival all these years. For if it were not for him pointing me in the direction that the world was moving, the twentieth century certainly would have destroyed me."

Gabby laughed, a short ironic bark. "So by trying to destroy you, he helped save the thing he most hated."

"I don't believe he hated me, not at the end. I believe he wanted to study me and wanted to render me harmless, neither of which I would ever allow," Luke said with a slight smile. "But I believe we achieved some level of mutual respect. At least I did."

I remembered that night in the old man's cold bedroom. I remembered the tears of Gabby's grandfather, the stony expressionless mask on my father's face, and most of all I remembered the tiny upturn of his lips as Abraham waved to the window and the old adversary standing out in the snow, always on the outside looking in. I remembered that night and felt a kinship with my uncle that I'd never felt even in all our travels and battles together. We were both destined to stand outside the window, looking in on a warm and normal life we could never truly know.

Luke turned to me almost like he felt me staring at him and nodded to me. I nodded back, then let the moment pass like a shadow in the night. I turned to Smith. "This would be a really good time to tell me you have a cleanup crew on retainer. Or at least a budget for this." I waved my hand at the entrails and puddles of blood and body parts strewn all over the bandshell.

"Yeah, lemme make a couple calls. I'll get the cleaners out here and get the movie shoot excuse planted with the security guards." He pulled out his cell phone and pushed a few buttons.

Flynn walked up to me and leaned on me, her arm on my shoulder. "Not a bad night, Harker. We got the bad guys and didn't lose any of the good guys."

"True enough, but where's Renfield? That was kind of the point of all this in the first place, wasn't it?"

"He's in the Suburban, out like a light. Augustus had him drugged to the gills, so your uncle stashed him in the car while we took out the vamps. What's so funny?"

I chuckled again. "Sorry, it's just ironic that after all this time tending to all of us, this whole mess was about us taking care of Renfield, and then he ends up sleeping through it all in the car."

So, of course, that's the moment the dapper little manservant decides to reappear. "I assume by the fact that you're upright that we won?" Renfield set a small red cooler down on the edge of the stage and passed me a beer.

"How in the world did you find a cooler full of beer?" I asked, twisting the top off and knocking down half the beer in one long pull.

"I put it in the back of the Suburban," Smith said. "I figured if we lived through this shit, we'd need one." He reached down and passed a longneck to Flynn, then popped the top on a bottle of his own. The four of us sat on the edge of the stage looking out over the lawn while Luke and Gabby talked about her great-grandfather.

"You're right, Flynn," Smith said. "This was a pretty good night."

"Yeah," I agreed. "We beat the big bad, and Gabby learned that not everything with fangs is a monster."

"Too often the monsters are the ones in suits, not a fang or claw in sight," Flynn said.

"That's what the police are for," Flynn said. "They take care of the things that walk in the daylight."

I raised my bottle to the others sitting with me. "And we handle the things that go bump in the night."

HELL FREEZES OVER

A Quincy Harker, Demon Hunter
Novella

CHAPTER 1

I smelled the blood from the front steps. For a murder that happened upstairs in the master bedroom at the back of the house, that's pretty bad. The smell of blood is visceral for me, probably because it's at the core of everything I am. From my dad's dalliances with Uncle Luke's "wives" back in Transylvania, to Luke drinking from both my parents and meddling around in my DNA, to everything I deal with on the job, blood is kinda my gig. But not like this. Not the cloying, nose-clogging, overwhelming stench of it that boiled out of the Standish house like fog rolling in off the ocean.

The coppery-hot scent of it crept into every nook and cranny and wrapped itself around me like a moist blanket, promising to flavor every meal I touched for the next three days. I hadn't smelled blood like that since the Somme, when the mud ran red for two years after over a million men lost their lives in 1916. Luke and I spent most of that year running all over the front rallying British and French troops and pushing back vampires and werewolves recruited by the Germans to attack in the night and demoralize the Brits. The Kaiser's boys had never encountered sheer British pigheadedness on that scale before. They died by the thousands, but nothing the Germans threw at them, military or magical, could make those stiff upper lips waver.

But the smell of blood pouring from the Standish house in waves took me back to France, and I could almost hear the screams of young men dying in the distance again. I snapped back to the present when I caught a young uniform staring at me. I walked up to him, flashed my Homeland Security badge, and said, "Where's Detective Flynn?"

He stiffened at the sight of my fed creds. "Upstairs, sir. I think she's still in the bedroom." I took a step for the door, then moved aside as a forty-something sergeant came hustling down the steps, turned left away from the cops gathered in the driveway, and threw up in the bushes. The cop on door duty took a small notebook out of his pocket, opened it, and made a tick mark on a sheet of paper.

"Running the pool?" I asked.

"Yeah," he said. "Sarge over there makes five."

"Mostly rooks?" I asked. Rookie cops were famous for puking at messy crime scenes.

"Not really," the officer, whose nameplate identified him as Vasquez, replied. "Two rooks, but everybody else has had some years on them. We even got one of the techs."

"Shit," I said. "Now I really don't want to go in there." I wasn't lying, either. The chances that this was something right in my wheelhouse were pretty high, and if it made veteran cops lose their cookies, it was going to be a bad night. Oh well, when you're the demon-hunting part-vampire magic-wielding nephew of Dracula, there aren't really that many uneventful evenings at home in front of the TV.

I squared my shoulders and went inside, keeping my Sight locked down tight while I observed the room with my mundane eyes. Small foyer, large family room off to the right dominated by a massive TV over a fireplace with a game system and controllers on a shelf. To the left was what looked like a formal dining room, with a table for six set with holiday dishes. There was a light layer of dust on everything there, so I figured it wasn't used much. I saw a door through the dining room open into a bright kitchen with nice tile floors.

I didn't pay too much attention to the downstairs, just enough to notice that there wasn't a drop of blood anywhere. If the scene had been as messy as everybody was saying, how had the killer gotten out without leaving a drop down here? I climbed the stairs to the second floor, regretting leaving my jar of Vicks VapoRub in the glove box.

I took a pair of booties from a box at the top of the stairs and slipped them on over my shoes. *You'll want to double-bag unless you're tired of those shoes,* came a voice in my head.

Thanks, I thought back, reaching for a second pair of shoe covers. Most of the time the voices in my head are either bad memories or delusions, but ever since I saved Detective Rebecca Gail Flynn from bleeding out by sharing blood with her, we were linked more closely than any two people ever should be. Unless we were both very careful about shielding, we were in each other's head all day, every day, which made for some truly awkward moments.

The stairs ended in a hallway that led left to a small bathroom and linen closet, then right to three bedrooms. Two of the bedroom doors were closed, with kids' names on the doors in bright wooden cutout letters. The door to the master bedroom stood open, with a uniform standing in the hall just outside.

"Flynn inside?" I asked, holding up my creds.

"Yes, sir, but I can't let you in there." He moved to block my path, and I managed to keep myself from laughing. Not only could I break every bone he ever cared about, but I could magically heal him, then kick his ass some more. But he was taking his doorman duties seriously, so I gave him a little credit there.

"You see that badge says Homeland Security, right? You know Flynn is on the same task force with me, right?"

"I do know that, sir, but this is our crime scene, and until somebody tells me different, nobody gets in without a CMPD badge or clearance from somebody over my head."

Somehow I still managed to keep from laughing. *Flynn, get out here*, I sent through the mental link we shared. *Your puppy is showing his teeth.*

"Let him through, Birk," Flynn's voice came from around the corner. "He's almost harmless, so he can come in."

"Good job, Junior," I said as I passed the uniform. "Now she's pissed at both of us."

Leave him alone, Harker. Flynn's voice rang in my head as I stepped across the threshold.

"I didn't start it," I protested as I stepped into the room. I froze as I caught sight of the scene. I took an involuntary step back and this time heard the *squish* of soaked carpet beneath my feet. I looked down, and my blue-bootied shoes were islands in a sea of crimson, two of the few things in the room that didn't look like they'd been painted with reddish-brown drying blood.

The mother and two children were in the bed, on top of the blankets, lying peacefully as if sleeping, or posed. She was a trim woman who looked like she did Pilates three times a week without ever breaking a sweat. Her blonde hair was pulled off to one side with care, like her husband didn't want it to get bloody when he murdered her. The irony of it was almost enough to make me scream.

Lying on either side of her were her kids, maybe eight and ten, maybe younger. I've gotten worse at guessing ages since nutrition had gotten so much better. All kids look like giants to me now. These two were as different as night and day — the boy dark with curly brown hair spilling over his face, and the girl slight and blonde, looking almost ethereal lying there.

Their eyes were closed, thank God, but their slit throats made a huge grin across their necks like some demented comic book villain. All three of them had their necks slashed from ear to ear, then long slashes up the inside of each arm and slices across the wrists, just to be thorough. Looking at the bloodstains on the woman's nightgown and the kids' pajamas, I guessed that the femoral arteries would be opened up as well.

I wish you were wrong, came Flynn's voice in my head. *But the doc confirms it – the major arteries in the neck and the veins in the arms were opened. They bled out in a minute. Two tops.*

The walls were a study in arterial spray-painting, with arcs of blood droplets reaching to within a few feet of the ceiling. The mattress was soaked, with blood dripping from the comforter onto the floor and pooling all over.

Sitting in one corner beside the bed, a butcher knife in his hand and a puddle of blood spreading out from his ass, was the man of the house, Darin Standish. Fortyish, Latino, trim, dressed in silk pajama bottoms and nothing else but blood. To put the icing on the cake, in his left hand, almost impossible to see clutched in his fist, was a rosary. *He was praying before he did this.* That thought ran through my head, and I almost lost my own lunch. If I'd eaten anything in the past six hours, it would have been gone that second. As it was, I had to take a few deep breaths through my mouth to keep my gorge down. I got myself together, gave myself a mental shake, and got back to the body.

From the position of the body, I was guessing that he killed his family, then sat down and cut the arteries in his own legs, slashed open one wrist, and made it halfway through his own neck before succumbing to blood loss. I was staring at a seriously dedicated suicide. I reached out to the body, stretching my senses just to edge of the mundane world, but sensed nothing malevolent in the room.

"You getting anything?" Flynn asked in a low voice. Our link was more secure, but she didn't like the idea of letting me inside her head on a regular basis. I didn't blame her; I wouldn't trust me with my deepest and darkest secrets, either.

"Nothing except nauseated," I replied. "This is as bad as anything I've ever seen, and I've been around the block once or twice."

"Yeah, it's awful. Look at that little girl, such an angel…" She was right, of course. The little girl was the place everyone immediately looked in a tragedy. And this one was more cherubic than normal, with apple cheeks even in death, a halo of blonde hair spread out on the pillow beneath her, and a tiny gold cross around her neck.

I mentally wrote off my pants as a total loss and dropped to one knee in front of the father, opening my Sight. The "real" world swam out of focus, becoming less immediate as my senses shifted into the magical spectrum. Nothing changed in the magical spectrum—no demonic taint, no dark magic sigils carved on the dad's aura, nothing to explain why this apparently happy man would murder his family in the most brutal way imaginable.

I stood up, turning my attention to the daughter. Sometimes nasty things from other dimensions can break free using a child's belief in monsters as the anchor point. But not here. It was like this child had never known fear a day in her life. The girl looked exactly the same through my Sight, just as innocent and beautiful, with her cross glowing in my Sight like a beacon, a ray of light in a murky Otherworld. I looked all around the room with my magical senses, then dropped my Sight and turned to Flynn.

"There's no magic here," I said, turning for the door. I squelched my way to the stairway and was about head down when Flynn caught me.

"What are you doing? Where are you going?" she hissed at me.

"Well, I was going to eat ice cream and binge-watch *Justified* on TV, but if you've got a better idea, I'm not married to that one."

"There is a dead family up there, and we don't have any idea who or what killed them. You can't just *leave*."

"Oh, I can. I promise I can. You're welcome to watch me just leave. Look, Detective, I'm the supernatural guy. I'm the one that believes in all the weird shit. You're Scully. You're the one that thinks the world is a normal place that operates under normal laws. So you should be ecstatic when I tell you this was a normal murder/suicide. So now, dear skeptic, I take my leave." I made my most florid bow, which was pretty good given the amount of time I spent in Europe, and once again tried for the door.

"Stop."

I stopped and turned back to Flynn. "I need your help. Even if this isn't anything more than a human nutball, it's as deranged a rat bastard as I've ever encountered. And that puts it right in your wheelhouse."

"I wish that were a little less true, but go on."

"So there's absolutely no evidence of magic here?"

"Let me look again," I said, and opened my Sight again. Using my Second Sight is like laying a filter over the world in front of me. Everything goes a little fuzzy, and I can see bright spots of color where magic was used, or where supernatural creatures touched this plane of existence.

The Standish's bedroom looked as mundane as any house I'd ever been in. There were the normal minor cold spots where ghosts passed through from time to time, but that could just have been grandparents looking in from the Other Side on the kids, or a curious spirit here and there. The little girl's cross glowed with a white halo of purity, like it was recently blessed, and the rosary in the father's hand radiated the same kind of minor blessing. But there was no hint of dark magic or demonic presence anywhere. I let my Sight drop and the room returned to ugly reality.

"Sorry, Flynn, there's nothing. It looks like they went to church recently, but that's all I've got. There was absolutely nothing supernatural about this murder. I know that's hard to take, but most of the nastiest things humanity has ever done have been like that—completely without supernatural help."

"I know. People are the nastiest creatures in the world."

"In a couple of worlds, Detective."

CHAPTER 2

I left a very disappointed Detective Flynn at the house going over details with the crime scene techs and working on recreating the events of the previous night. I had less than no interest in reliving someone's murder, so I went home. Even with the sun high in the sky, I was exhausted. Flynn's call had come in around eight in the morning, and I'd been fleecing an all-night poker game until after seven, so once I finally got home, I was asleep almost before my head hit the pillow. That's when I got my first hint that this case wasn't as mundane as it seemed.

I came awake seconds after I fell asleep. At least it felt that way. It was dark as the devil's own asshole in my room, which was odd since I distinctly remembered it being almost noon by the time I got showered and into bed. I looked around for a clock, but couldn't see one, then pawed the nightstand for my cell phone, with equal lack of success. With my eyes useless, I focused on listening to the room, but I heard no sounds of life, not even my air conditioner or the fan on my computer. Complete silence is so rare in today's world that I noticed it more acutely than I had in previous decades. But this silence was pervasive, like a blanket covering everything around me.

Finally, out of the edge of my peripheral vision, I caught a glimpse of some kind of low light, a glimmer or shine off in the distance. Distance? I was in my bedroom, which is barely fifteen by twenty. A decent room, certainly, but there was nothing in my whole condo that could be measured in anything resembling "distance."

Fuck, another dream.

I don't dream. At least, on a good night I don't remember them. On a bad night, I wake up right in the middle of them, thrashing about in my bed, sheets a sweat-sodden rope twisted around my middle tight enough to cut off blood flow to my feet, a scream caught in my throat, fighting with everything I've eaten for the past twenty-four hours to get up and out past my teeth. If I'm lucky I manage to get control of myself before I puke or piss myself. If I'm unlucky, it's another 3AM run to the all-night laundromat reeking like a homeless man on a two-week bender. They know me there.

I've seen some shit. I suppose it's impossible to get a century under your belt without seeing some shit, but my family tree, particular "gifts," and undeniable talent for sticking my nose in where it doesn't belong have put me in situations to see more shit than a sewer rat. And when I sleep is when all the barriers between the nasties in my mind and my memories crumble, and the worst things I've seen across over a hundred years and six continents come out to play.

Antarctica. It's what you were wondering. There's nothing fucking scary in Antarctica because there aren't enough people there. The whole fucking continent has about five thousand people on it in the summer, such as it is, and less than two in the winter. And they all chose to be there, and they all have enough shit to do just to stay alive and do their jobs to not fuck around with anything supernatural. Not enough time on their hands to get really stupid.

The other six continents? Full of assholes. Assholes who fuck with things that should be left alone and call up shit that people like me have to put down. And make me do shit that I have to live with forever, especially when I'm alone in the middle of the night without any whiskey to dull the screams that echo through the dark hallways of my soul.

I stood in the dark long enough for the glimmer of light in the distance to take shape, and I couldn't tell if I was moving toward it or it was moving toward me, in that weird *Pan's Labyrinth* way that things move in dreams without actually moving, but I realized the the light was the outline of a door, and I've known enough about lucid dreaming for long enough to know that I was meant to open it. So I did. I reached out my hand and opened the door.

And was immediately back in the middle of the Standish family's bedroom. The only difference was there was no blood and no dead people. It looked like the bedroom of a happily married middle class couple from Whitebread, USA. There were no signs of death or destruction, just a patterned white and mint green comforter that I had seen at Target a couple weeks ago and now was under no circumstances ever going to purchase, no matter how well Renfield said it matched my curtains.

I felt something warm in my hand, and I looked down to see the little Standish girl standing beside me, throat mercifully intact, looking up at me with blue eyes the size of saucers. She opened her mouth, but no words came out.

"What is it, honey?" I asked. She moved her lips, but again nothing.

I got down on one knee in front of her. "It's okay, sweetheart, nothing can hurt you here. Nothing can ever hurt you again," I said. I reached out a hand and stroked her hair. She opened her mouth, and blood poured out. Not arterial spray, but a waterfall of crimson down her face, painting the front of her nightgown and cascading to the floor. I skittered back, trying to stay out of the blood, but my hands squished in red-soaked carpet.

I scrambled to my feet, and the room looked like it did that morning when I'd first walked in. The eggshell walls were painted in some bastardized Jackson Pollack spatter, but only red. Red everywhere, all the way up to the ceiling and spattered across the blades of the white wicker ceiling fan centered over the bed. The little girl came toward me again, holding out both her hands, and now blood was flowing from her wrists down to her fingers, out of her eyes like tears turning her cheeks crimson, and blood streaked her legs from her cut arteries, puddling around her feet with every step.

I kept backing away, and she kept coming, an inexorable vision of death in red and angel-blonde hair. She stretched out her arms to me, silent supplication like a toddler begging to be held. I shook my head and backed away, away from the abattoir of the bedroom, away from the hemorrhaging little girl, away from the memories of blood coating every surface.

I felt something solid behind me and turned to see a giant door in dark oak, a wooden engraved surface stretching up high above my head, with a knob just barely within reach. I realized that somehow I was seeing this door through the little girl's eyes, and if I wanted to get through, I was going to have to get back to my normal size.

Let's be clear—I did not want to go through that door. As a matter of fact, if going back through the Industrial Revolution was one of the choices other than going through that door, I'd be lighting gaslights and heating my house with coal again in a matter of seconds. But I knew it wasn't an option. I had to go through the door before whatever piece of my subconscious dragged me into this shitshow would let me find the exit.

So I willed myself taller, and the door shrank to a more normal size. It was still a pretty massive door, all carved oak and antique brass hardware with crosses and fleur-de-lis carved and embossed into anything that stood still long enough. I gripped the knob and turned, and once again was transported. This time I was someplace cleaner, if no less uncomfortable for me. I was in a church. A huge sanctuary with dark stone floors, cushy benches for pews, and hundreds upon hundreds of people all kneeling.

I felt that warm little hand in mine again and looked down at the thankfully blood-free Standish girl gazing up at me in something akin to adoration. She beamed a smile up at me that made me forget at least a decade of the nastiest parts of humanity, and I couldn't help but smile back. That smile faded as I saw my shoes—nice loafers unlike anything I've worn since an unfortunate investigation into a Wall Street broker in 1983 who literally sold his soul to a demon for hot stock tips. Even back then I could have told him just buy Apple, but I've met the guardian angel that sat on Steve Jobs' shoulder, and that dude had some serious mystical horsepower behind him.

I walked down the main aisle of the sanctuary, kneeling and crossing myself in the middle before my diminutive guide led me down an aisle to sit next to a good-looking woman of almost forty. Thirty-eight, to be precise, because I'd read Annie Standish's brief bio in Flynn's head while I stood over her cooling body. That meant the khaki- and polo-clad body I currently inhabited must be Darin Standish, the late Mrs. Standish's apparently loving husband right up until the time he severed every major artery in her body and bled her like the first deer of the season, then sliced himself up like Christmas ham before bleeding out in the floor of his bedroom. A head of curly hair atop a shy smiling face leaned forward and waved excitedly at me—Clay Standish, excited to see his dad in a way only preteen boys can still be.

I turned to the front of the church and felt the world *shift* like it only ever does in dreams. Everything blurred, and suddenly we were all somewhere else. Or more correctly, we were nowhere. Or I was, because I was alone. The church and all the people — gone. The Standish family — gone. Even my little girl guide was gone. It was just me, standing in a foggy, featureless plain surrounded as far as the eye could see with nothing.

"Now what?" I asked, and found that I'd spoken aloud for the first time since the dream started.

A voice from above started to speak, and for a few seconds I just listened, trying to make out the words. I knew them, something about them resonated with me like something I'd heard all my life, just in a slightly different dialect or accent. Then the voice rose in volume, then rose again, then climbed to a scream, then a shrill shriek that bored into my brain like a dentist's drill and drove me to my knees. I clapped my hands to my ears and screamed in pain, but the din of the chanting was so loud I couldn't even hear myself scream. I rocked back and forth on my knees, screaming in time with the chanting, then collapsed sobbing into a ball, rolling on my side and shrieking.

Then something hit my face like a slap and I was awake, curled up in a fetal position in the floor of my bedroom, my sheets tangled about me so tightly they cut off circulation to my legs. I was soaking wet from sweat, but also freezing cold, like...

That's when I noticed Flynn lying sprawled on the floor on the opposite side of my bed, completely unconscious. I got up, fell to the floor again, my feet on pins and needles, disentangled myself from the sheets and crawled over to the unconscious detective.

"Flynn?" I asked, shaking her arm. Nothing. "Flynn!" I shook harder, probing her mind through our link. She was alive, but stunned almost to insensibility. Her eyes rolled back in her head and she started to shake uncontrollably. I didn't know what the hell was going on, but I knew shock was a real possibility, so I sat back against the bed, pulled her into my lap, and wrapped my arms around her. Her shivering continued unabated, so I reached behind me and pulled a blanket off my bed to cover us up. I used a corner of the blanket to wipe the sweat and water from my face, then I held Flynn tight to my chest, trying to let my warmth soak into her.

I focused my will and whispered *"Fiero,"* concentrating just on pulling up heat, not setting my entire bedroom on fire.

After what seemed like half an hour of sitting on the floor holding her to my chest, Flynn woke up.

Her eyes fluttered open, and I felt her consciousness twine into mine, like an old couple holding hands, comfortably connected. She looked up at me, gave me a warm smile, and said, barely audible, "This is nice, Harker, but you're not just wet, you're naked, too. And that means it's definitely not a roll of quarters poking me in the butt right now."

CHAPTER 3

A few minutes later we were both sitting on the couch in my den after I'd thrown on a pair of sweats and a *Preacher* t-shirt. I poured a healthy slug of bourbon in both coffee cups, ignoring Flynn's protests.

"You're off duty, have a drink. You are off-duty, right? What time is it? Hell, what *day* is it?" I asked.

"It's about seven at night, and it's Monday. Or Monday night, anyway. You slept the whole day away."

"It happens," I replied. "While I'm not strictly nocturnal, like Uncle Luke, I usually do my best work at night." I thought about that for a second, then decided there wasn't anything going to save that statement, and just let it die. "What else did you find out at the Standish place?"

"Nothing," Flynn put her coffee cup down and leaned back on the sofa. "It appears to be exactly what you said it was—a perfectly mundane murder-suicide. Sad but ordinary."

"It's not," I said, remembering that little girl's face looking up at me.

"What do you mean?"

"Well, it wasn't monsters in the closet that had me screaming on my bedroom floor," I said.

"Yeah, I was gonna ask about that, but I was waiting for the right time. Like a month or so past never seemed like a good call."

"Ordinarily that would be perfect. With the shit I've seen in my life, the last place you want to go running around is the dark alleys of my mind. But this time we kinda have to pay attention to the signals I'm getting because this wasn't a dream. This was a visitation."

"A visitation?" Flynn asked. "From who?"

"The little Standish girl."

"Emily?"

"Yup, in the flesh. Well, more like in the ether, but you get the idea."

"Why would the ghost of a murdered little girl come to you in a dream, Harker?"

"Fuck if I know," I said honestly. "Maybe her ghost sensed something out of the ordinary about me at the crime scene and followed me home, despite my wards."

"Wards?" Flynn looked around the room at the door, ceiling, trying to see what I was talking about.

"You can't see them without the Sight," I explained. "And the really nasty ones you can't even see with talent. The first layer just tells nasty and uninvited things to leave, that they aren't welcome here. The next layer backs that up with a little spell of banishment that sends most things short of an archdemon or major seraphim back to wherever it came from. The next—"

Flynn held up a hand. "Wait a second, Speedy. You're telling me you warded your apartment against *angels*? Why? Aren't they the good guys?"

"Technically, yes. I mean, they still carry out the will of God and all that shit, but ever since the Great War, they've had free will, so when they're not doing what the big guy wants, they come up with ideas of their own. Most of those ideas are really stupid, like New Coke and Jar-Jar Binks, but every once in a while they decide to do something truly dangerous, like try surfing. That's where we get tsunamis. So I warded my place against the Host from both zip codes, north and south. If I can go through my life without speaking to another angel, I'll be thrilled."

"Present company excepted, I hope," came a voice from the door to my bedroom. I turned to see a vision of loveliness in a white v-neck t-shirt and white yoga pants standing there. Glory's hair was tied into a long, loose blonde braid that spilled down and around one shoulder. Her blue eyes looked worried, and her normally Revlon-commercial lips were drawn tight.

"Morning, Glory," I quipped. Not even a hint of a smile. I must be in bigger trouble than normal. "What's up?"

"I should ask you the same thing," Glory said.

"Harker?" Flynn said from beside me. I looked over and saw her standing by the couch, gun in hand and trained on the angel in my doorway. "Who is that, and how did she get in here?"

The stunned look on Glory's face was almost certainly mirrored by my own. "You can see her?" I asked.

"Of course I can, she's standing twenty feet away from me. By the way, sister, there's about a zero percent chance of me missing from this distance, so let's keep all hands where I can see them, okay?"

"Put the gun down, Rebecca," Glory said.

"Not a chance, cutie."

"I wasn't asking," Glory said, then something in her voice changed. "Put the gun down, *now*." She put a little extra emphasis on the last word, the kind of emphasis that made her eyes flash blue lightning.

Flynn holstered her weapon, staring at her hands the whole time like they weren't under her control. Which they weren't, not completely. She looked at me for help, but I could only shrug.

"Rebecca Gail Flynn," I said, "meet Glory. She's my guardian angel. And I don't think she likes having guns pointed at her."

"It's rude," Glory said.

"So is popping into the middle of a conversation uninvited,"

Flynn shot back.

"Touché," Glory admitted. "Now that we're done fencing, may I sit?"

"I was hoping that this whole thing would degenerate into Jell-O wrestling, but if that's not going to happen, come on over." I waved Glory to a seat on the couch and I moved over to an armchair where I could keep an eye on both of them. "So what are you doing here, Glory?"

"I could ask you the same question, Q," the angel said.

"I live here."

"That's not what I meant and you know it. Why did you lock this little girl's soul to the Earth? What are you planning?"

"What are you talking about?" I asked. "I haven't done anything with anybody's soul, at least not lately."

Glory pointed to the corner of my living room, by the TV that usually just sat gathering dust unless the Panthers were playing and I happened to be awake in my condo. "I'm talking about the soul of a little girl sitting in the floor of your den playing with her dolls."

"What the actual fuck are you…" I opened my Sight and shut my mouth, deciding to see for myself what Glory was talking about. I immediately regretted it. Glory was telling the truth. I didn't know if she was even capable of lying, being an angel and all, but that was irrelevant in the face of the ghost playing dolls in my living room. Little Emily Standish looked just as angelic as she had in death, just as peaceful as she had in my dream, and just as goddamn creepy as you'd expect from a ghost in a bachelor pad.

"Glory, why is there an eight-year-old ghost in my den?" I asked.

"That's what I wanted to ask you, Q. And how can your little friend here see me? I'm supposed to be invisible to humans unless I decide otherwise."

"Flynn might not be exactly one hundred percent normal human anymore, remember?"

"Oh, shit, that's right. But she can see me? I didn't think the last one could."

"First, her name was Anna. Second, you weren't around nearly as much back then. Something about leaving me to live my own life, et cetera, et cetera, blah blah blah."

"That was before I had a century's worth of proof of exactly how dangerous you are to yourself and the rest of the universe when left alone for more than five minutes."

"I'm going to let that one go and say that I don't know if Anna could see you or not, because she never mentioned it. But apparently Flynn can see you, so maybe you two should shake hands, or go for coffee, or whatever. But can you please for the love of fuck do it after we figure out why I'm being haunted by a preteen murder victim?"

"Maybe she wants your help," Flynn said. Glory and I both turned to look at Flynn, who just shrugged. "It's kinda the logical answer, right? You wander into her murder scene, throwing magic around like some kind of scruffy superhero, and she notices you. You don't pick up on whatever she wants you to see, so she follows you home and shows you something in your dream that gives you a clue. Then you help me catch her killer, she goes to Heaven, and everybody's happy. Right?"

I looked at Glory, then back at Flynn. It made sense, in the perverse way things happen in my life. "Fine," I said. "Then we're going to need all your case files, photos, and everything you've got on the Standish family. If something from the dark side of the tracks killed these people, there's a good reason for it.

I hope."

"You hope?" Flynn asked, going to a briefcase on my dining room table.

"Look, sometimes things are just nasty. There's no real reason for what they do, they're just assholes. The same holds true for monsters and people. There might not be a reason for what happened to the Standishes. Could be they just ran into a monster with too much time on its hands."

"That covered up every single trace of any evidence? Come on, Harker, you don't believe that any more than I do," Flynn demanded.

"That's just it, Becks," I protested. "I don't know what I believe. Nothing about this crap makes any sense, least of all why there was a little girl walking around in my head last night."

"Well, here's what we have on the family. Annie Standish, thirty-eight, civil engineer at McFarland & Greene. Steady employee, nothing out of the ordinary. She had three days of PTO left this year, had already scheduled them for Christmas week. Married thirteen years to college boyfriend Darin. Two children, Emily and Clay, ages eight and ten. Studied at NC State, got her Master's at Clemson, where she met Standish. They both graduated, got married immediately, and went to work. Married almost ten years before Clay comes along. Easy delivery, no complications, she goes back to work a month later. Couple years later along comes little Emily. Same story, textbook delivery. These people have a friggin' storybook life, Harker. They're so nice and easy that they're totally boring. There's no reason for anyone to target them."

"Okay," I mused. "The wife was a civil engineer. Not exactly a high-risk profession. Pretty unlikely she pissed off any supernatural agencies with a bridge design. What about hubby?

What did he do?"

"He was a compliance manager for an investment bank," Flynn replied.

"I don't even know what that means," I said. Flynn looked at me, unbelieving. "Seriously, I have no idea what those words mean. Look at me, Becks, I was born when people still lit their houses with hurricane lamps, and most of my ridiculously long adult life has been spent either battling the forces of darkness all over the world, or studying arcane texts in dead languages. I'm an expert in a lot of shit, but modern banking is beyond me."

"He was the guy who made sure that the stock brokers weren't breaking any laws," Flynn explained. "He was almost a lawyer for the bank, making sure that no SEC rules were broken."

"So he wasn't boring enough to just be a banker or a lawyer, he was a half-banker, half-lawyer, all Yawnsville."

"Unless he caught somebody moving money illegally and shut them down?" Flynn theorized.

"The kind of people who launder money and murder people over it aren't often the same people who can mojo a husband into murdering his whole family. No, this wasn't a work thing. There's something supernatural here, or there wouldn't be a ghost playing tea party in my den. Did they go to church?"

"Our Lady of Holy Comfort, right here in town." I saw Glory start a little at the mention of the church.

"What is it, Glory?" I asked.

"I...I can't say, Q. Sorry, above my pay grade."

"What do you mean, you can't say? Is there something going on at that church? Do the angels know something?"

Glory stood up from the arm of the couch, where she'd perched through Flynn's recitation of the Standish family's boring life story. She paced my living room, shaking off sparkles of light with every step. Her wings rustled and she toyed with her braid just like a nervous human until I finally stood up and grabbed her by the shoulders.

"Glory, stop it." I gave her a shake, and she looked up into my eyes. If you've never locked gazes with an angel, I don't recommend it. There are things humans aren't meant to see, even humans with supernatural abilities. Maybe *especially* humans with a supernatural streak and really long lives. The purity of the soul staring back at me from Glory's eyes was like a mirror, reflecting every nasty thing I'd ever done, every impure thought, every vindictive moment and every commandment I'd shattered. I let go of her and turned away, dropping to one knee and trying valiantly to keep my dinner where it was supposed to be.

"You shouldn't do that, Q," Glory said from behind me.

"No shit, angel-face," I said when I was ninety percent certain I wasn't going to paint my carpet in day-old fast food. I coughed a little, wiped my mouth with the back of my hand, and got to my feet. "What's the deal with the church?" I asked.

"I really can't tell you. I would if I could, but I have orders I can't break," Glory said, looking miserable.

"Of course you can break them, G-money. You just open your mouth and tell me what I need to know."

"It doesn't work that way for us, Q. If we're given an order by one of the Host that outranks us, we can't disobey. Remember what separates humans from the Host? What caused the War in Heaven?"

"Free will," I whispered.

Glory nodded. "We've gotten a modicum of freedom in the last few millennia, but not much. I still couldn't tell you if I wanted to. Which I don't, because I don't want you to die."

CHAPTER 4

If I've learned anything from the past century of wandering the Earth, and the jury is certainly out on that question, it's not to bother arguing with supernatural beings. Angels, demons, faeries, and all those other kinds of magical creatures just see the world differently, probably because they aren't of this world in the first place. So when Glory told me she couldn't clue me in as to what was going on at the kid's church, I decided to go ask the folks on the other team if they knew what was up.

"Where are you going?" Glory asked as I went to my closet and pulled out a long black leather coat. Cliché, I know, but when dealing with demons and black wizards, it's best not to be too subtle. Not that I've ever been accused of being subtle.

"You can't give me the information I need, so I have to go follow up with other sources," I said. "No harm, no foul on your part, darling, but I *have* to know what's up with this kid and why she's suddenly decided to go tiptoeing through the tulips of my nightmares. Because, let's be honest, the inside of *my* head is the last place a sweet little girl like that needs to be walking, no matter how dead she is."

"He's got a point," Flynn said. "I've been inside his head, and it's ugly in there. But what are these other sources you're talking about? Sounds like something I'm not going to approve of."

"Which falls directly under the category of things I give zero fucks about. Sorry, Flynn, but you don't get a vote in this one," I said, checking the pockets of my coat for all the usual accoutrements. Salt, check. Silver stakes, check. Holy water, check. Flask of Macallan 18, check. Snub-nosed thirty-eight hammerless revolver, check.

"I don't think that's quite correct, pal," Flynn said, putting herself between me and the door. "You see, when you started hitchhiking in my head, we became partners. And this looks a lot like the kind of thing a partner needs to know about, unless she wants to suddenly find herself on her knees with a migraine in the middle of the police station, or grocery store, or wherever I happen to be when you start getting your ass kicked again. Which I do feel every bit of, by the way."

"Yeah, sorry about that," I said. "We should work on getting some better shielding set up. I've kinda developed a bit of a high tolerance to pain over the years. Knowing that you'll eventually get over it takes a lot of the sting out of even the most vicious beatings."

"Be that as it may, until we get that set up, let's work on you getting your ass kicked less, shall we? And the way we start working on that is by you not going stupid places without backup. So where are we going?"

I looked at her, then looked at Glory. My guardian angel was studiously being no help whatsoever, sitting on my sofa reading *The Way of Kings*. I didn't own the book, so I knew she brought it with her. That's angelic power, right there—strong enough to carry a Brandon Sanderson novel and still fly.

"I'm going to Mort's," I said. I squeezed my eyes shut and stood there, waiting for the explosion, but nothing came. I slowly opened one eye, then the other until I was looking at a very confused Rebecca Flynn.

"Mort's, the dive bar on Wilkinson?" she asked. So she did know it, but apparently she only knew the cover.

"Yeah, that's it," I confirmed. "Gotta go meet a guy about some information. I'll call you tonight. Or you call me if anybody else bites it."

"Hold it." Flynn pressed her back to the door. "Obviously Mort's is more than just a dive bar, so why don't you clue me in?"

"Mort is a demon who lives in the back room of the bar. He's a leech, feeding off the sadness and pain of the humans that come into his bar," Glory said with a snarl.

"His place is also a kind of informal safe haven and meeting ground for a lot of the things that go bump in the night around town. It's where people in the know go to sell a little extra piece of their soul for a few more years in the corner office, or a few extra points of profit on a business deal, or just to look better in a bikini for a few more years."

"So what are you going to do there? Won't most of the customers want to kill you on sight?" Flynn asked.

"Yeah, but Christy, Mort's manager, has a strict no murder policy, so I'll be fine."

"How does she enforce that if the clientele is as nasty as you say? With a demon in the basement and who knows what in the bar, I think one little bar manager might have more than she can handle," Flynn said. "I'm going with you."

"No, you're not," I said. "Don't worry about what Christy can or can't enforce. She's one of the most powerful witches I've ever met, so nobody messes with her."

"So you're going to a demon's bar run by a black witch to get information on a ghost? This doesn't sound crazy to you?" Flynn said.

"I'm over a hundred years old, super-strong, super-fast, know more spells than most D&D rulebooks, and Dracula is the first number on my speed dial. My definition of 'crazy' might be a little broader than most people. Besides, I never said Christy was a black witch."

"But she works for a demon."

"And my uncle is the most famous bloodsucking villain in literary history," I pointed out. "That doesn't mean much. I've never seen Christy do anything evil. To the contrary, most of what I've seen her use magic for has been protection of the innocent, or keeping the peace in general, both pretty white-magicky type things. Who knows? Maybe she just took the job there to keep an eye on Mort."

"You don't believe that," Flynn said.

"Nah, but there is a slim possibility. Look, you wanna come with me, fine. Just don't interfere unless I'm in real trouble, and don't eat or drink anything unless it comes from me or Christy. Even from a sealed bottle. A twist-off top will not keep out magic."

"Is there really anybody in there that's dumb enough to mess with your partner?" Flynn asked with a smirk.

I stopped and turned to her, working really hard not to grab her by the shoulders and give her a shake. "Rebecca, let me be real clear. I'm a badass as far as humans are concerned. Or mostly human, or whatever I am. But when it comes to the things that sit in the dark corners of places like Mort's bar looking for prey, I'm like a high school quarterback going up against Brett Favre. I'm not even in the same league as these things, so watch your step. Seriously. There are guys sitting at the bar eating peanuts and watching football that can turn your skin inside out without blinking an eye. And I don't have near enough mojo to throw down with them."

"So why are we going in there, if you know you might not be able to walk out?" The look in her eyes said she got the message, at least as much as anyone really can without seeing what a manifested demon can do.

"One, it's the only place in town where I can get the information I need. And two, they have excellent fried pickles. And you know how I love some fried pickles. But seriously, it's a Sanctuary. No one is allowed to raise a finger to another creature on the premises."

"And these monsters abide by that?" Her eyebrows were crawling up around the middle of her scalp at that.

"They need a safe place to drink and watch the game, too. Plus, remember the whole thing about being run by a demon and managed by the most powerful witch in three time zones? They keep a tight rein on the clientele."

"Then why are you so worried about me? If it's a Sanctuary, then nothing is going to hurt me while I'm there."

"Yeah, but unless you plan on staying there forever, which has been done, eventually you'll leave, and Sanctuary will no longer apply. So try not to draw attention to yourself. Any more than you will just by walking in."

"Not used to women?"

"Not used to delivery. You walking through the door is the demonic equivalent of Domino's knocking on the front door of a frat house."

"Oh," she said, and her voice was small and decidedly less enthusiastic. I hated to scare her because usually that's not conducive to shooting the bad things, but in this case, I wanted her afraid. Because if she was afraid, she wouldn't unwittingly violate any of the hundreds of little social mores that exist between predators like humans and demons.

We took Flynn's car because rolling up to a bar in my shitty little Toyota just never did anything to impress anybody. At least her confiscated Escalade made us look like thugs, and the long coat and hat pulled down over my face did nothing to dispel the illusion.

I knocked on the door, and an old-school peephole slid open in the steel-reinforced door.

"Password," a pair of red-rimmed eyes appeared in the hole.

"Open the fucking door, you dimwitted twat," I replied.

"Close enough. Come on in, Harker. Try not to break anyone this time." The door opened and a half-shifted werebear stood beside a small podium with a ledger on top. "Sign in," the bear said, motioning to the ledger.

"Are you fucking high?" I asked. "I'm not fucking signing anything, especially not here, of all fucking places."

"I never said you had to sign your real name. Nobody does. You'd be amazed at how many Donald Trumps and Mickey Mouses we have in the bar tonight."

"Fair enough," I said, picking up the pen and writing "Jimi Hendrix." I passed the pen to Flynn, who signed "Lucille Ball."

Mort's place looked like any stereotypical dive bar, only darker. Beer signs along the walls provided most of the illumination, along with a rectangular light fixture over the room's lone pool table and the glow of the jukebox in the corner. Mort's one nod to contemporary decor was a color-changing bar top, but I knew it was magic and not LEDs that made the colors shift with the mood of the inhabitants. I know because I cast the spell in exchange for a rather extravagant bar tab I'd run up on one of Luke's birthdays a decade or so earlier.

The bar was a deep blue when we walked in, tinged with green at the edges. Calm, with a hint of horny and depressed. That's about what I wanted to see when I walked into a demon bar. A couple spots of purple appeared at the corners of the twelve-foot expanse of blue as the inhabitants got a good look at me. Plenty of the denizens of Charlotte's underworld hate me on sight, so I wasn't surprised that I made enough impact to shift the bar's color. As long as most of it stayed purple, lavender, or blue I was okay. If more than a third of the surface went red, I needed to think about getting out of Dodge. Mort loved the early warning system, and it did provide a lovely up-light for the highball and martini glasses scattered all along its length.

I stepped up to the bar and Christy slid me a Newcastle and flashed me a smile. "Where you been keeping yourself, handsome?" she asked as she eyed Flynn.

Christy was a plump Asian woman in her forties with an easy smile and a slow temper, as long as you followed her rules. And her rules were simple: don't start shit in her bar. That was it. Follow that one, and you'd never see her dark eyes flash pupil-less black.

"Who's your friend?" Christy asked me.

"Detective Rebecca Flynn, Charlotte-Mecklenburg Police," Flynn replied, flashing her badge with as much subtlety as anyone can have flashing a badge in a demon bar.

"You do know you can lie about that shit every once in a while, right?" I asked. She looked at me like I was nuts. "You do understand that you don't have to tell every single bad guy in the city that you're a cop, don't you?"

"It makes it easier if I have to shoot anyone later. Identifying myself right off the bat means that if I have to blow somebody's face off, I have to fill out less paperwork."

"I can understand that," Christy said. "You should see the paperwork we have to run for the Alcoholic Beverage Commission."

"What the hell kind of crime lord's joint is this? Cops welcome, paperwork in order, what the shit? Am I on an episode of *Punk'd*?" I asked.

"I don't think that show's still on the air," Flynn said.

"Besides, Harker, I already knew Detective Flynn," Christy said, and both women shared a laugh, probably at my expense.

"Huh?" I said, confused. That was starting to be my natural state around Flynn, and I didn't like it.

"I worked vice a few years ago when I was new to the force. I did a couple of undercover cases here. There was something hinky going on with one of the regulars, but we never could pin anything on him. This was before I knew anything about the supernatural, so that's probably how he kept us from nailing him."

"Don't worry, we took care of him," Christy said. She turned to me. "You remember that incubus with a thing for little boys?"

"Yeah," I said, a glower on my face. "I remember that as soon as I was ready to chase him down and do lots of unpleasant things to him, he disappeared. I always figured you had something to do with it, but couldn't come up with a good way to ask."

"He's buried behind the sand trap leading up to the green on the fourteenth hole at the Country Club. And under the sand trap on the twelfth. And in the water hazard on eight. And—"

"We get it. He's in a lot of pieces scattered in a lot of places. Good job," I said.

Christy looked at me. "We don't shit where we eat, Harker. That's the first rule. This stupid fuck couldn't control his impulses, so we controlled them for him. Now, what can I do for you?"

"I need to know what's going on at Our Lady of Holy Comfort," I said, leaning on the bar.

Christy's face did something I thought impossible—she turned white as a sheet. The bartender's eyes got big, and she looked around as if to make sure no one overheard me. Useless since there were three vampires sitting at various tables around the room, and they could hear a fly fart in a hurricane a mile away. If any of those guys wanted to hear what Christy was saying, all they had to do was listen.

"You're gonna have to talk to Mort about that," Christy said, and my blood ran a little cold. I'd been going into Mort's for more than a decade and had never laid eyes on the big boss. I'd hoped to maintain that status quo for a little while longer, but it seemed like my luck was running like normal — shitty.

"What's the big boss got to do with this?" I asked, keeping my tone light but casting my eyes around the room using the mirror behind the liquor bottles to see if anyone was paying undue attention to us. All the other customers seemed to be firmly ensconced in whatever they were up to, be it pool, drinking or just not looking anywhere near me.

"All I know is I have directions that if anyone asks about that particular church, they go straight to the boss's office." Some of the color had returned to Christy's face, but I could see by the green in the bar top nearest her that she was still pretty nervous.

"Well, lead on, then," I said.

"It's the door between the two restrooms. He knows you're coming," Christy said. "She has to stay out here, though." She nodded at Flynn.

"Oh, hell no." The detective responded about as well as I expected her to. "No way am I letting this idiot go in there alone while I sit out here sipping piña coladas and fending off the unwanted advances of denizens of the underworld."

"Don't worry, sweetie, most of the guys in here wouldn't be caught dead with a human. A live one, that is," Christy said. "And it's not like it's negotiable. Harker is going to go back and talk to the boss, and you're *not* going with him. It's up to you two how much furniture and how much you get broken before we all come to that conclusion, but that's how this debate ends. So you want that piña colada now, or after I start throwing magic missiles around in here?"

Flynn looked an awful lot like she wanted to take her chances throwing down with Christy, and in a normal fight I'd give Flynn the edge every time. Christy tops out at about five-three and carries a few extra pounds on her, almost all of them in exactly the right places, while Flynn is tall, at least five-eight, and all lean muscle and Krav Maga classes. But all it would take is one well-placed spell, and Flynn's sleeping it off for the next day and a half, while Christy wouldn't even break a sweat.

Don't even try it, I sent to Flynn through our mental link. *You have no shot. I don't know if I could take her in a spell duel, and I know I can't take out her and the three bouncers watching us right now.*

"Fine," Flynn said after a long second, and I let out a breath. She turned to me, and I was surprised to see genuine concern in her eyes. "Please don't do anything too stupid. I'm actually starting to like having you around. A little. A very little."

"I'll try to refrain from abject stupidity for at least the next ten minutes," I said, turning to go through a secret entrance between the restrooms at a dive bar to have a chat with a demon about a Catholic church that my personal guardian angel was afraid to talk about. I apparently need a new barometer for "abject stupidity."

CHAPTER 5

After all these years, the monsters still find ways to surprise me. The last thing I expected when I stepped through the door Christy opened into the back room of Mort's was a magic show, but that's exactly what I walked in on. There was a small stage set up in one corner of the room, and on it a man in a tuxedo, top hat, and black cape with red satin lining. He was tall, thin almost to the point of gaunt, with a long face, the kind of face that always looks sad. His eyes were sunk in his face, and his cheeks were hollowed out, all of which gave his face a kind of beetle-browed skeleton look that would have been creepy even in the most innocuous of settings.

He was performing magic tricks for an audience of three — a little boy perched on a stool watching avidly, his feet tapping the rungs of the stool beneath him and his hair bouncing as the boy's head bobbed to the rhythm of the magician's background music. The boy was flanked by two bodyguards, both minotaurs in tailored double-breasted suits. They had huge double-headed axes strapped across their shoulders and Uzis in their hands. I didn't want to think about what was tough enough that they would have to unstrap those big axes. Usually a couple seven-foot bullmen with submachine guns was enough to deter trouble. Of course, it hadn't kept me out, so I guess they did have a point.

The magician juggled balls, then blew on each ball as it reached the apex of its arc, causing the balls to burst into multicolored flame, which he continued to juggle. He spun the balls of fire faster and faster until they blended into one long circle of fire, which the magician stuck his arm through, then another arm, then his entire torso, never letting the ring stop spinning until it settled on its hips and morphed again into a circle of solid multicolored light, flashing a rainbow hula hoop around his waist. He reached down once again, grabbed one end of the color loop, and flipped the stream of colors from around his waist into the audience, grabbing the tail of the rope at the last second when it dropped to the floor, a harmless length of connected handkerchiefs in all the colors of the rainbow.

The little boy on the stool clapped and laughed, then shot a pointed look at his bodyguards, who clapped politely. The magician bowed grandly from the waist, doffing his top hat as he did so. He came up with the hat held in front of him, top pointing toward the stage.

"For my next trick, I will pull a human out of this hat," he said, then began to wave his hand above the top hat's brim.

"Why don't you try something new and pull a living human out, Clive?" I called from the back of the room.

The magician's head snapped up and his eyes locked onto me like a missile guidance system. "Harker." His tone implied that he was slightly less than thrilled to see me.

"In the flesh, no thanks to our last meeting." I gave a little half bow, never taking my eyes off the man in the cape. It had been thirty years or more since I last saw Clive Hardwick, also known at the time as Zoltan the Spectacular, star of stages all over California. He was the real deal as far as magicians went; he had power in spades. It all emanated from the demon that lived in his top hat, of course, but Clive was allowed enough of a leash to use the demon's magic for card tricks and sawing the occasional woman in half.

Not as part of his show, you understand. Clive and his

demon just liked cutting people into little bits. I heard of some strange disappearances in the days after his show left town, and I followed Clive around from town to town for a couple months. I finally put an end to his private butcher's practice behind a magic and comedy club in Fresno, when I banished his demon and beat Clive to within an inch of his life. Clive got in a few shots, too, including one that left me with second-degree burns over more than half my body. He burned most of my hair off and a fair chunk of my face. It took six months and more than a dozen donations from Uncle Luke to put me back together. But when I walked out of the alley that night, I was damn sure the only one capable of walking.

Honestly, I thought he'd died. He was well into his sixties in 1983, and he hadn't exactly been the poster boy for clean living (not that I'm one to talk). So I was a little surprised to see him in Charlotte in the back of a bar where I was supposed to meet with a big-deal demon. And I was even more surprised to open my Sight and see that he had another demon living in his hat. That thing must have been the penthouse of pocket dimensions.

Clive didn't waste time. I always admired that just a little bit in a "you're an evil bastard and I'm probably going to kill you, but this one aspect of your personality is kinda cool" way. He didn't launch into a monologue about what he was going to do to me, he just summoned up a glowing purple ball of energy and threw it at me.

In the second and a half before the sphere hit me, I didn't have enough time to analyze it. I didn't know if it was eldritch energy, demonfire, angelfire, distilled dragonfire, regular fire-fire, or some other kind of energy. I couldn't tell, and frankly I didn't give a shit. I just dropped flat to my stomach and let the ball of bad intentions fly over me and burn a hole in the brick wall behind me.

"That's new," I said, dusting myself off. "Did you get an upgrade when your new hitchhiker moved in upstairs?" I motioned at his hat.

"My Lord Duke Dantalion granted me one his finest spell crafters for my service," Clive grinned as he stroked the hat. It was a little creepy, like he actually cared for the thing in there. I guarantee whatever demonlet Dantalion had sent up from the fifth circle didn't feel the same way about Clive.

"Nice to hear you and Dandelion are getting along so well," I said. My fingers were quickly twining together a piece of string I found on the floor with a couple of pop tops from beer cans.

"What are you doing there? I can't quite...oh, I don't care what you're doing, Harker. It will all end the same way, with you burned to cinders in this room. *Infernos!*" He thrust both his hands out at me, and a stream of fire shot out like water from a fire hose.

I finished with my makeshift bracelet and tied it to my wrist. I held up the representation of a shield and focused my will. "*Inverso!*" A blue-white half-sphere appeared in front of me, centered on my wrist. The fire-stream hit my shield and split, bending around my shield and spewing off harmlessly to the sides.

Unfortunately, the heat didn't go with it, so after less than a second of Clive's fireboats, my wrist started to smoke and blister.

This brought back unpleasant memories of our last meeting, so I tried something I didn't think of decades back in California. I drew my Glock and shot him three times. Or shot at him, rather. Clive flicked up a hand, and with a quick "*Dispersos!*" sucked all the kinetic energy from my bullets. The spent slugs dropped to the floor, harmless, but Clive had to stop his fire assault to save himself, so I got what I needed — breathing room.

"Come on, Clive," I called out, flipping a couple of tables and taking cover behind them. "You couldn't beat me decades ago, don't you think I've learned new tricks in all that time?"

"Ahhh, that's where you're wrong, Quincy," Clive called back from the DJ booth, where he was hiding. "I've not only learned a few new tricks of my own, I've got backup to help me make them more spectacular than ever!" With that, he pulled his hat off, waved his hand over the opening, and shouted "*Sica!*"

Daggers flew from the opening of his top hat. Dozens of them, all streaking across the room right at me. I ducked, and most *thunked* into the overturned bar table, some flew over the top, and a couple skittered along the floor.

I quickly stripped off my makeshift bracelet, added a couple of knots of my hair into the weave, focused my will on the scruffy little band of aluminum and copper, and whispered "*redirectus.*" I wrapped the bracelet around my fist, brass knuckles style, and stood up, throwing my hand at the stage like a punch as I came up. A wave of force pulsed out from my arm, catching the stream of deadly blades and reversing their course.

As usual, things didn't go exactly as planned. Not all of the knives reversed perfectly along their axis, so some went careening off in random directions. None of them headed in my direction, which was the good news. It wasn't great news for the kid sitting in front of the stage, though. While several dozen knives whipped toward Clive at ridiculous speed, a good six or so whirled and tumbled toward the boy, who sat watching our little magical duel with unrestrained glee.

I didn't think about who the kid was, or what kind of parent lets a cherubic, tow-headed little boy with glasses taking up half his face sit in the back of a demon's bar watching an evil wizard do parlor tricks. I didn't wonder about the obvious control he had of the goons surrounding him, goons who were already moving to intercept the missiles streaking toward their young charge. Missiles that were going to be way faster than any human's reactions. I didn't think about anything, other than *Oh shit, I kill this kid and Glory is going to have my balls for earrings.* My guardian angel likes kids, and getting one killed would put me on her shit list for most of an eternity, at least.

So I didn't think, I just acted. Describes a lot of decades for me, especially the 60s and those years in San Francisco and St. Maarten. I flung a hand out toward the kid and shouted "*Inertius!*" Immediately, all the forward momentum of the knives halted, and they dropped to the floor with a thunderous clatter. But since energy can't be destroyed, it had to be redirected somewhere, so I redirected it to Clive. Actually, Clive's shoes.

All the forward energy of dozens of knives flying through the air at blinding speed suddenly transferred itself to Clive's shoes, yanking his feet right out from under him and dropping him flat on his back and sending his hat spinning across the stage beside him.

The biggest problem was that Clive never cancelled his spell, so his hat was still firing knives at the rate of several blades per second. As it spun around the room, knives bounced and clanged around the bar, thunked into the table I ducked behind, and one buried itself into the shoulder of a bodyguard who finally wrapped himself around the little boy, who still sat clapping on his stool, laughing and shrieking with joy at the chaos and bloodshed around him.

The hat spun, spitting knives in every direction, until it came to rest on its side right next to Clive. That pointed the mouth of the hat right at the old magician's side and neck, which were promptly filled with razor-sharp four-inch daggers. The skeletal old magician tried to roll out of the way, but the hat just kept spewing sharpened death at him until he finally collapsed. When Clive died, his spell was broken, and after one last hiccup of blades, the hat fell still. I stood up from my cover behind the table, looking at the carnage Clive and I had wrought upon Mort's private room. There were knives poking out of almost every vertical surface and more than one horizontal one. Shattered glassware littered the bar and every tabletop, not to mention the spilled drinks and the utter destruction wrought upon the front of the jukebox. It must have gotten some spray from a fireball, too, because it was *wrecked*.

I stepped over to the hat, sprinkled a little holy water from a vial in my coat pocket into the depths of it, and murmured a quick exorcism. Clive's little buddy shrieked a number of rather unpleasant names at me, then let out one final shriek as my magic banished him back to hell. I tossed the hat over Clive's dead face and looked around. The little boy had scrambled out from under the body of a pincushioned guard and was now back on his stool, looking over the wreckage.

"You okay, kid?" I called out.

"I'm fine, Mr. Harker. But I seem to be in need of a new magician. This one has sprung a few leaks. Do you know anyone who would like a job?" The voice coming from the kid was way older than anything that should come from that body and I started to have a bad feeling about this little boy.

"No, I don't know of anyone right offhand. Let me guess, that's you in the little ankle-biter, isn't it, Mort?"

"Mortimer Jacobus Venesta, at your service, but I prefer Mort. My parents called me Jake, but that was so long ago that I'm the only who remembers those days. Well, maybe your uncle."

"How old are you?" I asked before I could remember never to ask a monster anything more than was absolutely necessary. You give away information just by the act of asking, so it's always better to keep your mouth shut when dealing with ridiculously powerful creatures from the lowest circles of Hell. Which I was pretty sure is exactly what I was dealing with.

"I came into this world somewhere along 1790, so I suppose your uncle has been here longer. And we won't mention my time before I came over."

No, we wouldn't. The last thing I wanted was to chitchat with a demon about his millennia in Hell. And that's what this kid was—the earthly vessel for Mort, the demon.

CHAPTER 6

"So, Mr. Harker, what can I do for you this evening? I assume you want something since it's been more than a few years since our last conversation, and that ended with a certain amount of broken architecture." Mort and I weren't exactly strangers, even though I'd never been to his place of business, and I'd certainly never seen him in this current body. We'd had a disagreement some years ago about the acceptable uses of fresh corpses that resulted in the death of a lot of ghouls and the destruction of a few automobiles and one small warehouse. I had almost forgotten about it, but obviously Mort hadn't. I decide just to breeze along like we'd never tried to kill each other and hope I could outrun him if it came to that.

"Yeah, I need some information," I said. I walked over to the seating area in front of the stage, picked up a toppled stool, and sat down across from the little demon host.

"What kind of information?" Mort asked.

"What's going on at Our Lady of Holy Comfort?" I asked. I figured no point in beating around the bush. He'd either tell me or not, and the fewer opportunities I gave the centuries-old demon to trap me into something with my words, the better.

The demon got a thoughtful look on his face, then he broke into a grin. "Oh yes, the Church of the Holy Blankie! I know that one, some big goings-on going on down there. Didn't your little guardian angel fill you in? Oh, I guess she wouldn't, would she?"

Her word was "can't" not "won't," but I'm not here to parse grammar with him, I thought, trying not to let anything show on my face.

"Not talking? Afraid I'm going to twist your words into some binding agreement that binds your soul to my service and traps you into wearing women's underpants for a century? Don't worry, Mr. Harker, I have plenty of people entering into agreements with me willingly — I don't need to trick people. And as far as underpants, I'm not interested in what type, if any, you wear."

"So what's the deal at the church, then?" I asked.

"Well, it's not that simple."

"Why not? You just went through this whole spiel about how you weren't going to make me do anything ridiculous to get the information, now you're telling me the exact opposite."

"I didn't actually say any of that." The demon kid folded his arms across his chest.

"And people wonder why demons have a terrible reputation as welshers."

"I'll have you know that I have never reneged on an agreement in five millennia of dealing with you hairless apes!" I'd struck a nerve, and decided to push my edge. Not the safest course of action, I'll admit, but if you're looking for someone to tweak a demon's nose in its own lair, I'm your guy.

"But you certainly took advantage of the ignorance and purposeful misunderstanding of your temporary business partners, didn't you?" I swear, dealing with demons is worse than faeries. Faeries can't lie, it's a genetic thing. So they've learned to obfuscate and evade with the best of them. Actually, they are the best of them. Demons are a lot like that, with more negotiations ending in eviscerations, and less arbitration.

"There might be a few souls currently serving thousand-year sentences as fulfillment on contracts they didn't read thoroughly,"

Mort admitted.

"So what do you want me to do?" I asked.

"You're not going to refuse to work for me on principle?"

"I don't have that many principles, Mort, and the ones I have are pretty flexible. So what's the gig?"

"I need someone killed," Mort said.

"What do you need me for?" I asked. "You've got to have dozens of killers wandering through the doors every hour on the hour."

"I do, but they can't take this guy out. He's got some real juice, magically speaking."

"Like Clive?" I asked.

"Yeah," the boy snorted out a laugh. "If Clive were actually talented, and ever had more power in his whole body than you have stored in your pinky finger."

"I typically don't just kill random people as favors for demons. That's a good way to really irritate a guardian angel, you know," I said. Since he already knew about Glory, I could use her as the "bad cop" to try and spin this negotiation to something I wouldn't hate doing.

"Oh, I don't think you'll mind killing this one. I've heard you have developed quite the soft spot for innocent young women? Well, this is right up your alley, Mr. White Knight. This magician, let's call him Danvar the Magnificent, goes through lovely assistants like some guys go through underwear."

"Not seeing the problem, Morty. So the guy has issues with women, and he fires a lot of assistants. What's the big deal?"

"I never said he fired the girls. I said he goes through them. He hires them, brainwashes them into mindless pleasure drones, uses them up, and when he's tired of them, he wipes their minds and leaves them in whatever city he happens to be in when he gets tired of them." Mort watched my face as his story unfolded, and the glee in his eyes told me that I wasn't nearly as good at hiding my emotions as I wanted to be, particularly when dealing with a demon. *Lock it down, Harker, or you're gonna get yourself killed. Or worse.*

"Okay, that's pretty bad. And it's definitely on the list of things I don't approve of. But why do you care? This guy sounds like the kind of guy I'd expect you to invite over for milk and cookies instead of hiring somebody to take him out."

"Pretty good, Harker. I never thought you'd be able to hold out that long without making a joke about the new body," Mort gestured at his chest. "The last one ran out of steam, so I had to go take over a new one. It was that or go back downtown, and I've gotten accustomed to the weather up here, if you catch my drift."

I did. I was a little nauseated by it, but I did. Mort's old body died, which happens eventually to bodies inhabited by demons, and he went to get a newer model. I could only hope that the kid who used to walk around in that body died before Mort took it over. Otherwise he was still trapped in there, his consciousness shoved off to the side while Mort used his body. Yeah, that's the guy I was working for. A real prince.

"So where do I find this magician, Mort? And how do I verify your story? I'm not just going to murder this guy on your say-so."

"Ri-ight," Mort drawled. "You've grown a pair of morals since coming to Charlotte. Or is it since you started running with that delectable little policewoman you left out in my bar to entertain the boys. Tell me, Harker, does she wear the handcuffs, or does she put them on you?" He leered at me, a disconcerting image coming from a kid who should be entranced by cartoons and comics, not sitting in the back of a bar hiring a hitman to take out an evil magician.

"You probably want to leave Flynn out of this, Mort, she can more than take care of herself." Just to be sure, I sent a thought her way. *You okay out there?*

Fine, but bored. Nobody out here is stupid enough to start anything with me. I thought I'd at least get to arrest somebody. I could tell from the tone of her thoughts that she really was bored, so that was reassuring.

"I'll look into him, Mort. I'm not making any promises, but if he's as bad as you say, he deserves anything I can do to him. One question, though. What did he do to cross you?"

"Why Quincy, old pal, can't I just want to help clean up my community?"

"One, we're not pals. And two, no, you can't. You've never cared anything about a community as long as you can make a profit and wreak some havoc. So since this guy is just doing exactly what you usually want people to do, I want to know what he did to piss you off."

"He killed my mom," the boy's voice came through for the first time, and all the hair on my arms stood up. "She went to see a magic show, and she didn't come home all night. A couple days later the police came to my house and told me my mom was dead. I'm not stupid, so I went on the web and looked it up. She was…raped a bunch of times, then she walked out in front of a bus and killed herself. So I called Mort to help me get the man that did that to her."

This was bad. This was more than bad, this was some epic awful. The boy wasn't just still alive inside his body with Mort wearing his skin suit, he'd invited the demon in to get back at the man who killed his mother. The worst part was, I couldn't blame him. I thought about some of the things I'd done in the past driven by grief, and summoning a demon wasn't anywhere near the worst of them.

"So, you gonna help us? Me and little Bobby here, I mean." Mort's voice returned, and it was easy to look in his eyes and tell that the demon was back in control. I shuddered a little, knowing now that the boy was a willing passenger to everything Mort was going to do with his life.

"Like I said, I'll check it out. If this is for real, I'll make sure Danvar the Molester's show has a shortened run."

"Bring me proof, and I'll tell you everything I know about Our Lady of Holy Comfort and what's going on there." He held out a hand, and I shook it.

I looked into the demon/boy's eyes, and they went human for just a second. He had blue eyes, the boy did.

"Please get the man that killed my mom, Mr. Harker. I don't want to be stuck in here forever for nothing."

Before I could say anything in response, its eyes went black again and Mort smiled up at me. "Happy hunting, Reaper."

I took my hand back and turned for the door. I stopped with my hand on the knob and turned back to Mort. "Mort, you know I'm not just a stupid human, right?"

"I know what you are, Harker. Maybe even better than you do."

"Then you know you do not want to jerk me around on this. Because if I come back here and I find out you've played me…"

"Spare me the threats, Harker. I stopped being afraid of humans somewhere around the Crusades. Now go be a good Reaper and kill something, won't you?"

I walked out, feeling not for the first time in my career like I'd made a deal with the devil. And that *always* ends well.

Flynn was sitting at the bar sipping on a Stella when I walked out. Christy was polishing a section of bar top as far away from where Flynn sat as possible while still being behind the bar. The wood and Plexiglas surface was glowing a deep maroon all around Christy, but faded to a cool blue-green at Flynn's seat. Whatever had Christy riled up, Flynn gave not a single fuck about it.

"What did you do?" I asked in a low voice as I stepped up beside her.

"Nothing much, just played a game of pool or two," she replied. I looked around, but the lone pool table was abandoned, and the green felt showed no new bloodstains.

"What happened?" I pressed.

"There was a disagreement about the break, so I did."

"You broke?" I asked. "What exactly did you break?"

"That guy's nose, and his brother's jaw. But they're fine. They're weres, so they heal fast, and I think they're jackals or something like that, so it was the only way to keep from killing them." Her voice stayed low and calm, but we were collecting some looks. A lot of people wouldn't mess with Flynn if they thought she was under Christy's protection, but everyone in town knew I was fair game.

"What about Sanctuary?" I asked.

"They touched me first, so I was clear. Christy's not happy about it, but she's a woman, so she's letting it slide."

"What do you mean, they touched you?" I was a little surprised at the anger I heard in my own voice, and I zeroed in on the lycanthropes drowning their pain in a couple pitchers of beer over in one corner.

"It's not a thing, Harker. And don't start trying on the shining armor. I don't need one, and the suit won't fit you anyway." She was right, of course. Rescuing damsels in distress never ended well for me. They always ended up inside my head.

"What do I owe you, Christy?" I asked.

"Six months of staying the hell out of my bar and a promise that I never see her again at all," the fiery manager shot back.

"Can't promise anything, so here's some cash for the beer you had to comp the dogs." I jerked a thumb over my shoulder at the weres. "But tell them to be more careful who they're sniffing around next time. All humans aren't created equal anymore." I dropped a couple of twenties on the bar and we walked out onto the street.

"Where to now, boss?" Flynn asked with enough snark in her voice that you could cut it with a knife.

"I need information, and Glory can't or won't give it to me," I replied.

"I thought that's what you went in there to find? Don't tell me I got felt up by two shapeshifters with dog breath for nothing."

My vision blurred a little red at the mention of the were-jackals mauling Flynn, but I blinked a couple times before she noticed. I hoped. "I got some information, but I need to confirm it. So I've got to go get help from the last person in the world I want to ask."

"Smith?" Flynn asked.

"Smith," I confirmed, and slid into the passenger seat. Flynn put the car into gear and we headed off to admit to my boss that he might know more than me about something magical.

CHAPTER 7

We pulled into the garage underneath police headquarters and headed to the elevator. "What's your plan?" Flynn asked.

"What kind of plan?"

"To get the information you need out of Smith?"

"Well, I thought I'd ask," I said, honestly confused.

Flynn looked at me like I'd grown another head. "Yeah, when has that ever worked?"

I stepped into the elevator and turned to her. "What are you talking about, Becks?"

"Look, Smith is the single most tight-lipped human being I've ever met—"

"The jury's still out about that whole human thing," I reminded her. "I, for one, am not a hundred percent sure what Smith is, but I don't think he's human. Not totally, at any rate." There was definitely something magical about Agent John Smith. He looked human from the outside, but there was something in the eyes that spoke of too many years for a normal lifetime. And he was definitely stronger and faster than a typical human.

The doors dinged open, and we stepped off into the second-floor offices of the Charlotte-Mecklenburg Police Department. I followed Flynn as we meandered through cubicles and hallways until we came to the small block of offices "temporarily" assigned to Agent John Smith and his Department of Homeland Security Domestic Terrorism Task Force. At least, that's what it said on our badges and business cards. In reality, we were one team of the government's Paranormal Division. Basically, if something went bump in the night, we bumped back. Harder.

Flynn went to her office and I stepped up to Smith's door. I raised my hand to knock and the door swung open on its own.

"Come on in, Quincy," Smith said from his seat behind his desk. He was dressed like he always was, in a pinstriped charcoal suit with a muted burgundy tie and an American flag lapel pin. He looked up at me over a pair of reading glasses that I suspected were just for show, and his gray-blue eyes locked onto mine.

"What can I do for you, Harker? How are things at Mort's?" He motioned to a chair, and I sat in front of his desk. I noticed immediately that the chair was low to the ground, giving Smith an uncommon height advantage. He's not a small man, but I top out several inches over six feet, so I usually look down on him a little. This time he was the tall man in the room. *Oh well, his room, his playing field.*

"Mort's fine," I replied. "Christy sends her best. I need to know about a magician by the stage name of Danavar."

Smith leaned back in his chair and looked at me. "Why?"

"Because Mort wants me to kill him. Says he's basically a serial rapist , and he's operating without Mort's permission. So he wants him dead."

"And you're now playing hitman for demons?" Smith asked, one eyebrow climbing toward his brush-cut gray hair.

"Mort has information I need," I said.

"Information on what?" Smith asked.

"Our Lady of Holy Comfort Catholic Church," I replied.

"What do you need to know?" Smith's eyes were flat, revealing nothing, but that was no different from every other day. Still, I felt like there was something underneath this conversation, something he was either waiting for me to ask, or something he didn't want to tell me.

"I need to know everything. Hell, at this point I'd settle for knowing *anything*. Something serious is happening there, something so big that Glory won't talk to me about it. No, scratch that. She's not allowed to talk to me about it."

"Which makes it completely irresistible to you," Smith observed.

"You're not wrong," I admitted. "So what's the deal?"

"I don't know. I've heard some rumblings, and I know Flynn's homicides yesterday morning were members there, but there's been nothing from my sources about the place."

"And who are your sources, Smith? Where is your thumb on the pulse of the dark underbelly of the Carolinas?"

"Let me tell you one thing, Harker. You don't ever want to know how I get my information. I promise you that."

For some reason, I believed him. Smith had the eyes of a man who's seen some shit in his lifetime. And since I've seen more than my fair share of shit myself, I didn't push. "Yeah, I didn't figure you'd know. That's why I went to see Mort." I let that one just lay out there, the assumption that a demon knew more than him was exactly the kind of thing that would grate at Smith.

"How's Christy?" he asked, not batting an eye. I hate inscrutable motherfuckers like Smith. They make me work twice as hard for every scrap of information.

"She's fine. Buxom. Badass. Still taking zero shit and giving zero fucks."

"Good to hear. I like that girl. Hate she got mixed up with a dick like Mort, but I can understand it, given the circumstances." He said that like I was supposed to know how Christy got tangled up working for Mort, but I had no idea. And of course, phrasing it like it was common knowledge meant that I couldn't ask what the deal was without revealing my ignorance, which would give

Smith insight into another hole in my knowledge. If he really knew at all and wasn't just playing me. Which I would never figure out without asking him about it, the one thing he'd just insured I'd never do. Bastard played the game better than me, even in his off-the-rack suits.

"So, how old is Mort this time?" Smith asked, taking a file out of his desk drawer and opening it.

"Looks like he's hopped into an eight-year-old," I said, trying but not quite managing to keep the disgust out of my voice.

"That's not cool," Smith said.

"No, it's fucking disgusting," I replied, the bile I felt making its way into my voice.

"That's not what I meant," Smith interrupted me with a hand. "I have an arrangement with Mort about his continued existence on this plane. 'No deals with kids' is very much a part of that arrangement. He and I are going to have a conversation about this." I had a distinct feeling that conversation wasn't going to be a whole lotto fun for Mort and would probably result in a fair amount of broken furniture. Or people.

"So why Danvar? And why you?" Smith asked.

"No idea," I replied. "I just know the magician is mind-slaving his assistants, raping them into oblivion, and then casting them aside. I don't think any of that would be a problem, except he picked up a woman in Mort's territory, and now Mort wants a message sent."

"And he wants you to send the message," Smith said.

"I think me killing Danvar is only part of the message. If the local monsters think I'm under Mort's control, they'll fall in line pretty quick. Between Mort and me, we pack some pretty serious punch. I wouldn't mess with the two of us."

"I wouldn't either," Smith agreed, more out of politeness

than any sincerity, I thought. I've watched Smith open fire on a dragon with a handgun and not back down a single step. It was an illusionary dragon, but he didn't know that at the time.

"But you can't kill Danvar," he continued.

I started a little. Smith was generally pretty hands-off on my life outside the cases we worked together. This kind of directness was a little unprecedented.

"Why not?" I asked. "Is he not really a child molester? I wouldn't put it past Mort to lie about that kind of thing."

"No, he's everything Mort described to you, and more. He drains the life force from women, abuses them inside and out, bleeds them of their happiness and their life force, then sets them loose on the world as husks—lifeless, soulless walking shadows that torment their loved one by their mere presence until a few months later they commit suicide."

"And eventually you'll get to the part that says why I *shouldn't* kill this asshole."

"Yeah, I will. He's my informant. I'm working on turning him to give me inside information about Mort and his operation. That's why Mort wants him dead. Not some suddenly rediscovered noble purpose bullshit about not wanting the poor kids to be victimized."

"Still seems like a pretty good guy to come down with a terminal case of dead," I said, reeling at the idea of Smith using somebody like that as a source.

"And most of the time, I'd agree with you. But I'm pretty close to bringing this douchebag over to the side of the angels, and part of that is him agreeing to cease his less savory activities."

"Smitty," I said, knowing full well he hated that nickname, "purse-snatching is a less savory activity. Fixing a horse race is a less savory activity. Sucking out somebody's life force and personality so you can live forever is just fucking disgusting, and this guy needs to be put down."

"No." Smith didn't bother meeting my gaze this time. He knew he was wrong, and he didn't care. When he finally looked at me across his desk, his eyes were cold, just gray chips in his stony face. "This isn't negotiable, Harker. Stay away from Danvar. I'm not asking."

"I didn't come here to ask permission, Smitty. I came here to see if this guy was as much of a threat as Mort claimed, and if you had information about the church. Since the answer question one is yes, and question two is no, I guess I'm gonna have to go kill the rat bastard."

Smith stood up. "Don't do this, Quincy. I'd hate for us to end up on opposite sides of this thing."

"Yeah, so would I. So stay out of my way," I said.

"That's not how this works," Smith said, leaning forward onto his fists.

He opened his mouth to continue, but Flynn flung the door open. "We've got another one," she said, gesturing to me.

"Another what?" I asked, standing.

"Another family slaughtered in their home. Let's go."

I turned back to Smith. "We'll continue this later." I followed Flynn out the door and down the hallway. "How long were you standing out there?" I asked as we stepped into the parking garage elevator.

Flynn gave me her best "innocent" look, which sucked. "I just heard the last few minutes. I felt the tension rising in you and wanted to be able to interrupt if things got stupid. I felt them moving toward stupid, so I interrupted. But we do have a case."

"Same M.O.?"

"Oh yeah. Bring a spare pair of shoes. This one's even worse."

CHAPTER 8

It was a good twenty-minute ride from downtown to the University area where the Nettles family home stood in a nice suburban neighborhood named Whispering Falls, or Rambling Brook, or Fallen Spruce, or whatever stupid collection of nouns the developed pulled out of the hat this time. Flynn parked in the driveway, right behind the crime scene van. I pulled my car in beside hers, then got out and jerked my head toward the CSI van. Those guys have been known to do nasty science-type things to people who get in their way.

"Don't worry," Flynn said as she opened the door and slid out of the car. "If this is anything like the Standish place, they won't be leaving anytime soon." Good point. When there's twenty liters of blood scattered around a house, it takes a while to process a crime scene.

I got out of the car and took a look around, first with my eyes, then with my Sight. In the normal spectrum, it looked like any other house on the street. Brick two-story, white shutters, white siding for the eaves, small front porch, large back deck that extended far enough out to be seen a little from the front of the house. An attached two-car garage sat off to the left with the doors closed, a sidewalk leading up to the front door, where half a dozen cops milled around. The perimeter was set for two houses back on each side, but that did nothing to stop the crowd of lookie-loos from gathering, phones at the ready, trying to get a gruesome or sad photo for their internet profile.

I walked up to a uniform taking photos of the outside of the house. He was noting placement of the kids' bicycles, tire tracks, things like that. "Hey, Officer…" I let the pause drag on so he'd hopefully take the bait and supply his name.

No such luck. I had to read his nametag. "Officer Aguirre, could you make sure you get photos of everyone along the tape as well?"

"Sure…" he trailed off as he took in my long coat, black t-shirt, no visible badge.

"He's with me, Aguirre. Just do as he asks," Flynn said, shooting me a look. I opened my Sight and scanned the crowd. Nobody stood out as a bad guy, but I wondered if the homeowner's association knew that one of their neighbors was an elf.

I followed Flynn into the house, and my nose was immediately assaulted by the coppery smell of blood, the salty tang of fear-sweat and other, less savory smells of death. I wandered through the downstairs, poking around the kitchen, checking the channels on the television, doing all the things I could think of to keep me out of the upstairs. Finally, out of excuses, I put on two pair of booties over my shoes and climbed to the second floor.

Flynn was right, it was worse than the Standish place. She was waiting for me at the top of the stairs. A pair of crime scene techs were visible in the master bedroom off to the left, so I turned right to look at the children's rooms. Just going from the decoration on the doors, they had a boy and a girl, just like the Standishes.

"Are we seeing a pattern, here, Flynn? Two kids, boy and a girl? Is that significant?" I asked, my hand on the door to the little boy's room.

"It could be," Flynn replied. "It's honestly too early to tell. We can't build a dependable pattern off just two crime scenes. To get a real pattern we need more data points, which means either — "

"This fucker has to kill again," I supplied.

"That," Flynn agreed, "or we find cold cases with the same M.O., either locally or nationwide. I contacted the FBI and sent them the details of the case. They're running everything we have through their database, so hopefully today we'll hear if there are any other cases like this in the U.S."

"Let's hope the answer is no," I said.

"Why is that?" Flynn asked. "I mean, I understand it on a human level. We don't want anyone else to have gone through this, ever. But that's not what you meant, was it?"

"No, it wasn't. If this is local, then it's probably something I can deal with. If this is a demon that's been traveling for years, with no significant weaknesses and a long history of getting away with this shit, there's a good possibility that it's either too strong or too smart for me to handle, which is not only bad for yours truly, but severely reduces our chances of stopping this thing before it's eaten its fill."

I turned the knob and stepped into the Nettles boy's room. If ever there was a stereotypical American boy's room, I was standing in it. A Cam Newton poster hung in place of pride over his bed, Cam in his "Superman" pose after scoring a touchdown. A huge Carolina Panthers head hung over a small desk with a stack of *Chronicles of Narnia* and *Harry Potter* books on it. Framed on the desk was a picture of the kid, Carey, I remembered his name finally, with a smiling Luke Kuechly in the picture with him. A single bed sat under a window, a military-style footlocker at the end of the bed. In the middle of the bed, tangled in the covers like he was sleeping with it, was a football. This was a kid who loved his Panthers.

I knelt to open the footlocker and felt a rush of cold across my arms. I looked around and drew back as Carey Nettles appeared, sitting on the footlocker with a somber expression on his face. I reached for the footlocker again, and Ghost Carey shook his head at me, putting his hands over mine. I felt the grave-chill again and drew my hands back.

"Hi Carey," I said, looking right at the boy. He started a little, obviously used to being ignored. I went on. "Most people can't see you, can they?"

He shook his head.

"Well, most people don't know how to look. My name is Quincy, and I'm one of the good guys. I know how to talk to people like you, and a lot of times I can help them move along on their journey. Do you know what I mean?"

He looked at me, sadness filling his deep eyes. He nodded slowly, then looked around the room.

"I know, it's a little scary, leaving behind everything we're familiar with. But it can be exciting, too, getting to see new things, right?"

He nodded again, a little less pain in his eyes.

"Carey?" I asked. "Can you answer a few questions for me before you go?"

He nodded.

"I know you can't speak to me, but I'll ask yes or no questions, and you can just nod, okay?"

He nodded again.

I took a deep breath. "Did someone hurt your family, Carey?"

The ghost sat on the edge of the bed, just looking up at me. After a long moment, he nodded.

"Was it someone you know?"

Nod.

"Was it someone who lives here?"

Nod.

"Carey, did your daddy hurt you and your mommy?"

382 | Year One § *Hell Freezes Over*

Long pause, then nodded. A single shiny tear streaked down his face. I reached out without thinking to wipe it away, but my hand passed right into his face, startling us both.

"I'm sorry, Carey. I didn't mean to scare you." The irony of my words was not lost on me, as I apologized to a ghost for me scaring him, but this wasn't a haunting in the real sense, this was a lost little boy who didn't know how to find his mommy and daddy. "I just have one more question, then I'll help you find your mom and dad." *Or at least your mom*, I thought. I only had a little bit of faith in his mother and father sharing an afterlife, but this wasn't the time or place to discuss that.

Carey looked up at me, trust shining on his ethereal face. He nodded once, telling me that he could be brave a little while longer.

I took a deep breath. "Carey, when your daddy hurt your mommy and you, was it really your daddy, or was there something else with him?"

I saw the boy try to say something and shook my head. I hadn't asked a yes or no question, and the mute spirit couldn't answer anything. I held up a hand.

"Hold on, buddy, I've got it. Let's try this—was it really your daddy who hurt you?"

Carey shook his head.

"So somebody else was with him?"

Another head shake. Well, that didn't make any sense. If he wasn't being controlled by something…wait a minute.

"Carey, was somebody else in your daddy?"

A vigorous nod. He grinned and gave me a "thumbs up." So it was as I suspected—his father wasn't evil, he was possessed. That gave me some direction, at least. Now to send this kid on his merry way.

"Carey, are you ready to go find your mom and dad?" The little ghost boy nodded.

I sketched a quick circle on the floor with a piece of chalk I found in the kid's desk. It wouldn't hold much, but I didn't expect Carey to try and jump into my skin suit, either.

"Step inside the circle, Carey." He hopped down off the bed and stepped into the circle. I spun out a little of my energy to invoke the circle, and a glowing white light snapped into being all around the edge of the circle.

Carey drew back, frightened.

"Don't worry buddy. I won't let anything hurt you anymore." I focused my mind and called, "Glory! Get your yoga-firm ass down here. I need your help."

"You know I can't get involved in this fight, Q. And stop checking out my ass, it's perverted."

"It's a nice ass, and what do you mean you can't help me?"

"We've talked about this. I can't help you on this case."

"This is different. All I need you to do is open a door to Heaven and let this kid in to find his parents. And I kinda need to know if they're in there." I talked fast, but it's really hard to confuse an angel. They're otherworldly smart and can tell when I'm lying. I didn't really expect Glory to do it, but when she sighed, I knew I had her.

A fair number of my most successful interactions with women over the decades have been preceded by a resigned sigh on their part. I'll take it. Glory waved her hands in the air, spoke some Latin phrases, and the fabric of reality split wide open. Searing white light spilled into the room, and I had to avert my eyes. I also had to cover them with both hands, and a second later I pulled a pillow off Carey's bed and pressed it to my face to save my sight. Heaven isn't something mortals get to peek into and keep their Earthly vision.

I heard Glory speaking more Enochian, then the light around me dimmed considerably. I put the pillow down and looked past Glory to see a couple in their early thirties standing in a pool of light. Carey's face lit up when he saw his parents, and I looked over at Glory.

"We all good?" I asked. She nodded, and I dropped the circle around Carey. He ran to his parents, who looked up at me with a smile. The mom held a preteen girl by the hand, presumably Carey's sister, and his father looked at me with a grateful smile. Whatever this man had done, it wasn't by his hand, and left no stain on his soul, or he'd never be allowed near the soul of an innocent child. Carey and his family vanished, leaving more questions behind than they answered.

"That was bold, Q," Glory said, waving a hand and sealing her portal. I reached out with a toe and scrubbed out the edge of the circle, dispersing the magical energy into the world and erasing any trace of me from the room.

"Didn't have to be, Glory. If you'd give me the info I need."

"I can't, Q. I really, really want to, but I can't. It's not my decision, and I don't get to contradict my bosses. You know that."

"Yeah, I know. That whole war in Heaven thing. Whatever, thanks for helping with that. I couldn't send him on myself because if I just banished him, there's no guarantee where he would have ended up."

"Thanks for doing that. I couldn't stand the thought of that little boy just wandering the Earth forever."

"Don't tell anybody about it, Glory. I've got a reputation to uphold. Which I will ruin forever if I stay in this room talking to nobody any longer. Get out of here, I've got a crime scene to investigate."

"Later, Q. I hope you figure it out. I really do." I could see in her eyes that she wasn't lying. Well, that and the fact that angels can't lie. They can't. Neither can demons. Both of them can obfuscate like motherfuckers, but they can't *lie*. The trick is getting either bunch to give you a straight answer, so you know what they really mean. This time I felt like Glory was being straight with me. She couldn't tell me what was going on, but that didn't mean she didn't want me to put a stop to it.

CHAPTER 9

The rest of the house was spirit-free, thank God. I spent a little time checking out the daughter's room, but there was nothing there. Just a preteen girl's room with posters of musicians I'd never heard of and actors that I couldn't tell apart. A stack of *Ms. Marvel* comics spoke to a budding love of geekdom and good writing, and my heart pulled a little at the pictures of Elizabeth Nettles riding a horse at some kind of camp, her kayaking with a huge grin, accepting some award at a school function. I couldn't find anything to indicate she was anything other than a well-adjusted twelve-year-old girl. Still no computer in the kids' rooms, so I'd have to check the family PC down in the dining room for anything dangerous, but I was pretty sure I felt a strikeout coming there, too.

I pulled the door closed to the daughter's room and turned to go into the parents' room and murder scene. The blood had soaked all the way across the threshold into the hallway, making me grateful for double-bagging the booties. The room looked almost like someone had rollered the walls in reddish brown paint, there was so much blood splatter. Where the Standish scene had been contained mostly to the bed area, this room showed signs of a struggle with overturned furniture and bodies scattered all over the floor and bed.

Carey and Elizabeth were in the bed, and that's where most of the blood on those walls came from. It looked like the kids were stood up on the bed, their throats slit, and the spray directed around the room for maximum coverage. Sandy Nettles was lying on the floor at the foot of the bed, barefoot and bare-legged. Dressed in an oversized t-shirt and panties for bed, she'd obviously come awake when her husband brought the kids into the room.

She put up a fight, too. She was away from the bed, and there was a shattered lamp and alarm clock lying on the floor against one wall. Looked like she threw things at her husband to try and get him to stop. My guess was, she could have thrown a tank at him and nothing would have stopped what was going to happen here. Whatever was doing this shit had more power than almost anything I'd ever run across, and that had me plenty worried.

Sandy lay in a pool of blood so deep the carpet couldn't hold it all, so there were literal puddles of her blood on either side of her head. Her throat was slit deep enough I could see her spine through her throat, and every other major artery had been opened, too. It wasn't overkill in the classic sense—it was too clinical, too cold. There was no rage here, just the need for a huge volume of blood. That was reminiscent of blood magic, but there was no other hint of magic anywhere in the room, not even on the husband's body.

Jim Nettles lay facedown on the carpet, most of his body's blood streaking out from his legs and wrists. I felt a second's relief that I didn't have to see his empty eyes staring up at me, accusing, demanding answers, screaming for justice that I couldn't provide. I gave myself a shake and snapped out of my pity party, remembering that I wasn't the dead one in the room, so I had it pretty good.

I opened my Sight and scanned the room quickly. It had the same clean energy as the Standish scene, an almost sterile feeling in the magical spectrum, which was really odd for a place where so much blood had been shed. I filed that away on my list of things to poke Glory about and kept looking around the room. I turned slowly in place, scanning the walls, ceiling and floor with my Sight, but nothing leapt out at me as demonic or even supernatural in nature. For all I could tell with my third eye, this was committed by a completely unassisted human.

If there hadn't been an identical murder/suicide less than a day ago, and if I hadn't been haunted by the ghost of a cherubic second-grader ever since, I would have walked away from this one, too. But I was being haunted by sweet little Emily Standish, who stared at me from the Nettles' closet door with her big, blue, accusing eyes. So I kept looking. There had to be something here, something I missed at the Standish home...*there*. There was just a glimmer of light coming from the dresser. I dropped my Sight and walked across the room. A jewelry box, a stack of folded clothes waiting to be put away, a wallet and change dish, and a couple of framed photos sat on the polished wood surface. *Here we go,* I thought. I opened the jewelry box and pawed through it, dumping the contents onto the dresser.

"Hey, you can't do that!" One of the crime scene techs rushed toward me all in a tizzy.

"Calm down, Chow Yun Fat, I'm working here." The Asian man stopped in his tracks, his jaw agape.

"Who the fuck are you? I'm totally reporting you. You can't just come in here while I'm working and make racist comments. I'll have your fucking badge, you asshole. I'll make sure you—"

I held up a hand. "*Obliviscor,*" I whispered, then blew the irate man a kiss. His eyes glazed for a moment, then refocused on me.

"What are you doing?" he asked again for the first time.

"I'm checking for surveillance," I replied. "Detective Flynn asked me to. Told me to turn the room over to you once I was done." I gave him one of those "what can you do" shrugs and turned back to the jewelry. My fingers brushed against a silver medal, and I felt a tingle through my fingers, like a tiny electric shock. I brushed aside more rings and brooches until I felt it again, then drew out a silver medal on a string of glass beads, with a small silver crucifix dangling from the end.

Whoever this fucker is, he's a nasty piece of work, I thought to Flynn.

Why? What did you find?

The Focus for his spell on the Nettles family. Bastard enchanted a rosary to lock them under his influence. I'm coming down.

I stomped through the assembled cops and crime scene techs on my way to the front door. Flynn stood in the foyer talking to a neighbor but broke away when I came down.

"Aguirre, finish taking her statement. I'm sorry, Mrs. Ravin, I need to speak with my consultant." She followed me out into the yard and across the grass to my car. I opened the trunk and sat on the bumper, pulling off the blood-soaked booties and stripping off my shoes and socks.

"I wondered about the sneakers," Flynn asked as she caught up to me.

"Stopped at Walmart on the way over," I said. I put the booties, sneakers and socks all in a big plastic bag, then scrounged around in the trunk for an old towel I kept back there for emergencies. I wiped the last of the blood off my feet and threw the towel in the bag with the bloody shoes. I grabbed my Doc Martens out of the trunk and pulled on a pair of thick boot socks to go with them. Flynn stood there silent for several minutes while I laced up my boots, then finally she broke.

"Well?" she asked.

"Deep subject," I replied, keeping my petty little grin to myself somehow.

"Don't fuck with me, Harker. I need to know what's going on."

I held out the medal. "This is a big deal," I said. "It takes a lot of power to corrupt a truly holy object, and saint's medals and crucifixes are inherently holy. Put them on a rosary, and one that's seen some use, and they are significant objects of faith, at least to the owner. This might not mean shit to the Buddhist guy across the street, but to Jim Nettles, this is probably the focal point of all his prayers. I'm guessing his mother died of cancer, probably sometime when he was newly married, or around thirty. He prayed with this rosary through that whole time and carried it for a long time after. Then his wife had a scare, and he started carrying it again recently."

"How did you get all that? Some kind of psychokinesis?" Flynn asked. "A spell?"

"Nah, more like old-school Sherlock Holmes shit," I replied. "Most of that psychokinesis bullshit is just that—bullshit. There are a few PKs out in the world, but most folks do it with magic. Strong emotions leave impressions on objects, and magic can bring those to the front. But this was all detective work. There were pics of a woman bearing a slight resemblance to Nettles in the house holding both kids as infants, but nothing more recent of her. And this necklace is about ten or fifteen years old and shows signs of a lot of handling. So he prayed with this thing a lot, but there aren't enough religious items in the house to make me think he did that recently. They did the church thing, but it didn't drive them. And St. Peregrine is the patron saint of cancer patients, so all that makes sense."

"But what about the wife? What makes you think she had cancer?"

"No, she was a survivor. It was the bras. There was a

mastectomy bra on the dresser with a prosthetic built in, and she wore a bra to sleep in. Speaks to a woman with confidence issues centered around her breasts, and some cancer patients have trouble letting their partners see the scars, so they wear their prostheses to bed. But her cancer would have been enough to get him to pull that old rosary out and pray with it again. I'd bet we find out that they started going to church again about two, two and a half years ago. Probably right about the time she was diagnosed."

"So what killed them?" Flynn asked.

"It's not the what. We know the what, or the who. Jim Nettles killed his family and then opened every artery and vein in his body that he could reach. What we don't know is the why, and we don't know what needs an offering of that much blood to break through the Veil. And we really, really hope it's still locked on the other side."

"How are we supposed to find out those things? Especially the bit about whether or not this big bad is still locked away?" Flynn asked, keeping her voice low to not attract attention from the surrounding cops. Most of them knew she was on some oddball assignment with Homeland Security. Most of them didn't know she was working for the real-world equivalent of the *X-Files*.

"Nothing came through here, it would have left a mark," I said with more confidence than I felt.

"You're full of shit." The problem with trying to lie, or even fudge the truth, with someone who is literally inside your head is that they are *literally inside your head*. Flynn felt every nuance of every word I said, so she knew I was lying.

"Of course I'm full of shit, Becks. I can't tell what kind of magic is causing this because *I can't feel any magic at all*. Do you know how fucked up that is? It's like walking into a room where you know people died, but you can't see what killed them. They're just dead. No bullet holes, no stab wounds, no ligature marks, nothing. That's what I've got—a fucking conundrum that's hiding in an enigma. And not only do I have nothing, but my best resource has been ordered not to help me. So we're fucked. So I'm going home, and I'm going to do what I do when I don't have any other options."

"Get drunk?"

"That too. No, I'm going to call Luke. Maybe he's seen something like this, or read about it. The bastard's been alive long enough to remember when Gutenberg first played with movable type. If it's in print, he's probably read it."

"Don't forget Renfield. He's a smart little dude," Flynn added.

"Good call. You sticking around here?"

"Yeah, I need to talk with the officer that found the bodies, get the okay from up top to take over the case from the local detective, smooth it over with those guys, all those political things that you don't have to deal with."

"Beauty of being freelance, Detective," I said, walking to the front of my car. "On the other hand, nobody's gonna reimburse me for the shoes I just ruined."

"Take it up with your rich uncle, Harker. I'll swing by later and see what you've figured out."

CHAPTER 10

"I can't say that I've ever heard of anything quite like that, Quincy, but that also stands to reason, doesn't it? I mean, if there was something forcing people to commit horrific murder-suicides, but it went to such amazing lengths to hide its supernatural origins, then we wouldn't know it was supernatural at all. The only way we would discover these crimes is if, as happened to you, someone were to become haunted by a victim, or by sheer process of elimination." Uncle Luke sat on my couch, a snifter of brandy in his hand, lecturing to the room. I've always thought that his talents were wasted on being one of the most famous monsters in history. If it weren't for the whole sucking human blood to live thing, he'd be a hell of a college professor. He even looked the part, with leather patches on the elbows of his corduroy jacket, his dark hair curled just a touch longer than his collar, and his refined features that spoke of good breeding and blazing intellect.

"What do you mean, process of elimination?" I asked, sipping my third scotch. After the second one, the smell of blood started to ever so slowly fade from my nostrils, supplanted by the peaty oakness of a good Dalmore single malt. By the third, the sharp edges on my memories were starting to soften, and I could close my eyes without seeing every detail of the Minnie Mouse nightshirt Sandy Nettles died in, the pink fabric bunched up high on one leg, showing an expanse of toned thigh streaked with blood where she died fighting for her life and her children.

"Well, I suppose we'd have to go through every single

homicide in the country and filter them out based on similar patterns in victimology, crime scene details, information about the perpetrators, and any other data points we can find," Luke said. "If we could access that kind of information, we could, theoretically, see if anything like this has every happened before. But we would need basically all the world's police departments to be networked, with the same type of cross-referencing and recording the same details. I'm afraid the task is so daunting as to be impossible."

"Eight," Renfield said from my desk across the room. Renfield took up residence at my computer almost as soon as we started talking about the murders and buried himself in the internet and the darknet. For a guy who knew about the deepest, darkest recesses of the web, he looked like a stockbroker. His light brown hair was a little disheveled, and there was an excited look behind his wire-rimmed glasses, but otherwise Renfield looked perfectly put-together in khakis, a v-neck sweater over a nice Oxford dress shirt, and loafers that I was pretty sure cost more than my car. This was a confluence of several things. First, Luke took very good care of his Renfields financially. Second, this Renfield had a bit of a shoe fetish, and lastly, I had a really shitty car.

Luke looked over at his manservant, the most recent to bear the name of "Renfield," now as much a title as an ode to my uncle's inability to remember his minion's names. "Exactly what are you talking about, dear boy? This recent trend toward *non sequitur* does not bode well for your continued employment. I understand that you humans decline at a rapid rate, but I cannot keep someone in my service once their faculties begin to fail, I'm sure you understand."

Renfield shot my uncle a withering look. "Just as I'm sure you understand that your inability to keep track of the conversation at hand has more to do with your personal deficiencies than any imagined failings on my part. There have been eight similar cases in the United States since the end of the Civil War, where nine fathers murdered their families in their beds over a period of weeks. Each instance culminated in a city-wide or regional tragedy resulting in massive loss of life. For instance, the Great Chicago Fire in 1871 came right on the end of a streak of horrific murders among the city's businessmen. Nine families were slaughtered, with the fire bringing an end to the streak. A similar streak of murders was documented in San Francisco—"

"Let me guess," I interrupted. "In 1906, right before the great quake?"

"Exactly," Renfield confirmed. "There were also similar catastrophes ending strings of mysterious family slayings in Boston in 1942 when the Coconut Grove nightclub burned; in 1913 in Dayton, Ohio, when the Great Dayton Flood killed over three hundred fifty people; and tracking through the last century and a half to the most recent, when Hurricane Katrina touched down in New Orleans, devastating the French Quarter and bringing to an end the activities of the Crescent City Ripper, as he was being called by the press."

"I never heard of that," I said.

"Neither did I, and I read the newspapers religiously," said Luke.

"But neither of you read the newspapers specifically published and targeted to the African-American community, I assume," Renfield said. Luke and I shrugged and nodded. Renfield nodded back and said, "I thought so. The Ripper never received any mainstream press coverage because he was killing African-Americans in a city with a high crime rate, so he remained largely unnoticed until Katrina hit, then he vanished."

"Let me guess," I said, "after eight families were slaughtered."

"Nine," Luke said. I looked at Renfield, who nodded. I turned a raised eyebrow back to Luke. "Nine is a holy number," he said. "It has power. Whatever is doing this is working to bring about something nasty, and it's getting better at it."

"You think it harnessed the power from the nine murders to cause these disasters? Including Katrina?"

"I don't know if there's enough blood magic in North America to create a Category 4 hurricane out of whole cloth, but there's probably enough power in a couple dozen deaths to steer one," Luke said.

"So you think whatever this is building to could be bigger than Katrina?" I asked.

"It would seem to follow," Renfield replied.

"But we're not near any oceans, and most buildings of any size have enough fire suppression to keep Mrs. O'Leary's cow out of business," I said.

"But there are fault lines running all through the Carolinas, and there is some precedent for magical events triggering seismic tremors," Luke said.

"What fault lines? Why haven't I heard about this?" I asked.

"They haven't been active in decades, but most seismologists agree the Charlotte area is long overdue for some seismic activity," Luke went on, ignoring me.

"So now we think that these murders are just building up what, psychic energy to trigger a giant earthquake?" I looked around to see if anyone was laughing. No one was. "Seriously?"

"Seriously," Renfield said. "Take a look here." He brought my laptop over to the couch where I sat across from Luke. He showed me some pictures with red and yellow circles on them, then overlaid those pictures onto a map of the Carolinas. One of the red circles was directly over Charlotte.

"I have no fucking idea what any of that means, except that it's gotta be bad," I admitted.

"Well, nephew, at the root of it, that's all you need to know. Something is killing people and is planning to use the energy from those violent and tragic deaths to trigger a giant earthquake that will wipe out the whole city and kill thousands of people."

"Fuck," I said, leaning back on the couch.

"My sentiments exactly," said Luke.

"So what do we do about it?" I asked.

"Well, you stop it, of course," Luke replied.

"Why me? Why don't you stop it?" I asked. Every once in a while I like to beat my head against the walls of the universe and rail against my destiny a bit. It never gets me anywhere, but sometimes makes me feel better for a few seconds.

This was not one of those days. Luke, of course, had an answer.

"Quincy, my dear boy, I am a legendary creature of the night, with a centuries-long tradition of striking fear into the hearts of humans everywhere. I do not save the world, I terrify it. You, on the other hand, are a white hat of almost mythic proportions. There are demon mothers in the sixth circle of Hell who use tales of your exploits to scare their children into obedience. You have saved more lives than Jonas Salk and Marie Curie combined. You are the greatest advancement of humanity since the pasteurization of milk. This, clearly, is your department."

We kept hashing around ideas, I kept hammering scotch, until finally I waved my uncle and his assistant off so I could crash for a few hours of drunken slumber. I dropped into my bed, only taking enough time to strip off my shoes and pants, and was asleep almost before my head hit the pillow. Of course, that's where the real shit started.

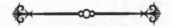

Emily Standish was standing at the foot of my bed when my eyes cracked open. She wasn't doing anything, just standing there with the preternatural stillness that only the dead can achieve. That's the one thing you eventually notice about dead people, how they don't move much. Even the animated ones, or the undead, like Uncle Luke. They don't have the constant motion of the living. There's no chest rising and falling with each breath. There are no twitching fingers, or tapping feet, or shifting of weight from one foot to another. There's no constant blinking, swallowing, eyes flitting from one thing to another. There's just... stillness.

I looked down at little Emily standing there, staring up at me with innocent, still eyes.

"What?" I asked, my voice soft, tongue thick with sleep.

Nothing.

"What do you want?" I sat up in bed, shaking the sleep off.

Nothing.

"Why won't you leave me alone?" My voice was louder now, sharper, echoing off the mirror above my dresser.

Nothing.

"Goddammit, what do you want?!? I'm trying, dammit, can't you see that? I don't know where to go! I don't know what to do! If you want me to do something, just fucking tell me!" I threw off the covers, surprised to find myself fully dressed.

"Help me," she said, stretching out a hand to me.

I couldn't resist, I stepped forward and took her hand. The room spun around us, twirled into a vortex of streaks and dashes of light twisting, whirling and spinning us until it stopped so abruptly that I almost fell over.

We were back in the church, but this time I was wearing Darin Standish's body. I remembered the polo shirt, remembered thinking how much I hate polo shirts and most people that wear them. But here I was, kneeling beside Annie Standish at the communion rail, bowing my head, then lifting it and opening my mouth as the priest put the wafer on my tongue.

The wafer dissolved as the priest spoke over my head, but instead of the normal Latin or English blessing, the priest began to chant in Ancient Enochian, the language of the angels. I've heard it before, most recently from Glory, but something about this was different. There was a power to these verses that was like nothing I'd ever heard or felt. Each word battered my eardrums and made the room spin. It was like Enochian, but as spoken by God himself, and nothing my mortal mind was capable of processing.

*"OLSON FVORSGGO HOIAD BALTON SHCALZON
PHOSOBRA ZOLRORITAN AZPSAD GRAATAMAL
HOLQ NOTHO AZIMZOD COMMAHT ANOBLO ZIENSO
THILGNON GEALD IDSBOBOLEH GRAMCASARM"*

I clapped my hands over my ears and clenching my teeth to keep the screams in. My stomach did a couple of rolling flips while my eyes teared up from the sensory overload. As quickly as it began, it was over, and I looked back up at the face of the priest. Except there was no face, just a cowled form standing over me with a brilliant white glow from where his face should have been.

The cowled not-priest reached down for me and pulled me up by my shoulders until I was at eye level. The glow coming from within his/its cowl grew until I had to shut my eyes against the brightness, but still the light hammered my lids with a relentless pounding. The priest leaned in close and put his not-face next to my ear, then whispered to me in Enochian, only this time I could understand it perfectly.

"Prepare thyself and thy world for the coming of my children,
For they come to usher in a new dawn.
They shall bring the light to the darkness,
They shall bring the fire to the water,
They shall bring salvation to the defiled,
They shall bring law to the evildoer,
They shall bring order to the chaos.
Prepare thyself, for the door is opening,
And there shall be no return to that which was before."

The priest-thing released my shoulders and I dropped back to my knees at the communion rail. I lifted my head, and I was back in the Standish house, kneeling on the blood-soaked carpet in an empty room. I turned, and little Emily stood in the door staring at the bed where she died.

"I know, sweetie, it can't be easy coming back here. I'm trying to figure out what happened to you, so I can make it right."

She shook her head.

"What, you don't want me to figure it out?"

She shook her head again.

"You do want me to figure it out?

She nodded.

Realization hit me. "You don't want me to try to make it right."

She nodded. "You just want me to stop whatever's coming?"

Another nod.

"Is it going to be an earthquake?"

Nothing.

"A fire?"

Nothing.

"You don't know?"

Nod.

"If we don't know what it is, how am I supposed to stop it?" I asked, feeling my frustration grow.

Nothing. I was never good with kids. Dead or alive. "Is there something here?" I asked.

She nodded, so I turned my attention to the room. It looked just like it had when I was first there, peaceful except for the incredible amount of blood. There were still little evidence markers lying around the floor where my subconscious had logged every piece of evidence, but my dream-brain had cleaned them up.

But wait, if I was dreaming, then I could bring all that evidence back, *in situ* as it were. I closed my eyes and focused my mind on restoring the crime scene to *exactly* how it had been in real life.

There it was. Lying under the bed, mostly hidden by the puddle of gore and the frilly dust ruffle. I dropped to floor level, ignoring the blood soaking through my pants, and reached out for it. I pulled it back into the light, then sat back on my haunches to examine it. It was identical to the one I'd found on James Nettles' dresser, except this medallion was dedicated to Saint Christopher, patron saint of travelers. But everything else was the same — the same glass beads, identical crucifix, and the same nasty spells bound to it.

"This is what I was supposed find, isn't it?" I turned on one knee to look back at little Emily Standish, but my perspective did that *shift* thing again, and I wasn't looking at Emily from the foot of the bed, I was standing in the doorway of the bedroom, and her father was standing by her bed, a huge kitchen knife in hand.

"No!" I shouted, and charged the room, but ran into a wall of invisible force. Darin Standish looked up at me, and his eyes were bright with glee. He knew what was coming, and he knew exactly how much he was going to enjoy it. I pounded on the barrier, but couldn't break through. A tiny part of me still knew I was dreaming, but the rest of me didn't care as Standish pulled his daughter up into a sitting position in bed, then nestled in behind her like he was giving her a hug. His glittering eyes never left mine as he dragged the blade across her throat, cutting almost all the way to the spine. I drew back all my strength to attack the barrier, focused my will to level it with a spell centered on my fist—

And woke up on the floor of my bedroom, with my fist encased in Glory's right hand.

"Quincy, STOP!" the angel bellowed, and she put the power of The Word behind it. I froze, hand in mid-punch, and felt all the power, rage and terror drain out of me as my eyes caught sight of the crumpled Rebecca Flynn lying against the far wall, knocked out cold with a trickle of blood coming from one ear.

CHAPTER 11

"Becks!" I yelled, and ran across the room to her side. Well, in the movie in my mind, that's what happened. What really happened was, I yelled her name and tried to run to her side and I sprawled across the carpet in my bedroom because I was lying on the floor tangled in my sheet. Then I realized that I was butt-naked, again, so I pulled the sheet around my midsection and eventually made it to Flynn's side.

"Becks," I said, shaking her shoulder, trying to rouse her without doing any further damage. I turned back to Glory. "Is she all right?"

Glory closed her eyes for a second, then opened them again. "She's fine. Not even concussed, which is surprising given how hard you threw her against the wall."

I gaped at her. "Wait, what? I did this?"

"Do you see anyone else here, Q? I'm an angel, I don't kick human's asses unless they really deserve it. Like murderers, televangelists, or you, almost every day."

I shook Flynn's shoulder again, then sent a tendril of thought out to her. *Flynn, you in there?*

Fuck, my head hurts. What did you hit me with?

Yeah, sorry about that. I was having a nightmare.

I know.

"You know?" I was so surprised I spoke out loud.

"No screaming," Flynn groaned. Her eyes fluttered open, and she immediately raised a hand to cover them from the light.

"*Obscures*," I said, and gestured toward the ceiling light. It popped and the room fell into darkness. I heard broken glass tinkle against the inside of the light fixture.

"Oops," I said. "I'll get that later. Rebecca, are you okay?" I turned back to my partner/police liaison, who was trying to pull herself into more of a sitting position against the wall, with little effect.

"You wanna sit up?" I asked. She nodded and I got up on my knees. I leaned forward, put my hands under her armpits, and lifted her into a sitting position.

"Better?" I asked.

Flynn nodded, then giggled a little.

"What?" I asked.

She pointedly looked down, then raised her eyebrows. "We've got to stop meeting like this. People will talk," she said with a little laugh.

"Don't worry, the secret of your torrid affair is safe with me," Glory said. "But really, Q, put that thing away before you put someone's eye out."

"Leave me alone, angel. I've gotta piss. Something you wouldn't know anything about, existing on rainbows and good wishes like you do." I stood up, holding the sheet around my waist, and walked back to my dresser. I pulled out clean underwear and picked up the jeans I wore the day before off the floor.

"You okay for a second, Becks?" I asked.

"Yeah, do what you gotta do." She waved me off from the floor.

I nodded and walked into he bathroom, leaving the sheet at the door. I took care of business, then washed my hands and face. I stared into the mirror for a long moment, looking deep into my own eyes.

What the fuck are you doing, Harker? I asked myself. I worked hard to keep my thoughts on lockdown, what with my connection to Flynn being enhanced by proximity. *You know you can't touch her. She's human, and that never ends well for anyone. Luke would kill you just so you wouldn't go through it again. And God himself only knows what Glory would have to say about it.* I stood there a minute longer, until I felt like I had control of my emotions, then I pulled on my boxers and jeans and stepped out into my bedroom.

Glory and Flynn were sitting on the end of the bed, Glory holding a glass of water and patting Flynn on the back. I walked into the room and leaned against my dresser.

"Good morning, Detective Flynn, so nice of you to stop by," I said. "Again."

She looked up at me and gave me a little wave. "Hi."

"We've got to stop meeting like this," I said.

"No shit, Sherlock," Flynn replied.

"No, Rebecca, I'm serious," I said. "This is twice you've come into my apartment uninvited, and twice that it's almost gotten you killed. I don't know how you missed it, but I have the ability to toss around pretty heavy amounts of magic, and all my dreams are awful, especially lately, since this little brat won't stay out of my goddamn head!" I pointed to the corner of the room, where Emily Standish stood watching the proceedings in silence.

"Harker, I'm sorry." Flynn looked up at me and I could see her eyes were rimmed with red. "But I know exactly how bad your dreams are, because *they keep waking me up.* Every fucking night, I've got to meander through my own dreams, never knowing when I'm going to get plucked out of my subconscious and dropped into the middle of yours. And you're right—your head is a fucked up place that I would avoid walking through if I could. But I can't. I have no more control over this shit than

I do the weather. So you might as well give me a key because if I wake up one more time from that goddamn Standish house, I'm just coming straight over here and yanking you out of your dream. And start sleeping in boxers, for Christ's sake. I'm tired of looking at your johnson."

I stood there staring for a minute, then turned, pulled open the top drawer of my dresser, and grabbed a key ring. I tossed the ring to Flynn, who caught it on the fly, then just stared at it.

"What is this?"

"I'll never understand women," I said. "You asked for keys. Here's a set of keys. But pay attention to the key ring."

"What's the deal?" Flynn asked, holding up the key ring. It looked for all the world like just a ring with a pink stone hanging from a chain. Which technically, it was. It was also a little more.

"That's rose quartz," I said. "That particular crystal is tuned to my magic. When you go to unlock the door, touch the crystal to the knob first. It'll disarm any wards I might have in place, and give you a sense if I'm in the middle of a casting or a summoning. The crystal will take on different colors depending on what's going on in here. White, blue, green, pink, yellow, purple—those are all fine. You can come in and nothing will blow up. If the stone glows red, be very careful. There's something going on that could be dangerous. If the stone turns black, then you have a decision to make."

"What's that?" Flynn asked.

"Whether or not what's outside with you will kill you, or destroy a significant portion of the free world. Because whatever's going on behind the door certainly might," I said.

"This is not the kind of romantic passing over of the key that I've had with guys before," Flynn quipped.

"I'm still half-naked. If you'd feel more comfortable doing this after wild monkey sex, I'm sure I could oblige," I said, probably a lot less than half-joking.

Flynn blushed to the roots of her hair, and Glory covered her mouth to hide her laughter, albeit poorly. "I think I'll pass," Flynn said, then reached for the water Glory was holding and downed the rest of the glass.

"So now what?" Flynn asked after she had her more prurient instincts under control. Or maybe they were instincts toward uncontrolled laughter. I sometimes have a hard time with modern humans.

"Now I need Darin Standish's rosary. It was found under the foot of his bed." Flynn's eyes widened, then she nodded as she remembered the dream.

"I can get it. What do we need it for?"

"I want to confirm that it's the same magic that's on the one I took from the Nettles house."

"Sounds like a — wait, you took evidence from a crime scene?" Flynn's voice went up a full octave as she realized what I said.

"That's my cue," Glory said, then vanished.

"It's not like there will ever be a trial, Becks," I said. "Remember, the killer was also the last victim? And whatever we find out about who killed these people, we'll never go after it in a court of law. So yeah, I grabbed Jim Nettles' rosary. Now I need to compare it to Darin Standish's so I can confirm the two murders are connected. Then I need to go see a man about saving a soul."

"Whose soul are you saving, Q?

"My own, maybe," I said. "Now go get me the rosary while I take a shower and get cleaned up."

"You have no idea what time it is, do you?" Flynn asked.

"Remember, Becky-lass, we old farts need lot less sleep than you young whippersnappers."

"Well this young whippersnapper isn't going into the office at four in the morning just so you can hocus pocus over a dead man's rosary. It's going to have to wait until morning. I'm going home, and I'm going to get a few more hours sleep. Then I'll bring you the rosary."

"Wanna crash here?" I asked, pointing toward the bed. "I know, it looks like a bomb went off in here, but I changed the sheets like two days ago."

"All that talk, and now you're trying to get me into bed," Flynn said with a tease in her voice.

"Don't worry, Becks, your virtue will be intact. I'm not sleeping. I've got some translating to do from this dream. But if you want to grab couple hours without driving home—"

Flynn was already barefoot, having kicked off her shoes the second I made the suggestion. "Done, Q. And thanks," she said, pulling her sweater off over her head and moving her hands to the waistband of her pants.

"Now shoo," she made waving motions at me, so I grabbed a clean shirt, socks and boots, and went into the living room. I fired up the computer, started searching out Enochian texts, and tried very hard not to think about the gorgeous police detective lying in my bed not thirty feet away.

CHAPTER 12

I waited about forty-five minutes to make sure Flynn was completely out, then I put on my boots and grabbed my car keys off the table by the door. I closed the door silently behind me and pressed my thumb to the center of the knob, activating my "away" spells. Anything with even a touch of ill intent would get a nasty surprise if it tried to get through that door.

"Where do you think you're going?" the voice behind me asked.

I turned and saw Glory in my hallway, leaning against a wall.

"You should do your cone of silence thing," I said. "Unless, of course, you want all my neighbors to hear us fight."

"What are we going to fight about, Q?" Glory asked.

"About me going to wake up the priest at Our Lady and ask some difficult questions about his recently deceased parishioners," I replied.

"We're not going to fight about that," Glory said.

"Oh, why not?"

"Because you're not going," the angel said flatly.

"Remember that whole thing about going where angels fear to tread?" I asked. "Well, that's kind of my life's motto, Glory. Whenever there's something too dirty or scary or morally ambiguous for you and your lot to figure out, Harker takes care of it. Demon summoned to Earth got loose and now threatens all of creation? We can't touch it, because a human summoned it, and humans have free will. But Harker can take care of it. Lion of Judah smoked too much ganja and let it slip that he's the key to bringing about the Apocalypse? There's that pesky free will again, better call Harker.

"You see, Glory, I know exactly the limitations of what you and yours can do, because I've been the one pushing your boundaries for almost a century. And I know that you and your harp-playing bosses don't want me to talk to the priest at Our Lady, so that's exactly what I'm going to do.

"Because no matter how much your pals upstairs might want this all swept under some supernatural rug, I made a promise. I made a promise to a little girl who died wondering why her daddy hurt her. And I'm going to keep that promise, no matter what. So you can lead, follow, or get out of the way because I'm going to go see a man about a murder."

"You know I could stop you," Glory said, the sadness writ large on her face.

"I know you can try," I shot back.

"Q, please stop this before it goes too far."

"Too far? Eight people are *dead*, Glory. How much further do you want it to go? Do you want me to wait until whoever's sucking up the magical energy of human agony and death releases it into a giant earthquake or fire or whatever? You want me to wait until the body count gets high enough for you? No dice, Glory. I'm going to go talk to this priest. And I'm either going to get some answers, or I'm going to figure out the rest of the questions."

"And there's nothing I can do change your mind?" Glory asked.

"Outside of actually fight me, no," I said.

"Fine," she said, and stepped aside to leave me a clear path to the elevator. "Just be careful. I almost like you, Harker. I'd hate to have to watch you go to Hell." Nice, my guardian angel thinks I'm going to Hell if I die. That's reassuring.

Half an hour later, I pulled into the parking lot of Our Lady of Eternal Comfort Catholic Church. It was still pitch dark, so I was more than a little surprised when the first door I tugged on was open. I walked through the side door right into the sanctuary, just before the altar. There were a few lights on, but not many. A silence hung heavy over the church, almost anticipatory in nature, like something I felt in London right before a bombing run was coming during the blitz. The energy was anything but peaceful, and I rubbed my arms in a vain attempt to lay the hairs down.

I caught a flicker of movement out of the corner of my eye and turned to see a man's back duck into a small room at the back of the church. I saw a small green light come on over the door and realized the priest had entered the confessional. *Perfect.*

I made my way to the back of the room, stopping before the priest's compartment. I touched the wooden door, making contact with the door and frame at the same time. I gathered my will and whispered "*combino.*" The wood blended together along the crack, effectively sealing the door. I was pretty sure I could let him out when I was finished.

I opened the door and let myself into the other compartment of the confessional and sat down. I looked at the low, padded rail, then thought better of it. Kneeling has never been one of my things, and I didn't feel like I was starting today.

"Welcome, my son. What is troubling you tonight?" The priest's voice through the grille was soothing, warm and compassionate. It didn't sound anything like the bellowed Enochian from my dream, but who knew what evil lurks in the hearts of men, right?

"How did you know I came for confession?" I asked.

"It's 5AM, son. There are only three reasons someone comes

into a church before dawn. They're looking for a place to sleep, they're looking for something to steal, or they've got something to confess. You're too well-dressed to be homeless, so I'm choosing to err on the side of virtue over larceny."

I gave a little chuckle. "Well, you're right, padre. I'm not here to crash, and I'm not here to steal. I'm here looking for answers."

"Many come through our doors seeking answers. I have hope that I can provide you with what you seek."

Man, this guy was good. He had the whole sincerity thing down cold. "I hope so too, Father."

"What can I do for you, my son?" He asked.

I focused my attention on the face past the grate and said "I need to know what happened the Standish and Nettles families." The priest's head snapped up and I saw his eyes go wide through the mesh screen.

"I'm sorry?" he said, as though he were having trouble hearing me.

"I said, I need to know what happened to the Standishes and the Nettles. You remember them, right?" I growled through the screen. "Parishioners here, brutally murdered this week, father killed his wife and children then opened up every vein he could reach? Am I ringing any bells here?"

The priest turned and jiggled the handle a little, ready to leave. Unfortunately for him, there wasn't really a door anymore.

"Yeah, that's not gonna work," I said.

"What did you do?" he asked.

"I might have fused the wood together at the doorjamb. I'll let you out when I'm done with my questions. Now, what do you know about what killed these families?" I asked.

"Nothing," the priest replied. "I just heard about Annie and her family this morning, and then for the same thing to happen to Jim and Sandy...well, it's terrible. I can't understand why anyone would want to hurt them. They are both lovely families, well-liked within the church, and..." He looked up at me, and his eyes narrowed. "Are you with the media? I will not have these families turned into some kind of spectacle just for your ratings or sales numbers."

I liked this guy. If my dreams weren't pointing toward him as a mass murderer and perhaps the vessel for the destruction of my entire city, he seemed like somebody I could drink a beer with. But everything I'd seen showed him up to his eyeballs in this shitpile, so I had to stay on him.

"I'm not with the media. I'm with the police." Not exactly true, but I've been lying to priests since my first confession somewhere along about the time electric light bulbs were starting to catch on. I pressed my badge to screen, then took it down before he got a good look at it. *No need to waste time explaining exactly what the Department of Homeland Security's Paranormal Division was,* I thought. "I know you knew the families. I know they were members here. What else can you tell me about them?"

"Nothing," he said, and his voice shook with emotion. "They were all members, yes. The children were active in Sunday School and Vacation Bible School in the summer. Jim Nettles played on the church softball team. Annie Standish volunteered with our annual coat drive in the winter. Darin Standish, I didn't know him as well, but he came to services once or twice a month, and was always friendly. There's no reason for anyone to want to harm these people."

Except you, or whatever's living in your skin, I thought. "Padre," I said, letting a little menace creep into my eyes. "I know there's something going on with you and these families. The only point of convergence is right here at your pulpit. So think about it.

What is it that got these people killed? What happened here last Sunday?" I opened my Sight to watch his aura while he replied. It glowed with a steady yellow light, purity tinged with blue for a protector. This was a man who genuinely cared about his flock. So why did he cast a spell in an ancient magical language to make Darin Standish and Jim Nettles murder their families?

"Nothing happened, I swear it! Sunday was a perfectly normal Mass. The Nettles family were all at the morning Mass, and the Standishes attended the later service. Carey was very excited; he was going to see his first Panthers game with his father that afternoon. I told him I hoped he got a football." He did, too. The ball I found in his bed was an official NFL ball, one of the ones Cam Newton, the Panthers quarterback, gave to kids in the stands after he scored a touchdown.

I heard a choked sob from the screen. "Why would someone do this, Detective? Who *does* this to a family? To children?" The only change in his aura was a tinge of red with his anger. No black, no gray, no nasty greens and browns that indicated guilt, or possession, or lies. He was the real deal, a pastor genuinely upset at losing members of his flock.

"I don't know, Father," I said, reaching up and touching the screen where his hand was pressed. I felt nothing, not even a tingle of malicious magic. This man was as holy and God-touched as anything I'd ever encountered. It didn't make any sense.

"I don't know," I repeated, "but I'm damn sure going to find out." I opened the door and stepped out, touched the other door and released my spell, then scanned the sanctuary, reaching deep with my Sight to find something, anything that could point me in the direction of whatever was turning God-fearing, football-loving Catholics into some of the worst butchers of humanity I'd ever seen.

I walked the sanctuary for several minutes while the priest cried and prayed in the confessional. The whole time I paced the room, I scanned it for some demonic taint, some evidence of dark magic. There was nothing. Not even a mischievous pixie or a disgruntled brownie upset by the cleaning crew. It was the most blessed building I'd seen in years, and that made it all the more perplexing. Because something in this church was turning men's hands against their own families, and I couldn't for the life of me figure out what it was.

Then my phone rang, and I was forcibly reminded that it wasn't my life at risk.

CHAPTER 13

"This better be a real emergency," I said into the phone. "Like the Krispy Kreme on Sharon Amity is out of glazed doughnuts, or something equally important."

"Where are you?" Flynn's voice was heavy with sleep.

"I went to church," I replied.

"Did anything burst into flames?" Even sleepy, she was still a smartass.

"Both my ass and the building are still intact. As a matter of fact, as holy places go, it might be the most sanctified place I've ever set foot. I'm pretty certain that I'm the most unholy thing to set foot in the church in weeks."

"Well, something there has been doing a number on people, because we have another dead family, this one right off Wendover, not three miles from the church."

"Goddammit," I muttered. "I was literally *just* inside the place, for the last hour and change. There is no way anyone there did anything magical, black or otherwise, within the last month. It's cleaner than the friggin' Vatican," I said. Admittedly, there's a *lot* of magic thrown around the Vatican on any given Sunday, so maybe that wasn't the best analogy, but Flynn understood where I was coming from.

"I'm on my way to the new crime scene. I'll text you the address."

"I'll see you there," I said, then slid my finger across the screen, ending the call. The text from Flynn came in moments later. I dropped the address into my GPS app and found the house, less than five minutes away. I opened my car door and slid behind the wheel, preparing to go walk through my third incredibly violent crime scene in as many days.

After a few seconds, I put my head against the steering wheel and closed my eyes. Visions of the Standish and Nettles homes flashed before my eyes: pictures of abandoned kids' rooms, mothers with their throats cut so deeply they were almost decapitated, dead fathers sitting on their bedroom floors staring at the carnage they had wrought.

"Fuck that noise," I said to myself, and cranked the car. I pulled out into traffic away from the crime scene. It was time to start getting to the bottom of this shit, one way or another. And it looked like it was definitely going to be "another."

A quick Google search on my phone showed me that Danvar the Magnificent was playing at The Laugh Laboratory, a comedy club styled after a mad scientist's lab located in the NC Music Factory, a renovated mill turned into a set of nightclubs, restaurants, and party zones. I expected the place to be pretty much deserted at dawn, and I wasn't disappointed. The parking lot was empty except for a couple of pickup trucks with Super Clean Party Clean-Up logos on the side, and a green Mini Cooper with a scruffy looking dude asleep behind the wheel. I thought about rousing the sleeping beauty and sending him home, but if he was drunk enough that he shouldn't drive, but smart enough to actually *not* drive, I figured I was doing the world a favor by letting him sleep it off.

I looked around, saw no sign of the cleaning crew, and walked around to the back door of the Laugh Lab. It was locked, of course, but that didn't matter to me. I thought about picking the lock, just to make sure I still could, then decided that kneeling in front of a doorknob in broad daylight was exactly how I never wanted to start a conversation with a nervous cop or security doofus.

I pressed my hand to the deadbolt and whispered *"recludo."* I felt the tumblers click into place through my fingertips and turned the knob easily. The door whispered open, and I ducked through into the (hopefully) deserted club.

For once, things went my way and the club was empty. I navigated a maze of tables and chairs, meandering through to the dressing room off the side of the stage. Behind a thin black curtain was a short hallway with two doors on one side and one at the end. The first door had a simple piece of white tape on the door reading "Opener." The second door said "Employees Only," and the door at the end of the hall had an honest to God gold glittery star on the door above a small printed piece of paper that read DANVAR THE MAGNIF. I guess they ran out of room on the page to make truly magnificent.

I tried the dressing room door, but it was also locked. A quick spell, and I was inside. The dressing room was spacious, way more room than one assistant-raping magician needed. A makeup counter with lights surrounding the mirrors dominated one wall, covered in flowers in vases and bouquets just lying around. A long couch sat under a series of photos of famous comedians and magicians on the opposite wall, and a small fridge with a microwave on top sat next to the door. A small door marked "restroom" stood closed at the back of the room, but it was on the makeup counter where I found what I needed.

"Here we go," I said, opening the makeup kit. I pawed though the various concealers, blushes, and creams until I found what I was looking for—a small black plastic comb. I plucked a few hairs from the comb and sat down cross-legged in the floor.

From my pockets I pulled out a selection of spell components and set them on the floor in front of me. Four candles for the four points of the compass, check. Knife, check. Chalk, check. Matches, check. String, check. I drew a hasty circle around myself, then placed the candles at the cardinal compass points. I lit each candle in turn—North, East, South, West—for positive spell casting. If I were casting a spell intended to harm, I would have drawn the circle widdershins and invoked the candles backwards, but this was a simple finding spell, nothing dark about it, except my intentions for Danvar once I found him.

I plucked a few hairs from the comb and set them on the floor in front of me. I drew my knife and cut my thumb, squeezing a few drops of my blood onto the hairs, then placed the blade of the knife across the hairs. I focused my will on the blade, blood and hairs, muttered "*contineo*," and released my will onto the knife. It blazed with white light, then flickered to darkness. I picked the knife up and stood up, slowly turning inside my circle. As the point of the knife neared the northern compass point, it began to glow, brightening as it zeroed in on a direction. I continued to turn, slowly rotating past the direction the knife indicated I should go. As I got further away from pointing north, the glow faded more and more until it was dark. I turned in the other direction, reversing course, and as I neared north, the blade shone once again, confirming the spell worked.

I reached out with a foot and scrubbed out the edge of my circle, feeling an inrush of energy as the protections dissipated. I flicked my fingers, and the candles went out, snuffed by my will. North. Danvar was somewhere to the north of me. Didn't make sense, all the decent hotels were to the southeast, in downtown. Unless Danvar purposefully didn't stay in decent hotels.

Decent hotels mean decent security, and means that people

aren't used to hearing screams from the rooms next door. But north, north led to the University, which was also pretty clean-cut. Then it came to me—Sugar Creek. There were a lot of cheap hotels near the intersection of Sugar Creek Road and I-85, and a lot of them weren't the type of place to report the occasional loud noise in the middle of the night.

I left the Laugh Lab the way I came, equally unnoticed, and got back in my car. The guy sleeping in his Mini was gone, and I pulled out of the Music Factory without seeing another soul. I turned left onto Tyron, heading north to Sugar Creek with a dagger blazing merrily away on the passenger seat.

My gut was right. The dagger kept glowing like a firebrand as I turned left onto Sugar Creek, then cruised into the parking lot of the Imperial Extended Stay Motel right beside the interstate. The parking lot was mostly deserted, with the construction workers that took up most of the rooms in the hotel out on job sites. I pulled into a parking spot beside a banana yellow Cadillac with New Jersey vanity plates that read MAGICMN.

The dagger kept glowing as I pointed it toward the door, so I figured my intuition and magic had led me to the right place. I dispelled the location charm with a wave of my hand and a pinch of salt from a McDonald's bag crumpled up in the floorboards behind my passenger seat. The spell was effective, but there aren't very many times when you really want to be carrying around a knife that glows like a roman candle.

I stepped out of the car and leaned on the bumper of the Cadillac. A moment's concentration and I whispered *"aqua,"* sending my energy into the gas tank of the car. With no other magical changes to the car, it wasn't going to run very well with a tankful of clean water. Danvar's getaway handled, I stepped up to what I thought was his door and kicked it in.

Sometimes I forget my own strength and the shoddy nature of modern construction. The door didn't just open, it flew off the hinges and slammed into the TV sitting on the end of the dresser. The TV toppled forward and shattered on the floor, and I heard another thump and a muffled shriek as a body hit the floor.

I stepped through the door and looked around. Danvar the Magnificent was lying on his back on the floor between the bed and the wall. In front of him was the ubiquitous cheap hotel round table covered with playing cards, an empty Wild Turkey bottle, a single overturned yellow plastic cup, and a huge glass bong with a naked mermaid on the front with the carburetor protruding from her legs.

Danvar was a remarkable sight, the finest example of not wanting to see behind the curtain that I'd ever encountered without demonic involvement. He lay flat on his back, turtled in a cheap hotel chair that had apparently gone over with him in it when I kicked the door in. His skinny legs stuck out of his white striped boxers, and his arms flailed the air unconstrained by anything more than a yellowed wife beater. He looks to be at least seventy, gaunt to the point of being skeletal, with a lush white goatee his only visible hair anywhere.

"What the fuck?" Danvar bellowed from the floor.

A skinny woman in nothing but black lace panties stood up from the floor on the far side of the room. I quickly surmised that she was the cause of the thump and squeal I heard when I "opened" the door. She looked to be about twenty-five, with brown hair and a birthmark just to the left of her bellybutton. I figured she was the new "assistant."

"You want to leave," I said to her.

"I can't leave my master," she replied, casting a loving glance in Danvar's direction.

"Can you at least go lock yourself in the bathroom until the crashing and cursing stops?" I asked. She nodded and did just that.

"Who the fuck do you think you are, shitbait?" Danvar asked me, coming to his feet and getting untangled from the chair and table.

"You're Danvar the Magnificent, right?" I asked, focusing my will around my right hand.

"Yeah, I'm Danvar. And I believe I asked you who the fuck you are."

"I'm Quincy Harker, motherfucker, and this is my town. Maybe you've heard of me?"

"Nope," he said, diving onto the bed, his hand darting under the pillows and coming out with a small black revolver.

He squeezed the trigger, but I was ready. I held up my hand and shouted, "*Perfringo!*" The magic enveloped the handgun, and it blew up. That did a number of bad things to Danvar, including blowing his fingers off. One whizzed by my ear, splattering bloody mist all over the right side of my face. One blew backward and smacked Danvar in the forehead, and I think the rest were reduced to tiny pieces by the explosion.

Danvar collapsed onto the bed, howling and clutching his wrist. He held up the damaged stump and shrieked at me. "What the fuck? What the fucking fuck?"

While I admired his devotion to the f-word, I quickly grew tired of hearing him scream, so I stepped forward and punched him in the jaw, really hard. His eyes rolled back in his head and he flopped back onto the bed, out cold. I looked around the room, and it was pretty well destroyed. The door was bent at almost forty-five degrees and was laying in the closet. The table and chairs were overturned, and they were the least damaged things in the room. The TV was crushed into the carpet, and the room's occupant was bleeding all over the comforter. All in all, a good start to my visit.

CHAPTER 14

Danvar the Magnificent woke up in his boxers and wife beater, tied to a chair in a cheap motel with his own belt and neckties, with a towel duct-taped to this wrist to staunch the bleeding from his missing right hand. It was not his best morning ever. Then there was the matter of the wizard sitting on one of the beds in his motel room juggling balls of fire.

Danvar's eyelids fluttered open, and he shook his head to clear it. He let out a groan, then tried to move his right hand. His eyes flashed wide open then, and his mouth opened to let out a scream.

"Don't do it," I said, flicking a fireball at his face. It stopped three inches from his nose and exploded, showering the scrawny magician with little licks of flame. He let out a little shriek and tried to move away, but his ankles and wrist were secured, so he was going a whole lot of nowhere, and fast.

He looked over at his latest victim, who sat on the bed filing her nails and watching the whole proceeding with the kind of detached disinterest that is only found in the deeply unconcerned or the tragically damaged. I'd looked in her eyes, and she definitely fell into the second category.

"Amelia, untie me," Danvar demanded.

I laughed, and the little bastard's attention locked back onto me. "What's funny, you little illusionist? She is my assistant, and she will never sit by and let you torment me so."

"First off, jackass, I'm about as real as it gets, so don't even think that any of this is illusion. Secondly, her name is Amanda, you rotted prick. And third, she's totally saved you already. Who do you think cauterized your stump so you wouldn't bleed to death?" Danvar's eyes went back to his right arm, so I flicked out my fingers and severed the rope holding that hand down.

He held up his handless arm and gaped at me. "What kind of monster are you?" he asked.

"I don't really know. I might even be human. But here's what I do know. You're a magic-wielding assclown who kidnaps women and brainwashes them into being your sex slaves and assistants, then when you get tired of them, you wipe their brains and dump them wherever it's convenient. Somewhere along the way you pissed off a demon named Mort, who hired me to kill you in exchange for information I need."

Most of the time when someone's lost a lot of blood, like a hand, they get a little pale. The level of pale Danvar hit when I mentioned Mort was far beyond blood loss. I'd blown off his hand, tied him to a chair, and as much as told him I was going to torture and kill him. But one mention of the little demon club owner, and the Magnificent One was shitting in his boxers.

"I don't know what you're talking about," Danvar stammered.

"Don't bother lying to me, Danvar. What's your real name, by the way? I feel stupid calling you by your lame-ass stage name."

"Rupert," Amanda said from the bed. "I looked in his wallet once while he was sleeping. He never told me, just made me call him Master, or Magnificent, or SuperCock." Every word out of her mouth was just tossed out there with no inflection, like she was reading from a teleprompter, or like the computer voice in a cell phone.

"SuperCock?" I looked at Danvar. "Everything I learn about you makes me hate you a little more. Look, I'm not an assassin. I've killed plenty of people in my time, but I don't make a habit of doing favors for demons, and I usually only kill people who are actively trying to kill me. So let's make a deal—you tell me everything you know about what's happening at Our Lady of Comfort Catholic Church, and I won't kill you."

"You'll let me go?" SuperCock asked, and by the light in his eyes, I knew he didn't understand exactly what that would entail.

"Oh sure," I said. "I'll let you go. I'll cut off all access to magic, and I'll probably make you impotent just out of some twisted sense of justice, but I'll let you go."

"Fuck yourself," he grumbled.

"Biologically impossible," I replied. "I'm gifted, but not in that level of either endowment or flexibility. So do want to tell me about the church, or do you want me to just shoot you?" I drew my Glock and leveled it at his forehead.

"Wait! Stop! Don't shoot! There are people who will miss me. Powerful people." His eyes narrowed. "I can put you in touch with them. Maybe they know something about your church."

I looked at him. Really looked him over. He was giving off all the normal signs of being terrified, but none of the standard tells people give off when they lie. "How do I get in touch with these people?"

"In my phone," Rupert said. I grabbed the phone and opened up the contacts browser.

"You really should lock your phone. I mean, anybody can access your personal information this way," I said. "Who am I looking for?"

"I don't know his real name, but he's in there under Smith. That's the name he goes by here."

My stomach sinking, I scrolled through the numbers until I got to the name Smith. Sure enough, the number was familiar. *Fuck.* I pressed SEND and then switched the phone to speaker.

Smith's gruff voice filled the room after the first ring. "What do you want, Rupert? I told you that we'd contact you when we needed you to move again. For now, just work on getting back in Mort's good graces and stay the fuck out of sight. The guy that's looking for you is the real deal, and he will kill your worthless ass if he catches up to you. I'm trying to talk him down, but he's a stubborn fuck. So what do you want?"

"Hi Smitty, stubborn fuck here," I said.

"Goddammit, Harker," Smith said. "Do not do anything stupid. I need that fucker to get close to—"

"I don't care, Smitty. He doesn't know shit that can help me, you don't know shit that can help me, my fucking *angel* can't tell me anything that will help me, so the only thing I can do is go to Mort, tell him I killed this sorry motherfucker, and see what he knows."

"Harker, I am *ordering* you—"

"The fuck you are," I said. "The list of people I've taken orders from in this lifetime is pretty short, and your name is nowhere on it. But don't worry, I'm not going to kill your precious rapist informant, Smitty. I'm gonna take the pieces of his hand I blew off back to Mort and hope he buys that as proof that I killed SuperCock here."

"SuperCock?" Smith said, and I shook my head.

"Long story involving his latest victim, who's at this location and is going to need a lot of fucking therapy before she can— Goddammit! Fuck!" I swore loudly at the gout of blood that squirted across the phone's screen. I looked up and Amanda was kneeling on the bed, right behind Danvar, with her nail file buried to the hilt in his eyeball.

"Never mind, Smitty," I said. "You traced this call, right?"

"Yeah, I'm about three minutes away. I've got a breach team

and an ambulance with me."

"You'd better call a meat wagon, too. Our victim just opened Danvar's carotid artery with a nail file, then stabbed him in the dick a couple times before burying her cosmetic implement in the magician's eyeball."

"Fuck," Smith's voice was a little awed.

"Yeah," I said. "Impressed me, too. But look on the bright side, I don't have to lie to Mort about Danvar being dead." I turned my attention back to Amanda. "No, sweetie, you probably should just leave the nail file in his eye now."

She looked back at me, confusion all over her face. "But I broke a nail when I stabbed him. How am I supposed to take care of that?"

I turned back to the phone. "Drive faster, Smitty."

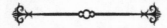

Two minutes later the parking lot was full of black SUVs and flashing lights. Smith stormed into the room, his flat-top quivering with rage.

I stood up as he walked in. "Smitty, I'm sorry," I said. "I really had decided not to kill him, but I guess hearing that set Amanda off, and she—"

Smith nailed me right under my jaw on the left side of my face with a right cross that landed hard enough to slam my mouth shut and drop me straight backward on my ass. I sat there for a second looking up at my assailant, who was also kinda my boss, then I got to my feet.

Smith stood there breathing hard, his nostrils flared and his heart beating fast enough for me to hear it without enhanced senses. He didn't speak, just clenched his jaw and fists and squared up for a fight. I took a deep breath and looked down into his face. I could almost see the lightning in his storm-gray eyes.

"That's your one," I said. "I figure every friendship, or business relationship, or partnership, or whatever we are, gets one shot at the other. One punch, with good reason, and you've got one get out of an ass-kicking free card. You just used yours. I deserved that for fucking up your operation."

I stepped forward, until we were almost touching. I felt more than saw the agents behind Smith move their weapons to the ready position, or thumb the safeties off, or if they were really smart, twitch a little closer to the door in case they had to run.

When I spoke, my voice was low, and had all the sincerity of my century on Earth behind it. "But let me be very fucking clear. If you ever lay hands on me in anger again, we will throw down. And I will not hold back. And only one of us will walk away from that fight."

Smith looked up at me, his five-ten and stocky frame bulked up to my six-four lean form. Our eyes locked, and before either of us spoke again, volumes were said and received.

"That day's coming, Harker. But you're right. Today ain't that day. Now get the fuck out of my crime scene before I change my mind."

Of course I didn't move. I'm not smart enough to walk away from trouble, or an armed government special ops team with a leader that wants to beat my head in. Instead, I pointed to Amanda. "She needs help. Serious help. The kind that takes years, costs serious money, and keeps people in rooms with soft walls until it works. You gonna make sure she gets that?"

"She'll be well taken care of, Mr. Harker. That's why Agent Smith brought me into this case." I looked past Smith and saw a heavyset woman in a business suit standing in the doorway. She carried a briefcase instead of a gun and wore pumps instead of combat boots, but this woman exuded the same type of confidence that the special operators around her did. She was either one of the best in the world, or thought she was.

"And you are?" I asked.

"Dr. McColl," she replied, stepping forward and holding out her hand.

"Don't look like any Irishwomen I've ever known," I said, shaking her hand.

A grin split her face, and a broad white smile stood out in stark contrast to her ebony skin. She laughed, and said, "I married an Irishman. Sergeant Sean McColl, 82nd Airborne. We met in Iraq."

"He on the team, too?" I asked, only to see her face fall.

"He didn't make it home from Iraq."

"Sorry to hear that," I said. I sensed something more to her story and remembered something I'd heard about from Luke a few years back. "Djinn?" I asked.

"Yeah," she replied. "His unit stumbled upon a Djinn ruling a small village like a king. Sean objected, and the Djinn wiped them out. The Army called it a 'training accident.' Even crashed a pair of helicopters to cover it up."

"But you didn't buy it, poked around into too many rabbit holes, and ended in the Freak Squad," I finished her story.

"Pretty much covers it," she agreed.

"Doctor McColl helps civilians and our personnel alike deal with the aftereffects of encountering the supernatural for the first time," Smith said.

I chuckled a little.

"Something funny about that?" McColl asked. I could tell she was sensitive about her work.

"No, not at all," I said. Might have been useful for me, if my first encounter with the supernatural hadn't been *in utero*. "I guess when you've walked the walk as long as I have, the supernatural isn't so super anymore. Anyway, I'll leave you to the cleanup. I've got a crime scene to walk, a demon to interrogate, and a ghost to lay to rest. Good to meet you, Doctor. And Smith, we'll finish this later."

"Count on it, Harker."

CHAPTER 15

I was in a foul mood when I walked into Mort's, which is exactly the wrong mindset to be in when you walk into a room where most of the inhabitants want to eat you, kill you, maim you, or some combination of three. The second I stepped through the door, the room fell silent, except for a pair of twenty-something weres, maybe foxes, making out in a back corner. The anger was rolling off me in waves, and I'm sure every sensitive being in the room felt it. I stepped up to the bar as a couple of humans scurried for the door, their eyes never leaving me.

Christy came over to me, a Stella in hand. "Here, take the edge off," she said, sliding the bottle to me.

"Why, whatever do you mean?" I asked.

"Harker, I like you, for no good reason, I might add. But understand that my rules apply to you, too, and if you break Sanctuary out here, your safe passage will be revoked, you will be banned, and you will be removed from my bar. With extreme prejudice. Everyone in here will get a shot at you, and I don't care how good you are, I don't think you're walking out of that. So please, before you start something, understand that I *will* finish it, no matter how unpleasant that becomes."

I thought about it for a minute, then decided that if two people usually on my side think I'm far enough gone that they have to threaten me with epic ass-kickings unless I get my shit together, then maybe the problem isn't with the rest of the world, maybe it's with me. I sat down on a stool, drank my beer, and brought my emotions under control.

"Sorry, Christy. This case is a motherfucker, you know?"

She leaned on the bar. This had the dual effect of bringing her close enough to talk without the whole bar overhearing and pushing up into my eyesight some of the most expansive and impressive cleavage this side of the Mississippi. "They're all motherfuckers, Harker. That's why motherfuckers like you have to deal with them. If this shit were easy, the mundanes could handle their own problems. But it's not, and they can't. So come on, Ethel. Put on your big girl panties and do the job."

I gave her a little half-smile and said, "Is that supposed to be motivational? Because if so, I think that job at Hallmark is out of the question."

"Nah, the look down my shirt was motivational. The talking was just cover." She reached under the bar and buzzed open the door into the back room. "Go on back. And remember, there's no Sanctuary back there, that's only for the public part of the bar. So be careful."

I drained the last of my beer and set it on the bar. "Thanks, Christy," I said.

"You're welcome, Quincy. Good luck."

I'll need it, I thought as I walked back into Mort's lair. My mind as racing as I stepped into the room that not twenty-four hours before had looked like nothing so much as a theatre, but now was a nicely-appointed office, with a full wet bar, dark hardwood floors, a pair of leather couches in a seating area, an oak desk the size of a small car, and floor-to-ceiling bookshelves, all filled with leather-bound volumes with gold lettering on the spine.

Mort sat on one of the couches, a can of Coke in his hand. A pair of minotaurs stood behind him. I couldn't tell if they were the same minotaurs from earlier or not, but they didn't have any obvios perforations, so I assumed not. I'll admit to being a touch speciesist, but I've never cared enough to learn to recognize individual minotaurs.

"Harker," Mort nodded, and raised his Coke can to me.

"You know that's creepy as fuck, right?" I said, sitting down. I turned to the nearest minotaur. "Get me a Coke, would ya?" He glared at me, then looked over at Mort.

"It's fine, David. Just get one from my mini-fridge." The minotaur turned and walked over to a section of wood paneling that wasn't covered in bookshelves. He pressed a piece of moulding, and the panel slid out of the way to reveal a small refrigerator. He opened the fridge, grabbed a Coke, and closed everything back up. He brought me the soda and handed it to me without comment.

"Thanks," I said. The minotaur grunted.

"Now that you've peed on the hydrant by being an ass to my security, can we get on to business?" Mort asked.

"Sure," I said. "Danvar's dead." I didn't elaborate because I wanted to get my information and get out. "Now what's going on at the church?"

"Hold on, Harker," Mort held up a hand. "Our deal was that you kill Danvar. Did that happen?"

I didn't say anything.

"Did you kill Danvar, Harker?" Mort's voice got low. "And know that I can tell if you're lying." Of course he could.

"No, I didn't kill him. But he is dead."

"What happened, Harker? How did he get all dead if you weren't the one one doing the killing?"

"His latest assistant," I said. "She opened his carotid with a fingernail file then jabbed it through his eyeball into his brain. All I did was blow his hand off. And beat him up a little. She did the rest. Sorry," I said. I was about as unsorry as I could possibly be, but maybe with enough contrition, I could get Mort to tell me what was going on at the church anyway.

No such luck. "Oh, that's too bad, then, Mr. Harker. Our agreement was very clear — you kill Danvar, you get information. You didn't hold up your end of the deal, so I am understandably disappointed, and unfortunately for you, under no obligation to tell you anything about the happenings at Our Lady of the Holy Comfort."

"You're not," I agreed. "But I was hoping that since you got the end result you desired…"

"Oh, but I didn't," Mort protested. "I didn't care a whit about Danvar living or dying. I had a rather sizable wager on whether or not you would murder a man in cold blood. I counted on your single-mindedness and general misanthropy to carry the day, but apparently I was mistaken."

Great. I was the subject of a supernatural bet. And I was the cause of Mort *losing* said bet. Pretty much guaranteed I wasn't getting the information I needed easily.

"All right, Mort, what's it going to take?" I asked, sipping my Coke in what I hoped looked like an "I don't give a shit what the answer is" pose.

"What is *what* going to take, Mr. Harker?" Mort grinned at me.

"What's it going to take for you to tell me what you know about what's going on at the church?" I asked, wondering what my chances were against two minotaurs and a demon. I figured I was 50/50 against either one, but both was going to stretch the limits of my creativity.

"Oh, that?" Mort asked. "That one's so easy I'll do it for free. Nothing." Mort finished his soda and tossed the empty can back over his shoulder. The minotaur, obviously used to such behavior, caught the can on the fly. Mort just sat there, grinning at me like the cat that ate the canary.

"What do you mean, nothing?" I asked.

"I mean nothing, Quincy. I know absolutely nothing about that church. I've never been nearer to it that passing by on the road, and no one has mentioned anything about it in the bar. Not just recently, but ever. That's what I know, Harker—not a goddamn thing." He leaned back in the couch and crossed one leg over the other and put his hands behind his head. He was grinning to beat the band, and it all started to sink in.

"You played me," I said. After all these years, all the warnings to other people about dealing with demons, and I make a rookie mistake like that. I felt my face flush as it all sank in.

"About time you figured that out," Mort replied.

"You fucking played me, Mort."

"You are absolutely correct, Q."

"You just wanted to use me to kill Danvar, didn't you?"

"Finally! He gets it!" Mort threw his arms wide, as if to give the world a big hug. "I'm so proud of you, pumpkin!" He stood and walked over to me. "Come on, Q. Let's hug it out."

That was it. My vision went red, and every bit of restraint I had went out the window. I threw a straight right that flattened Mort's nose and knocked the demon six feet backward to land on the couch again. He shook his head, ran a hand over his bloody nose, and glared up at me.

"That was a mistake, Harker. Your last one. I never promised you information about the church. I just told you I'd tell you everything I know. Well, I held up my end of the bargain. If you don't like the outcome, well, that's what you get when you make a deal with the devil. But to lay hands on me? In my house? I don't give a good goddamn who your uncle is. That. Doesn't.

Happen."

Mort was on his feet, and I watched with my mouth open as his form shifted, stretched, and grew from a harmless-looking little boy to an almost seven foot tall behemoth with muscles on top of muscles and a bloodthirsty grin stretching from ear to ear.

"You like this version? It's Bobby 2.0, the upgraded version. This is what Bobby could grow into with proper diet, exercise, a steady diet of protein and anabolic steroids, and a decade or two of mixed martial arts training. Or he could just let a demon live inside him and he gets to look like this whenever I need him to beat up an annoying business associate. Like right now. Hold him, boys."

The minotaurs charged me, but I wasn't going to make it that easy on them. I ducked under the grasp of the one on my right and stepped inside his reach. I kicked his knee sideways, and the big man-bull dropped to the floor. I grabbed him by the horns and steered him around between me and his buddy, then planted a foot in the middle of his back and gave him a shove.

In the move in my mind, this resulted in the minotaurs going to the ground in a tangled ton of bullman-flesh, leaving Mort for me to deal with one-on-one. In reality, the second minotaur vaulted the first one like an Olympic hurdler and charged me, horns-first.

I sprang straight up, grabbed a ceiling joist, and swung out into the seating area, landing on Mort's coffee table. This put me within striking distance of Super-Mort, and he caught me in the ribs with a sweeping sideways blow that took me off the table and flipped me backwards over one of the leather couches onto the expensive-looking rug. I took a minute to make sure I bled on the rug, then came to my feet, flipping the couch at Mort as I did so. He caught it without even a grunt, and it was a seriously heavy wood-and-leather sofa.

Mort swung the sofa around like a baseball bat, and I dropped to my stomach. He quickly reversed grip and swung the huge piece of furniture down at me. I rolled onto my back and got my hands up in time to keep from getting crushed, but still was faced with a giant pissed-off demon swinging hundreds of pounds of decor at my head.

I gripped the sofa with both hands, focused my will and shouted "*Infiernus!*" The wood frame and leather burst into flames, and I let go of the couch and rolled to my right. I came up on one knee in front of a minotaur, and I pulled my Glock as I came to my feet. I pressed the pistol to the underside of the monster's jaw and squeezed the trigger four times. The pistol spat 9mm slugs into the bellman's jaw, and they rattled around in his brainpan, generally making a mess of things. I stepped back to let the dead minotaur drop to the ground and turned to Mort.

The 'roided out demon-child was holding the flaming sofa, looking at it like it was a new toy. That's when I realized the error of my ways. If you're going to use something as a weapon against a denizen of Hell, fire probably isn't the best choice. Mort was born in fire, so setting stuff on fire around him just made him comfy.

It didn't do much for me, though, so when Mort chucked the couch at my head, I dropped my gun, rolled forward under it, spun around, and shouted "*Aquas!*" at the flying sofa. A stream of water sped from my hands like a fire hose and soaked the couch, putting out the fire and filling the room with noxious smoke. With a moment's concealment, I drew a knife from my boot and opened my Sight to find the other minotaur. He stood out against the smoke, limping around trying to find me to rip me limb from limb. He wasn't moving very quickly. I'd obviously done some damage with my kick, so I circled around him and sliced through his hamstring.

He dropped to one knee and I stepped up behind him, pressing my knife to his ear. "You can live or you can die tonight, Bessie. You want to live?"

He nodded.

"Then you drag your busted-up leg the hell out of this room and you never raise a finger to me again, you understand?"

"Mort will kill me," the minotaur whispered.

"Only if he makes it out of here, which I do not intend to let happen. So who are you more afraid of, the guy with the knife in your ear, or the guy that might kill you someday."

"Y-you," the big monster stammered, and started limping towards the door. That left me Mort, who was throwing more furniture around trying to find me in the smoke. The air cleared a bit, and Mort found me sitting atop his desk, legs crossed, wearing my best unconcerned with the world look.

"There you are, Harker. Time to die!" He charged me, and I sat there cross-legged as he ran right through me.

I dispelled my illusion and gave Mort a little whistle. He turned and charged me again. This time I went to the rafters again, using the bar joists in the room as my own personal jungle gym. Mort followed me swing for swing, until I got to the wall and jumped off, jumping ahead to the wall and bouncing off. Mort tried, but he was a little heavier than me, so he ended up with both feet buried in the drywall. His upper body flipped backward, and Mort was hanging upside down by his feet. Still buried to the knees in the drywall and concrete.

That was the opening I'd been looking for. I grabbed a hunk of sidewalk chalk and sketched a hasty circle on the wall, trapping Mort within. I called up my will, focused it on Mort, and said,

"*Vade in domum tuam.*"

Mort looked at me and said, "Go home? That's the best banishment you could come up with?"

"Fuck off, Mort. I'm tired," I said, then grinned as the circle began to glow with an infernal red light. "Besides, it worked, you sonofabitch."

The circle glowed faintly, with a bright blue-white light, then it shifted to a blinding yellow flash, then the circle was empty, and all that was left of our encounter was a smoldering sofa, a thousand pounds of dead minotaur and a circle burned into the wall with a pair of footholes in it. I looked around the destroyed office, then walked back out into the main bar.

Every eye in the place turned to me as I stepped out of the private office. "So, Mort's dead," I announced. "And I'm in a shit mood. If anybody's feeling suicidal, this is the time to step up. Otherwise, I'll be leaving."

I stopped at the end of the bar where Christy stood, bar rag in hand, polishing the same square foot of bar she'd been polishing when I walked out.

"Is he really dead?" Christy asked.

"No," I said. "You can't kill a demon on this plane. But he is banished, so he'll either have to be summoned back here, or find a hole to crawl out of on his own. There aren't very many of those left, I've seen to that over the years."

"Then I'd better get the summoning circle ready," she said.

"Wait, what?" I stammered. "You're going to call him back? Why? You have a chance to run this place on your own, or at the very least get out of here and live free of Mort."

She gave me a sad little smile, like I was the slow child in first grade who couldn't understand why Dick ran after Jane. "Q, it doesn't work that way. This bar isn't on Earth. We're in a pocket dimension just outside of Hell's sixth circle. Mort is a mid-level seventh-circle demon, which makes him stronger than all but the very toughest sixth-circle demons. He was the one enforcing the Sanctuary here, not me. All my power comes through me, from Mort."

"Why? Why in all the hells would a demon run a bar for Earthbound monsters?"

"It's different. Nobody else was doing it, and it was a diversion. Torturing souls gets boring after a millennium or two, so he wanted something to change it up. And by moving in on the sixth circle, he insured—"

"That no one would challenge him because anyone strong enough to take this place from him would be too busy trying to move up in Hell's hierarchy to care about this little dive bar," I interrupted.

"So Mort got to play in the mortal world a little, got to wreak havoc on Earth and the sixth circle, and stayed pretty invisible to his seventh circle kin," Christy finished.

"That's a lot smarter than I gave him credit for."

"Not smart enough to leave you alone, no matter how often I warned him," Christy said.

"You warned him about me? Why?" I was thoroughly confused.

"You're one of a kind, Harker. There's never been another being like you in the history of the universe. Part human, part vampire, with a moral compass that changes directions like humans change socks and enough magical knowledge and power to be truly dangerous. You're a singularity, and those are either extremely valuable or extremely powerful. But they are always extremely dangerous. That's you, Q, in a nutshell."

I thought about it for a second, then opened my mouth to

speak. But nothing came out. A singularity? That was gonna take a while to wrap my head around. I closed my mouth and nodded.

"I'm gonna go summon my boss back from Hell. You should probably be gone when I'm finished."

I nodded again and headed to the door. I never looked back, because you never know what might be behind you, but nothing jumped me before I opened the door and walked back out into the deserted parking lot. I call that a win.

CHAPTER 16

"How bad is this one?" I asked Officer Aguirre when I stepped up to the door.

"Those boots might survive," he said, looking down at my Doc Martens. "Detective Flynn is upstairs. She's been waiting for you a while."

"Yeah, I had some stuff to do," I said.

"Whatever it was, I hope it included getting your affairs in order, because she is *pissed.*"

I chuckled and said, "Aguirre, a woman may some day be the death of me, and it might be Detective Flynn, but it won't be today. I'm good to go in?"

"Yeah, go ahead."

I'm here, I sent to Flynn.

About damn time, she replied. Aguirre was right, she was pretty grumpy.

Anything new?

No, same shit, different beautiful dead babies. Get back here and do your mojo thing so you can tell me you don't know shit.

I bit off a smartass reply, put my head down, and headed up the stairs. No matter how much fun winding Flynn up is on a normal day, this wasn't it. There were dead children upstairs, again, and I didn't know what was killing them. And if I didn't figure it out by tonight, we'd wake up to four more bodies tomorrow morning, and the morning after, until either our killer changed his plans, or Our Lady of Holy Comfort ran out of four-person families.

That wasn't a comforting thought.

The Lemore house was a little different from the other two crime scenes. It was a sprawling Dilworth ranch, with all the bedrooms arranged on the left side of the house, with an entryway into a formal living room front and center. The garage, mud room, and kitchen were at the end of the house on the right, and that looked like how most people entered and left the house. Dinner dishes were loaded into the dishwasher, but it had never been run. Maybe the mother was waiting for a full load and died with a dishwasher half-full of unwashed dishes. That struck me as sad, somehow, that those dishes would never get clean.

Through the kitchen was a smallish dining room with a bedroom off it that was converted into an office. Then we had the den, or great room, or whatever the real estate agents call them nowadays. It sat right behind the formal living room and was dominated by a fireplace with a huge TV hanging above it. A couple of discarded game controllers lay on the floor in front of the fireplace, and I could just hear the dad's voice telling the kids that he wasn't buying another one when theirs got broke because someone stepped on it. The whole place was just like the other two—a Donna Reed slice of heaven dropped into the middle of the twenty-first century.

I turned left and made my way down the hall past the guest bathroom to the bedrooms. The door to the master bedroom was open, but I wasn't ready for that yet. I knew what was waiting for me in there: a pile of cops and crime scene techs all trying to be professional while holding back tears and nausea, dead children looking like little sleeping angels, a mother who died knowing she couldn't save her babies, and a father who somewhere in his consciousness must have been raging against whatever force made him destroy everything he'd ever built, and no clues. Never any clues, no hint who was behind this unnecessary, spiteful suffering, no arrow pointing the way for me to direct my rage. Just more goddamn questions.

I opened the door on the right instead and stepped into the little girl's room. Her name was Jeannie, judging by the sparkly blue letters on the door, and she loved *Frozen* and all things having to do with that movie. I stepped into a suburban winter wonderland, with walls painted pale blue and covered in snowflakes, to a white plush rug and ceiling painted with white and glitter to look like stars sparkling through a snowfall. Emily Standish sat on the bed, looking up at me with her big, sad eyes, holding the hand of a gorgeous little girl I assumed was Jeannie Lemore. Jeannie wore a *Frozen* nightshirt that hung almost to her feet. She was around ten, forever trapped on the verge of transitioning from a little girl to a teen heartbreaker. Her black hair was done up in cornrows adorned with pink, white, and blue beads that I could almost hear click against each other as she played.

"Hello, Emily," I said. "You must be Jeannie," I said to the other little girl. She nodded.

"Can you tell me what happened?" I asked, kneeling down to be on eye level with the girls. Jeannie's brown eyes were big and round, almost too big for her face, the kind of eyes you knew would show all the secrets of her soul when she got older. Except for the obvious, of course.

She shook her head. I looked to Emily, who just looked back at me. Emily raised a hand, held it out to me, and I touched fingers with her. Nothing happened, and I looked back at Emily, who just sat on the bed, ethereal and inscrutable.

"What is it, honey? I can't touch you here. I can barely even see you..." I closed my eyes at my own stupidity.

I opened my Sight and reached out to Jeannie, pressing my fingers to the sides of her head. In the physical world, my hands passed through the space where Jeannie sat and my fingertips touched, but in the world outside, my fingers pressed to the girl's temple, and her eyes flickered up to lock onto mine.

I felt myself falling backward and almost broke contact with Jeannie's head to catch myself, but remembered what I was doing and let myself fall into the contact. I tumbled head over heels, closing my eyes to keep from losing my breakfast, which shouldn't have been much of a concern since I hadn't eaten in a day and a half.

When I stopped moving, I opened my eyes and saw that I was back at the communion rail in Our Lady, kneeling between a lovely woman in a pretty green dress and a little boy in a short-sleeved dress shirt and khakis. The part of me that was Jeannie Lemore instantly labeled these two "Mommy" and "Dwan." I didn't even know they made khakis for eight-year-olds, but I'm not exactly part of the khaki-wearing set. I watched as the priest stopped at the family next to us, said a few words, placed the communion wafer on the man's tongue, and moved on to the man with us, who Jeannie-me identified as "Daddy."

The priest pressed his hand to Daddy's forehead and began to speak, not the normal rhythmic Latin that always lulled Jeannie to sleep, but a harsher tongue, more sharp edges and guttural sounds than Latin. I knew it to be Enochian, the ancient language of angels and demons. That's how I knew there was something wrong with the church, because the priest was speaking the tongue of demons. But when I went to investigate, there was no hint of demonic activity anywhere, much less in the priest. Everything about him screamed "holy" to the high heavens. But where would a legit holy man in modern North Carolina learn a magical language that has never been widely spoken on Earth and hasn't been spoken at all in the US since the 60s? Where could he learn a language that died thousands of years ago if not by the very creatures that spoke it?

My eyes snapped open and I came back to myself, kneeling in Jeannie Lemore's bedroom and staring into the eyes of her ghost. "You did it!" I said to the little girls. "I understand now, and I know how to stop it. I hope."

The two little girl ghosts looked at each other, then they stood up from the bed, joined hands, and walked through the wall of the house. When they reached the wall, a portal opened up, and they vanished in a flash of purest white light. I fell backwards on my ass in the middle of the floor, then scrambled up and bolted toward the master bedroom.

"Flynn!" I yelled as I hit the hallway. "Flynn, where the fuck are you?!?"

She turned from her examination of the parents' dresser drawers. "What is it, Harker? What do you want?"

I pulled her aside and said in as much of a whisper as I could manage, "I figured it out. You've got to come with me. Right now. We're finishing this. Today."

"What the fuck are you talking about, Harker? What did you find? Who's doing this? Where are we going?" She fired questions at my back as I dragged her down the hall and out the front of the house.

"You drive, my car sucks," I said, yanking open the door to her unmarked car and reaching out to slap the magnetic bubble light onto the top of the car. "Haul ass, Flynn."

We sat there.

"Well?" I said. "Let's go!"

"Where, jackass?" Flynn asked. "You haven't even thought it

at me yet."

"Fuck. Sorry. The church. We've got to go the church. The fathers are all being possessed, and I know how to stop it now."

She put the car into gear and pulled out onto Queens Road, lights flashing. She turned right toward Third Street and then looked at me sideways. "I thought you'd checked the place for bad mojo and there was nothing there."

"I did. There is no demonic possession at the church. It's as sanctified a place as I've ever known."

"Then what's making these men murder their families? What are we going there to kill, Harker?"

"We're going to church to kill an angel, Flynn. What else?"

CHAPTER 17

This time we walked into the church through the front doors. I stepped into the sanctuary and spotted a couple of little old ladies kneeling in prayer, the sweet kind of women who probably went in to pray for the souls of their dead husbands every day before volunteering in the daycare until it was time for cutthroat bingo in the fellowship hall in the afternoon, then dinner at Golden Corral before watching Pat & Vanna and going to bed at eight o'clock because there wasn't anything worth staying up to watch on television since they took *Dallas* off the air.

"Get them out of here," I said to Flynn. She peeled off and started hustling the ladies down to the church Family Life Center for cookies and milk or whatever. The priest I spoke to in the confessional was now standing at the communion railing, and he turned as I walked down the center aisle. He spun around, a wide smile on his face, resplendent in his black robe.

He was a young priest, almost certainly under forty. His hair was longer than I was used to on priests, long and wavy, curling just a little bit over his collar. His blue eyes and crisp jawline were guaranteed to make him a hit with the young women of the congregation, and the couple days' stubble he sported made him approachable enough for the men not to hate on sight.

"Quincy Harker, so good to see you again," he said, throwing his arms wide and giving me a huge smile.

"Padre," I nodded. "Or is there another name I should use?"

"We don't really do the whole 'name' thing," he said. "But if you need to call me something, how about Dominus? I could live with that, I suppose." He waved his hands and his entire body was enveloped in an otherworldly glow, and his eyes became orbs of pure lightning. Other than that, you couldn't really tell him from a normal person.

"Not really in the mood for pizza right now, Domino's. But if it's an ass-whooping you're looking for, just let me know. I've got one right here with your name on it."

"Oh, Quincy, let's not fight," the angel/priest said. "I'm not here to destroy you. I'm here to recruit you."

"Recruit me?" I said, honestly baffled. "For what?"

"There's a purge coming, and I need a stronger vessel. My ethereal energy will burn this body out in a matter of days, weeks at the most. But your body is different." Dom walked through the gap in the communion railing and sat down on the polished oak.

"Thanks for noticing, I've been working out." I ran a hand over my abs, but the angel didn't laugh or give me any indication that he was anything other than batshit crazy.

I decided on a different tactic. "What was that about a purge?" I slid sideways into a pew, as much for cover as support. "Like some kind of war? Don't you remember what happened the last time there was a war in Heaven?" I didn't, of course, since it happened a couple bajillion years ago.

"But this will not be a war in Heaven, nor anywhere. I have no interest in overthrowing the Father, or in taking over His domain. I just want to be rid of you cockroaches down here, and I want you to help me."

"What cockroaches? Humans? And did you miss the part where I *am* a human?" I asked.

At least mostly human, Flynn's thoughts echoed in my mind.

All the parts that matter, I sent back an image of me in my towel. Flynn blushed.

Quit flirting, we've got serious trouble, Flynn replied.

Yeah, no shit. A psychotic angel wants to recruit me to be a general in his war on humanity. You gotta get out of here. If he catches sight of you, he'll either send you to Hell or just will you out of existence.

Flynn's thoughts froze for a second, the psychic equivalent of her mouth dropping open. *He can do that?*

And worse. He's a seraph, one of the Host. The big deal of angels. I can't hope to beat him, just maybe get lucky and send him back to Heaven where he can do less harm. So get out of here.

I'm not leaving you to fight him alone.

You're just going to get me killed if I have to watch out for you. Now get the fuck out of here!

Fine.

Flynn?

Yeah.

Pray for me.

I cut off the mental connection between me and Flynn and turned my attention back to Dominos.

"Girl problems?" the angel asked.

"I got 99 problems, dickhead, but she ain't one," I replied. He looked confused. I don't know that I expected a seraph to be a Jay-Z fan, but I was reaching for any common ground here.

"Why do you want to destroy humanity?" I asked.

"You breed too fast, make too much noise, and have captured too much of the Father's attention for too long," he replied.

"Oh, so this is like a jealous big brother kind of thing. I get that. I had siblings. You hate them a lot of the time. They make Mom and Dad give them all the love, and you feel all ignored. But then one day, they're gone, and you're all alone, and you don't want anything more than to be able to sit down with your shitty little brother and have a beer with him. So if humanity is your little brother, you could probably wipe them out, but you'd miss them eventually. I mean, the cosmos would be just way too quiet without them, right?"

He looked pensive for a moment, and I wondered if that bullshit spiel had actually worked. He lowered his head, as if overcome by emotions. I even saw his shoulders shake once, twice, then he looked back up at me.

"That was the stupidest thing I've ever heard. And I was here when your kind first learned to use fire."

We're clear. Take this motherfucker down. Flynn sent an image of her and the old ladies sampling the communion wine in the church kitchen.

I'll try. If I don't make it out of here, feed my cat.

You don't have a cat.

Well, if I get out of this, remind me to get a cat.

"Yeah, but I distracted you long enough for the civilians to get clear," I said. I focused my will and said "*clavum,*" throwing my hand in his direction. A stream of spikes shot from my palm, streaking straight at the angel's face.

He laughed and floated into the air, my spikes flashing under his feet to shatter against the pulpit. "You'll have to do better than that, Harker," he said. He held out both hands wide from his sides and cast bolts of white energy in my direction.

I dove behind the pew and covered my face in my hands as the wooden bench turned to splinters that cascaded down over me. I kept my face covered and scurried along the floor to the end of the row. I hopped up and shouted "*Infierno!*" at the angel, pointing my hands at him like I was throwing a basketball. A globe of fire materialized between my fingertips and streaked toward Dominus.

He laughed and took to the air, easily dodging my fireball,

which struck the pulpit and spread fire across the front of the church. The carpet started to burn, and the communion rail was engulfed in seconds.

I jumped a couple of pews and dropped to the floor again as Dom threw another bolt of force at me. Another pew blew to splinters as I rolled forward along the stone floor. I hopped up and flung my hands at him again. I shouted *"Ningor!"* and the air over the angel coalesced into a roiling mass of white clouds, which immediately began to dump ice and snow upon the pissed-off seraph. It didn't do much more than annoy the angel, but at least the sanctuary wasn't on fire anymore.

Dom flew left, right, and sideways, but my little storm cloud followed his every move. Finally, after trying to dodge the blizzard I dropped on his head, Dom landed at the front of the church and directed his attention upward. As he focused his attention on dispelling the storm, I sprang over the pew in front of me and charged the distracted angel.

I've had worse ideas. I'm sure of it given the number of times I've ended up in hospitals in my life. So running straight at a demented angel who wants me to join his army might not be the stupidest thing I've ever done, but it definitely makes the top ten. He flicked out a hand, and I ran into a brick wall. An invisible brick wall made completely from the angel's willpower, but nonetheless, I dropped straight back and flopped to the floor like a fish out of water.

"That's your best shot, Harker? Just charging at me like a bull? Maybe I didn't make it clear—I just need your body, and I don't really need it to be alive when I'm in there. Frankly, it would be easier if I just killed you and took over right now." He raised both hands over his head, and that white energy enveloped his fists, growing to a sparkling orb the size of a beach ball. Then he brought both hands down over his head like he was chopping wood and I was a reluctant hunk of oak. The ball of energy flew at me, promising to blow me to bits the second it hit. My life flashed before my eyes, and in my considered opinion, I hadn't slept with nearly enough redheads. I closed my eyes, waiting for the bolt of angelic fire to hit me right between the eyes.

CHAPTER 18

Except it never hit. A streak of white flashed in from the ceiling of the church and hurled itself between me and the white-hot fireball half an eye blink before I was incinerated.

"Cutting it a little close, aren't we?" I asked my guardian angel.

"Can we hold off the smartass comments until I'm maybe not on fire?" Glory replied as Dom's power crackled along the shield of wings she surrounded me with. I smelled burning feathers and shouted "*Aquos!*" A thick cloud of steam erupted from Glory's back as a hundred gallons of water materialized around the angel.

"Thanks," she said.

"No problem," I replied. "I assume you have a plan for how to deal with our flying friend up there?" I pointed to Dom, who had taken off and was now floating above the sanctuary.

"I do, but I don't wand to spoil the surprise," Glory said, then unfolded the cocoon of wings she'd saved me with, and flew up to face the psycho seraph.

"Hey, Domino's, why don't you pick on someone your own species!" Glory called.

"If there were anyone here with even an iota of my power, I would happily do battle with them. As it is, I have to settle for you." He threw bolts of power at Glory, which she avoided without breaking a sweat.

"That the best you got? You're gonna have to go back through Gabriel's boot camp if you can't take out one little guardian," Glory taunted.

Dom threw more bolts of energy, and now Glory had to expend a little energy avoiding them. The whole time, I watched her left hand. When she dodged one particularly close blast, I stood up and shouted *"Tempestus!"*

Hurricane-force winds shot from my hands, buffeting Dom around the ceiling and providing the opening Glory needed. She charged the distracted seraph, landing a punch on his chin that knocked him into a midair flip, then she reversed course and hit him from above with both feet, driving Dom to the floor.

I charged the pulpit again, this time with no intention of tackling the angel. Instead, I veered to the right and the last minute and grabbed a hunk of sidewalk chalk from one jacket pocket. I knelt on the floor of the church and drew a shaky circle around the downed angel, then focused my will into the chalk and invoked the circle. A flash of blue-white energy pulsed along the lines, and the circle snapped to life around the shaken angel.

"What the heaven do you think you're doing, mortal?" Dom asked, reaching out with a finger to touch the circle. The magical boundary crackled on his outstretched finger, and he snatched back the scorched appendage, sticking it into his mouth and sucking on it in a very human gesture.

"I think I'm locking you away until I figure out what to do with you," I said.

"And I think I know exactly what to do with him," Glory's voice came from above me. She floated to the ground right beside me and glared at the imprisoned angel.

"Release me, Glory," Dom said with a smile.

"Kiss my ass, Dom," Glory replied, extending the middle finger of her right hand.

"Sorry about that, Dom," I said. "I'm a bad influence on angels."

"That's the damn truth," Glory said, and held up a fist. I bumped it, and we stared at Dom, who fumed inside the circle, then turned to Glory with rage in his eyes.

"Guardian, I order you to release me. As one of The Host, I command you." He flared his wings out as far as he could in the circle and put enough of his power into the words to make his eyes glow white.

"There's a problem with that, Dom," Glory replied. "You're no longer one of The Host."

"What?" the imprisoned angel said.

"Huh?" I added, equally eloquent.

"I just came from Gabriel, you poor misguided bastard. He sent me down with a message, and Uriel loaned me something to deliver it with." Glory stretched her arm into the air, and suddenly there was a flaming longsword in it. She swung the sword down, then up, then down again, slicing through my circle like it was nothing. She raised her arm again, opened her hand, and the sword vanished.

Dom's eyes flickered, then the fire went out and his mouth opened wide in a howl of pain and rage that shook the windows in their frames. His wings, the pride of every angel, lay on the floor of the pulpit, trapped inside the circle with Dom, just a pile of useless feathers now. The suddenly former angel dropped to his knees, gathering the feathers to his body, but at his touch, they turned gray and melted into a fine dust that drifted away on the currents of air.

"What have you done to me?" Dom shrieked.

"I just carried out the sentence, Dominus," Glory said, and her voice was heavy with sadness. "You did this to yourself the second you took the Father's work onto yourself. We carry out the will of God, not the will of The Host. We don't make decisions of life and death, Dominus. The second you did that, you abandoned The Host and all we stand for."

"We? Who the heaven do you think you are, *Guardian*? You've no right to call yourself one of The Host."

"I don't?" Glory asked. "Do you not recognize me, Dominus? I know it's been a few centuries, but have I changed all that much?" She spread her wings, and Glory was surrounded by a yellow-white light so bright I had to turn away and cover my face with my hands.

When the glow faded enough for me to turn back to her, she had folded her wings and was back to being Glory, my everyday, run-of-the-mill guardian angel. Dom, however, was on his knees in the circle staring up at her in adoration like she had just cured cancer or invented pizza.

"You," he said, and the love in his voice was like the sum of every mother speaking to every newborn throughout history.

"Me," Glory replied, and the sadness in her tone made me think of every single Tom Waits song ever, all being played at the same time. Glory raised her right hand, looked down at the kneeling former angel, and said, "I'm sorry, Dom. I don't know where we failed you, but perhaps the Morningstar can heal you and make you fit for service again."

Her hand flashed a blinding white, and Dom disappeared in an explosion of sulfur and red-tinged smoke. My pitiful little circle vanished from the wood in a blaze of burnt chalk, and there was no trace of our fight except for a lot of splintered pews and the stench of brimstone on the pulpit. Lying on the floor where Dom had been, blissfully unconscious, was the priest I had met the day before.

I picked up the priest and laid him on a padded pew, smoothing down his robes and putting a hymnal under his head for a pillow. Then I turned to Glory.

"What the ever-loving fuck was all that?" I asked, crossing my arms and staring at her.

"Here's what I can tell you, which isn't much. Dominus was insane. He acted alone, without knowledge of The Host or anyone else."

"Anyone?" I asked, eyebrows climbing.

"I don't get into what The Father does and doesn't know. I always assume that He knows everything and sometimes just waits for us to figure things out for ourselves. He does like His children to be independent, you know."

"Then he must fucking *love* me," I muttered.

Glory took hold of my chin and turned my eyes to hers. I looked deep into them, really looked for the first time, and behind the blue I saw more than I could process. I *saw* the love, the compassion, the forgiveness for every stupid, hard-hearted and small-minded thing I'd ever done. I stared into her eyes until I felt like my heart would burst, and then I tore myself away, tears rolling down my face.

"That's just how I feel about you, Quincy Harker, and I have nothing like the capacity for love that Father has. So yeah, he fucking loves you. And don't you forget it."

I stood there for a moment, trying to pull myself together. When I could speak again, I looked back at her. Fortunately, she had de-magicked her eyes, so I could look at her without being overwhelmed.

"So it's over? The murders? The magically-induced unnatural catastrophes? All done?"

"All done. No more murders, and no more using the death of innocents to manipulate the Earth's energies. And hopefully Dominus can be rehabilitated."

"In Hell?" I raised an eyebrow.

Glory looked at me like I was a particularly slow first-grader. It was a look she'd used before. I've given her plenty of opportunities to perfect it over the years. She said, "Hell isn't for punishment, Quincy. The punishment is being away from the presence of the Almighty. The redemption comes in the hope to some day earn the right to be in His presence again. If Dominus truly repents and learns from his mistakes, he may one day become part of The Host again. That is our most sincere hope."

"Our? I thought being part of The Host was like a rank thing, and Guardians were a step below."

"Usually that's true." Glory gave me a little smile. "But you're a special case. You get into a little more trouble than most humans, so you require a higher level of guardian. So you get me." She gave me a dazzling smile, the kind that's supposed to distract me from asking any questions she doesn't feel like answering. I knew she was playing me, but I let her. She wasn't going to tell me anything more about her status among the angels, or about the attention I was receiving from Heaven, so I figured I'd just chalk it up to a win and move along.

"Yeah, I got you. Ain't you the lucky one?"

"I am, Harker. I truly am. Peace be with you, my friend." Glory gave me a quick hug, then vanished in a stream of sparkles.

"Kid definitely knows how to make an exit." I grinned and turned to the door.

Let's get out of here, I sent to Flynn.

Did we win?

We're still alive, so yeah, we wo,. I replied.

Meet you at the car. You're driving, she thought at me.

Drunk on communion wine?

Fuck off, Harker, that shit's stronger than I thought.

I've never heard anybody slur their thoughts before, Becks.

Just open the car door, asshole.

I looked back at the church, and as the sun flickered behind a cloud for a second, I thought I saw the figure of little Emily Standish standing in the doorway. She gave me a little wave, then turned and walked through a patch of sunbeam, and was gone.

"Peace be unto you, little one," I murmured, then walked to the car and rode away.

About the Author

John G. Hartness is a teller of tales, a righter of wrong, defender of ladies' virtues, and some people call him Maurice, for he speaks of the pompatus of love. He is also the best-selling author of EPIC-Award-winning series *The Black Knight Chronicles* from Bell Bridge Books, a comedic urban fantasy series that answers the eternal question "Why aren't there more fat vampires?"

John is the author of the Bubba the Monster Hunter series of short stories and novellas, the Quincy Harker, Demon Hunter novella series, and the creator and co-editor of the *Big Bad* anthology series, among other projects.

In 2016, John teamed up with a pair of other publishing industry ne'er-do-wells and founded Falstaff Media, a publishing conglomerate dedicated to pushing the boundaries of literature and entertainment.

In his copious free time John enjoys long walks on the beach, rescuing kittens from trees and recording new episodes of his ridiculous podcast *Literate Liquors*, where he pairs book reviews and alcoholic drinks in new and ludicrous ways. John is also a contributor to the *Magical Words* group blog. An avid *Magic: the Gathering* player, John is strong in his nerd-fu and has sometimes been referred to as "the Kevin Smith of Charlotte, NC." And not just for his girth. He can be found online at www.johnhartness. com and spends too much time on Twitter, especially after a few drinks.

For more information about appearances, signings, and other silliness, feel free to follow John on Twitter (@johnhartness), or on his website www.johnhartness.com.

CPSIA information can be obtained
at www.ICGtesting.com
Printed in the USA
LVHW01*1959100518
576714LV00007B/97/P